I0788168

PIECES

A Novel by Sondra J. Hardy

CHAPTER ONE

New Orleans

September 1933

I'm Violet Booker, and I'm expecting a child with Clarence Margaret. We didn't plan this; it happened because we fell in love. However, there's a complication: his wife, Maria. She's a Hoodoo practitioner feared by many and rumored to have the ability to hurt people without touching them.

After my mother found out about my affair with Maria's husband, we had a terrible fight. It ended with me having a busted lip and being kicked out of my home. Now, I'm on a train to Harlem, New York, to stay with my aunt and uncle. I feel scared and alone. My dream of becoming a teacher is now lost, and everyone is disappointed except Clarence.

There is a woman named Maydell Scott who lives in the community. She spent over ten years in a roach-infested flophouse. She is known for being loud, smoking cigarettes, and drinking so much hard liquor that many men would be embarrassed. Usually, she disappears at night and comes back about an hour before noon to have a cold, three-day-old coffee. Often, she passes out on her bed but wakes up, washes herself in places where it counts, dresses, and heads back into the city with her gambler boyfriend from New York.

Maydell Scott boldly questioned why Clarence was not in her bed since last night, noting she woke up alone again. She suspected he rushed out to return home before his wife, Maria, woke up. Standing confidently with her legs apart, she rubbed herself and hurriedly approached Clarence as he entered the town's only grocery store serving Black residents. She shamelessly wrapped her arms around his neck, lifted her dress to show her underwear, and pressed herself against his tall, muscular six-foot-four frame. Unaware of his wife watching in shock, she suddenly tried to kiss him, sticking her tongue into his mouth, but he turned away and pushed her back.

"Don't act like you don't like it, Clarence!" she said, laughing and straightening her dress.

Clarence's wife clenched his arm tightly, overwhelmed with anger. This was the third time this so-called "Morceau de poubelle" trash had acted up! "Sale de deux bits! Sale pute, tu sens comme un poisson pourri - You two-bit whore! You unclean whore who smells like rotten fish!" Maria shouted in her native French Creole, pushing Maydell away from Clarence.

At that moment, Maydell aggressively pushed Maria, a petite woman who is only five feet two inches tall, causing her to fall and scrape her elbow.

"So, what are you gonna do now, half-breed?" Maydell taunted the woman, who is half-French Creole and Black. "You can't even speak English properly! Get up, half-breed! Get up! Deewww it!" She laughed and mimicked Maria's French Creole accent.

Suddenly and unexpectedly

"Stop it!" Clarence yelled as he stepped between the two women, mainly to shield his wife. Passersby, horrified, couldn't believe their eyes as the two women fought with closed fists; Maria, the fair-skinned woman, was winning and shouting in French Creole. Some onlookers watched the scene unfold.

"Maydell, you'd better get going before the law shows up. We don't want trouble, so get the hell outta here!" he said, shielding his wife, who was trembling, bleeding, and clutching the blood-stained sleeve torn from Maydell's dress. "Oh my God, Maria, your elbow is bleeding badly," he exclaimed. He took his handkerchief and pressed it firmly against her wound to control the bleeding.

"Owwweee! My eye, I can't see out of it!" yelled Maydell, bleeding heavily. She also had a large cut on her face from Maria's scratch. "She's gonna pay for what she did to me, that half-breed Creole Black bitch!"

Maria, in a surprise move, lunged at Maydell once more, catching her off guard. This time, her weapons were her pointed fingernails, which she used to target the same area she had wounded earlier. She scratched Maydell repeatedly until Maydell fell backward.

Maydell collapsed onto the dirt road; her face covered in dirt and blood. She gradually got to her feet and noticed a burning sensation under her right eye.

"Oh my God! Jesus! My eye! You scratched my eye and face! I'm bleeding! Help me, Clarence!" she screamed, clutching her bleeding face and signaling Clarence to help her up.

"Get outta here, Maydell! Leave my wife and me alone!" he shouted as he quickly wrapped his arm around Maria and walked away.

"She's paying for this got-damned dress!" Maydell yelled at them as she staggered away, holding her face. "Half-breed, I'll come to your door tonight to get paid for the dress you ruined, and I'll also take your husband! I was the one he wanted. I'll be over later to see you out, and I'll be in! I'll be your kids' new mama!" Maydell staggered toward the flophouse where she stayed.

Walking silently, Clarence held Maria close to calm her down after the incident, but she couldn't shake her suspicion of her husband. Why is this woman trying to get close to my husband again? And why did she say such nasty comments about moving into my house and becoming a new mother to my children? The nerve of that sale pute!

"How do you know that gutter trash woman?" Maria snapped angrily, pulling herself away from him.

Stopping, Clarence tightly held her arm. Sweat from the midday sun shimmered on his Nubian brown skin. He was a captivating figure, and Maria loved to look at him.

"Look at me," he said in a tone so low and deep that Maria stopped walking to listen.

"That woman is loose and twisted up in her mind. She has never been married and has no family here. No man wants her because she's been with every man in this town and probably elsewhere, too!"

"Even you, amour?" she asked softly, gazing intently into his eyes.

"What you should have done was stay out of it and let me handle what was necessary to send her on her way! She knows we're married, so let this go and let's go home!" he said, dismissing her with a wave and storming off, distancing himself from Maria.

Maria watched her husband walk slowly and deliberately, but she eventually sped up. She was worried he would never respond to her questions. The heat was getting intense, and sweat was streaming down her face. Although her hair was tightly tied back, it was now messy after the violet brawl. She wiped her forehead with a bloodstained handkerchief belonging to her husband, smiling at it as she tucked it into her bosom to absorb the sweat on her chest. She checked inside her dress pocket to make sure that the sleeve from Maydell's dress was still undisturbed and ready. After patting her pocket, she quickened her pace to catch up with Clarence.

By the time they got home, it was as if nothing had happened earlier. Their children, three sons named Kempton, Joseph, and Sampson, along with their identical twin daughters, Izelle and Rosetta, were happy and relieved to see their mother and father, who had been away since early morning.

Maria took pride in her children, especially the fact that the twins were fluent in French Creole. Sometimes, they would even switch to French Creole while doing household chores and cooking.

"Mère, what happened to your arm!" Izelle asked, alarmed when she saw the bloody wound on Maria's elbow.

"Rein, mes belles filles – nothing, my beautiful daughters," she said, kissing each of them twice on the cheek and hugging them close.

"I tripped over a rock on my way home. Your father helped me, and it's already improving—see? Isn't that right, Clarence?" she asked, looking directly at him.

"That's right, it's over, and your mother will be fine," he said.

"We have something to tell you all," Eighteen-year-old Kempton announced. Clarence and Maria looked on, stunned by the bloodstains on his overalls. The wet blood had the foul odor of a recently slain wild animal. Maria felt her knees weaken and her grip on the twins' wrists tighten.

"What happened to you?" Clarence asked, his voice raised—no response from Kempton.

"I asked what happened to you, boy!" Clarence said, gripping Kempton's arm so tightly that he grimaced in pain and struggled to free himself, but Clarence refused to loosen his hold.

"Clarence, you're hurting his arm! Let him go! Stop it!" Maria pleaded as she held onto her daughters. Clarence ignored her pleas. Something was wrong, and he needed answers.

"Boy, I asked you what happened, and this is the last time I'm gonna ask you. What did you do?" By this time, father and son were standing face-to-face. Clarence was breathing hard and bracing himself to hear the worst.

"It was me," Sampson, their youngest son, admitted.

"Joseph and I took your rifles, and we went back into the swamp to hunt the boar we tried to kill last week."

"What?" Clarence exclaimed in disbelief, letting go of Kempton's arm.

"That boar we tried to kill last week, which escaped, nearly killed Kempton. It suddenly appeared and ran straight at him," he stammered.

"I shot it twice in the head. After it fell dead, Joseph shot it two more times to be sure it was done. We then tied it up, ran a pole between its legs, and carried it home. It took all of us to bring it to the barn, skinned it following your instructions, and now we're preparing to cut it into pieces for hanging in the smokehouse and selling some of the meat, except for what we keep for ourselves. We take what is best for our family first. We meant no disrespect, sir. We're all sorry." He kept looking at the ground, bracing himself for the worst.

Clarence looked at his sons. He loved them and would do everything in his power to keep them all safe. But right now, a mix of anger and relief consumed him.

"Come here, all of you," he said, motioning everyone to get closer to him. Everyone gathered around Clarence.

"Listen to me. You all heard from your mother and me what happened to your friend Johnathan? He was like a part of this family. He played here with you since you were little ones."

Everyone nodded in agreement. The twins buried their heads into Maria's chest and began to weep. She hugged them close to her.

"Yes, sir," the sons replied.

"He was y'all's friend, a very mannered and good boy, went to school, and never caused any trouble to anyone around here. He loved his family and all of you, as he didn't have any brothers or sisters. However, just like you boys did today, Johnathan went hunting in those thick swamps all alone. That's very dangerous because anything can happen there. You never go in those swamps alone. He went without his father and his uncles. He left early in the morning while his mother and father were still sleeping. By nighttime, he still hadn't come home. On Sunday morning, his father, Allen, and his brothers, all armed with rifles, entered the swamp. They searched for two days for Johnathan. Well, we all know what happened next. He was found on that third afternoon by Mr. Louis, Mr. Drews, and their boys when they went fishing. Johnathan had half of his head blown off." Clarence paused and cleared his throat, thinking of Jonathan, who played with his sons just days before he was murdered, and how Johnathan's father screamed and collapsed at the sight of his dead son.

The image was haunting. The twins were sobbing now. Their friend Johnathan, whom they both had a crush on, was gone forever. They all remembered the details of the funeral. Johnathan's mother, Mavis, fainted at the service, and his inconsolable father was heartbreaking. A week later, they both moved north to Philadelphia, never to return to New Orleans again.

"I'll not have that happen to my sons or my daughters," Clarence said, his voice shaking. "Don't any of you go into those swamps ever unless I'm with you and or if your mother says it's okay for us to go, do you all understand? I'll not have any of my children floating dead in the swamp!" Clarence shouted with fear etched in his eyes

"Yes", they all said in unison, even Maria answering and nodding her head yes. This scared Maria because she had never seen Clarence behave in that manner.

She was clinging to her daughters even tightly to comfort and protect them. Then everyone drew closer to Clarence, who outstretched his arms, and everyone held onto one another.

"We need to cut up and clean that boar right away before it spoils in this heat, then get it in the smokehouse. After about two weeks, we'll start selling off the meat. And sons, you all did very well, not only killing that thing but keeping each other alive. Now, let's get on with our day because it's getting late. We got a lot to do before sundown, and we have church tomorrow."

Clarence and his sons started towards the barn and smokehouse, each one talking at once, telling their father about the kill. Clarence turned to look back at Maria and his daughters, tipped his hat, and smiled at them. Once inside the barn, he and his sons began the intense slaughter of the dead beast, which weighed 500 pounds. *That thing could have killed my son*, he thought as he examined the long, sharp tusk. He stood back and marveled at the way his sons were skillfully butchering the boar. He was grateful that they all made it home alive despite their disobedience.

"I'll be right back," Maria said as she made her way to the door. "Izelle and Rosetta, please start dinner. Cut the potatoes into pieces, and finish boiling the beans and rice. Then cut and season the two chickens. We'll have biscuits for Sunday, but cornbread for tonight. I need to go out back to clean up. *"Dépĉhez-vous maintenant! -* Hurry now!" And then she was gone.

"Oui Mami!" they said after their mother left. Then they quickly put on their aprons and began their assigned tasks.

Maria waited until everyone was out of sight, attending to their tasks. The first thing she did as she walked towards the tool shed was to examine her wound. The bleeding stopped as she carefully removed Clarence's handkerchief. It was still very sore but not painful. She stopped by the large, galvanized basin that held rainwater for bathing. She had previously put a mixture of herbs in the water: rue, comfrey root, verbena, mistletoe, and benzoin were tied in a white cloth bag and left inside the basin. If anyone got scraped or cuts, Maria would dip a clean cloth into the mixture and press it against the wound, which was precisely what she did on her elbow. Within two days, the wound will heal.

"*Reconnaissant À Vous Seigneur mon Dieu, I am grateful to you, Lord my God, for sparing the lives of my sons Kempton, Joseph, and Sampson,*" she whispered in prayer. She remembered how she had sewn a small, discreet flannel red bag into the seams of her sons' shirts, as well as inside their pants and the weapon sacks that held knives and bullets for their rifles. They took the flat bags as patches to repair holes in the inseam of their shirts and pants. They never questioned Maria about what they were and why the red patches were sewn there. Little did they know that the small pouches contained quince seeds. The seeds, along with the herbs of mullen and feverfew, protected them all from harm, especially from wild animals.

It's now time to protect my family from the thief who is trying to destroy my family. Maydell must go. Maria quickly began the work. Deep in the corner pocket of the tool shed, where Clarence kept tools for the farm, was a box she concealed from everyone. She went inside the shed and locked it behind her. She opened the box, which revealed the tools needed to rid herself of the thief forever.

Maria took the torn and tattered sleeve of Maydell's dress out of her dress pocket. Putting it to her nose and smelling it, she pulled her head away and wrinkled her nose in disgust with the overpowering odor of rancid sweat, sex, cheap perfume, and stale tobacco smoke. Looking inside her apparatus box, she began gathering her supplies: thread, needles, square-headed pins, Kufa dust, black mustard seeds, wood-stick matches, chicory, wood chips, Balmony, Spanish moss, a cigar, and a small cast-iron cauldron. She filled the cauldron with wood chips, lit the wood stick match, and began a small fire. As they began to burn, she began creating a doll using the sleeve of the dress. Carefully cutting angles to resemble a head, neck, arms, torso, and legs, Maria worked very quickly. "The *la riddance of this poubelle* will happen before sunrise tomorrow morning," she said out loud. Ten minutes later, the doll was done. "*Merveilleux-*

wonderful!" she exclaimed, clapping her hands at her work. The small doll, made from a dress sleeve, was stuffed with herbs and was ready for the next preparation. She laid it on the ground and took a short, sharp-tipped stick and scraped out of her fingernails the dried blood and skin from the fight. Slowly and deliberately, she scraped off the residue, specifically concentrating on scraping off the flecks of blood and skin onto the belly of the doll. She did this until each one of her fingernails was clean. Next, she counted out six square-headed pins and pushed three in the mouth of the doll and three in the belly: one to the left, center, and right side. One by one, she pierced the pins into the doll firmly and wiggled each one, especially the one in the center.

Satisfied, she then lit the cigar, put it into her mouth, and inhaled, taking in four long draws, and blew the smoke directly into the doll's face, holding it up, making sure the smoke consumed every inch of the doll's body. This was repeated thirty more times until the entire shed was filled with sweet-smelling smoke. The wood chips were now in a low but hot flame. The doll was then dropped into the cauldron, where it began to burn. Maria carefully tied a white turban on her head and recited her petition:

"Maydell, you vile and filthy pute of lust, your mouth is full of lies that nobody can trust.

After the humiliation in front of my husband today, you'll now be reduced to ashes, and forever you'll pay. You will smell smoke that you won't even see, and it will cause you to flee. The smoke will make you choke, making your belly feel like swamp mud.

Then you'll vomit rotten-smelling blood; nobody can save you or take you to your sickbed. Maydell Scott, by sunrise you'll be dead".

Rocking back and forth with her eyes tightly closed, Maria chanted the petition three more times until she no longer smelled or heard the crackle of the contents burning in the cauldron, which was now reduced to ashes. The cigar she smoked was reduced to nothing as well. She looked inside the cauldron again. Everything, including the stick, was burned down to ashes, and the pins were now blackened. Maria carefully gathered up the remaining tools. She wrapped them back into the sackcloth, put them inside her box, and returned them to the corner side of the shed. She then took out a black, tattered piece of fabric and laid it on the ground. Turning the cauldron upside down, she emptied the contents onto the cloth, even the charred pins. Giving the cauldron one more tap with the side of her hand until it was void of everything, she returned the cauldron to the corner with the box. The black cloth was then folded into a small packet bound with twine. Everything was done.

Maria stepped outside and hurried into the fields. She picked up a sharp stone, dug a hole, and buried the contents. Satisfied, she returned to the house. As she opened the door, the tempting aroma of cooked food made her smile. She paused in the doorway, watching her daughters set the dinner table and speak fluent French Creole, a language she had taught them when they were five. She admired how quickly they learned. Soon, they were blossoming into young, beautiful women excelling in school and their chosen fields of study.

And therefore, I'll not have a puta like Maydell destroy this. I'll curse anyone who tries to break my family.

"Mère, is everything alright? Where were you?" Rosetta asked, handing her mother a cup and saucer of hot water with a thick slice of lemon. "We were very worried when we didn't see you for a while," she said as she encircled Maria's small waist in a firm hug.

"Je vais bein-bein ma belle Rosetta, I'm doing fine, Rosetta, I can smell dinner from outside! It smells wonderful!" Maria exclaimed as she put the cup and saucer down on the table. "I see you went ahead and made biscuits, Izelle. Thank you for doing that."

"You're welcome, Mère," Izelle said. "I poured hot water and your favorite soap into the basin in your room. I know you didn't have time to wash before dinner. You can leave me your dress, and I'll put it away for the wash on Monday."

"Thank you, I'm going to wash right now. Your father and brothers will be here by the time I'm finished."

Maria headed straight to her bedroom. In the center of the small room, a basin big enough for her to stand in, soap, a washcloth, and a towel to dry off with. Maria took off her sweaty dress, which also faintly smelled like cigar smoke.

"I wish this basin were big enough for my whole body!" she murmured to herself, sighing as she picked up the washcloth, soaked it in warm water, lathered it with soap, and quickly washed to avoid making everyone wait and having dinner get cold. She had already heard Clarence and her sons outside washing with a pail and rainwater, then changing into clean clothes. The bloodstained overalls and shirts would be left outside, wrapped in a sack, until Monday. After their baths, everyone would eat dinner, go to bed early, and be ready for church tomorrow morning. She thought to herself that on Monday, there would be much more to do as she finished her bath, dried off, and looked into the large dresser Clarence had made for her as a wedding gift. She selected a clean, crisp house dress. She looked at the other six dresses and thought about her luck in having these six handmade, clean dresses. Many women nearby owned only three work dresses and a "good" dress for church or special occasions; all those hours of sewing as a seamstress over the years had paid off.

"Merè?" Maria didn't hear the soft knock on the door or the noise of Clarence and their sons, who were already in the house.

"Yes, come in," she said. Rosetta and Izelle went in, followed by Joseph.

"We're all waiting for you," Rosetta said as she bent down and collected Maria's dress and undergarments.

"We'll put these out back for Monday, and Joseph will throw out the used water." Izelle left the room with her sister.

Joseph, her middle son, has been different over the past month. He appears distracted and much less talkative. His behavior changed after the death of his best friend Johnathan, whom he had known and played with since childhood. He has become more withdrawn, and she has heard him crying several nights in a row.

"Joseph," Maria called to her son.

"Yes, Ma?" he said, lifting the pail without looking at her.

"How did you all do at butchering that boar? Will you have a lot to sell after it's been smoked?" she asked, motioning for him to sit beside her on the edge of the bed.

"After gutting it, we divided the meat into sections and weighed each part. Some is hanging in the smokehouse. Daddy plans to burn the raw skin to prevent any odor and to keep wild animals away. The barn was stained with blood, but we cleaned it up good and burned the bloody rags."

"Joseph, I hear you crying and walking around the house at night sometimes," she said, wrapping her arm around his shoulders.

Tears began to well up in his eyes as he looked straight ahead.

"We had planned to attend college together," he said softly. "He was the reason why I was doing so well in school. He helped me understand science, including the soil and how plants grow in it, as well as when they should be grown, especially with our vegetables on the farm. Jonathan was so smart. Why would those evil white men kill him like that? I heard they shot him, and half of his head was gone," he said, wiping tears from his face. "I also dream about him," he added, looking down at his hands.

"What are your dreams concerning him? Share with me, son,"

"He looks different now, happier, and he mentioned he's no longer in pain or scared. He also said that where he is now, nobody can ever hurt him again."

"Go on, Joseph, keep talking," Maria encouraged, listening with keen interest to her son's story.

"Well, he said for me to go to college and not worry about the money because it would be found somewhere hidden, and the Big-Red would show you where it is," he said, looking at her.

Maria frowned, appearing clearly confused.

"Before he left, Johnathan told me he loved Izelle and planned to marry her after college. He said they often went to the barn to kiss, and after their third kiss, he told her he loved her. He believed that with time, she wouldn't be so sad and would marry someone else, and they would be together for many years. Johnathan also said Izelle's future husband would look just like him, only older. That's when it started getting very sunny and painfully bright. He said it was time for him to leave. I kept asking him to wait because the sun was hurting my eyes, but he just smiled and told me to close my eyes so I wouldn't be affected by the brightness. I did, and then I woke up. The next morning, when you and Daddy went to the store, the sun was shining directly on my face".

Maria observed Joseph, who kept his gaze fixed on the wall. The situation was overwhelming, even for her.

"Joseph," Maria said while holding onto him. "Jonathan wanted to tell you that he's okay where he is, and you know what?"

"What, Ma?" he asked, turning to face her.

"Nobody can ever hurt him again. Tonight, you'll sleep peacefully, I promise. When you wake up, you'll start feeling better each day. I hope you continue to do well in school. You need to go to college," she declared firmly. "Now, let's go; everyone is waiting for us." Maria hugged him, and he remembered to go outside to empty the water pail before joining the family for dinner.

Maydell. The nasty scratch on her right eye and face needed bandaging. The sting of the medicine Ole Lizzene, the eighty-year-old flophouse owner, dabbed on her wound was so painful that she cried out, and her other eye welled up with tears.

"You know you owe me another two dollars from last week, Miss Maydell," the old woman said in her deep-rooted southern drawl after she dressed the wound. "So, when Imma git it? I needs to have the money if yo gonna stay heah, "

"You'll get it! Shut up, old woman, and leave me the fuck alone!" Maydell yelled, rushing to her room and slamming the door behind her.

"Not going out tonight," Maydell murmured to herself after bandaging and packing the wound to prevent bleeding. "Shit!" she hissed, glancing at her bandaged eye in the mirror. She appeared hideous, especially with fresh blood seeping through the bandage. It was clear the injury was a deep gash, and she would need to change the bandage soon.

"Half-breed bitch!" she shouted, unaware of who might hear her. "The half-breed will pay for what she did to me! I need money to fix this damn hole of a room!" The gambler, a stout man about five feet ten and weighing nearly three hundred eighty pounds, known as High Roller-Gunn, planned to play cards again at the Black-owned bar. Dressed in a suit and carrying a gun on his belt, Gunn won every game he played. Even top players from New Orleans couldn't beat his quick wit. Every other night, he found a new card game, new opponents, and a fresh victory. He owed over a thousand dollars and promised her dinner, a new dress, and shoes. If he won tonight, he'd head to Harlem, New York, where he told her Black folks worked hard all day, made good money, and lived faster than in New Orleans. He was leaving tomorrow morning with three others seeking a better life up North; the men would handle the driving. Only one woman was traveling with them, Lena Collins. Beautiful and eager to escape New Orleans and her marriage, Lena had tried for years to have a child but failed. She was fed up with her husband's control and decided to leave with Gunn. If her husband, Wayne Collins, tried to come after her, Gunn would quickly stop him with his gun.

Gunn said he was leaving on time, and if you weren't ready, it was good got-damned riddance. Maydell would miss the life-changing opportunity. A bandaged eye and a deep facial gash would soon get infected, pus forming, leaving a nasty scar. Gunn didn't want to be seen with a woman on his arm who would also bear a scar. She felt tears well and began to sob. Her thoughts turned to Clarence Margaret and his empty promises, which quickly proved to be lies, recalling the last time they were together. She had told him she loved him, how he made her feel dizzy with his touch, and how he squeezed her in ways that left her wanting more. But once she expressed her true feelings, Clarence left as soon as she fell asleep in his arms. All she had now were memories of his touch, his deep kisses, and his tight embrace from last week.

Clarence was more caring than Gunn, who, after several rounds of drinking scotch, positioned himself on top of her, spread her legs wide, and forced himself inside for ten minutes. When it was over, he would fall asleep drunk, and she would quietly leave, taking fifteen dollars from his pocket. She dared not look in the wallet on the table with his winnings, as he counted every dollar and warned that even one dollar missing would lead him to threaten her with a gun. He claimed that the fifteen dollars was her share, and in a corner was a bag containing a new dress, stockings, clean panties, and shoes. Thinking beyond that, she contemplated later going to Clarence's house to tell his wife and children everything, hoping Maria would become so distraught she'd leave her husband and take her children, revealing the truth about their three months together and Clarence's taste for her, she thought, smiling through tears. They would get married a year later, so his children would have grown accustomed to her by the time of the wedding. As his children grew up and moved on to improve their lives outside Louisiana, Clarence would want a fresh start with a new family. They would have a child immediately after the wedding, another right away, then wait two years before having three more, each a year apart. It would be tough at first, but Clarence would be with her for the rest of his natural life, she thought wickedly. Yet, the harsh truth stared back at her in the cracked, dirty mirror; the bleeding had stopped, but left a fresh bloodstain.

Now drunk, Maydell staggered to the table and poured herself some of Lizzene's homemade hooch, which was so potent that even High Roller-Gunn would be knocked off his happy fat ass. She snatched up the half-full, dirty glass on the small table near the bed, took a sip, closed her eyes, and grimaced as the hot, flavorful liquid went down her throat. It made her feel warm.

After her third glass, the room started spinning, causing her to pass out on the soiled bed-bug-infested cot she slept on.

"I'ma gonna go see Clarence later," she drunkenly declared to herself out loud. *"When I wake up, I'ma see him and her. She's gonna hear the got-damned truth."* Then she fell into a deep sleep.

Two hours had passed. It was eleven forty-five at night, and a sharp smell of smoke tingled in her nose along with a cough that woke her, filled the air. She quickly got up, threw open the door, and ran out of her room barefoot, desperate to escape the rooming house and save herself. She stopped, noticing no visible smoke anywhere, but she still struggled to breathe, heaving and gasping, which only made her choke and gasp more, so she staggered down the hallway, confused about the source of the smoke, she stumbled down the hallway into the dimly lit parlor, where three tenants and their women were engaged in lustful kissing and loud moaning, unaware of their surroundings — especially the couple on the chair. The man was sitting with his trousers around his ankles, while his female partner straddled him, eyes closed, head thrown back, clearly enjoying the roll and grind of her hips.

The couple in the corner stopped what they were doing when his woman quickly looked up and saw Maydell. She hurriedly pulled her dress down, tapped his shoulder, and pointed her finger in the direction of where Maydell was standing. He looked and quickly zipped up his pants.

"What do you mean, rushing up in here and interrupting us?" he asked, annoyed. His woman now stood behind him, looking over his shoulder.

"Don't you smell smoke in here?!" Maydell shouted, coughing and hacking uncontrollably. "Get out! There's a fire in the house!" Her coughing worsened, and the smell of smoke grew stronger as Maydell grasped her throat. Then she did the unthinkable: she lifted her dress, spread her legs, stood still, and started to pee right on the floor in front of the guests.

"What the fuck!" Owen, the tenant, yelled at her. "What the fuck are you doing, pissing on the floor, Maydell?" The stunned guests all stood there, staring at her.

"She's crazy!" Sara, Owen's woman, whispered, clutching his arm tightly. Everyone watched in horror as a steady stream of urine pooled into a large puddle on the floor, and guests hurried to cover their noses against the foul smell. Maydell's dress was soaked in sweat and urine, and her coughing had become relentless.

"*Oh my God!*" screamed Sara.

Maydell stopped coughing, then let out a loud groan, clutching her stomach. Bending over, she vomited blood that poured from her mouth. Then her eyes rolled back, and she collapsed headfirst to the floor. Violent twitching and convulsive movements seized her body, then stopped. She heaved her last breath. Her lifeless eyes remained open, as if she saw something terrifying, yet they were fixed on nothing. Maydell Scott lay in her pool of piss and blood, dead.

Before going to bed with Clarence, Maria checked on their tired children. She then cleared the dinner table and ensured Clarence and their sons inspected the barn, animals, fires, smokehouse, and that everything was securely fenced. She quietly approached Joseph's bed, watching him sleep. Earlier, she had placed a cup of hot chamomile herbs in his wash water, told him to wash, and made him drink chamomile tea after dinner. As he slept, she softly recited Psalms 121.

When she finished, she placed the family Bible in her sons' room, near their beds, and made sure to include a slip of paper inside the Bible to mark the verse.

Maria went to her room and lay down beside Clarence. Their eyes were closed, but she sensed he was still awake. Today brought a mix of feelings for everyone in the family. By the end of the day, everyone was exhausted but hopeful for better times ahead. The evening was hot, even with a breeze that offered some relief. Maria sat up and took off her nightgown.

"How's your arm?" Clarence asked, rolling onto his side to face her.

"I'm feeling much better, but it's still a little sore. It'll be better in a few days, though," she answered. After a few moments of silence, she spoke up.

"Those children are our lives, and no one will tear this family apart, especially not some no-good two-bit whore."

"Maria, nobody will ever take the children or me from you. Don't even think about such a foolish idea, because I'm not going anywhere." He pulled her close and kissed her deeply, and she responded with a gentle moan.

Already naked, he took her breast in his mouth while caressing the other. The sensation felt like both pain and pleasure, and she didn't want him to stop. She spread her legs for her husband, who was now on top of her.

"Now, Clarence, now!" she cried out, gritting her teeth. Gripping his broad shoulders, he looked into her green eyes and thrust into her with such a long and powerful motion that Maria gasped, surprised by this unexpected response from him. The full, slow, and methodical movements began gradually and increased in speed until they were nearly over. Gritting his teeth and tilting his head back, Clarence exhaled a long breath and remained inside Maria until he couldn't hold it anymore. Carefully pulling himself out, he rolled onto his side, drawing Maria closer to his chest, and held her tight.

"Je t□ aime tellement - I love you," she whispered to him.

"And I love you, Maria", he said.

Sleep eventually overtook them. Maria dreamed of eating fried fish. She then woke up and looked at Clarence, who was sleeping soundly. Turning to the window, she quietly got up and gazed at the sky, where a new moon shone. She smiled, feeling that tonight marked the end of one life and the beginning of a new one for her and Clarence. She stroked her belly, knowing from her dream that a new son would be born in a few months. She returned to bed, held Clarence, and fell asleep again, drifting off into a dream.

CHAPTER TWO

Wash-Day Monday marked the start of a new week, and everyone in the household woke up early. Izelle and Rosetta walked to school with their brothers, following the household rule. Joseph was visibly improving; he was sleeping better and no longer crying at night, thanks to the tea Maria prepared for him after dinner. His academic performance was also improving; according to his science teacher, he could enter the Science and College of Agriculture in two years if he maintained his focus. Maria and Clarence were pleased with his progress. Kempton, however, was uncertain about his future, which worried Clarence, as Kempton was about to graduate from high school. Meanwhile, Sampson was determined to expand the family business, selling meat and vegetables from the farm.

"Sampson, I will teach you everything about hunting, slaughtering, gutting, cleaning, and smoking wild hogs in the smokehouse to sell to locals. But eventually, you'll want some places that cater to our community to buy only from you," Clarence said, pointing at his son's chest to emphasize his point. "The most important thing you need to learn, especially if you intend to own and run this family business, is how to add, resolve problems, divide, and ensure you get paid on time. Let me ask you, Sampson: if you have people working for you, how much will you pay them? How many will work for you when you begin?"

Sampson looked at his father, shrugged, and remained silent.

"Uh-huh, boy, you need a plan. Things will be very different when you run this family's farm. Let me ask some more questions. If our people are going to come to you for the food we grow for their restaurants or stores, will you have a delivery truck, or will you sell directly from here? If you deliver, how many trucks will you have? Who will drive them? Learn to plan and think about these things, because the best way to do so is to do extremely well in your arithmetic lessons, count money, and go to college like your brother Joseph. He will study the soil, and you should learn about business. If I have to work seven days a week to pay for your college education, I will. I want to see all of you succeed," Clarence said firmly to his fearless son, Sampson.

"I will, sir," Sampson said as the two walked down the road together.

"I'll see you all when you get home from school. Be good, everyone," he said as he watched his family join some of the other children their age, all walking together. The heat was already rising, and it wasn't even eight o'clock yet. He waited until the children were out of view, then headed toward the house.

"Coffee? I've kept it hot, and we can also have some of the biscuits from yesterday," Maria said as she poured a cup of coffee for Clarence.

"Thanks," he said as he took a quick sip and bit into the warm, buttery biscuit.

"It's already getting hot outside, and I have a lot of work to do in the garden. The tomatoes, collards, and sweet potatoes need watering, harvesting, and packing into bushel crates for sale. I haven't decided yet whether to sell from the back of the truck or to send word around that we're selling the vegetables here on the farm and that we're taking orders for boar meat locally. When the boys return home and finish their homework, I'll have them help me harvest the sweet potatoes because, by then, I'll be too tired to work alone. It seems like everything will go smoothly, and we'll make good money whether we sell here on the farm or in town."

Maria watched Clarence as he kept sipping his coffee. Things seemed fine, but something felt wrong. Maydell's comment about taking on the role of the new mother to her children and Clarence's wife stuck out. Maydell appeared so sure of herself. However, if everything went according to plan, Maydell wouldn't be involved much. "Bonne putain de débarras, good riddance, whore."

"Did you say something?" Clarence asked, as he looked over at his wife.

He smirked and asked, "You said something in Creole twice. What's going on with you? You've been quiet since Saturday, well, until Saturday night."

The details of that evening still lingered vividly in her memory. When she and Clarence awoke early on

Sunday, their passionate encounter confirmed to her that she was expecting a child. The idea of another baby seemed perfect for their family, especially since the boys were growing up, and in a few years, the girls would start school to hone their sewing skills and then marry. One more child now, and another the following year, will complete their family. If Clarence were employed and the farm was thriving, two more children would be a welcome addition. However, her thoughts were suddenly interrupted by something more serious.

"I need to ask you something," she said, biting into her biscuit. "What was Maydell talking about, saying she would move in here and be the mother of our children, Clarence? What did she mean? Did you have an affair with her?"

Clarence paused his eating long enough to glance at his wife, who was now so upset that she was heaving and staring at him. He could have sworn that for a moment he saw her green eyes turn red.

"Answer me!" she yelled.

"I thought I told you that nothing was happening and that I didn't mess around with her! Got-damn it, Maria, stop bringing this up!" he said, getting up from his chair.

"Ah-no, mon amour," said Maria, who wasn't backing down from discussing how she was feeling. "Something doesn't feel right. I noticed that when you wouldn't answer me when I asked you if you were messing around with that pute!"

"Stop it!" Clarence snapped as he pushed himself up from the table and angrily poured his coffee down the sink. He then turned to push his chair back forcefully, causing it to shake and startle Maria, who quickly moved away. The argument grew more heated; she accused him, and Clarence denied it all. Maria raised her voice, shouting and screeching louder than Clarence as their voices intensified. Luckily, no neighbors were nearby to overhear their accusations about infidelity. Suddenly, both of them heard knocking at the door.

They paused briefly to glance toward the curtained door and saw the shadow of a woman in a white work dress, a blue purse hanging at the crook of her arm, and a headscarf tied tightly on her head. Clarence approached the door.

"Audine? Oh my God! We haven't seen you in a while, c'mon in!" he said, shifting the topic as he warmly embraced her and guided her into the kitchen.

"I understand," Audine Booker said, returning the hug. "You don't need to worry about mentioning my late husband, Ruddell's name. It's been five years since he passed, and I know I have to move forward with my life now."

"Good morning, Maria," Audine said with a smile.

"Good morning, Audine," Maria said tersely, giving a quick nod. "Please have a seat." She gestured to the chair beside her as Clarence pulled out the seat for Audine to sit in.

Audine, a forty-year-old woman, was exhausted. The temples of her pulled-back hairline revealed telltale signs of gray. She had wrinkles on her forehead, giving her a perpetually worried look. Her dull, brown eyes, which once sparkled, now seemed lifeless and hollow. Her gray-and-white hospital uniform showed the hard work she was doing. Old sweat stains were turning yellow under both armpits of the uniform. Faded bloodstains and grease spots decorated the front. It's a wonder she could keep working at that hospital amid death, sickness, and patients screaming in pain. One word summed up Audine at that moment: despair.

"Let me pour you some coffee, Audine," said Maria.

"Thank you, Maria. I haven't eaten since last night," Audine said. Without waiting for Maria to offer a biscuit, she shamelessly helped herself to the tasty treat.

"I forgot to bring my lunch, and we don't have time to eat. It was also a busy night at the hospital," she said, as she hurriedly shoved the biscuit into her mouth.

"Oh? What happened?" Clarence, suddenly intrigued by a distraction from his earlier encounter with Maria, listened with interest.

"You all know Maydell Scott?" she asked, taking a quick sip of the piping hot coffee.

"Yes, we know her, don't we, Clarence?" Maria said, her gaze not leaving him.

"Well, she's dead," Audine said as she added more sugar and milk to her coffee.

"What?" Clarence asked in disbelief. "We just saw her on Saturday! What happened to her?"

Around one in the morning, she was brought in by a group from the flophouse where she stayed. Humph, it was quite a sight. She was covered in blood, and one of the tenants who helped carry her in, what's his name?" she asked, glancing around the kitchen. "Owen!" she suddenly remembered, exclaiming.

"What do you mean she was covered in blood?" Maria asked.

"Was she shot or stabbed? What exactly happened?" Audine's story drew sudden interest as she kept talking.

Audine recounted how Owen told the doctor that Maydell rushed into the parlor where he and his friends were entertaining female guests. She was shouting that she smelled smoke and that a fire was burning inside the house. Owen claimed there was no smoke or fire, saying he and his guests had been in the parlor for hours, drinking and enjoying music.

"So, Maydell was saying there was a fire when there actually wasn't?"

"Yes, that's right," Audine said between bites of the biscuit. "Owen thought she was crazy. But what was even more interesting was that big bandage over her eye. Nobody knew how it got there. The flophouse owner, Ole Lizzene, went to visit her sister earlier that day, so there were no answers right away. But when she returned later, she told Owen that Maydell had gotten into a fight earlier on Saturday. She didn't say who she got into a fight with. All I heard is that when the doctor removed the bandage, it was already infected; pus and blood oozed out everywhere."

Clarence asked, "So, what happened with this smoke and fire?"

"Oh, yes," Audine continued. "What Owen also told the doctor was that Maydell wouldn't stop coughing."

Clarence whispered, "Oh my God," in a hushed voice.

Maria stayed silent, slowly sipping her coffee while paying close attention to Audine's words. *Everything I did after the fight with that pute was successful.*

"Well, the situation got worse," Audine continued. "According to Owen, Maydell pulled up her dress and peed right in front of everyone! And if that wasn't enough, she clutched her stomach, bent over, and threw up blood. Then she fell to the floor headfirst and died. Most likely, she cracked her skull because she hit the ground so hard. The women began screaming, and one of them collapsed at the sight of so much blood. Owen and the other men carried the woman and took her friends to another room so they could move Maydell to Owen's car and take her to the hospital. But when they arrived, it was already too late. She was dead."

"What about Maydell's family?" Clarence asked.

Audine asked, "What family?" as she reached for another biscuit. Owen explained that Maydell was kicked out of her mother's house at seventeen, mainly because she was often causing trouble there. One day, when her mother returned home, she went looking for Maydell and found her in bed with her mother's second husband. Maydell seemed to have a fondness for him because he always had money and bought her nice things, associating with her usual preference for handsome men like the gambler High Roller-Gunn. She was supposed to leave with him for New York the night she died, but that plan evidently didn't come to pass. So, she doesn't have any family to bury her.

"Humph, maybe the High-Roller will bury her," Maria said, smirking.

"That's enough, Maria," Clarence said sharply.

Maria cast a sharp glare at her husband, feeling hurt and confused that he would openly humiliate her in front of Audine. Something isn't right, and I plan to find out what it is, she thought, pressing her lips together.

"The hospital will take care of her remains. It's common, women, I mean folks like her, who have no family," Audine said as she reached for a third biscuit.

Maria glared at Audine, spreading butter on it, then hurriedly put it into her mouth. It's like she hasn't eaten in weeks!

"I didn't come here to deliver bad news about Maydell, but to ask if you both could help me. I need a big favor," Audine said.

Maria and Clarence exchanged glances, bracing themselves for her request. What could she possibly be asking for? Money, food, or a place to stay?

As you know, my husband Ruddell passed away five years ago. Since then, I've been working at the hospital to provide for my daughter, Violet, and my son, Mason. I want to tell you, Maria, you're very fortunate to have your husband here helping you run this farm. Look at how you're living—better than most Black people here. You have a large house, plenty of food, all this land, and even a smokehouse! How did you manage to afford all this?" she asked, studying the kitchen with renewed interest.

"Hard work over many years," Clarence said, pointing to himself. "My brothers and I saved every penny we earned from this farm after our mother and father passed away. When my brothers died, everything was left to me."

"Oh my, I see," Audine said enviously as she kept glancing around the kitchen, examining every detail of Maria's decor, the neatly arranged pots and pans, and how spotless it was compared to her own home.

"Ruddell kept everything he earned. He didn't hold back anything. He even worked on Sundays when he should have been in church with me and our children. The people he worked for worked him to death," she said, tears welling up in her eyes.

"I'm truly sorry, Audine," Maria said, gently reaching out to hold her hand. "What can we do to help you?"

"We all know what happened to Jonathan Davis," she added weakly as she blew her nose.

"Jonathan and our son Joseph were the best of friends," Clarence said, looking down at the floor. "That young man had a very bright future ahead of him. He was like a brother to Joseph, and thanks to him, Joseph excelled in science and arithmetic. We miss him deeply, but Joseph misses him even more."

"What happened to that child was horrible," Audine said, shaking her head. "I saw him brought into the hospital. Half of his head was blown off. Several nurses fainted when they saw his injuries, whip marks on his back, bruises on his face, and his eye was missing. The mortician explained that his eye was shot out. My God, none of us is safe! But I want to ask if Clarence can stay at my house while I work the third shift. Since Jonathan died, we're very scared, especially for my children. We have nothing to defend ourselves with. You both have sons who can handle rifles. Violet, Mason, and I have nothing."

Before Maria could even answer or understand what Audine was asking, Clarence responded to the request.

"Of course, Audine," Clarence replied. "Everyone on this stretch of the road now knows that Jonathan's murder serves as a warning for all of us to stick together and protect our families, friends, property, and one another. So, yes, I am more than happy to help you and your family."

"God bless you, Clarence," Audine said as she held his arm. "Could you start next Wednesday and return on Thursday? Those are my third shift days. If you need help with your farm, Mason can come by on Saturdays until three in the afternoon, so he can be home for dinner and prepare for church on Sunday. I'm lucky to have weekends off."

"Wednesdays and Thursdays work for me. What time should I be at your place?

"I have to be at the hospital at seven-thirty in the evening, and I get off at five-thirty in the morning. I'm home by six o'clock. You know, I am so happy that Wayne Collins, who goes to our church, also has the same shift and picks me up and drives me home, or else I would have had to walk to the hospital," Audine said, smiling.

"Wait a minute," Maria interrupted, clearly annoyed with Clarence for excluding her from the conversation. "Why can't Violet and Mason just stay at his house while Wayne's wife watches them?"

"What wife?" Audine quipped.

Maria was now confused as the furrow of her forehead deepened as she anticipated an answer. *And how dare Clarence agree to this without a discussion! What has gotten into him?*

"Did you hear about what happened to Wayne's wife, Lena? She ran off with that gambler, High Roller-Gunn! Wayne told me he came home from work and found a note on the table. In it, she apologized but said she was done being his wife, that she hated living in Louisiana, and wanted to leave. She mentioned she would send the divorce papers once she reached Harlem, New York. Audine said disgustedly, "He was heartbroken. I went over to help him clean up since she had left the house a mess. She took all the savings, about one hundred and fifty dollars, stored in a wooden box under their bed, along with nearly all their food and her clothes. All that was left for Wayne was two dollars and the bed they shared."

"That's just terrible!" Maria exclaimed. However, she couldn't help but wonder if something similar might happen to her. Would Clarence suddenly leave, like Lena left her husband? The idea sent a chill through her, prompting her to stand up and pour another cup of coffee to warm her up.

"Well, I gotta go," Audine said as she took the last sip of coffee. "I've been here too long and don't want Violet and Mason to worry. Besides, I need to do laundry and prepare dinner for tonight. No wonder they call it Wash Day Monday," she said, rising from her chair to stretch her swollen legs after sitting there for an hour.

Maria and Clarence followed her to the door to see her out.

"God bless you," Audine said warmly as she hugged Clarence. "I'll see you next Wednesday at six." Waving goodbye to both, she stepped outside. They heard a car horn and the rumble of an approaching vehicle. Wayne Collins had arrived. Audine entered the front seat and shut the door. Wayne honked and called out greetings to Clarence and Maria, who waved back as they headed to the road to go home. After their departure, Maria and Clarence re-entered the house.

"It's getting late, and there are lots of chores to finish," Clarence said as he tilted the cup to drain the last of his coffee. "The smokehouse is doing well, and by Saturday, we can have folks over to buy some smoked meats, tomatoes, eggs, sweet potatoes, and corn. I have a feeling that we're gonna do good if folks come out here first before they go to the market."

He was met with silence as Maria busied herself clearing the table and placing the dishes in the sink.

"What's wrong with you now?" he sighed, exhausted by the arguing. It was becoming quite irritating, and with everything happening, these petty fights were unwelcome at this moment.

"What's wrong?" she asked, turning to Clarence while drying her hands. "What's wrong is that you first told Audine you're going there to watch her kids. I'm not happy about that at all!" she said, slamming the dish towel into the sink. "What about our family, Clarence?" Maria asked, her voice trembling with fear.

"This is our neighbor and friend, Maria. Just in case you need a reminder, I worked with Ruddell for years, right up until the week before he passed away! Have you also forgotten that he was my best man when you ran away from your mother to marry me? My God,

Maria, what has gotten into you?" Clarence's heart was pounding as he rested a sweaty hand on the cupboard to steady himself.

"I haven't forgotten how Ruddell was there for us, Clarence!" Maria shouted. "What really angers me is that you didn't include me in this important decision, which will impact our family. How could you be so self-centered!"

"You know what? This isn't getting us anywhere," Clarence said, raising his arms in frustration. "I'm tired of all this fighting and just want to move on with my day. When you can act reasonably, we'll talk. Until then, you're behaving like a child." He then left, slamming the door behind him.

Maria stood stunned in the kitchen, her eyes wide. Did this really happen? A deep sense of trouble washed over her, like an intruder had invaded her space. She felt humiliated in front of Audine Booker; a petty gossip who dares call herself a church-going woman. The audacity of Audine, riding around in a car with Wayne Collins, who is still married despite not living with Lena!

"I've got a lot of work to do today," Maria said aloud, affirming herself. Then she returned to the kitchen to begin her tasks. After placing the heavy pot filled with red beans and onions on the stove to simmer, she chopped the sausage, which would cook once the beans were tender. In about fifteen minutes, the house was already filled with wonderful aromas. However, thanks to Audine's greedy appetite, all the remaining biscuits were gone, so there would be no dessert of sweetened wild blackberries drizzled with warm butter and sugar, a delicious mixture her Grande Mère used to make. Wiping away the tears of her morning frustration, Maria got busy. After an hour, everything was finished.

The kitchen was spotless and peaceful, and the scents of the beans and sausage she prepared for dinner filled the house. She grabbed the egg basket and went out to the barn to collect as many eggs as the big red hen had laid for the day.

Maria approached the barn, feeling the noonday sun's intensity, even hotter than earlier. A breeze was absent, leaving the thick humidity unrelieved. Inside, she found Clarence in the large barn his family had owned for over sixty-nine years. The barn was massive, once housing horse stalls, but due to cost and maintenance, Clarence and his brothers sold all ten horses and two mules. With the proceeds, they bought a truck to transport vegetables to the New Orleans wharf. Any remaining money was used to buy a car for church trips, a rare luxury for their Black family. Clarence was busy sorting overflowing bushel crates of vegetables, over eighty-seven bushels. Due to the heat, he wasn't wearing a shirt, and sweat streamed down his forehead, back, and torso, his Nubian skin glistening. Maria gazed at her husband in admiration, captivated by his effort. He looked up and caught her staring at him.

"Hey," he said, returning to count the large pile of sweet potatoes and mark everything on the small scribble pad of paper he held.

"Hello," she greeted, coming closer. "You've gotten a lot done since this morning. It seems many items will be sold. I hear most people prefer buying from us rather than visiting the store in New Orleans, where we're not exactly welcome. So, have you decided to sell here, or will you head to the wharf to sell everything in New Orleans?"

"I've thought about this a lot while working out here," he said, wiping his brow. "We'll sell everything outside the barn since it's easier, I won't have to pack everything into the truck and make the trip back home before nightfall, especially with the boys. We'll tell the children to inform their teachers, so everyone knows. I also spoke with Deacon Frank Boone from the church about fifteen minutes before you arrived. I told him that since he works at the hospital, he can inform Audine, and once she knows, the entire hospital will get involved. He'll also invite some church members. We plan to do this Saturday morning and close at five. I believe we'll raise a lot of money, and I feel good about it. Since Sampson wants to do this for a living someday, he'll learn a lot by helping me. I also intend to talk to his arithmetic teacher to see if he can come observe how Sampson manages the money; it could be useful as extra homework or part of a thing".

Maria exhaled deeply, feeling relief, yet she winced at Audine's name. Ruddell and Clarence were close friends, but Audine's penchant for gossip, meddling, and mood swings was overwhelming. Was she truly a good friend? Probably not. By now, the words of her overhearing the argument were likely everywhere, including at the hospital where she worked. It was undoubtedly a topic of discussion during her ride home with Wayne.

"Maria, we need to talk, honey. Come sit down," Pulling up an extra chair from the corner and sitting next to him.

"This fighting between us needs to end. We've been arguing for weeks, and it isn't good. Our children overheard us even when we were in the barn, shouting. Audine tends to gossip, and I'm worried that everyone will find out once she gets to work," Clarence said quietly, lowering his voice.

"Afraid of what, Clarence? Is there something you're not telling me, maybe the truth about Maydell?" Maria asked, closing her eyes and sighing. She was convinced that something indeed happened between them, but without Clarence confessing, there was no point in continuing the conversation, at least for now.

"You know what?" Clarence said, standing up. "This ends now. My answer to your question is no. I wasn't messing around with Maydell. She was always trying to cause trouble, especially when she had her eyes on married men, men she knew she couldn't have. That was just her way of pretending."

"Pretending what, Clarence? That she would come here, marry you, and stay with our children while pretending to be their mother? My God, that woman was crazy!" Maria exclaimed. "But what really bothers me is that you also left me out of the discussion and decision about going to take care of Audine's children, leaving us behind! Do you realize how dangerous that is, especially after what happened to Johnathan? How could you put this family in such danger? How, Clarence?" Maria quickly stood up, causing the chair to fall to the barn floor and frightening the family cat, which then ran out of the barn.

"Maria, come back over here and sit down!" Clarence said as he picked up the chair, slamming it back into place. "Sit down!"

Maria, initially hesitant, looked at her husband with hurt and anger before reluctantly sitting beside him.

My reason for deciding quickly was because Ruddell would have wanted me to do so. He and I were friends even before you and I met. He helped me bury my brothers and in many other ways, which kept me from losing this farm. Also, don't forget that Ruddell was the one who found the preacher who married us secretly in the middle of the night, just before your mother planned to force you into an arranged marriage with a French Navy officer. Without him finding that preacher, you all would have been on a boat to France, in that arranged marriage with someone you never met! So, we owe Ruddell that much. Do I think he married the wrong woman? Yes, I do. We warned him that Audine had a big mouth, but he married her anyway. For a while, she even spread rumors that you were a French mistress not married to me. Ruddell quickly set her straight, warning that if she didn't apologize, the wedding would be off," Clarence said, gazing at her.

Remembering all those years ago brought back many memories, especially one in particular: the arranged marriage her Mère had planned, set to take place early that fateful day. Her Mère had arranged a beautiful wedding with a lavish lunch afterward. Then, Sunday morning, after attending Mass at the Catholic church, Maria, her new husband, and her Mère would sail off to France, never to see New Orleans or Clarence Margaret again. Clarence was right to tell the truth about that, but Audine spreading that horrible rumor all those years ago was enough to make her turn away from her, even after all this time. That explained why she was being extra kind after she and Ruddell married and why she was always so complimentary.

Now I know! Not only does she have a big mouth spreading gossip, but what a liar she is! Oh, that wretched woman! And already, underneath a man still married, even though his wife, Lena, is no longer living in their home.

"I remember everything, Clarence, but there's got to be a way for us to be looked after. Our sons know how to use rifles on wild animals, not people. I'm terrified, Clarence," Maria said softly.

Here's what I'll do. I'm going to talk to Ricks and his men to see if they can drive by when you're alone with the children, because until I talk to Audine to find out how long she needs me, I'm not leaving this family unprotected. Clarence said. "Let me talk to him, hopefully today if he drives by, because he never travels alone without some of his men in the car with him and several carloads following him. Some of those men are former hardened criminals. Those rednecks and yahoos are afraid of them, but they all know their place. I'll handle this.

"Alright, let Audine know you can handle Violet and Mason, but ask her how long this is going to go on. You have a family right here that needs to be looked after," Maria said as she stood up.

Clarence said, "There's something else I need to tell you."

"What's that?" Maria asked, looking back at him.

"I'm sorry. I should have discussed this with you first," he said. "Come here," he beckoned Maria. Instead of sitting back, she lifted her dress and straddled the chair to face her husband, then began kissing him passionately. Clarence quickly removed her dress top, revealing her bare breasts, which he started to kiss. She moaned loudly, and with his other hand, he fondled her breast, pinching her nipple between his thumb and finger, making Maria react intensely.

Putting her arms around his neck, she stood so he could remove her panties and then sat back down on his lap. She felt his hardness through his work trousers, and sensing what she wanted, he unzipped his pants and slid halfway out of them.

"Sit here, Maria," he said, pointing to his male hardness that was waiting for her. She slowly eased herself on him until Clarence was completely inside her. The slow grid soon picked up, and Maria arched her neck back as Clarence was tasting her breasts now one at a time, and then gave her a sharp nip at her breast that made her gasp. Clarence's pace was now so fast that they both breathed hard, moaning, and Maria was grasping onto him tighter. He clapped her buttocks with an open palm, making her moan loudly.

"Did you like that?" he asked huskily.

"Oui-yes, Clarence, again!" This time, he smacked her buttock harder, held his hand there, and circled it again with his open palm, then smacked harder again:

whap! Maria shrieked with pleasure, and Clarence held her tightly to make her slide even deeper inside him.

"Faster, Maria!" he commanded through his gritted teeth, erasing all recent fights from their minds. As Maria neared climax with her husband, trivial concerns no longer mattered. She loved her husband; she and the children were well provided for, and in about a month, a new life would be created. If they continued to have such moments in the barn now and then, who knows? Two or even three more children might join the family. The thought of another baby feeding at her breasts made her deliriously happy.

"Maria!" he shouted, reaching a violent climax that made her grip her husband's shoulders until she was ready to let go. Both were covered in sweat, breathing heavily, and barely able to move.

"I love you, Maria," Clarence said breathlessly as he cradled her head in his hands. "Don't ever think otherwise. I'm only devoted to you, nobody else."

"I love you, too, Clarence. What you said earlier makes it clear that we need to look out for each other. As long as we're all protected, I believe we can get through this," Maria said, deeply kissing him.

"Let's go into the lake to clean up," Clarence said, slowly easing himself out of Maria. "There's no time to fill the washtub. Let's just run in and get out of the water quickly."

"Clarence, I don't know. Joseph said he saw a big water moccasin in the lake," said Maria. Maria remembered seeing a water moccasin bite a child several years ago. It was horrifying to watch as the snake stayed latched onto the child's little hand. After it let go, the child was dead.

"We'll be okay because we won't stay in the water for long," he said as he collected their clothes and two towels he always kept in the barn. They walked to the lake holding hands. After placing their clothes and towels under a tree, they held hands again and ran toward the water. Initially, the water was icy, but the rushing sound was calming.

"This is what I want with you forever," she whispered, clutching his neck and looping her legs around his waist. However, she caught sight of it out of the corner of her eye, the black snake resting on the rocks, its size seemingly unusually large as it slid from the rocks into the water toward them.

"Clarence, we need to leave the water now! The snake Joseph saw just went into the water and is heading straight for us!"

Clarence grabbed Maria's hand, pulling her out of the water swiftly, and they both ran to the tree where their clothes were. They stared at the lake, unaware of their nudity, as the snake continued swimming further into the water until it disappeared from view.

"Oh my God, Clarence, I've never seen a snake that long, especially a moccasin," Maria said, trembling.

"That's unusual to see a snake that long in these parts. Keep the kids away from here. If we fish over here, we're all bringing a rifle. My God, one bite, and that thing will kill someone fast and painfully," said Clarence as he took a towel and handed it to Maria. "That thing is old. Nothing that big and long is a young one. Well, come on, Mrs. Margaret. I guess you forgot all about what you needed to get in the barn," he said, patting her backside. "Let's get outta here; we've got a lot to do before the kids get home. Oh, and by the way, Ricks may come over."

After they quickly dried off and folded the towels, Clarence draped his arm over Maria's shoulders, and she held onto his waist. They arrived at the barn, and Maria grabbed her egg basket, heading straight to the hens. The big red hen, which consistently produced up to ten eggs, was crucial for steady sales. To protect her, she was kept in a special, high-up spot in the barn where predators couldn't reach her. The family dog, a large and aggressive mutt, would alert with loud growls and continuous barking and attack if needed. To collect eggs, Maria had to climb a steep ladder to reach the hen carefully. She finally reached the top step, where the hen was resting on her nest. But something was unusual; the hen usually was very jumpy when someone approached, but now she was perfectly still, facing the right side of the wall, as if transfixed by something.

"Good afternoon, Red," Maria greeted as she reached beneath the hen to gather eggs. The hen suddenly spread her wings and jumped off the nest, exposing fifteen freshly laid eggs.

"Bien! Good!" exclaimed Maria as she carefully collected the eggs and gently descended the ladder. She meticulously counted the eggs to ensure none were damaged. Elated, she set the ladder back and looked up to check on the hen. Maria couldn't believe what she was seeing. The hen had returned to the nest facing the right side of the barn wall, remaining perfectly still. But there was no time to waste.

"I'll see you back at the house for lunch, Clarence," she called out as she walked out of the barn.

"Hey, how about some ham and fried eggs?" Clarence asked, wiping sweat from his brow.

"Yes, she replied. I'll call you once everything is ready," she called back to him as she exited the barn and headed toward the house.

She carefully stored the eggs in the icebox and began preparing dinner. After forty-five minutes, she had baked four pans of cornbread, and the rice and beans with andouille sausage were simmering. The whole kitchen was filled with a wonderful aroma.

As Maria stepped outside to call Clarence, she noticed several unfamiliar cars, even though Clarence had mentioned that Ricks might visit. She recognized his car, but the others were unknown to her. Suddenly, fear seized her, and she quickly ran to the tool shed. She moved to the corner where the rifles were stored and grabbed a pistol from a special wooden box Clarence had bought years ago, which she always kept loaded. Holding it firmly and aiming downward, she hurried toward the barn. In just a short moment, she saw another car parked alongside the others, increasing her fear. She ran toward the barn without regard for who might be inside, determined to protect her husband. She reached the barn and burst through the door.

"Afternoon, Maria," the deep but familiar voice said. A circle of men surrounded Clarence while several of them looked at and selected vegetables that Clarence had picked and packed in the bushel boxes. The entire barn, filled with men from the surrounding community and from farther south of New Orleans, began to sound more like an outdoor market. Several of the men were already sipping beverages from flasks, talking, laughing, and handing over money to Clarence, who stuffed many bills inside the leather bag he used when selling in the open market down by the wharf. Except for a man she spotted, whom she had never seen before, he was sitting in a corner with a long, sharp machete that he was sharpening meticulously. Maria tightened her grip on her pistol and Clarence's arm.

"Oh him," said the man, known in the community only as Ricks, gesturing toward the man sharpening the weapon.

Don't worry about Jacquè Pierrè. We call him Jack because many of the men here can't say his real name. He's a Creole man who speaks a little English and mostly French Creole because his folks are from a place called Haiti. I've never heard of it, except that he knows how to use that machete besides just cutting meat," Ricks said as he pulled out a flask from his back pocket and took a long sip.

Maria was stunned but also very happy that someone besides her knew how to speak French Creole! After she heard what Ricks had to say, she decided to approach the mysterious man who sat frozen with his long, deadly-looking weapon.

Ricks. He stood five feet six inches tall, a dark-complexioned man who always had a lit pipe in his mouth and wore the same hat since the day he escaped prison. Ricks was a murderous man who was not to be crossed. Even most of the rednecks and yahoos feared him because of what they heard he was capable of if crossed the wrong way. The rules applied for both sides: stay on your side, stay out of the way, and move along. The thirty men inside the barn were all friends of Ricks. They all had something in common: prison. All of them had served hard time, from petty theft to murder.

Ricks was a former convict who claimed he was set up during a card game. According to his story, he was drinking heavily and losing, so he folded in the first round. The hostess, who was serving fried fish and whiskey, helped him into her bedroom, where he passed out on her bed. Hours later, when he woke up, his head was pounding from whiskey and cheap wine. His pants were around his ankles, exposing himself, and he was shocked to find a gun in his hand. The house was eerily quiet from the last time he remembered. Just before passing out, he recalled the smell of frying fish, the loud laughter of the card players as they slapped down their cards, and the hostess guiding him into the bedroom. A burning smell filled the house, and in his drunken state, he staggered into the room where the card game was happening and, to his horror, saw the eight card players and the hostess dead. Each was shot twice in the head, and six white police officers stood in the room, their angry faces turning toward him, guns drawn.

"Don't move!" shouted an officer, pointing his gun at Ricks. "Put the gun down and raise your hands so we can see them!" Then they descended on him like locusts, slamming his face on the filthy kitchen wall, hoisting him up, snapping handcuffs on his wrists, and then shoving him headfirst into a waiting police car.

After a month, the trial concluded, and Ricks was sentenced to thirty years of hard labor. Two days later, the sentence was enforced immediately. While working in a field, he and four fellow convicts he had befriended devised an escape plan.

"The plan is to distract the officer on the horse. When he loses his footing, we run. Those two convicts nearby are always fighting," Ricks said, nodding toward the two who were already shouting and escalating into a confrontation. "I told one of them to start a fight so the others would join in. That's when we make our escape." He explained this to the four who nodded in agreement. Suddenly, the two convicts on the other side of the field started a heated argument that quickly turned into a fistfight. The other convicts ran toward the chaos and joined in beating the two fighters, prompting the officer to dismount from his horse, leaving his rifle behind as he ran away. One of the escapees grabbed the gun and ran behind Ricks and the others. Over the following weeks, they found shelter with several families who knew Ricks and two of the other escapees.

Later, it was revealed that Charlie Poke, one of the card players on that tragic night, was losing badly, which led to an argument. The opponent he argued with drew a nine-inch straight razor and threatened Poke's life. However, Poke acted faster, pulling out his gun and shooting all the players at the table, including the hostess. Ricks avoided being shot because he was asleep in the next room. Poke then stole all the money, entered Ricks's bedroom where he was sleeping, and left the gun in his hand.

Three weeks after the murders, Poke was found dead while attempting to do the same at another card game. The shooter, who also carried a gun, knew about Poke's role in the earlier murders of eight card players and the hostess. He was well-prepared.

After ten years, twenty-six of Ricks's former cellmates eventually located him and quietly resumed their lives.

"We wanted to tell you that we know who killed Jonathan," Ricks said, sitting in the chair placed in the center of the group. Maria gripped Clarence's arm more tightly. One of Rick's men pulled out another chair so Maria could sit down.

"We came here to tell you personally that no one will ever see those men again," Ricks said, crossing his leg and removing the pipe from his mouth.

"Tell us what happened," Clarence said.

"Well, a few weeks after Jonathan was buried, our friend Alan Beaks here was in town sweeping the walkway in front of old man Franklin's store where he works," gesturing to a tall man with a deep jagged scar running from his forehead to his partially closed right eye. "Welp, a father and his son were talking loud enough for Alan to overhear what they were saying."

"We sho nuff taught that young nigger a lesson, yes sirree! Hah!!!! Your grand-daddy's whip he used to use when he was an overseer back in those days tore the black offa that boy's back! I enjoyed hearing him scream Oh, please stop, sir! You're hurting me! Yo grand-daddy showed me how to raise that whip, whirl it up in the air, and then *boom*! Strike it on that boy's back as hard as you could! Yass Suh! When his hide started coming off his back, I knew it was your turn to show me what I taught ya!" the father said, laughing.

"Yeah, daddy!" "Soon as we told him to walk to the water, I told him you ain't walkin' fast enuff! Now run into that water, boy!" Soon as he got deep enough, I pulled that rifle and squeezed that there trigger, and bam! One to the back of his head! Oh, my Gawd, daddy! That thing gotta a lot of power 'cause half of that boy's head went flying everywhere! I took one more shot just for fun, but I missed. It was okay, 'cause that first shot was the best one!" the son said, laughing.

"The son and his daddy didn't think Alan was listening. They kept talking and laughing about how they killed poor Jonathan. But you see, one thing that boy should've done was to shut his big mouth," Ricks said as he cleared his throat and adjusted his sitting position. "He told exactly when and where they would return to the same fishing spot where they murdered Jonathan. Well, Alan kept pretending to sweep and clean until Old Man Franklin told him he could leave for the day and return early the next morning. Alan shared everything he had heard with me, and that's when I gathered everyone and decided to pay them a visit at the fishing spot. We wanted to give them both a taste of what they did to Jonathan. We also brought Jack along," Ricks explained. Jack looked up briefly to glance at everyone, nodded, then returned to sharpening his machete.

Ricks recounted how Lenny Gray from their group went fishing, and sure enough, at precisely the right time, they saw him walking toward the fishing spot. When the father spotted Lenny, he ran over shouting at him, but Lenny pretended not to hear. The father then yanked the fishing pole from Lenny's hands and told him to leave immediately, or he and his son would kill him, just like they did to that boy a few weeks earlier. The father then ordered Lenny to leave.

"Well, Len glanced at both of them and said, 'Vengeance is mine.' The son told Len to shut up, then raised his hand with the club ready to strike. Suddenly, the first shot was fired, hitting the boy right in his hand. The club flew out of his hand so quickly that he screamed like a little girl!" described Ricks.

Everyone in the barn laughed as Ricks continued the story.

"The father rushed to help his boy, and then another shot rang out—boom! It hit him right in the back of the shoulder, causing him to fall on his ass. Then we all came out with our guns and rifles. Some of my men emerged from the bush, others jumped down from the trees, and two hid behind a large rock. Jack, with a machete in one hand and two knives clenched between his teeth, ran towards the boy, frightening him so much that he started peeing his pants and crying."

"So, what happened, Ricks?" Maria asked, her chest heaving, not out of pity for the murderers, but for her son's best friend, wishing they suffer twice the pain Jonathan endured. *"J' espère que ces salauds ont souffert!"* *I hope those bastards suffered!*

"Well, it gets better, yes, ma'am, it sho nuff do get better," Ricks said as one of his men handed him a flask. He took a quick sip of the whiskey, replaced the cap, and kept on going.

"After they were shot, we surrounded them. I went to the father, and I says to him, " Are you okay? His son says to his father, *"Don't answer that dirty nigger, daddy!"* Like I said, that boy had a big mouth, cause two of my men went on either side, one to the left and one to the right, and they stood on his arms so that he couldn't move. Jack took a short ax out of his pocket, raised it, and in one clean chop, cut off the right hand and then the left. The boy started screaming, and damn, so much blood. Woo! Jack took the hands and put them in a sack. Then the boy's father started screaming and hollering that he was sorry and that they didn't mean to kill Jonathan, but he should've remembered and obeyed the rules around here, or he'd be alive. But no sooner than he finished saying that Jack goes to the father, raises the ax high, and then swings the ax, and cuts the man's foot off. Blood goes everywhere, and then does the same with the other foot, and puts it in the bloody sack. The screaming between the two was like they were trying to scream over each other," said Ricks.

*Served them right. Now Jonathan can rest in peace,
Clarence thought.* "I hope those fuckers suffered,"
Clarence said through his clenched teeth, as he shifted
his stance in the chair so that Maria was now sitting on
his lap, her head heavily resting on his shoulder. He kept
listening to Rick's account of what had happened.

"Yes, indeed, son," replied Ricks. "After that, two of
my men lifted the father, and the other two took the son,
and I hope those bastards suffered. They dragged the
father and son to Jack's boat and threw them in. I
stepped in, sat down, and lit my pipe to smoke. Jack
took the father and placed his bloody legs over the
edge of the boat to let the blood drain into the water.
He did the same with the son, making him put what was
left of his hands into the water to drain the blood.
Afterward, Jack paddled the boat further into the
swamp."

"We said we was sorry," the father said weakly, bleeding profusely from his wounds.

"Do you think we should forgive you and your boy after what you did to one of ours?" Ricks asked, lighting his pipe, taking a few puffs, and exhaling the fragrant smoke. "That young man had a lot of promise. You took him from his mama and daddy. That was their only child. Losing him drove her outta her mind, especially having to witness half of her son's head blown off. When they cried, we all cried!" Ricks yelled, fists clenched.

"But I said we was sorry." the father said, who was now weeping.

"Shut up, Daddy!" the son shouted. "That nigger had no business being in a place that belongs to us!" Before he could say something else, he went silent when Jack took a hammer and smashed the son's nose in, flattening it to a grotesque, minuscule piece of bloodied flesh. The son was unconscious.

"You know what? I told you that son of yours has no manners and doesn't know when to keep his mouth shut. We had to do this for Jonathan, and now both of you have to leave," Ricks said to the father as he took another draw from his pipe.

The boat drifted further into the swamp. Jack sounded a sharp whistle, attracting the alligators' attention. It seemed as if they recognized the sound and became alert.

"Time for this ride to end, boys," Ricks said to the unconscious son and his father. Moving closer to the semi-conscious father, Ricks took a draw from his pipe and blew the smoke into the face of the father, who let out a weak cough. Grabbing the father's hair and pulling his head back, Ricks coughed and hacked up from the depths of his throat a thick wad of slimy brown mucus and spat into his face. Then he signaled Jack to deliver the meal to the alligators. Jack effortlessly picked up the son and threw him overboard. The moment the sound of the body hitting the water happened, the alligators swam into the water, and a frenzy ensued as the body was torn to pieces. The largest alligator seared off his head, and a piece of his leg and torso were in shreds. Blood was all over the water. The father was next, and this time the frenzy was worse than when the son was thrown in. The sounds of his skull being crushed, severed legs, and arms were horrific. Ricks and Jack watched in silent amazement as the smaller alligators were biting each other to get scraps of the bloodied flesh. When there was nothing left except the blood in the water, it was over. Jack let out another high, shrill whistle and began to chant in Patois to the alligators and then began to row the boat back to the fishing spot, which was another five miles away from the depths of the swamp. The men were waiting with fresh buckets of wash water and clean clothes for them to change into, so that Ricks and Jack could wash away the blood and the evidence of what had happened a few hours ago. The bloodied dirt was collected and thrown into the water, the bloodied clothing of Ricks, Jack, and the four men who held the father and son down were burned, and the ashes were scattered amongst the various parts of the wooded area that surrounded the water. All evidence of what happened disappeared.

After the meeting in the barn, Ricks, his men, and Clarence began doing business. Jack even assisted Clarence with cutting meat, impressing him with his skill at slicing it into thin, even pieces while leaving enough for Saturday's gathering. After Maria told Jack about the event in Creole, he said he would be happy to teach Clarence's sons how to butcher meat with the large knives and machetes he had brought from Haiti.

Maria hurried back to the house, praying along the way that the food didn't burn, because if it did, the Wash Day Monday meal would be just ham, eggs, and potatoes. When she stepped inside and headed toward the kitchen, she suddenly stopped to see the back of a woman in a yellow dress, bent over and looking inside her oven.

"Oh my God! Who are you?" Maria yelled at the intruder.

The intruder quickly pulled herself up from the oven with a pan of hot cornbread. Facing Maria was Audine.

"Audine!" Maria exclaimed in exasperation as she walked toward her. The nerve of that woman letting herself in!

"I'm sorry to intrude, Maria. I knocked on the door several times and received no response, so I checked the barn to see if you were all right, especially after the fight between the two of you. I saw you and Clarence were together without clothes, and I noticed how you sat on him and bounced, with him spanking you and you asking him to do it again, which made you cry out. I saw you stretch your neck back while he rubbed that spot where he spanked you, turning red from the force. Then he took one of your breasts into his mouth, nursing like our babies do, making baby sounds. You called out his name, and he responded, even shaking. Afterward, you gathered your clothes and towels and went to the lake. I followed discreetly, hiding behind a large rock and watching you wash each other and kiss. Then I heard you scream 'snake!' and ran back to the house. I hid in your bedroom until I saw Rick and his men arrive, and you ran to the shed, grabbed your gun, and went up there. I was scared but didn't want the house to burn. I kept busy stirring the rice and gumbo and even ate some cornbread—your cooking is excellent, Maria, it was very tasty! Watching you both made me miss Ruddell so much. We didn't do anything like what you and Clarence did in the barn. I wish Rudell would clap my behind as hard as Clarence did yours; I miss being held by him".

Maria remained frozen in stunned silence as Audine revealed her secret. Did she really stand in my kitchen and tell me she saw my husband and me being intimate? Oh my God, she's disgusting!

"Audine, how dare you come into my house uninvited! How dare you touch the food my family is going to eat tonight, and how dare you watch me and my husband have private moments to show our love!

You're a nasty, disgusting, wicked gossip who can't keep your mouth shut! You're always meddling in others' affairs! Leave my house!" Maria said, opening the door for Audine to go out.

"Not so fast, Maria," Audine said calmly, remaining in her place. "I have some bad news for you and Clarence. Wayne's wife, Lena, has been murdered. Wayne needs to go to New York, and I will be going with him. There's no reason for him to travel alone to a place he's never been. So, honey, Clarence should come to my house on Sunday evening because it will take us three days of driving, stopping for rest, fuel, food, and bathroom breaks. Wayne was smart enough to keep written directions from friends at our hospital, in case we needed an overnight place to rest, gas, food, or a place to use the toilets. These directions include places that will accommodate Black travelers so that we won't face harm. We plan to stay a week after Lena's funeral. After that, I'll need Clarence to watch Violet and Mason for a few months until Wayne recovers from his grief. By then, I hope to be Wayne's new wife. Maybe he'll do what Clarence does for you. Who knows, maybe I'll even give him a child Lena couldn't. I'm not that old! I've overstayed my visit, so please ensure Clarence is aware of my extended stay on Sunday. We'll see you at church too, so I'll remind him then. I'm going to walk down the road where Wayne will meet me. Goodbye, Maria."

After slamming the door behind Audine, Maria sat down at the kitchen table. Her morning had been overwhelming with rapid events, and now the summer heat made her feel nauseous. She hurried to the sink just in time to vomit. Using the boiling water from the stove, she cleaned the sink and added lemon juice to eliminate the smell. Sweat dripped from her forehead, and she could only sit quietly. The doorknob turned, and Clarence entered.

"We just earned a lot of money!" Clarence exclaimed. "Ricks and his men bought meats, vegetables, and even added five dollars extra for two more bushels of sweet potatoes. They also promised to spread the word about the gathering on Saturday and said they would bring their wives and more people. Today alone, we made one hundred dollars!"

"Clarence, Audine just brought some bad news," Maria said, sounding exhausted.

"What? Was she here again? What happened?" Clarence asked as he sat down.

"Lena Collins is dead."

CHAPTER THREE

Harlem, New York

September

Lena. Lena's journey lasted a week of driving to Harlem, New York. High Roller-Gunn and the other two male passengers shared driving duties and had directions to various stops for food, accommodations, gas, and restrooms. Before leaving for New Orleans, Gunn received written driving directions from some of his gambling partners in Harlem, who had previously lived in the South. Many Louisiana businesses refused service to Black people needing food, lodging, or restroom facilities due to segregation laws. Gunn kept his gun handy and was prepared to shoot anyone who threatened him. Initially, the drive was lively and celebratory, with Gunn entertaining everyone with stories of his gambling exploits, causing Lena and the other passengers to laugh heartily. However, as they left the outskirts of New Orleans, the mood shifted. Hot days turned into unbearably hot nights. The addresses, provided by Black New Orleans bar owners, were in such remote locations that Gunn grew paranoid, suspecting passengers might try to steal the five-thousand-dollars in the suitcase on Lena's lap. Occasionally, he would stop on isolated roads, seize the case from Lena, and count the money with her holding a candle so he could see the stacks, with his loaded gun between them. They finally arrived in Harlem on a Friday morning.

"Bet you all have never seen anything like this before! Just look at these tall buildings!" he exclaimed, gazing up at the towering structures that represented the vibrant sights and sounds of one of the largest and busiest cities the three sleepy passengers were about to encounter.

Gunn, finally home, puffed on a lit cigar clenched between his decaying teeth. Lena, still half asleep, yawned as the bright sun shining directly into her eyes from the passenger side caused her eyes to hurt. The noise outside the car snapped her fully awake. The two other men in the backseat, Cornelius Bookman and Alfred "Al" Meckford, were still sleeping. As she blinked to focus, she observed the busy walkway on 125th Street: Black people hurriedly walking to their jobs as housekeepers, shop owners, and various other roles. Storefront owners were sweeping outside, women holding their children's hands to escort them to school, and cafés filled with customers shouting their orders for eggs, bacon, toast, and coffee costing twenty-five cents. Those in a rush grabbed a hot biscuit with butter in a brown paper bag, while several men hurried from the café to catch buses about to leave. Lena thought, So, this is Harlem.

"Alright, everyone, wake up and get the fuck out of my car!" Gunn yelled as he tried to get his five-foot-eleven, 380-pound frame out of the driver's seat of the 1930 black and silver chrome Cadillac he had purchased with cash a year earlier during a poker game that earned him a $1,000 winning hand.

Gunn approached the other side of the car where Meckford was sleeping and pounded on the window with his hand, startling Al Meckford. Known from New Orleans to Georgia for his dynamic piano playing, which could invigorate even the most reserved worshipers into a spiritual frenzy, Al's reputation was well established in Black churches. One Sunday afternoon after service, he was caught in the Pastor's office passionately kissing his fifty-nine-year-old lover. Al's pants were unzipped, and his lover was on his knees, fondling him, causing Al to moan loudly. The Pastor and eight deacons burst in and found them in the act. Al was instantly fired and physically ejected from the church, along with his lover. That Monday, the lover left the rooming house permanently. The owner handed Al a handwritten note from him, explaining that they couldn't continue and advising Al to find happiness elsewhere, perhaps with a suitable woman. Inside the envelope, there were two hundred dollars in worn twenty-dollar bills. The owner, disturbed by the letter, told Al to pack his things and leave immediately. After hearing from friends who played cards with Gunn, the High Roller, that Gunn was only taking three passengers to New York, Al quickly decided to join Lena and forty-two-year-old Cornelius

Bookman, a single, struggling barber, for the ride. Harlem seemed like the fresh start he needed.

"I told you to wake up and get out of my got-damn car!" Gunn yelled, roughly grabbing Cornelius, pulling him out of the car by his shirt sleeve, and throwing him onto the walkway. Al, now fully alert, quickly slid out of the back seat behind Cornelius. Gunn motioned for Lena to exit as well, and she obeyed promptly. The three passengers then stood facing Gunn.

"You're in Harlem now, and things aren't like they are in New Orleans," he said, relighting his cigar and blowing out a puff of smoke. "People here are different. So are the clothes, the music, the food, and the money. This is where we live, work, eat, and sleep," Gunn said, pointing to the many tenement buildings lining the dirty street.

"Take this," Gunn said, reaching into his pants pocket to count out one hundred twenty dollars, then handing the two of them a split of sixty dollars in cash to Al and Cornelius.

"Put the large bills in your shoe," he advised as he moved to the back of the car, opened the trunk to retrieve their suitcases, and handed them to Al and Cornelius. "Be careful out there—lots of pickpockets and desperate thieves. Your best bet is to find a rooming house and hide your money in a place where thieves won't find it. Cut a hole in your pillow to keep your money in, and sew it up when you're done using it. Okay, see you around, and good luck." They all shook hands, and then Al and Cornelius walked down the street until they were out of sight.

"Grab your shit, and let's head inside," Gunn said, gesturing towards the dilapidated building ahead. "This is where you'll stay."

"This is where you live?" Lena asked, surprised at the run-down, filthy tenement she saw as his home. She had imagined him living somewhere much nicer, not this.

"Stop asking me stupid questions!" he snapped at her. "Yes, I live here. What the fuck did you expect, a castle? Hurry up and grab your shit because I need to sleep and be somewhere later tonight."

He brushed past Lena, who was stunned not only by his admission but also by his brash reply. His mood constantly shifted. During the drive to New York, he would make everyone in the car laugh so hard that he'd pull over for them to get out and laugh until tears rolled down their faces. But moments later, he'd be shouting at everyone that it was a mistake to bring everyone with him to New York. He drove for hours, shouting and waving his gun. Even when they begged him to stop at the next gas station that served Black people and had a clean bathroom, he ignored them and kept driving. Poor Al. He begged and cried for High-Roller to pull over so he could pee, but Gunn acted as if he didn't hear him and kept going.

"Hurry up! I ain't got all got-damned day waiting for you! Once we're inside, my place needs cleaning. The dishes are dirty, and I need you to cook. After the meal I had in New Orleans last week, I'm sure you can make me a whole mess of red beans, gumbo, shrimp, and ham," he said with a grin.

He pulled the key from his pocket, opened the door, and switched on the light. The three-room home, consisting of a bedroom, small parlor, and kitchen, was appalling. Clothes were scattered on the bed, the floor, and piled so high on a chair that they obscured the view. Lena looked into the corner of the kitchen and gasped at the dead, smashed cockroaches on the wall. Two rats darted across her shoes and disappeared into a hole in the wall. Lena screamed.

"Oh my God, this place is a mess! No, no, no! I'm not here to clean or cook! I'm your guest, not your maid!" she firmly declared. "I'm leaving to find a place like a rooming house for unmarried colored women around here. I will not stay in this shit-hole!"

Suddenly, a punch to Lena's nose caught her off guard. She fell onto the filthy floor, blood spurting from her nose. Gunn yanked her up and slammed her against the wall. Her once cute, slightly pointed nose was now grotesquely flattened, black and blue, with blood pouring out of it. He then punched her in the mouth, breaking her front tooth. She slumped to the floor, covering her face and crying hysterically.

"When you're finished, clean up this fucking mess that you made. Lesson number one: do as I say, keep your mouth shut, and you'll be okay," he snarled, sharply kicking her side. Then he left, slamming the door behind him.

Lena clutched her side and whimpered in pain, trying to get up but collapsing back down. She saw where her tooth had landed on the dirty floor after she spat it out. Her nose was swollen, making it hard to breathe except through her mouth. A million thoughts raced through her mind, especially about her husband, Wayne. As she sat there, crying and thinking, four brown rats scurried across her feet and went into a hole in the wall.

CHAPTER FOUR

In the weeks after the horrific beating and Lena's arrival, she felt trapped in Gunn's squalid dwelling. She no longer perceived herself as beautiful; the confident woman had become a frightened one with a missing tooth. The beatings persisted, and Gunn only left her alone to cook and clean. The once disorderly kitchen was now spotless, free of rats, and the walls were thoroughly cleaned. When Lena cooked, the entire space filled with the aroma of a New Orleans kitchen. On Mondays, she always made red beans and rice, but she had to use a different type of sausage from the butcher since Andouille wasn't sold in Harlem. Many people who encountered Gunn often asked about the whereabouts of that "Red Gal" from New Orleans, who made the building smell so good on Mondays. However, each Monday was also a day of tears and sorrow, recalling Washday Mondays and her memories of Wayne. Wishing to return home and apologize for her disloyalty, she would often break down and cry. On days when Gunn was in a good mood—winning money, talking, and laughing—he showered Lena with gifts: new dresses, shoes, stockings, undergarments, expensive perfumes, and trips to get her hair done. He wanted her always dressed and perfectly styled. Even shopping with her, Gunn would pick out all the foods he liked, especially those he remembered from his time in New Orleans.

On his bad days, he would sit and stare at the wall in the living room. Suddenly, the beatings would begin and end with him slamming the door, leaving Lena alone for days.

"I need you to do something for me, Suga," Gunn said as he mopped up the last bits of scrambled eggs and bacon with a piece of toast. "You need to take a small teaspoon of this here stuff that my friend gave me to give to you," he added as he pulled out a small bottle from his pocket. "Gimme that spoon over there,"

Lena immediately got up, went to the drawer where the utensils were kept, and handed him the spoon.

He uncapped the small, ornate-looking bottle with a strange top. He poured a little of the clear, thick liquid onto the spoon.

"Open your mouth," he said, standing up.

"What is that?" Lena asked, staring at the spoon he was offering. "I-I-I don't want to take something I don't know anything about," she stammered weakly.

In an instant, Gunn grabbed her hair from behind and yanked her head back, preventing her from moving as she shrieked in pain.

"Open your got-damn mouth!" he shouted. Lena whined loudly, but that made him tug her hair more, causing her to tilt her head back and open her mouth as wide as possible. He took the spoon and pushed it into Lena's mouth.

"Swallow it, and you'd better not spit it out!" he shouted into her ear.

Lena squeezed her eyes shut as the thick, clear liquid now filled her mouth. The taste was bitter, and it burned her throat as she swallowed. She coughed and gagged. Gunn covered her mouth with his hand until her coughing subsided, then released her.

"Imma come back in a few hours. Clean up this place and change the bed sheets. Make the bedroom smell nice for me tonight because I have a surprise for you. And oh, make sure to wash and scrub yourself good down there," he said, grabbing her crotch. He pushed her aside, causing her to stumble into the chair, then slammed the door and left.

Lena slumped into a kitchen chair, coughing, and sipped her remaining coffee, adding more sugar and milk. The burning sensation subsided after a few sips, and she started to feel better. Clearly, he was out for the day, collecting hundreds of dollars owed by gambling houses across Harlem, Brooklyn, and Queens. He also gathered debts from petty gamblers at salons, basement speakeasies, and, of course, the number runners. Gunn owned them all. Those who didn't pay faced either violence or death. When individuals won money during his time, he appeared to take his cut of the winnings. This happened three times a week, especially on weekends, when card games ran from Friday night to early Sunday morning, often lasting until just before sunrise.

Some gamblers played all day Sunday into the evening, leaving them broke. Gunn was there to collect every dollar they lost to him. When he'd come home, he'd slip into bed naked and wake Lena with his sloppy, drunken kisses. His stank body and breath would reek of stale liquor, tobacco from cigars he smoked all night, cheap perfume, and sex from the whores he slept with.

Lena needed to visit a Black doctor nearby to treat gonorrhea, which she had been infected with twice.

"I'm sorry to have to deliver this news, Miss Collins. After this happened twice, I doubt you'll ever conceive or carry a healthy pregnancy," the doctor told her as he injected the penicillin into her buttock.

After visiting the doctor, she was convinced that this was her punishment for leaving her husband, their marriage, and their church.

Last week, she recalled him climbing into bed, and the memory caused her to wince.

"Open your legs wide for me, Lena," Gunn slurred drunkenly. He fumbled as he climbed on top of Lena, roughly grabbing her breast and suckling it vigorously. "You remind me so much of my mama when I used to nurse from her as a baby. The only difference is you don't have any sweet milk for me to drink."

He continued to make harsh nursing and slurping sounds until he forced her legs apart and entered her. After five quick thrusts, it was finished. Gunn, frustrated with his poor performance, demanded she fulfill him, pointing at his flaccid manhood. When she initially refused, he grabbed her hair, slapped her hard, and held her head until she complied. However, it still wasn't enough, leading to the worst beating he had ever given her. She woke the next morning with bruises covering her body.

Lena gathered the plates and utensils, then washed, dried, and put them away. She swept the floor, checked for any dead rodents, and changed the bed sheets as instructed. Going downstairs to the washwoman's place near the front entrance, she was to give 'Miss Paula' the two dirty sheet sets, pay twenty cents, and exchange them for two fresh sheet sets and bed pads for the week. She knocked on Miss Paula's door, and the small woman, standing only four feet eleven inches tall, opened it.

"Good morning," Miss Paula said flatly. "I suppose that you're here with more soiled sheets," she added as she took the bundle from Lena.

"Yes, Miss Paula. I'm here to pick up two sets of fresh sheets and two bed pads for next week. Here are twenty cents for the set," Lena said as Miss Paula handed her the fresh sheets and pads.

"Thank you," Lena said as she turned to leave.

"You need to leave him," Miss Paula called after Lena. "He's an evil man. Leave him before something bad happens," then she shut the door.

Lena wondered if that woman was right. The faded bruises, black eyes, and missing front teeth all told the story of what was happening.

The red beans and rice with sausage were finally simmering. After Miss Paula left, Lena felt a dull ache in her stomach. At first, it was mild, but soon the pain grew so intense it frightened her. The sharp discomfort made her bend over and cry out. Suddenly, a rush from her bowels forced Lena to run to the shared bathroom down the hall. As she hurriedly pulled down her panties, she didn't have time to clean the pee-stained toilet seat. Her body released waste uncontrollably, causing her to moan in pain and tears. It felt as if her insides were on fire. Lena sat on the dirty toilet for forty-five minutes until her bowels stopped. Feeling weak and exhausted, she got up, flushed, and washed herself at the small sink.

Lena opened the bathroom door and saw several tenants waiting for her to leave, wrinkling their noses at the lingering smell. She felt extremely embarrassed as she closed the door to the apartment. Once inside, she boiled water, poured it into a deep basin, and mixed it with cold water until the temperature was warm enough for her to stand in.

She scrubbed herself thoroughly, paying special attention to her buttocks, where she had to sit on the dirty commode seat until she felt clean. After washing everything, it was as if nothing had happened.

It was approaching eleven o'clock at night. The food she had spent the day preparing, feeling weak, was left untouched on the stove just in case Gunn came in hungry. It was either leaving the food out for him or waking up to another beating. Exhausted after using the bathroom again later that day, Lena finally drifted into a deep sleep.

Something felt wrong. She was haunted by a nightmare of a tall, bald, naked, faceless man with unusually large hands, which disturbed her deeply. The sensation was so vivid it woke her up. As her eyes fluttered open, she realized she was not dreaming, just like in her nightmare, a tall, bald, naked man was looming over her. He looked at her with a crooked smile and jagged teeth, some missing. The intruder was not

Gunn. In the faint light, Lena saw he was younger with almond-shaped eyes, but his eye color terrified her. She tried to scream, but he was quick and covered her mouth with his large hand.

"Don't scream," he said softly and raspily. "Gunn's in the next room. He told me I could come in and show you something, so stay quiet and keep your mouth shut!"

Terrified and wide-eyed, she quickly nodded in agreement as the intruder smiled and gently withdrew his hand from her mouth.

Once he took his large hand away, Lena rolled to the other side of the bed and sprinted toward the door leading to the kitchen. She grabbed the doorknob, opened it, and saw Gunn sitting at the table with a cigar clenched in his teeth, a glass of whiskey nearby, and a big stack of cash, seemingly unaware of everything happening around him.

"Help me!" she screamed. The tall, unclothed intruder pressed his large hand over her mouth once more, then seized her around the waist and kicked the door closed. He lifted her and forcefully pushed her onto the bed with a loud thump. After a moment, Gunn opened the door and stood there.

"You ain't going nowhere!" he hissed. "This man paid me good money to have you for the night. Don't let me or him regret it. Be nice to him, Lena, or there will be trouble." He nodded at the intruder, known as Devil Man, then left, locking the door behind him.

Devil Man got into bed next to Lena, who was curled up protectively and crying hysterically.

"Shh, stop it," he said, as he smacked her bare behind so hard, she yelped in pain.

"You liked that, didn't you?" he said with a threatening smile. Lena continued crying and stayed silent.

"Lie on your back and open yo legs".

Lena didn't respond, and for that, he grabbed her, climbed on top of her, and spread her legs open using his knees. She immediately felt his extremely long hardness. He took one of her breasts and did what Gunn would do to her when he nursed on it relentlessly, making the same slurping noises, except Devil Man was louder. When he bit her nipple, Lena shrieked. Covering her mouth to be quiet, he looked into her eyes.

His unnaturally red eyes seemed to burn with intensity. She had never met anyone as frightening as him. Suddenly, he pushed his enormous length inside her again, causing her to scream.

"Be quiet, gal, because the more you scream, the more it's gonna hurt. Just stay quiet!" Then, as he gradually found a steady rhythm, he increased his speed. Lena closed her eyes tightly, hoping it would end soon. After thrusting deeper and faster, he grabbed her breasts firmly and let out a loud groan. His body was covered in sweat, and he shivered uncontrollably.

"Turn over," he demanded breathlessly.

"What will you do to me?" Lena stammered. "I want you to leave! You've gotten what you wanted, so please go now!"

A sharp slap across Lean's face silenced her. Devil Man pulled out a long, dirty rag from under the pillow, then roughly pressed Lena's face onto the bed and gagged her with the rag.

"Don't scream because I'm not here for trouble. I just want to get what I paid for".

Devil Man grabbed her by the waist, lifting her so that her knees bent and her backside was raised, facing him. Lena trembled, overwhelmed with fear about what would happen next. As he touched and squeezed both sides of her buttocks while speaking rapidly in an unfamiliar language, she felt him stretch her. Then, Devil Man inserted his prolonged, hard erection inside her, causing agonizing pain. All she wished for was death to find peace.

As her screams grew louder, Devil Man's influence within her intensified. Lena then sensed a warm gush emerging from her behind.

Oh no-oh my God, no! I've made a big mess! She thought through her tears. She felt a steady flow of loose feces and blood coming out of her onto the sheets. The room now reeked of his filthy sweat, sex, her blood, and shit.

"We're finished," Devil Man said as he carefully moved away from her bloody backside. As he slid off the bed, he pulled her with him. Then he hoisted her to her feet and untied the rag from her mouth. Grabbing her hair, he forced her head back and pressed his tongue into her mouth. Lena gagged at the unpleasant taste.

"Better clean this mess on the bed, 'cause there's a lot of blood and shit," he said. "Gunn told me he gave you that stuff this morning. That stuff was to make sure that you wouldn't get shit all over the bed or on me. Otherwise, he would have killed you. Since this was yo first time getting it in yo ass, the blood was to be expected. But look, I'm ah coming back again tomorrow night. Once you're used to it, you might even like it and love me. Then I'm ah gonna take you away from that fat fuck," Devil Man said, smiling at her before quickly dressing. He then approached Lena, who stood with her arms crossed over her chest, her head bowed low in shame and pain.

"Bye, Suga," he said, clapping her behind hard again with his large hand, this time more forcefully. He knocked on the door, indicating to Gunn that he should open it. Devil Man stepped out, and Gunn quickly slammed and locked the door behind him. Both of them had left, leaving Lena alone in the dark room. She shuddered and sobbed as she looked at the bed, stained with shit and blood. Every part of this day seemed to have gone wrong.

That's why Gunn made me take that horrible-tasting concoction! It was a laxative! That low, filthy son of a bitch! I have to leave here soon, or I'll end up dead or just kill myself. Lena thought through tears, biting her swollen bottom lip. She turned on the light and was horrified to see a bloodstain and wet, loose feces in the *middle of the bed. Quickly, she stripped the sheets and small cover to protect the cheap, stained mattress. She crumpled the soiled sheets and placed them inside the used pillowcase. Using fresh sheets and pillowcases from this morning, she hurriedly made the bed and discovered a surprise: Miss Paula had tucked in two extra heavy cotton pads to protect the mattress. Afterward, she went to her perfume box, chose the scented rose water, and sprayed it on the sheets and herself to mask the earlier smell. As she bent to put the bottle back, Gunn stood directly behind her.*

Without saying a word, he punched her in the face so hard that her other front tooth was knocked out, and then she collapsed against the wall. Lena lay on the floor, bloody and unconscious, for the rest of the night.

"Get up." Lena's eyes fluttered; everything blurred around her. She felt a sharp headache as she held her head and struggled to breathe through her swollen nose. Blood stains marked the floor and wall. Suddenly, her memory of last night resurfaced, causing her to whimper in pain while clutching her head.

She saw her other tooth in the corner, which had been knocked out of her mouth.

"I need to go uptown to collect some money owed to me by several people who have been hiding out for six months. I now know where to find them," he said while adjusting his .38 caliber at his waist. "You should cook some food, clean up this place, and remove those dirty ass sheets outta here and give them to Miss Paula. Make sure she gives you two more clean sheets. Oh yeah, my friend who visited last night wants to see you again tonight at eleven. C'mon, get up!" he said, hoisting her to her feet.

"Ouch!" Lena exclaimed, pulling her arm away from him. Her eyes adjusted to the natural light in the bedroom, revealing that it was ransacked.

"Shut up and get over here!" he exploded, grabbing her arm. Lena saw what he was holding: the spoon with the laxative.

"No, no, no! I won't take that shit again! It made me sick! No!" she screamed.

Her slap on the face knocked her off balance, causing her to stumble against the wall. Gunn moved closer, but Lena decided to fight back. She kicked his leg, but it didn't have the desired effect. He then lifted her to her feet, grabbed her in a chokehold, and pried her mouth open with his hand. She bit his finger until she tasted blood.

"You high-yella fuck-bitch, you bit my finger! Now you're gonna get it! Take this shit now!" Taking the bottle with the laxative that fell to the floor, he managed to bite the cork and open it with his teeth. He spat the cork on the floor, held Lena's head back, poured the bitter liquid down her throat, and kept her mouth closed until she stopped struggling with him.

"This place better be clean when we come in tonight. He's paying a lot, so don't fuck things up for me," he said, shoving her as he left. He slammed the door shut and walked out. After hearing the front door close, she hobbled to the kitchen sink, spat out the laxative, then turned on the tap. She cupped water in her hands, rinsed, and spat repeatedly until the bitter taste disappeared.

Lena, tears streaming down her face, desperately thought, 'I have to leave tonight! I can't keep going like this.' She decided to return to New Orleans to plead with Wayne to take her back. Even though he's stubborn, she believed he was forgiving enough to mend this—she had to try. As she looked at her naked body, she was shocked by her injuries: dark bruises covered her torso, bite marks marred her breasts where Devil Man had bitten her, and two bruises between her legs indicated he had forcibly spread her, leaving her sore. Her once-beautiful face was marked with a black eye; her nose was broken and flattened, she now had two missing front teeth, her lower lip was cut and crusted with dried blood, and her hair was tangled. She dropped the sheets and cried, but quickly reminded herself there was no time for tears. Gathering strength, she planned her escape. She washed her face, pinned back her hair, and wrapped a cloth around her head to hide her messiness. When she looked in the mirror, the dried blood was gone, but her black eye remained. She collected the soiled sheets and left.

Firmly gripping the stair banister, Lena slowly descended the stairs. Each step was painful, and she grimaced as she walked. Looking at her right leg, she noticed a large black and blue bruise. She wished she had a longer dress to hide the reminder of what happened to her. At the last stair, she exhaled in relief. Finally, I made it! She thought as she let go of the banister and hobbled to Miss Paula's door to knock.

Miss Paula had two large wooden crates by the door. Dirty sheets were placed in the left crate, and for urgent stains, like blood or feces, you would knock on the door to personally hand over the soiled sheets, pay her, and receive clean ones in exchange.

Miss Paula opened the door. She was the widow of the late Arnold Overman, a handyman for the tenant building who also helped build it three decades earlier. Arnold and Paula lived on the first floor rent-free, under the condition that they worked; Arnold handled repairs, and Paula managed the daily laundry. This arrangement lasted until Arnold's death fifteen years ago. Now, at eighty years old, Paula still does the laundry and continues to live there rent-free.

"Good morning, Miss Paula. I have three sets of soiled sheets for you today. Uh-uh, Mr. Gunn would like three sets of fresh sheets. He didn't leave me any money to pay you, but can he give it to you tomorrow?" she asked, keeping her head down in hopes that Miss Paula wouldn't notice her black eye and split lip.

"You don't need to pay," Miss Paula said as she took the sheets from Lena. "Mr. Gunn left me enough money to cover the next six months, so there's no need to worry." Miss Paula examined the sheets closely, then brought them to her face for a quick sniff. She wrinkled her nose at the strong scent of sex and feces.

"Blood," she said, staring at the bundle. "And I also know how everything got on these sheets," she whispered, motioning Lena to come inside her flat. Lena hesitated but eventually went in.

"Have a seat, Lena. I've got coffee, eggs, and a few fresh biscuits. I'll get us some plates and be right back." She hurried to her small kitchen to prepare breakfast. Lena hesitated but sat in the big chair, feeling unexpectedly at ease. She looked around and saw a cozy, tidy room decorated with photos, probably of her family: two sons, a daughter, and her husband. Everyone in the pictures appeared taller than her. To the right, in the adjoining room, was the kitchen, featuring a small table, two chairs, a stove, and a washing machine with rollers. Several shelves on the wall held various soaps, scrub brushes, lye, starch, and bottles of scented toilet water in rose, lilac, and lavender scents.

So, this is what she uses to make the sheets smell so good after they've been washed. Lena thought, fascinated, as she stared at the colorful bottles with flower petals inside, secured with cork tops to keep them tightly closed.

She also saw a small ladder that she used to reach laundry items that were too high for her to reach. In the left corner of the kitchen was a wall-mounted ironing board, with an iron resting on a large brick when heated. Lena sat, mesmerized by how tidy everything was and amazed that such a petite woman could manage such a hectic operation serving over twenty-five tenants.

"I hope you enjoy adding cream and sugar to your coffee because black coffee gives me such stomach pains," Miss Paula said as she placed the tray of food and hot coffee on the small round table in her parlor.

"Oh, Miss Paula, you didn't need to go to all this trouble. I really shouldn't stay too long. Mr. Gunn might return soon, and I have a lot to do. I should be leaving," Lena stammered as she started to stand.

"Lena, sit down. I need to talk to you because I know what's going on. Plus, Gunn has a lot of people to collect from-I saw that gun tucked into his waistband. He'll probably be killing people to get his money and spending time with those whores. That's how you got sick," Miss Paula said as she sat down to eat. "I've seen everything, and you need to leave tonight before something bad happens. Finish your breakfast and listen to what I'm about to tell you," she said, gesturing for Lena to eat. Lena looked at her, stunned by what she had just revealed.

How did she know I got sick? Lena wondered shamefully as she took a sip of the piping hot coffee.

"I've lived here for over thirty years, knowing many locals, especially the Black doctor, dentist, and midwives who delivered half of Harlem's children. The doctor who treated you feels like a son to me. I remember when he went to medical school and graduated top of his class. My late husband, Arnold, helped him find his current office, built him a beautiful wooden desk, and a locked box for his money when he cared for patients. He told me you came to him twice for shots for that nasty disease Gunn caused. There's no doubt Gunn was the source, considering the devious characters involved. He also said your last infection has permanently prevented you from having children. I'm so sorry, Lena," Miss Paula said gently, holding Lena's hand.

Tears of pain and hurt filled Lena's eyes. She was overwhelmed by the thought that she might never have a family with her husband, Wayne, and the fear of being alone to care for herself as she grew older was heartbreaking. If Wayne doesn't reconcile with her, what will happen then? As these thoughts consumed her, Lena started to cry.

"Don't cry," Miss Paula said gently. "You'll get through this. Drink your coffee and have your breakfast before it cools. I have much more to tell and show you. Just sit back and listen to me."

Lena sat in the chair, took a few more sips of hot coffee, lifted a forkful of fluffy scrambled eggs to her mouth, and listened as what was about to be revealed to her was about to be shared.

"His real name is Martin Gunn. His mother, Ophelia, was very young, only fifteen years old. Her family disowned her after she showed up this big", Miss Paula said, gesturing at her belly. "She was involved with a thirty-five-year-old married man who, upon learning about Ophelia's pregnancy, left his wife and children, abandoning Ophelia and her baby. Her birth was difficult, requiring two midwives—one early in the morning and another late into the next day. When he was finally born, he was a large, constantly crying baby, day and night. Ophelia nearly went crazy trying to quiet him. The only way to soothe him was feeding him her breast milk, which he refused to give up even as he grew older. He wouldn't eat solid food unless it was supplemented with her milk. After he turned five, this habit persisted. Every day, Ophelia would lift her shirt, and he would run to her, smiling to nurse—even after her milk dried up, he kept pulling her shirt himself!" Miss Paula said, taking another bite of her eggs and a warm, buttered biscuit.

"Oh my God, Miss Paula! So, he was nursing from his mama even after her milk dried up, until he was five years old?" Lena said, astonished by the revelation.

"Oh yes, and you haven't heard the worst of it all, Lena." Miss Paula said, taking a sip of coffee. "When he got older, Ophelia would take him by the hand and have him come into her room. Then she'd sit on a chair, lift her top, show her breasts, and say to him, "Are you ready for your mother's milk? Then he'd go to her and drop to his knees at her feet and say to her: *"Yes, Mama, I want your milk."* Then he'd go to her breast and nurse on them like he was a baby! Lawd have mercy, that nasty woman! Then one day, when he came home from being out on the streets gambling all day, but at the exact time to feed on his mamma's breasts, he quietly went into her room, and guess what? There she was sitting in her chair, her shirt completely off, and another man was on his knees nursing on her breasts! Well, Gunn stood there watching, and they didn't even know he was standing there. He couldn't stand seeing another man at his mother's breast, so he reached into his pocket, took out a straight-edge razor, and went straight up to that man from behind, yanked that man's up from his mamma's breast, and slit his throat! Oh Jesus! All that blood that came gushing outta that man's neck! His mother screamed, and Gunn threw the razor on the floor and ran off!"

"Oh my God, Miss Paula!" Lena exclaimed, eyes wide with nervousness as she sipped her coffee. She was trembling so badly that Miss Paula gently took the cup and saucer from her trembling hands to prevent them from falling.

"So, what happened to that poor man and Ophelia?" Lena asked.

"Right after Gunn ran out, I had to stay quiet, run downstairs to my place, lock the door, and pretend I was washing sheets until his mamma stopped screaming. Then she ran down the stairs, knocked on my door, and shrieked for me to call the police because she had killed a man!"

"Wait a minute," Lena asked, bewildered by this new revelation. "You saw all of this? How?"

"Yes, I saw everything and more. She told the police she murdered the man and that the razor was hers. They arrested her, and she was jailed. Without a lawyer, the jury quickly found her guilty, and the judge sentenced her to life. However, she died two weeks later from pneumonia. Gunn didn't find out she was dead until a week afterward. He then moved back into that flat and has stayed there ever since. It took my husband and me months to clean the blood off that wooden floor. Have you ever seen that rust-colored circle on the bedroom floor?"

"Yes, I have! I tried scrubbing it off, but it just won't go away. Why is that?" Lena asked, frowning.

"That's because it was that man's blood! You could never scrub it away," Miss Paula said as she began taking the plates into her small kitchen. Lena sat there, shivering as if a cold wind was passing through her. I need to leave. After hearing all this about Gunn and his mother, no wonder he's crazy! she thought, standing up from the chair to leave.

"I already know whatcha thinking," Miss Paula said as she returned. "It's still early morning, giving you enough time to leave, but not until tonight. However, before you go, there's one more thing I need to show you. C'mon, hurry!"

"Look inside there," Miss Paula said softly, guiding Lena to the front door and pointing to a specific spot before opening it for them to step outside. Lena obeyed and gasped. The small opening was just big enough to see the entire front entrance of the tenant building.

"You can see who comes and goes?" Lena exclaimed.

"Yes," Miss Paula said proudly. "Because I am small, my husband didn't want me opening the door to anyone when he was away at work, especially if I was alone. He made a notch in the door large enough for me to see who's outside and built a small platform for me to stand on so I could look out. The door is always kept locked. He told me that at night, if I peek through the hole, I should make sure all the lights inside are off so no one can see the glow or me peering out!" She chuckled. "I miss him very much, but that hole in the door allowed me to see who's coming in. I even saw the man Gunn killed. I saw you the first day you arrived here, and I saw that tall man who hurt you last night."

Lena continued to stand, looking at Miss Paula.

"But c'mon, honey, we need to get going because we have a lot to do to get you out of here."

Miss Paula locked the door, and the two women quickly headed upstairs to the second floor. Lena winced, holding her head with her palm, unaware of the intensifying throbbing pain and the swelling of her badly bruised leg. Pain was secondary; her focus was on escaping this hellish place, which she swore she would never return to, even if it meant sleeping on the streets. Lena marveled at how this small, agile woman could almost run up the stairs, prompting her to quicken her pace to keep up. When they reached Lena's door, Miss Paula paused.

"C'mon over here," she beckoned as they moved down the hallway a few steps from Lena's door and faced a gnarled wooden wall with cracked, peeling paint. Miss Paula reached into her pocket and pulled out a tiny, curved silver hook attached to a reed-thin strip of leather. She carefully guided the hook into a round groove embedded in the wall. With a gentle pull, the wall opened. It was a door designed to blend seamlessly with the wall. Lena was baffled at what she saw.

"Shh, be very quiet and take off your shoes. I don't want any other tenants to hear us," Miss Paula whispered. "Go on in."

Lena stepped into the small, narrow space that was very dark. How could she see in here? Lena wondered, trying to feel around to avoid bumping into anything, but she stayed cautiously still. Miss Paula then gave the door a gentle pull so it would close quietly behind them.

They both stood in the pitch-black darkness of the tiny space.

"Now, move to my left side and place your eye right there," she said, standing on her tiptoes and guiding Lena's hand to a spot only she knew in the dark. Lena obeyed.

"Oh my God! Jesus!" Lena gasped as she looked into the bedroom where she and Gunn were sleeping. "Miss Paula, how? I-I don't understand! You can see us in the bedroom!" she stammered.

"Yes, I see everything in this small room. That's how I knew about Gunn's mother and him feeding off her, how I saw Gunn murder that man, and how I constantly see all the nasty women coming in here. That's also how I saw him beating you. You don't think I noticed the marks on your arms, your face, and what he did to your mouth, causing you to lose your front teeth? Lawd have mercy, you poor child. I was upstairs crying, praying for the Lawd to stop Gunn from beating you so much," Miss Paula said. "Do you know why he made you take that stuff?" she asked.

"No, I don't. I do know it made me very sick, and I swore that he'd have to kill me before I'd swallow that shit again. No ma'am, uh-uh," Lena said, shaking her head defiantly.

Miss Paula looked at Lena and said, "I saw that tall, devil-like man and what he did to you." She then took Lena's hand and squeezed it. "Gunn wanted you to use that terrible medicine that kept you running to the toilet, as that evil man plans to return and do it again! I overheard him tell Gunn that he'd pay extra if he could come back around eleven tonight, after Gunn finishes collecting money and while you're asleep — just like last night when he did that awful thing to you. I heard your screams. So, I've decided to help you escape. Let's go to the bedroom now."

Miss Paula ran her hand along the door, locating the hole where she had embedded the hook to open it. Lena stepped outside. Paula re-secured the hook into the groove, closed the door, and put the hook back into her apron pocket. Lena then opened the flat door, feeling beads of sweat forming on her lips. Fear overwhelmed her, causing her to tremble uncontrollably. This is it, she thought. I have to escape, or I will die here!

"Come on, Lena! Grab your suitcase and pack what you can carry! Do you see all the boxes over there?" Miss Paula asked, pointing at the boxes next to the bed. "When you leave here at ten tonight, start moving the boxes. Behind them is a window with stairs leading to three alleys in the next three buildings! Gunn was using those boxes to hide the windows and prevent you from escaping. Then, you need to run as fast as you can, up to ten blocks, to the small store where everyone goes in the morning. A black car will be waiting there, driven by a man named Evans. You tell him your name, get in the car, and he'll drive you to a safe place. Gunn will never find you. But remember, you gotta be in that car by ten-thirty, no later! Evans has to return the car to the white people he works for."

Lena was speechless and overwhelmed with gratitude that this angel before her was guiding her to freedom. She felt deep love and admiration for her bravery in helping her escape her captor. Lena stepped forward and embraced Paula, tears streaming down her face.

"Miss Paula, thank you so much for saving me! I don't know how I can ever repay you," Lena said, wiping away her tears.

"Just thank God above that you'll be free, Lena," Miss Paula said, hugging her again. "And listen to me: if you need anything, tell Evans. But Lena, if something happens and you don't make it, come back to me. Knock on my door three times, quietly enough that only I'll know it's you. I have to go now because I gotta wash the sheets, get them dried, and act as if nothing happened. God bless and keep you, honey."

They embraced once more before Miss Paula left, knowing Lena might never see her friend again. There was no time for reflection; it was time to pack and go. Lena moved to the corner of the small bedroom and grabbed her little brown suitcase, a gift from her mother when she got engaged to Wayne. She thought, "As soon as I leave here, I will work long enough to save enough money for a train to New Orleans and to return to my husband." She opened the suitcase and reflected, "I should have been more patient and worked harder to have a child with him. Once we can repair our marriage, I'll visit my dear friend, Maria, to ask for help. I'll do anything!"

As she nervously finished packing, she quickly made the bed, tidied up the room, and started preparing a meal of sausage gumbo, cornbread, and rice. This way, he will believe everything is normal until he notices that I am missing.

Nine-thirty. Everything was finished. Lena was trembling so badly that she was stumbling around the flat. She glanced at the towering pile of boxes nearly reaching the ceiling! Moving them would take hours! she thought in panic. She scanned the room and noticed a chair stacked high with Gunn's sour-smelling shirts, socks, and soiled underwear. He had told her never to disturb the pile of clothes.

Lena, with all her strength, swung the mound onto the floor. Sitting in the center of the chair was an old, worn cigar box. As Lena reached to remove it, she found it somewhat heavy. She lifted the lid and opened it.

"Oh my God!" she exclaimed, covering her mouth. Inside the box, rolls of money were tightly secured with twill and labeled with paper markers, each representing $1,000. The dates ranged back to 1920, when Gunn was just starting his gambling days. Lena hurriedly counted each roll, finding a total of fifty-eight, amounting to $58,000. She quickly grabbed two rolls, worth $2,000, closed the box lid, and carefully packed the money into her suitcase. She laid the rolls neatly between two skirts before snapping the suitcase shut.

She then dragged the chair beneath the tall stack of boxes. Her leg throbbed with pain as she carefully lifted her pain-free leg and slowly raised the other. After enduring the beatings, her body protested, but she kept going, throwing each heavy box to the floor with a loud thud. About halfway through, her back ached badly, making her cry out, yet she pushed on until she reached the top of the window. After tossing five more boxes down, the window was entirely uncovered. Freedom! Looking outside, she saw the rain pounding and the wind whipping the storm. She tried to open the window, but it was stuck.

"Oh no, no, no!" Lena screamed, disregarding who might hear her. Then she grabbed her suitcase and hurled it at the glass window. The window shattered, sending glass shards scattering across the floor. Her sturdy Oxford shoes helped her as she carefully lifted her bruised leg until it reached the first step of the three-story tenement building. Holding the wall for support, she slowly lowered her left leg and guided it down onto the stairs, ensuring both feet were safely on the steps.

The howling wind caused the rain to fall sideways, soaking Lena already. It was a fierce storm, and suddenly a loud thunderclap and intense lightning struck. Lena was scared. Ignoring her fears, she tightly gripped her suitcase and carefully descended the stairs, barely seeing anything. When she reached the bottom step, she moved to the edge of the alley, cluttered with trash and debris. She peeked around the corner to check if it was safe, but then she saw a familiar black Cadillac in front of the building. Oh no! As she stepped closer for a better look, she saw two men run into the building: High Roller-Gunn and the intruder from the other night: Devil Man! They weren't supposed to return until eleven! she thought.

Lena felt nauseous, but as soon as they entered, she turned right and ran for her life. The cold rain hammered down, drenching her. She kept sprinting, aware that time was running out. Despite her leg pain, she pushed herself harder, visions of home, her husband, and safety in New Orleans fueling her determination. Tears streamed down her face, blinding her as she failed to notice a crack in the walkway, causing her to slip and fall, sending her suitcase flying. Just minutes from freedom, Lena lay on the muddy walkway, groaning in agonizing pain. Her forehead was badly scraped, her hand and knee cut deeply. She slowly tried to stand, but her knee buckled, and she fell again. She saw the suitcase sinking into the rainwater. Remembering the money inside, she gathered her strength, got up, and hobbled to the suitcase. She grabbed it and limped the last six blocks to the market, where Miss Paula had said a black car awaited her.

If you can't make it, turn back. When you reach my door, knock softly three times; I will hear it because my bed is next to the door. Miss Paula told her.

There it is! The black car was parked in front of the market. Overcoming her pain, Lena started running as fast as she could.

"Wait!" she screamed, but the thunder and heavy rain drowned out her shouts to the driver to stay. Moments later, she saw the car drive away from the curb.

"No, No, No! Wait!" she screamed, chasing after the car. But it was too late; it sped down 125th Street into the night. Lena stood there, dazed and bleeding from her wounds, then collapsed on the sidewalk, oblivious to the rainstorm, sobbing.

It's two o'clock in the morning. Rain, thunder, and lightning illuminated the sky, keeping Miss Paula awake beneath her blanket, her head resting on a soft pillow and freshly laundered sheets. She was terrified. Earlier that evening, she heard the crash of the window Lena broke, followed by Lena's unsteady footsteps going down the wobbly wooden stairs to the three alleys. If Lena listened carefully, she would be only ten blocks away after the third alley, which leads to the market where Evans would be waiting in the car to take her to the church's safe place. However, by the time she heard the window crash, it was already past ten o'clock, and to make matters worse, Gunn's Cadillac and Devil Man pulled up in front of the building just as Lena was leaving. After Gunn and Devil Man went upstairs, Gunn was heard loudly unloading obscenities to the point of him screeching and throwing his belongings against the walls.

"So, where the fuck is she, Gunn?" Devil Man yelled. "I paid you $250 last night to keep that high-yella gal all night into tomorrow! And here you are, just standing there on your big fat ass, telling me she's gone out the got-damn window? Fuck you, Gunn! Where the fuck is my money? Give it her, you fat fuck!"

"I ain't got your fuckin money, and it's time you got the fuck outta here. Shit, I should've charged you at least five hundred dollars for her! I'm not giving you shit! Now, get the fuck outta my place!" shouted Gunn.

Gunn reached into his pants pocket for his .38 revolver, but he was too late. Devil Man lunged at him, smashing his large fist into Gunn's nose, catching him off guard. Gunn stumbled back against the wall. Devil Man then grabbed Gunn by his shirt, pulled back his arm, and struck him again on the jaw. Gunn fell back against the wall and collapsed to the floor, unconscious. After delivering a brief beating, Devil Man quickly took Gunn's fully loaded revolver.

Rummaging through his jacket pocket, Devil Man retrieved a wad of five-hundred-dollar bills, likely contained within the extra bills. As he sifted through the debris of broken window glass, scattered boxes, and Gunn's soiled clothes, he noticed a cigar box. Assuming it contained cigars, he picked it up and opened it.

"What the fuck?" Devil Man saw the money-wads tied up in twine and immediately counted each roll. Fifty-six thousand dollars. That was enough money to get out of Harlem and move somewhere else! Devil Man went up to Gunn, who was still unconscious, and with the heel of his shoe smashed Gunn's mouth until it was a bloody pulp.

"That should prevent you from running your big mouth again, you fat fuck." Devil Man said, then spat on Gunn, slammed the door, and left.

Miss Paula, who was out of bed, heard the violent fight between Gunn and Devil Man. Gunn lost after a loud thud against the wall. Yes! Finally, a man was up there whooping his fat ass! Hah! She heard one last punch that knocked Gunn to the floor again. She then heard the door slam, and through the peephole, she saw Devil Man walking down the stairs, holding a cigar box and a large wad of cash. He paused, looked in her direction, and smiled, showing grotesquely decayed and missing teeth. Miss Paula quickly jumped off her wooden block, ran to her bed, and pulled the covers over her head. Eventually, she fell asleep.

At first, she thought she was dreaming or if it was the soft rolls of thunder signaling the end of the storm. Miss Paula sat up and heard the sound again. Three soft knocks on her door.

Oh no, Lena! She failed, Paula thought as she got out of bed. Her heart sank with fear and sorrow, feeling overwhelming heaviness, but she had to let this wayward soul in to protect her until Evans could retrieve the car. However, she wasn't sure when that would happen. Miss Paula approached the door without peering through the peephole.

"Lena, I'm so sorry, honey. Come inside," she said as she opened the door. There stood Gunn, with a blood-stained shirt, a terribly flattened nose, a black eye, and a mangled mouth from the beating by Devil Man.

"Wh-what do you want here at this hour, Mr. Gunn?" she asked, backing away from him. "It's very late, and you need to leave!"

"Where the fuck is Lena!" he shouted, pushing her aside and storming in.

"I-I don't know!" Miss Paula said, stammering as she nervously clutched at her robe.

"The fuck you do, you old bag of shit! My money is all gone, and so is she! Now, where the fuck is Lena?" The disheveled and wild look in his eyes said it all. He wasn't leaving until he got information about Lena. His madness was apparent—Devil Man had stolen the money while he was unconscious, and Lena escaped.

"Get outta here now! Do you hear me? Leave!" Miss Paula yelled. "I always knew you were crazy, just like your mama, you nasty piece of shit! You were up there as a grown man, nursing on her breast like a child! I saw you kill that man while he was doing the same thing! Instead of facing your punishment like a man, you ran away and let your mama take the blame! You're a murderer and a coward!"

Suddenly, Gunn pulled out a short pick-ax, which he had concealed in his back pocket. He hit Miss Paula on the head, causing her to collapse to the floor.

"Oww!" she screamed, holding her head, which was bleeding profusely. Gunn went after her, striking her head and face repeatedly until her nose split. He raised the ax above his head, striking the last blow, cracking her skull. Her entire body, which had gone into convulsive twitching, now stopped. Gunn stared at the bloody body and let the ax pick drop to the floor. Then he left, leaving Miss Paula in a pool of blood, dead.

125th Street was flooded, with rain impairing visibility. A large black car stopped by the walkway, and a well-

dressed Black man in a chauffeur's coat, gloves, umbrella, and hat pulled low over his eyes opened the umbrella and hurried over to a woman huddled at the corner market.

"Lena!" the stranger shouted. Lena, who had been hunched outside the market for two hours, was soaked, cold, and feeling defeated. *Is this one of Gunn's henchmen coming to find me?* She wondered, clutching her small suitcase to her chest. She glanced up at the tall Black man who loomed over her diminutive frame.

"Come on, Lena! I'm here to get you out of here! I'm Evans, and I need to get you out of this rain! C'mon!" He extended his hand to her. Lena's eyes were wide, but after standing in the freezing rain for over two hours, she was too exhausted even to notice Evans, who took her hand and led her to the car. He opened the door and helped her inside.

"Let me take that for you," Evans said as he reached for the suitcase, but Lena, still clutching it tightly to her chest, shoved his hand away. She shook her head so forcefully that rainwater soaked into her hair and splattered against the passenger side window.

"Okay, I understand," Evans said as he tipped his hat and closed the door. He ran to the driver's side, got in, shut the door, and glanced back to check for oncoming cars. Then he accelerated and drove into the darkness outside Harlem.

A terrifying thought crossed Lena's mind. What if this isn't Evans? What if it's another one of Gunn's monsters who would suddenly turn on me for more beatings and another attack by Devil Man! As the car sped up, Lena suddenly reached for the door handle, ready to jump out.

"No!" Evans shouted. He sharply turned and slammed on the brakes. Lena started to open the car door, but Evans, being tall and having a more extended reach, quickly pulled her back, preventing her from opening it. "Have you lost your mind? Do you want to get yourself killed?" Evans asked, gazing sternly into Lena's eyes.

"Let me out of here! Let me go!" Lena shouted, struggling to pull her arm free from Evan's strong hold.

"And where will you go at this hour, Lena? I know everything that's happened to you. Miss Paula, who's part of our church, called me last night and shared everything that's been going on with you since you came to Harlem. She asked me to come and get you before that damn Gunn guy ends up killing you. I'm going to release your arm and show you my driver's license to prove who I am — I'm not here to hurt you, but to help you." Lena remained motionless; her eyes filled with terror.

Evans released her arm, then went into his coat pocket and carefully withdrew his wallet, pulling out his driver's license. Lena quickly snatched the wallet and confirmed that his name was Evans Walter, with his current address listed in Brooklyn.

"I waited at the corner market for you," he said, taking his wallet back. "It was nearly ten o'clock, and I needed to return the car; otherwise, my boss would have fired me for not bringing it back on time. When I went to the Manhattan hotel where he was staying, the desk clerk handed me a note from him, instructing me to pick him and his wife up the next afternoon because their party was still ongoing. So, I drove back to Harlem as fast as I could through all this rain to find you. When I saw a woman huddled against the market doorway, I knew it was you because of how Miss Paula described you. I'm taking you somewhere safe, where Gunn won't find you."

"I-I'm really sorry, and I feel so ashamed," Lena said, lowering her head. "I thought I was being deceived and that you were one of Gunn's friends trying to take me back there." Then Lena began to cry, sobbing uncontrollably.

"Miss Paula would never do something like that, and I'm nothing like Gunn or his friends. What he needs is a real man to put him in his place, so don't worry, because you're going to be safe," Evans said confidently, his eyes fixed on Lena. Then they drove away as Lena held the tiny suitcase even more tightly to her chest, watching Evans drive. After an hour, they arrived in front of a tenement building that looked completely different from the ones in Harlem.

"Okay, we're here," Evans said as he turned off the ignition. He exited the driver's side and rushed over to Lena, who was sitting nearby. The rain had grown heavier during the hour-long ride, and it was now freezing. Sharp, needle-like raindrops fell from the night sky, causing Lena to shiver from the bitter cold. She was wearing only a thin dress, and her shoes were soaked.

"Lena, come on!" Evans urged, reaching out his hand to her as they stood outside the car. "The rain and wind are getting worse, and it's cold! Get out of the car!"

As he tried to take the suitcase out of her arms to help her out, Lena snatched it away, remembering the wad of money tucked inside.

"No!" she snapped sharply at Evans. "I got it, it's mine." Lena thought to herself, not trusting anyone, especially to take her belongings — particularly the money — from her suitcase. She reached out with her free hand, asking Evans to help her out of the car. Evans looked at how tightly she was clutching the suitcase, frowned, and noticed her distrust.

They both hurried up the stairs toward the building ahead. Lena saw bright lights shining through the windows, which were covered by heavy curtains. Evans seemed to be familiar with the place; when he opened the door, sounds of singing, shouting, jumping, and women beating tambourines filled the air. Lena stepped closer to observe and saw women dressed in white swaying, praising God loudly, jumping, and wildly flailing their arms in a sacred dance unique to them and the Lord. Her heart pounded with happiness and raw emotion. The piano was playing energetically, causing everyone to stand. This storefront church was in a Holy Ghost frenzy, and the musician and singer was none other than Al Meckford, the passenger she had traveled with from New Orleans, Louisiana!

"What is this place?" Lena asked breathlessly, clutching her soaking wet dress to her chest.

"It's the church that Miss Paula and I are part of. She's a deaconess, and I serve as an usher. She shared with me, the Pastor, and several members what was happening to you, Lena. She said she couldn't watch what was happening to you anymore, so we all devised a plan to get you out of that hell-hole," Evans whispered close to her ear, holding onto the crook of her arm so she could hear him.

Lena started to cry. Miss Paula is my angel, my saving grace, and someone who loves me! Oh, thank you, God, for sending her to me!

"Don't cry, Lena," Evans said softly. "You need to change out of those wet clothes and shoes before you get sick. Come over here and follow me."

Evans led Lena to the left side of the church and opened the door. The room was spotless, filled with the smell of fresh flowers and a faint hint of perfume. She looked across the room and saw that it contained many items for women of the church who needed a place to calm down when overwhelmed by the Holy Spirit. Two cots, covered with sheets, pillows, and blankets, sat on a wooden divider. A pitcher of water was placed on a woodblock between the two cots. At the foot of each cot, there was a box filled with white smocks, head coverings, slippers, towels, extra blankets, and toiletries.

A large bag with her name on it was also at the foot of one of the cots. Lena looked up at Evans, curious about what was inside the bag.

"The women gathered a dress, undergarments, shoes, some sandwiches, and pie. On the desk over there, there's still hot coffee from sitting by the radiator. I'm about to leave, but I suggest you stay here until the service ends. Just change out of your wet clothes and put them on the floor next to the radiator to dry, along with your shoes. Feel free to eat, lie down, and rest. The service will last quite a while, especially with this rain and cold, but I'll check on you later to make sure you're okay. Goodnight, Lena. I'm so relieved you're safe, and tomorrow I'll visit Miss Paula to tell her you made it," Evan said with a broad smile.

Evans quickly moved to the door and then disappeared. Lena stared at the door as the music and tambourine sounds grew louder. She placed the wet suitcase near the radiator and looked inside the bag with her name on it. Inside, there was a plain blue dress, undergarments, shoes, a tignon, and slippers. Lena laid them all out on the cot and began to undress, removing the soaked clothes that clung to her skin. Kicking off her wet shoes, she used the towel provided to dry off. After putting on dry clothes and tying her hair with the extra fabric to make a tignon, she secured it tightly. She then looked further into the bag and found two chicken salad sandwiches and two slices of sweet potato pie. Lena hadn't eaten since morning. She unwrapped one sandwich, took a big bite, and closed her eyes as she chewed. The sandwich tasted wonderful. She rose and approached the desk where a cup of coffee sat. It was still hot. She blew on the cup, sipped carefully, and immediately felt her body warm again. After fifteen minutes, she finished the sandwiches, half the pie, and the coffee. Lena went to the lamp, then knelt beside the bed and offered a long, heartfelt prayer of thanks. When she finished, she climbed into the surprisingly comfortable cot. Pulling the covers over her, Lena closed her eyes. Despite the loud piano music of Al Meckford, shouting women, singing, church members pounding tambourines, and nonstop handclapping, Lena finally drifted off to sleep.

Two weeks after her escape, Deaconess Deloris "Dee-Dee" Franklin and her husband Nickford were kind, God-sent people. After that unforgettable night of fleeing Gunn's filthy hellhole, the couple—whom Lena met for the first time after waking up that night at the church—took Lena into their home. Dee-Dee's husband Nickford owned a corner diner known for serving fresh, hot coffee all day, sweet potato pie every day, Dee-

Dee's beef stew with hot buttered cornbread or a biscuit, and the lunch crowd's favorite: chicken salad sandwiches. Finally, Lena had a clean place to stay, work, and find peace. She joined the church that Evans helped her return to, and the congregation warmly welcomed her. In the weeks following Lena's escape, Evans visited the diner during her half-hour break for coffee.

"I still can't believe Miss Paula is gone," Evans said sadly as he settled into the chair opposite Lena, who had placed a steaming cup of coffee in front of him.

"The day after I picked you up, I visited Miss Paula to let her know that you had arrived and were in good hands. When I arrived, I saw the police and a large crowd at her place. I stepped out of the car to see what was going on," Evans said, looking down and hunched over, slowly stirring his coffee.

"I asked the cop what happened. He said that one of the boarders knocked on Miss Paula's door after not seeing or hearing from her all day. Several people went to her place and knocked on the door, but she didn't answer. After about three o'clock in the afternoon, someone tried again. The tenant noticed that the door wasn't locked all the way, so he went in and found Miss Paula dead. The cop said that Miss Paula died of a horrible head injury, her nose was severed, and the murderer stabbed her left eye." Evans stopped stirring his coffee and sat, transfixed at the steaming cup of coffee.

Lena, sitting and gazing at Evans, covered her mouth in shock as tears welled up in her eyes. Her chest trembled, and she burst into tears openly, unaware of the stares around her.

"This is all my fault!" Lena said through muffled sobs. "I should have stayed put and kept this to myself. She'd still be alive if I had just stayed silent." Evans stood up from where he was sitting and then sat down beside her, wrapping his arms around Lena to comfort her.

"No, Lena," Evans said softly, offering her his handkerchief to dry her tears. "We both know who did this to Miss Paula. We can't prove anything, and honestly, white police don't care much about us here. If someone gets hurt or killed, they either turn a blind eye or don't come up here at all," Evans said angrily, glaring out the window. "After her family was notified, they came from Florida to identify her at the morgue. Her children didn't like her being alone here, especially because she was so tiny. But she insisted on staying in Harlem to visit her husband's grave now and then. Well, now they're both at peace," Evan said with a heavy sigh.

"Gunn did this," Lena said, dabbing her eyes.

"Yes, I know," Evans said quietly, taking another sip of his now-cold coffee. "People I've talked to who live in the building said they hadn't seen him for weeks. Some tenants and members of our church kindly cleaned Miss Paula's flat. I also found out that two brothers moved into her flat immediately after her, taking over everything—collecting rent and doing laundry for the tenants. Even if Gunn doesn't know your whereabouts, you still need to be careful where you go. While New York is big, Harlem is small enough that people tend to figure things out. Everyone knows everyone."

"I know, and I plan to return home to New Orleans next Monday. I've already told Dee-Dee and Nickford. I needed time to think about what I truly want, Evans," Lena said, taking his hand. "Things just didn't work out for me here in Harlem. When I was in New Orleans, I dreamed of being happy with my husband, having a family, raising children, and growing old together. But I haven't achieved any of that. Instead, I became disobedient in my marriage, left my husband and our home to be with someone I thought I'd fall in love with, and divorced my husband. I imagined building a new life here, but I ended up with a beast who killed my friend," Lena said, pressing her fingers to her forehead. "I will never forget her as long as I live. I'm heartbroken that I was the cause of her death. One day, he'll pay for what he's done—both to Miss Paula and to me. I hope my husband will forgive me and take me back."

"I believe things will eventually work out between you two, but it won't be easy. Remember how you left your husband to be with Gunn, thinking you would be better off with him, only to find out Gunn was a terrible and evil man. Both of you will need time to work things out. Lena, you endured so much living with Gunn, my

God," Evans said as he finished his coffee and looked at his pocket watch.

"I've got to go now." How about I take you out for coffee tomorrow? Then on Monday, I can drive you to the train station and help you with your suitcases."

"I'd like that," Lena said, getting up and gathering their coffee cups. "You were my true friend who saved my life on that terrible night. I'll never forget you."

Evans asked as he headed toward the door of arriving customers, "Are you going to be okay going home tonight?"

"Yes, I'll be fine. Dee-Dee and Nickford are going to the church tonight for service and will help the others in preparing for the morning. I aim to finish cleaning, lock up, and be done by nine. After that, I'll cook for Dee-Dee, pack my things for Monday, and then head to bed. I'll see you at church tomorrow."

They shared a warm embrace before Lena headed back to work. The rest of the day was bustling with crowds coming and going.

By nine o'clock, the diner had been cleaned, the money for the next day counted, and it was closed. Lena said her goodbyes to the workers as several waitresses stayed behind to wait for their dates.

The walk back to Dee-Dee and Nickford's place was just fourteen blocks. It wasn't unusual to see the many cars and people still out and about late in the evening. Many Black residents living on this side of Harlem, away from 125th Street, would head to dance halls or jazz clubs to listen to music performed by rising stars or already famous entertainers. I'll miss all of this, Lena thought sadly, as she watched people rush to enjoy the Saturday night festivities. At least people were still out this time. Back home in New Orleans, I'd be in bed sleeping and up early for church. Maybe I'll return here someday with Wayne and the children we'll have, to visit Harlem, the church I joined, and spend time with Dee-Dee and Nickford. By then, Gunn will probably be in jail or dead, and I don't plan to believe what that doctor said about never having children. If anyone can help me have a child with Wayne, it's my friend Maria St. Laurent. Once I get back home and clear things up with Wayne, I'll visit her.

The fourteen-block walk helped her gather her thoughts about what to say when she returned home to Wayne and later visited Maria. After climbing the two flights of stairs, Lena inserted the key into the door, only to find it partially open, with the hallway into the parlor shrouded in darkness. A sense of unease washed over her, and she grasped her throat in sudden panic.

Dee-Dee would never leave the door unlocked. Suddenly, panic hit her as her heart pounded. Lena's hands trembled as she felt along the wall in the dark, searching for the lamp on the round table near the couch in the parlor. She found it, pulled the cord, and turned on the light. Relieved, she moved to close and lock the door. Perhaps Dee-Dee was in a rush and forgot to lock it, Lena thought, feeling reassured.

"Hello Lena," the male voice said.

Lena instinctively turned toward the voice and gasped when she saw who was behind her: Gunn. She screamed and desperately tried to unlock the door to escape, but Gunn quickly blocked her path. With no escape, Lena collapsed to the floor, trembling and whimpering, reminiscent of her childhood.

"Lena, Lena, shhh," Gunn whispered, bending down to her and gently placing his finger on her trembling lips to quiet her. "Please don't cry. I'm not here to hurt you. I came to tell you how sorry I am for all the terrible things I've done and to ask for your forgiveness. I just want to talk to you, and then I will leave. You'll never see me again. Finding where you were staying was difficult for me," he said, lifting her to her feet. "Want to know how I tracked you down? Well, one of my men, who works for me, regularly goes to Nickford's restaurant for coffee. He told me he saw you working there and followed you to that church you attend. He tried to stay but had to leave after about twenty minutes because those women kept shouting and screaming Jesus' name over and over again. Said it gave him a bad headache, so he left, found me, and here I am!" Gunn chuckled.

"Don't touch me, get out!" she screamed. She managed to break free and ran into the kitchen to grab a knife for self-defense, but he grabbed her arm, pulling her out forcefully, and threw her onto the couch. Lena tried to stand up again, but Gunn pushed her down so hard she hit her head against the wall, resulting in sharp pain and a feeling of heaviness.

The familiar pain she felt at his filthy, hell-hole of a flat hit her again as she held her head and rocked back and forth, moaning loudly.

"Lena, please sit down and listen. I want to apologize. Can you sit quietly and let me speak for a moment?" He was pacing back and forth, sweating heavily. As he moved, his footsteps pounded the floor, causing the walls and floor to shake.

"I promise that once I finish here, I'll leave and leave you alone. Besides, I have a new woman who wants me badly, Lena. She's just like you-so beautiful. I'll hurry so you can go to church tomorrow and I can spend more time with her," he said with a grin. Lena didn't respond.

She gazed at Gunn with wide, blinking eyes, her head pounding from pain. She wondered how the hell he got in here? All Lena could do now was pray that, by some miracle, Dee-Dee and Nickford would come through the door.

"Lena, before I forget, these are for you." Gunn walked behind the couch and pulled out an armful of roses. Lena sat, stunned by the gesture. "Please take them," he said, extending the roses to her. Too frightened to accept them, Lena turned her head to avoid looking at Gunn. He shrugged, placed the bouquet beside her, and sat down.

"Lena, I'm truly sorry for how I treated you," he said, pressing his white handkerchief to his sweating forehead. Lena glanced at him and noticed the remnants of a black eye, still swollen and partly shut, with a grotesque purple hue. It was clear someone had beaten him badly. Lena thought bitterly, if only whoever did this had killed him.

"I was a complete fool and acted like a big asshole. I should never have treated you that way, attacking you as if you were a man on the street. I know I hurt you deeply, and I am truly sorry. Please, Lena, forgive me, and then I'll leave. You won't see me again after tonight," he said, his chin trembling as if he might break down.

"What did you do to Miss Paula? She was found dead. The police said someone murdered her. It was you, wasn't it?" Lena asked, feeling a newfound boldness.

"No, no, no! She-she was already dead!" Gunn shouted, rising from the couch and beginning to pace again.

"Liar!" Lena screamed, breaking into uncontrollable sobs. "You killed her!"

"Listen, listen, listen to me!" Gunn sputtered, changing the subject. "I forgot to give you something!" He hurried to the kitchen table and grabbed a box with a bow. "Open it," he ordered.

"Are you fuckin' crazy?" Lena said, clearly pissed off that he changed the subject.

"Open it for me, please?" Gunn begged as he handed her the box.

Lena stared at him in horror and disbelief, knowing he lied about killing Miss Paula. This crude, self-absorbed, murderous liar was there offering a gift. If accepting the gift would get him out of here, I'll do it, she thought angrily.

Snatching the box, Lena headed into her bedroom and slammed the door behind her. Before opening the box, she thought about retrieving the key to lock the bedroom from inside, so when Dee-Dee and Nickford returned, they would see Gunn and tell him to leave. Her hands trembling, she searched all the chests of drawers for the bedroom key.

Oh my God, where is my key? Lena checked each drawer one by one until she looked through them all and found no key. Lena felt nauseous, and weakness overtook her legs before she collapsed on the floor in despair.

"Are you okay?" Gunn asked from outside the floor.

"I'm fine!" Lena snapped. "I'll be out in a moment."

"Okay!" Gunn replied cheerfully. "I hope you like the gift. By the way, Lena, your purse fell to the floor and everything spilled out. I've arranged everything back inside, especially that key you've been looking for. Don't take too long; I'm waiting. I also hope you're fine with me eating some of the cake from the kitchen, it looks so delicious! I'm gonna make coffee for us too. It'll be just like old times, honey."

Lena slowly rose from the floor and had to grasp the edge of the armoire to steady herself as she stood in disbelief that he had found the key!

"Oh no, no, no!" She wailed.

"Oh, c'mon now, Lena, don't sit there fretting. Tell you what, if you open the present, come out and show me, and have one dance with me, and I'll leave. Please come out, Lena."

Lena tore open the box, tossed the tissue papers onto the floor, and pulled out a black dress with a high collar. The dress looked very plain, made of heavy silk, with long sleeves and buttons at the back, which meant she would need help to fasten it. She noticed a faint smell coming from the dress. When she lifted the sleeve to smell it, she grimaced. The pungent odor of heavy underarm sweat made her wrinkle her nose in disgust and pull back quickly. It was clearly worn by someone else! The style was outdated by about twenty years; it was his mother's dress!

She threw it on the floor, looked inside the box, and saw a pair of used heels. The shoes had signs of age and wear; they were his mother's. She felt disgusted.

Lena faced a difficult decision: either put on the dress and shoes so he would leave, or confront something worse. She picked up the dress from the floor, undressed, and put it on, slipping into the oversized shoes. Looking in the mirror, she was horrified to see that both the dress and shoes were too large. The black dress, despite its color, bore rust-colored stains at the waist. Lena thought, "Oh my God, this is the dress his mother wore when Gunn murdered the man she was with, it's blood-stained!" In horror, she stormed out of the bedroom, slamming the door behind her.

Gunn was sitting on the couch, eating a large slice of cake. Crumbs were scattered everywhere as he took loud slurps of his coffee. He looked up and saw Lena glaring at him.

"You-you look so beautiful, honey!" Gunn exclaimed as he took the napkin from his neck and stood up. He reached out to touch Lena.

"No, don't touch me!" Lena said harshly as she backed away. "You said you'd leave after you saw me in this."

"Yes, I know. You're so beautiful, and I can't help but keep looking at you. You remind me of my mother in that dress, and she was stunning. I loved her dearly," he said hesitantly. "I'll leave afterward, but could you do me one last favor? Would you dance with me? I know we never had the chance to go out because I was harsh to you, but I want to make amends. After this song, I'll be gone." Suddenly, he moved behind her and grasped her waist firmly. His large body overshadowed her petite frame. He held her so tightly she could barely breathe, yet she could feel his breath on her neck. Lena closed her eyes tightly, wishing for this monster to leave. She felt her bladder loosen, but tried her best to hold it.

"Do you remember this song?" Gunn asked as he began to sway to the steady tune playing on the radio. The vocalist singing the song brought tears to Lena's eyes, mostly recalling the day she left New Orleans. The same song was playing when she met Gunn. But now she feared for her life. As they swayed, Lena's eyes suddenly widened. She felt him getting hard as he pressed against her, his breathing growing heavier.

"You know, Lena, when you left me, you left my place a huge mess," he said with a heavy sigh. "I was really burned up at you and my uh-friend who came back to see you again paid a lot of money. Well, things got bad between us. During the fight, he beat the shit outta me. Even gave me this," he said, pointing at his black eye. "You see, while I was out on the floor, almost dead, he took fifty-six thousand dollars. But you know what broke my heart, Lena? You. You stole two thousand dollars from me. Now, why'd you do that?" he asked as he began to press down on Lena's ribs.

"I can't breathe; you're hurting me! Let me go!" Lena protested, struggling to wiggle free from the death grip as she wheezed to breathe.

"Shhh," Gunn whispered into her ear. "Listen, baby, I forgive you and don't blame you for what happened. Honestly, I'd run away too. Let's just put this behind us.

I'm going to leave now." He loosened his hold as Lena freed herself. She bent over, coughing and clutching her ribs. "But before I go, please tell me you forgive me. All I want is to leave here as a forgiven man," he said, walking up behind her.

"I forgive you," Lena said between coughs and gasps for air. She was in severe pain, worried that he had broken her rib. "Now, get out," she added between coughs, clutching the edge of the couch arm.

"Thank you, Lena", she heard him say.

But at that moment, everything happened so fast. Lena felt him grab and pull her hair from behind, stretching her neck back as far as it could go. Then she felt the sharp edge of a razor slicing through her neck. The pain was excruciating. She tried to scream, but blood began to bubble out of the deep gash, and her breathing became a garbled mix of wheezing air mixed with blood. Lena felt herself losing consciousness as well as feeling her life spilling onto the floor.

Gunn forcefully shoved her down, causing her head to hit the floor with a loud thud. He glared at Lena's lifeless, bloodied body and stared into her empty eyes. Turning away, he went into the kitchen, rinsed the nine-inch straight razor he always kept in his back pocket, and washed the blood from his hands. After drying them, he folded the razor and slipped it back into his pocket. He then turned off the stove burner he had used earlier for coffee, rinsed his coffee cup, and put it back in the cupboard. In Lena's bedroom, Gunn found what he was looking for: a brown suitcase she carried when they left New Orleans. Inside, he found two thousand dollars that Lena hadn't touched, still neatly tied with the same twine knot he had used over twenty-five years ago. After snapping the suitcase shut, Gunn picked up the bouquet of roses Lena had tossed on the floor. He closed the door to the room and returned to the living room, where Lena lay dead. He placed the roses next to her hand, then reached into his suit pocket and pulled out a handwritten card that read, *"Sincerest Condolences,"* which he set on top of the roses. Finally, he went to the small table in the corner, where he kept his hat, and put it on.

"Rest in peace, Lena," he said, tipping his hat to the corpse. He snapped off the lamp and left as the radio played.

CHAPTER FIVE

Harlem, One Week Later

"It was truly a dreadful murder, and we all mourn your wife's loss deeply. She intended to come home to see if issues between you could be resolved, acknowledging her mistake in leaving you," the church pastor told Wayne Collins, who sat grief-stricken across the table. Audine grasped Wayne's hand firmly, providing her support. Since Lena's death, he had been crying uncontrollably and blaming himself. Despite her composed exterior, Audine secretly felt a surge of joy.

Good riddance, I'm so glad she's gone! Serves her right for running off with a two-bit criminal! My God, she was a married woman spreading her legs wide open for that immoral fiend while my poor Wayne was home alone and heartbroken. Well, thank God for me, hah! I'm here now! When everything is settled, when we get back, I'll give us a year before we become Mr. and Mrs. Wayne Collins. Violet will be at college to become a teacher; her brother, Mason, is getting older and will be able to take care of himself, and I'll start trying for a baby right away. There's no sense in us working all the time and coming home to just a house with no children. Wayne deserves a new family, and I intend to provide it for him. Six months after the first baby arrives, we'll have another one. Four children, hah! What a wonderful ending, thank you, Lena! Audine thought gleefully as she shifted her weight in the uncomfortable wooden folding chair that had splintered. The chair was way too small for her wide hips. She pretended to wipe tears from her eyes, made loud, noticeable sniffling noises, and kept her head low, constantly tugging at her black velvet hat to hide her broad smile.

"You know what, Wayne?" the Pastor asked. "What was so mysterious was that someone sent me an unsigned card with instructions that Lena's funeral expenses should be paid with the cash inside. Wayne, that envelope contained one thousand dollars. In another card, the sender told me to give this to you." The Pastor said as he handed a thick envelope to Wayne.

Wayne, with trembling hands, took the envelope that read: 'To the husband of Lena Collins.' He looked at it, then glanced at Audine, who casually shrugged. Carefully opening the envelope, Wayne extracted a card decorated with a single cross and sealed with tape at the edge. As he tore it open, a wad of twenty crisp, new fifty-dollar bills spilled out.

"What! Oh my God! Who sent this?" Wayne exclaimed with wide eyes. 'There's a thousand dollars in here!"

"Wayne, when we get back to New Orleans, put that money in the bank so it stays safe, you hear me?" Audine whispered, leaning close to his ear.

Wayne missed Audine's words and only looked at the cash before suddenly breaking down and crying. The Pastor watched Audine closely as she swiftly tucked the money into her purse. After closing her purse, she crossed her legs, grinned broadly, and remained oblivious to the Pastor's gaze.

The Pastor thought bitterly about her presence with him, hoping Wayne truly understood what he was facing. He considered her a desperately wicked woman, shaking his head in disapproval. A week later, Wayne and Audine returned to their home in New Orleans.

CHAPTER SIX

New Orleans

"Everything was paid for," Audine said as she took a sip of steaming hot coffee. She looked longingly at the uncut sweet potato pie in the center of the table. Wasn't Maria planning to serve the pie? she wondered, glancing at Wayne, who was sipping his coffee before refocusing on the pie.

Audine and Wayne sat at the table in Maria and Clarence's kitchen. Clarence went to stay with Violet and her brother Mason, much to Maria's annoyance. However, after Violet befriended the twins, she gradually warmed up to her. She also noticed that Violet quickly learned French Creole after hearing the twins speak it. Violet was a very intelligent and articulate young woman who proudly shared her ambition to become a schoolteacher. Besides her intelligence, she was also strikingly beautiful.

Audine continued, "You should have seen it—Lena looked stunning, almost as if she were sleeping. The funeral director carefully selected the right shade of makeup for her face, and her hair was perfectly styled. The woman she stayed with chose a beautiful blue dress with long sleeves, although I don't understand why it had such a high neckline, as she was already wearing pearls and gloves, which seemed a bit odd. Personally, I think it was overdone; once the casket is closed, who's going to see her?"

"There was a very good reason she was in that dress and pearls," Wayne said flatly as he set down his coffee cup. "Lena's throat was deeply slashed, and based on what the funeral director told me, it would've been better if she had worn the dress with the pearls because of the visible wound. Whoever did this wanted her dead. I hope she didn't suffer."

"Oh my God, Wayne, we're so sorry to hear this", Maria said, getting up to hug him.

"I still can't believe she's gone, and we're so sorry you had to go through all this, Wayne. Just remember that Maria and I are here for you," Clarence said, placing a comforting hand on Wayne's trembling shoulder.

"Thank you all for everything," Wayne said, his eyes reddening and beginning to tear up. "Lena and I went through tough times during our marriage. She left me, and I partly blamed myself for many things I said and for not trying hard enough to keep her happy. If I had done better, she might still be alive."

"Wayne, you wouldn't have expected she was going to leave, especially with that New York gambler who came here. From what I heard, Maydell was all over him, humph! Look at what happened to her, and now Lena. I heard the gambler hasn't been around for weeks, and I also heard the place where Lena stayed with him was filthy! Lena stayed there with him and- "

"Audine, please!" Wayne yelled loudly.

"Oh-oh, I'm terribly sorry. Please forgive me, Wayne. I know I have a habit of speaking out, and I didn't mean to hurt you. I'm sorry, honey," Audine stammered, grasping his hand. He nodded, his head bowed low, and his shoulders sagging.

Maria was amazed by how openly affectionate Audine was towards Wayne, and she was equally surprised by how quickly Audine grew closer to him.

She's not wasting any time! Maria thought suspiciously as she watched how Audine was all over him.

Audine's open affection was suddenly interrupted when all of Maria's children and Audine's children, Violet and Mason, burst into the kitchen where everyone else was seated. They were talking and laughing, with Mason, Audine's son, seemingly engaged in an animated discussion with Joseph. The two had become close friends and often talked. Maria watched Joseph fondly, noting that he was sleeping better and doing well academically. His last report showed four "A's" and two "B's," which Maria found impressive and was very grateful for.

Her daughters were right behind the boys, and they could hear them speaking French Creole with Audine's twenty-one-year-old daughter, Violet, who was replying to them in the Same Language. As soon as Maria saw her, her body suddenly stiffened. She took a quick breath through her nose and closed her eyes. Violet was stunning. Standing five feet nine inches tall with a slender build, she had her hair slicked back into a tight, single braid. Her almond-shaped eyes gave her an almost exotic appearance, as if they belonged to someone from an unknown land. She was always smiling, showing a set of perfect white teeth. Without realizing it, this young, beautiful woman commanded attention wherever she went.

Violet and twelve other young women were preparing for an exam in two months. The twins taught her basic words and sentences in French Creole. By the end of three weeks, Violet was engaging in lively conversations with them.

Maria stared intensely at Clarence, who was looking at Violet, feeling a hollow ache in her stomach. Something isn't right, she thought as she sat up straighter in her chair.

"Mère, I'm so happy you're home! I missed you so much!" Violet exclaimed as she ran to Audine and embraced her. "The twins have taught me a lot about speaking French Creole, and Mr. Clarence shared many insights about soil, like when to plant certain vegetables, and how rain and sunshine help them grow. Thanks to Mr. Clarence, I'm confident I'll pass the science portion of the exam. Many girls are struggling with science, but since I am quickly learning French Creole, I decided to attempt the extra credit part of the exam. That section involves simple sentences, reciting the alphabet, counting, and having a short conversation in French with a teacher, who will be available if we want to test in that part."

"Did you all hear what my daughter called me?" Audine asked, rising and hugging Violet tightly.

Audine beamed with pride as she heard her daughter call her 'mother' in French Creole. "See, I told you my daughter is smart! She's going to pass all her tests, become a teacher, and help our children learn to read, write, and even speak different languages! Oh, I'm so proud of you, Violet!" Audine rested her head on Violet's shoulder and gazed into her daughter's eyes with love and pride.

"Everyone, let's go outside so I can show Mr. Collins the smokehouse and share how well everything's growing on the farm. Wayne, I have so much to show you, and if you need anything, just let me know what you want, and my sons and Mason will load your car," Clarence said.

"Thanks, Clarence", Wayne said as he rose from his seat to go over to shake hands with Clarence. Everyone except Maria's daughters and Violet, who stayed behind, followed Clarence and Wayne outside.

"Violet, come with us so we can teach you more words in Creole. We'll pretend we're shopping in a grocery store, and we'll also teach you the names of vegetables, fruits, and meats," Rosetta said to Violet, who appeared eager and interested in learning more of the language. She followed Izelle, who already had paper and pencils ready for everyone, as she led the way into their room.

Audine and Maria were alone in the kitchen. After an awkward silence, Maria finally decided to speak.

"Can I offer you some more coffee?" Maria said.

"Yes, and I'd also like a slice of that pie too," Audine said, her gaze flickering between the different objects in Maria's kitchen.

"You know, you and Clarence really have everything," Audine said as she eagerly started eating the thick slice of pie Maria served.

"What do you mean by that, Audine?" Maria asked, raising her eyebrows in confusion. "Because all of this is the result of Clarence and my years of hard work, saving every penny and ensuring our children are cared for. So, if you think these things were handed to us, you're very mistaken."

Now that Lena's dead and Wayne has inherited that money, I intend to move forward with him. He's likely to ask me to marry him any day now. Once he does, I'll need a wedding dress made. Can you do that for me?

Maria was about to take a sip of coffee, but set her cup down on the saucer and looked up at Audine, who was smiling brightly and flicking pie crumbs from her fingers onto Maria's clean floor.

"What? Wayne just buried his wife, and you already think of moving on so quickly? My God, Audine! He's still mourning Lena, and what's worse is that the woman who did the laundry near Lena's hiding spot was found murdered! Audine, why are you rushing into all of this?" Maria asked, angry and stunned by the sudden revelation.

Audine picked up the napkin from the table, gently dabbed at her lips, and made irritating smacking sounds. After setting the napkin back down, she fixed a stern gaze at Maria.

"You seem to forget something. Lena left Wayne, not the other way around. Yes, Wayne is a man, and Lena couldn't stand being at home as his wife. All he wanted was for her to be there when he got home, attend church, and have children with him. Humph, she couldn't even do that! She didn't even try harder to have babies for that poor man. Yet, she had the nerve to leave Wayne and go to New York, a place she'd never been before, with a stranger and that gambler, whose name was uh-uh-High Roller-Gunn, yes, that was his name! Humph! It seems she preferred living under his coattails instead of her husband's. That nasty woman was most likely spreading her legs wide open for that man and maybe even more men if she needed money! I'll tell you one thing for sure; Lena deserved it. She had no business leaving her husband like that. If she had worked things out with Wayne, she'd still be alive. I also learned that the undertaker had to sew her mouth shut because her two front teeth were missing, probably punched out by the gambler, hah! What a stupid woman she was! Like I said, she's dead, and I plan to make Wayne a very happy and satisfied husband. Once we're married, I plan to have three children for him.

Timing will be key, so I'll plan the wedding soon so we can start having children each year until the third one arrives," she said, snapping her fingers. "Oh, and by the way, I still need Clarence to come over until Violet gets into that women's college in Virginia. Imagine that Maria and I will have five beautiful children! That is—uh, unless you're going to have another child. After seeing you and Clarence in the barn, I wouldn't be surprised if you're expecting right now! Then I'll have to have another one to keep up with you!" she said, throwing her head back and laughing loudly.

Enraged by the lies Audine was spewing at her dinner table, Maria stood up and calmly approached Audine, who was unaware of her. As Audine reached for a second slice of pie, Maria suddenly grabbed her wrist with a firm grip, causing Audine to drop the knife and pull her wrist away from Maria's painful hold.

"*Ouch*, you hurt me!" Audine lamented, shocked by Maria's gesture. She looked at Maria, horrified.

"Shut up, Audine!" Maria snapped through clenched teeth. "How dare you come to my house and talk about Lena like that! Lena was my friend and our neighbor. You have no idea what she was going through, especially with Wayne and the difficulty of not having children! She was also fed up with being stuck in that house, doing nothing but cleaning, cooking, and listening to the radio all day. It seemed like Wayne only wanted to work, eat, and come home — that was it. He kept asking her why she hadn't had children or why it was taking so long. Lena told me all of this!" Maria slammed her fist on the table, so close to Audine that her coffee cup spilled, drenching Audine's dress.

"That's exactly why she left Wayne! She was humiliated and fed up with Wayne's impatience, and now, of all people, you're sitting here telling me that you and Wayne plan to marry, have children, and try to be like my family? What's wrong with you, Audine? My God, Wayne just buried Lena, and you're happy about it? What kind of woman are you?" Maria exclaimed, glaring with disgust at Audine, who was fidgeting with a lace handkerchief, trying to clean up the coffee spilled on the table and her dress.

"Why are you raising your voice at me?" Audine asked, rising from her seat and tossing aside the handkerchief. "I'm telling you the truth! Lena had to be a loose woman to go all the way to New York, knew no one except that gambler, and then got herself killed, humph! I'll say how I feel, and that is this: she deserved what she got, and I'll be the one giving Wayne the family he deserves! I don't care how you feel about it, Maria! I deserve to be happy just like you!" Audine yelled, standing up and facing Maria with her fists clenched on her hips.

"What-what is going on?"

Maria and Audine looked toward the source of the voice. It was Violet, standing with Izelle and Rosetta, watching as the intense disagreement unfolded.

"Oh-uh, where did you all come from?" Audine asked, facing them. "I thought they were teaching you French, Violet."

"We heard both of you yelling, and we were getting scared," Rosetta said as she nervously grabbed and held Izelle's trembling hand.

"We were teaching Violet new French words that she might be tested on, but you both were talking loudly and then yelling. Is everything okay, Mère?" Izelle asked, walking over to her mother and hugging her.

"It's fine. Mrs. Booker was just about to collect Violet since she's leaving right now," Maria said, glaring at Audine in disgust.

"Come on, it's getting late, and Wayne is quite tired, as am I. Why not show me how much French you've learned from the twins? You girls are truly becoming lovely young women! Once Violet passes her exam, she'll make an excellent teacher. After that, she might head north to find a great place to settle down and-"

"Ma, please," Violet urged, touching Audine's arm gently. "Miss Maria is correct; we must go now because I need to review the new words Rosetta and Izelle taught me. The test is in two weeks, and I'm competing against twelve other girls who also aim to pass it," she insisted quickly.

"You're right," Audine said. "Maria, thank you for the coffee and pie you served. I'll make sure to call you soon to discuss what we talked about. When I leave, I'll remind Clarence to come over to watch Violet and Mason. It seems Clarence has been helping Violet a lot, especially with science and other things."

"Thanks for coming. You and Violet take care," Maria said unenthusiastically.

"I'm looking forward to more French lessons with Izelle, Rosetta, and Miss Maria. Thank you for welcoming me into your home," Violet said. She then approached Maria and gave her a hug, which Maria returned with a brief and gentle hug.

As Audine and Violet left, Audine beamed with a broad smile while watching her son, Mason, and Wayne chatting and smiling as they walked with Clarence and his sons.

"I'm sorry things got a bit noisy in your kitchen, Maria," Audine said, glancing over her shoulder. "I still see us as friends. You and Clarence were kind neighbors to Wayne and me. Clarence, in particular, has been wonderful by coming to my house to watch Violet and Mason, which has really touched my heart."

"How much longer will this last?" Maria asked sharply. "I need my husband home because conditions are getting worse in some parts of Louisiana, and we're not safe alone, especially at night. So, tell me now, how much longer will this continue?"

Audine, smirking as she walked toward Maria, leaned in close to her ear.

"After Wayne and I get married, we'll live together. I plan to quit my job because I expect to have a child by then, just like you." She patted Maria's belly. "What? You thought I didn't know?" Audine said, then walked over to Violet, linking arms with her.

Maria was shocked as she saw Audine engaging in a lively conversation with Violet, who then approached Wayne. Violet put her arms around Wayne's neck, hugging and squealing playfully while he helped her into his car. Wayne was carrying a large basket of vegetables, while Mason and Joseph transported smaller baskets of sweet potatoes. Kempton, Clarence, and Sampson carried multiple sacks of smoked meats, including chicken, ham, and bacon slabs. Clearly, Audine and her family would not go hungry.

"Thank you, Clarence," Wayne said as the trunk was closed after the last sack of hams was carefully loaded inside. "Clarence and Maria, you've both been a blessing to me and Audine. That trip to New York was one of the hardest things I've ever faced. Lena is at peace now, and it's time for me to move on without her," he said, voice trembling. "God bless you both, and thank you." Wayne shook hands with Clarence and each of his sons. He then got into the packed car, started it, and drove away.

Izelle and Rosetta went straight to their room, where they immediately started their loud, cheerful chatter. Maria watched from the doorway as her sons ran to the barn to collect their fishing poles and pails for a trip to the lake. Clarence, meanwhile, stared at Wayne's car, which was no longer there. He then noticed Maria glaring at him, her green eyes flashing quickly and her jaw clenched in a fury he had never seen before. She spun around and stormed back into the house.

"Maria, wait!" Clarence shouted after her. She ignored him and stepped into the house, shutting the door with a loud bang. Clarence quickly blocked the door and grabbed her arm. "What's wrong with you?" he demanded. "You've been acting crazy lately, yelling at me and our family, slamming things, and I heard you and Audine arguing all the way out at the smokehouse! What's going on?"

"Let go of me!" Maria snapped bitterly as she pulled her arm free from his tight hold. "Clarence, I see everything now," she said, settling into the chair. "I watched how you looked at Violet, and it's not right for you to stare at her like that! She's a smart young woman, but she's not one of those loose women who hang around the juke joints in a town like Maydell. You remember her, don't you, Clarence? You didn't think I knew about you and her?" Maria asked boldly, crossing her legs.

"What does Maydell have to do with anything, especially with Violet?" said Clarence. "She's a very smart woman I am looking after, along with her brother, Mason. I'm also helping her with much of the science for that test she needs to pass. I've been teaching her everything from the type of soil needed to grow certain vegetables to when they take root. I swear to God, Maria, I'm tired of all this fighting! I'm not putting up with this nonsense anymore; things will change around here soon because I won't let this family fall apart because of us!" Clarence said sharply as he headed for the door.

"You're right, Clarence," Maria sighed deeply. "But before you head back outside to fish with our sons, things are going to change around here, and quite soon. Come back here, because I have something to tell you."

"What? Is there something wrong with our children?" he asked.

Maria slowly rose from her chair.

"There's a reason behind my recent actions, and I sincerely apologize to you and our family. I would do anything to protect this family. Once everyone understands the reason for my behavior, they'll see things differently, and so will you," she said.

"What are you saying?" he asked.

She moved closer to him, clasped his rough hand, and pressed it gently against her belly.

"Clarence, we're expecting another child. The night we made him; I had a dream where I ate fish and wore a blue dress. That's how I know we're having a son. If my adding up is correct, he'll arrive in June." I'm now far enough along to know the due date, but I'll see Mrs. Wade, the midwife who delivered all our children, on Monday. I deeply regret my behavior and apologize to you and the family.

Clarence, grinning, swept Maria into his massive arms, and she wrapped her arm around his neck.

"When did this happen?" he asked.

"Several weeks ago, I can't recall exactly, but after my last monthly, my breasts started swelling, and I began noticing small signs similar to when Rosetta and Izelle were inside me. He will be coming to us in June," she said, smiling through tears.

"No doubt it happened when we were in the barn, Maria, because after that, we were doing it every night. I can't keep my hands off you," Clarence said, holding her tighter.

'That's possible, but we should prepare for this. A year after he's born, I want us to have one more. That way, our family will be complete, and our son will have someone here to share with him besides us. It wouldn't make sense for him to be all alone," Maria said.

"You have everything planned and figured out, don't you?" Clarence said, gazing intently into her eyes. "There's something I meant to tell you for a year."

"What was it that you wanted to tell me?" she asked, frowning.

"I wanted to have two more children. Our sons are growing older, and so are our daughters. The farm is doing well, so what's the harm of having two more? After that, our family will be complete. Would you be okay with that?" he asked.

"Yes, of course, I'd be fine with that, Clarence!"

"We need to share this wonderful news with our children. I'll go get the boys, you get Izelle and Rosetta, and then we'll all meet in the barn to share the news".

"Why the barn?" Maria asked, perplexed by the suggestion of the meeting site.

'That's where we made our son, and after he's born, we're going back there again to make our daughter," he said, kissing her deeply.

"Je t'aime tellement, Clarence. I love you so much," Maria said.

"I love you and thank you for our new son," Clarence said. Then he left to go to the lake.

This is probably one of the happiest days in my life, Maria thought with a smile. After all this time, Clarence also wants two more children, just as I do! I refuse to let Audine's words about my dear friend Lena ruin this day. If Wayne asks her to marry him, she won't have any children with him because she isn't the right woman for Wayne.

"Mère?" Izelle said.

Maria spun around to find Rosetta and Izelle standing behind her in the doorway, startling her.

"Oh my!" Maria exclaimed, surprised to see her daughters. "How long have you been standing there?"

"Long enough to hear you're having another baby!" Rosetta said. "Is it true?"

"Oui-yes. We're expecting a new baby in June. I'll need both of your help when he arrives. Are you happy for me?"

"Oui! Oh Mère, we're so happy, a new baby!" Rosetta said.

The twins hugged Maria as they all spoke in French-Creole.

Maria asked, "Your father wants us all to meet in the barn so he can tell everyone. But don't tell them you already know, okay?"

" Oui, Mère, we won't say a word. We'll pretend to be surprised. But why the barn?" Rosetta asked, first glancing at Izelle, then at Maria.

"Uh, Rosetta, let's go. I'll tell you why", she whispered into her sister's ear, smiling.

"I'll be there in a moment. I want to clear the dishes off the table". Maria said.

"Don't take too long, Mère!" Izelle said.

They left, and Maria remained in the doorway, observing her daughters as they headed toward the barn. Izelle was whispering something to Rosetta, causing her to halt with a stunned expression and cover her mouth. She probably shared details about the moaning they had been hearing late at night when they were supposed to be asleep.

Well, they're older now, and when they get married someday, they'll do the same. Maria thought to herself with a smile as she started clearing the kitchen table. Then she noticed a delicate lace handkerchief crumpled on the table, Audine's handkerchief, which she had used to blot the coffee she had spilled.

Maria knew exactly how to handle this, a smile forming on her lips. She folded the ivory handkerchief and tucked it into her bosom, then left the kitchen and went to the barn where everyone was gathered. There, she and Clarence would share the news of their upcoming addition to the family.

CHAPTER SEVEN

The return journey to Audine's house was peaceful, aside from Audine's constant lively chatter, with others replying politely with yes or no. After roughly thirty minutes, Wayne's car arrived and halted in front of her house.

"Home at last," Audine said softly, a weary smile on her face as she took Wayne's hand. She looked at him with exhaustion, but he avoided her gaze, quickly pulling his hand free, turning off the ignition, and stepping out of the car.

"Mason and Violet, let's bring these bushels of vegetables inside. After you put them away, I'll be leaving. It's been a long day, and I'm very tired," he said as he walked to the back of the car, opened the trunk, and started removing the bushel baskets.

"Yes, sir, Mr. Collins," Mason said as he stepped out of the car to meet him. Violet followed behind.

"Are you coming, Ma?" Violet asked as she adjusted her dress.

"I'll be inside shortly. You and Mason help Mr. Collins with everything," she said with a smile. "When he's finished, tell Mr. Collins to meet me in the car; I need to speak with him."

Audine nervously glanced in the rearview mirror, watching Violet, Mason, and Wayne chatting. Wayne said something that made all three laugh as they hurriedly carried the baskets in and out of the house.

Why was he so quiet during the journey here? Since leaving Maria and Clarence's house, his mood has changed completely. He never pulled his hand away like that when I reached for it! Audine thought anxiously. *Tears began to form in her eyes and then flowed down her cheeks as she searched for her handkerchief to wipe*

away her tears.

Where is it? Where is my handkerchief? She

wondered, searching for it in her purse with confusion.

Wayne stepped out of the house, hugging Violet, and

then she went inside.

Wayne slammed the trunk closed and then got into the car, staring forward with his hands tightly on the steering wheel.

"Audine, I need to talk to you," he said.

"Uh-about what?" Audine asked, concern flickering in her eyes as she looked up at him.

I believe you know damn well why I need to talk. It's about you and what comes out of that mouth of yours! When we were at Maria and Clarence's house, you kept talking about terrible things involving my wife, Lena. I heard it all! I had to step outside to the car to show

Clarence something, and I overheard your conversation with Maria, or rather, your yelling!

"Wayne, honey, let me explain. Please, sweetheart, I just wanted to tell Maria that I am so sorry," Audine stammered.

"Shut up, Audine! You're not sorry," Wayne said with disgust. "First, you sat there at the table bringing up details about Lena that I never wanted to hear again. It was clear that whoever murdered her had beaten her so badly that she lost two teeth. The truth is this, Audine: Lena was a good woman with a fragile soul. Like many married couples, we had our fights. She was also deeply hurt because she couldn't have a child. Part of that was my fault, because three months into our marriage, I was the one pressuring her to start a family. She agreed because she loved me and wanted a family with me," he seethed, pointing to himself.

"I failed Lena. She told me every month that nothing had changed and there was no baby, which made me impatient and envious of our friends with children. Each year, we heard about friends expecting one, two, or even three children, but for us, there was nothing. The night before she left, we argued about everything. She said she was tired of people asking why we didn't have children after eleven years of marriage. The last time I saw her alive, she told me I deserved better and said goodbye. I never realized I'd never see her again. That's why I'm so hurt by what you said about her—you run your mouth too much! You're rude and mean-spirited. When you started visiting me after Lena left, I thought you were a wonderful woman who could help with my home, cooking, cleaning, and attending church. I even imagined claiming your children as my own because I loved them so much. I envisioned you becoming my wife, and us having a child each year for five years, since Violet would be a teacher and Mason was growing into a good young man, so I knew he'd go to college like Violet. But because of your mouth, you ruined everything for us," Wayne said bitterly, his gaze cold.

Audine sat frozen, struggling to process his words. Shock, disbelief, and pain churned within her, twisting her stomach and making her feel sick. She desperately wanted to say something, but her throat was dry, and all she could do was stare at the man she was falling for, who was about to leave her life. Did he really say he thought I'd be a good wife and wanted a family right away? Those are exactly the things I want! she thought, panicking.

"Wayne, please forgive me," she exclaimed desperately, overwhelmed with grief. "I'm sorry for what I said about Lena; I had no right to speak so cruelly about her. I didn't realize you and Lena had so many problems. You're right, Wayne. I have a habit of speaking without thinking, and my words can be hurtful. Please don't leave me!" she pleaded, upset at the thought of him leaving forever. She hid her face with her hands, crying loudly and intensely, her body shaking uncontrollably.

Wayne sat frowning at Audine, who was loudly sobbing. Frustrated, he shook his head, took out his handkerchief, and set it on her lap. She took it and blew her nose.

"Thank you," she whispered gently, slipping his handkerchief into her purse and snapping it shut. She gazed downward, avoiding Wayne's eyes. They sat silently, neither looking at the other.

"Are you okay?" Wayne asked as he reached over and placed his hand on her forearm.

"I think I'll be okay, but I still feel very ashamed of what I said about Lena. It will never happen again. I'm going to call Maria and apologize for saying such horrible things. I didn't realize that Lena was her friend," she said, avoiding eye contact with Wayne.

She asked, "Can I ask you something?"

"Of course," he said.

"Are we still going to see each other? I'm so sorry, I promise I'll never do it again. I love you, Wayne," Audine said, gazing at him with her eyes still red from crying and blinking rapidly.

Wayne's jaw dropped. *Had she not heard me? She just insulted my wife, who is gone forever, humiliated me in front of our friends, and now she's telling me she loves me?* Wayne thought, his eyes widening in disbelief at Audine.

"Uh, look, Audine," he said, clearing his throat. "It's been a long day for both of us, so I think we should head home. I'll come by tomorrow to pick you up. Please pass along my goodnight to Violet and Mason, and take care."

"Can I kiss you, sweetheart?" she asked softly, leaning in to kiss him.

"Goodnight, Audine," he said briskly as he started the car. "I'll see you."

Audine experienced a sudden, sharp pain in her chest, instinctively clutching it while averting her gaze. She quietly opened the car door and stepped outside. As soon as she shut the door, the car drove away, and he disappeared.

Audine stayed where she was until she heard his car engine fade. Letting out a heavy sigh, she slowly walked toward her house, tears prickling her eyes. She wiped them away and then went inside.

Violet, Mason, and Wayne are wonderful together; they are MY family, she thought while she looked around the small kitchen. All the vegetables and meats were put away, and the empty bushel baskets were stacked neatly in a corner.

"You okay, ma?"

Audine flinched, surprised by Violet's gentle words.

"Oh-uh, Violet, you gave me a scare! I thought you were studying?"

I stayed there for a bit. I went into the kitchen to make coffee just in case Mr. Wayne came back. That's when I overheard your argument. I didn't like what I heard, especially what he was saying about what you said about his wife, Lena. Why would you speak about her that way?" she asked, puzzled by her mother's comments about Lena.

"Violet, let's sit down and talk because you're old enough to understand what's happening," Audine said as she sat down, gesturing for Violet to join her. "Maybe Wayne was right about me," Audine admitted sadly. "I tend to run my mouth, but I was simply saying my feelings. I already miss him, and thinking about him leaving me or being with another woman terrifies me. Oh my God, I have to get him back, I'll do anything! I love Wayne very much, and my dream is to marry him and build a new life and family together. I want to give him the family he deserves, humph! Unlike Lena, who failed to do so. I only told the truth about her leaving Wayne," Audine said, biting her bottom lip.

"Nobody was there on that terrible day when he returned home and saw everything gone! It was me who helped him forget about her-ME! And I was the one he started falling in love with," she said, pointing to her chest with conviction. "But now he's very angry, and he doesn't want me anymore! All I ever wanted was another chance at life with love, a new husband, and a new family, that's all I ever wanted!"

"Ma, what can I do?" Violet asked, noticing her mother's shoulders slumped and her rubbing her temples.

"You're a smart and beautiful woman who will make a wonderful teacher. My God, Violet, you learned another language so quickly!" Audine exclaimed with admiration.

"Once you pass that exam, think about finding a job where you can help teach other Black children to do well, so they won't have to scrub floors or toilets, work as maids for white families, or toil as I do. Humph! At least

Clarence's wife, Maria, doesn't need to work! Clarence owns a large farm, has a big house, and they're probably expecting another baby! Why can't I have all of that! Now you see why I need to have Wayne back?" she said, her jaw now tightening.

Violet looked at Audine in disbelief at her sudden admission. So, this is why she wants me to pass the Teacher's Exam, it's all part of her selfish plan to be just like Clarence and Maria! she thought, stunned.

"I'm really sorry about you and Mr. Wayne," Violet said suddenly, letting go of Audine's hand and standing up. "Knowing you, I'm sure you'll find a way to figure this out."

Audine quickly looked up, her mouth dropping open at Violet's unexpected words and the accusatory tone in her voice.

"I have a lot to study because the exam is next Friday, and Mr. Clarence is coming tomorrow night to help me with a few questions I have. He's been a big help with things I don't understand, and I plan to score high on that part of the exam. So, I'll see you tomorrow. Good night".

Violet left the kitchen, went into her room, and closed the door behind her. Audine, who was momentarily speechless, sat with her arms crossed in her small, worn-down kitchen. She recalled sitting in Maria's spacious kitchen earlier, longing for the size and abundance of Maria and Clarence's home and farm, and wishing she could have what they had.

Why am I unable to have what Maria possesses, a caring husband, children, and another on the way? This feels unfair! she wondered, her stomach clenching as *she swayed back and forth. Then Audine wept again,*

silent tears of resentment streaming down.

CHAPTER EIGHT

Violet lay awake the night before, her mind restless. Each time she turned in bed, she woke up again. Unable to sleep, she sat at the edge of her bed, reviewing the notes she had taken when Clarence explained more about soil color differences. "The darker and richer the soil, the better crops will grow," he said to her last night, just before she turned in. However, she understood the real reason for her restlessness: she was falling in love with him.

"Miss Booker, are you ready?" the exam proctor asked impatiently.

"Yes, sir," Violet replied, clearing her parched throat and folding her sweaty hands in front of her.

"Begin," he said.

"My name is Violet Booker, and I am twenty-one years old. I have lived in New Orleans my entire life. I aspire to become a schoolteacher because many local children only attend school up to the third grade before working in tobacco or sugar cane fields. I want these children to have the opportunity to complete high school and, for those who are able, attend college. I also hope to emulate Elizabeth Jennings Graham, who founded New York City's first kindergarten for colored children, which was operated from her home. She passed away in 1901".

The exam Proctor sat, mouth agape in shock that this woman, the only one who took the extra credit portion of the foreign language exam, articulated what she said in perfect French Creole. During the second part of the exam, she correctly named twenty-eight items on the table. When she finished, Violet stayed in place and looked at the proctor, whose incredulous stare expressed disbelief that this Black woman had not only passed that section of the exam but had done so flawlessly and fluently.

"Is there anything else I need to do on this part of the exam?" she asked.

She was met with icy silence. Then the proctor finally snapped to attention and loudly cleared his throat.

"Ah, yes, yes. You've finished this portion of the exam. You can leave now".

"Thank you, sir," Violet said. She moved to the corner chair to gather her belongings.

"Your results will be ready tomorrow. They'll be handed over to the Pastor of your church, which you and six others belong to. Those who have passed will first attend the teaching college in Virginia. After two years, another exam will be administered, and if you pass that exam, you'll be offered teaching positions in New York, Washington, D.C., and New Jersey," the proctor said.

Violet thanked him and departed, heading outside to start the twenty-mile walk home, which she felt anxious about. She was the last to leave the building, as the others only completed the written exam and skipped the foreign language extra credit part. A truck that looked familiar was parked a few feet from the building, belonging to Clarence, who promptly got out to greet her.

"So, how'd everything go? Think you passed everything?" he asked, wiping his forehead and neck, slicked with sweat.

"Everything was easy, at least for me," she said confidently. "When we reached the agriculture section of the exam, I noticed many girls leaving. I heard some crying because they either didn't know the answers or didn't even try. After I finished, the exam proctor told me I could take the foreign language section in a separate room with a proctor fluent in French and French Creole, or I could leave. I chose to take the verbal part of the exam."

"So how was that? Was the French hard to figure out?" Clarence asked, raising his eyebrows in interest.

"Well, I first had to tell the proctor who I was, where I'm from, and why I want to become a teacher. I told him this in French, but used French Creole instead of proper French, as he mentioned. You should've seen his face when I was finished!" she said, laughing. "Then I had to identify twenty-eight items scattered on various tables. After it was over, he said the test results would be given to our Pastor. I guess we'll find out on Sunday who passed, since those who pass will have to go to Virginia for two years and then take another exam. Once they pass, we'll receive offers from schools in New York, New Jersey, and Washington, D.C., where we'll be teaching," Violet explained. Then suddenly, her gaze slowly shifted downward.

Clarence asked, puzzled by her shift in mood, "After sharing all that wonderful news, why do you suddenly seem so sad?"

"I'm not sad," she replied, gazing into his gentle eyes. "I'm just scared. If I pass this exam, I'll be moving far away from everyone. Also, my mother made it clear she wants me out," Violet said.

Clarence, alarmed by the admission, was also repulsed. He had grown fond of Violet, but he was also developing new feelings for the young, beautiful, and brilliant woman standing before him.

"Get into the truck. I'll drive you home so we can talk about this. I've known your mother for years, but what she's doing to you is just downright wrong," he said angrily.

Clarence opened the truck door, assisted her inside, then got in himself, turned on the ignition, and drove away.

"Violet, you're a smart young woman, and I believe you will be a fine teacher to help many children who drop out after sixth grade to work in the fields. That's why I'm hard on my children to do well in school, because one day, they're gonna run the farm. By then, I hope things will have improved here," he said, sighing deeply.

"Thank you, Mr. Clarence. I've never left New Orleans; it's my home. But I'm grown now, and if I pass the exam, I'll teach these children, so they'll want to grow up to become teachers, doctors, nurses, lawyers, or landowning farmers like you, running their own businesses," she said, looking at him while he drove. She touched his forearm, and Clarence felt a tingling sensation where she touched him. He kept his attention on the rural, unpaved, and bumpy road.

"Mr. Clarence, I know I shouldn't say this, but ever since you came to look after Mason and me, I've been grateful. But when you started helping with the agricultural part of the exam, I began to like you even more. If I have to leave New Orleans, I might never see you again, at least not like this," she said, her voice trembling as she wiped away a tear. With one hand on the steering wheel, he reached out with his right hand, and they entwined their fingers, holding tightly. Clarence sped up the truck. When they arrived at Violet's house, he helped her out, still holding her hand until they were inside.

"Where's Mason?" Violet asked.

"He's on the farm with Joseph," Clarence said.

"Mr. Clarence-"Violet stammered.

"From now on, call me Clarence when we're alone," he whispered huskily, gazing into her eyes. He had been waiting for the perfect moment to express his feelings for her over the past few months. It would've been easier if not for Maria's announcement of their sixth child's arrival; how could he possibly find the right time to tell Violet? He pulled her into his arms and kissed her deeply, his tongue exploring. Violet responded by opening her mouth to his. "Take me to your room," Clarence said. Her eyes sparkled with desire as she took his hand, led him to her small bedroom, and shut the door behind them.

CHAPTER NINE

Clarence eagerly explored the softness of her mouth with deep, sweeping strokes of his tongue. Violet moaned as she experienced every thrust.

"We can stop this now if you want, Violet. We shouldn't be doing this, especially with my wife expecting a baby. But if you tell me no, we can stop now before it's too late. I'll gladly come up with an excuse to your mother, and she'll have to find a way to take care of you and Mason," he said, tilting her chin up to meet his gaze.

Violet's breath caught in her throat as she thought, *I'm here with him, and if I say no, I'll never see him again.* The concern flashed across her face, and her heart tugged at her. Without a word, she unzipped his pants, unbuckled his belt, and pulled them down to the floor.

Her fingertips explored the prominent, aching bulge of his underwear, revealing a long, thick erection. Clarence then slipped off his shirt and stood before her. Pleased by the sight, Violet smiled, running her fingers down his chest, her eyes sparkling as she watched his rustic, honey-colored eyes urging her onward.

"Violet," he whispered. "Once we do this, we can never turn back, and we must never tell anyone, ever. Do you understand?"

"Yes, Clarence, I understand. I've often wondered what it would be like to be with you this way. I don't want anyone else; I only want you," she said, her eyes filled with longing.

Clarence hurriedly started to undress her. He unbuttoned her blue dress and took off her undergarments. She stepped out of her worn Oxfords, revealing her narrow feet. He paused to look at her and admired her splendid figure.

"You're absolutely beautiful," he whispered, caressing her swollen breasts and firmly grasping her buttocks, causing her to close her eyes and moan loudly. He then delivered a firm slap to her buttock with his open palm. Violet was initially surprised by the unexpected gesture, yelping in surprise. Though it didn't hurt, the stinging sensation left her wanting more.

"Get the sheet that is on your bed and spread it on the floor," he said as he released her.

Without hesitation, she did what she asked of as she pulled the sheet from her neatly made bed. He took her hand and placed it on his erection. Guiding her hand, he closed his eyes as she aggressively grabbed him with both her hands, feeling the hardness rise in him.

"Violet, lay down on the floor," he said.

She followed the instructions and lay on the sheet. The hardwood floor was uncomfortable but necessary since their tiny bed couldn't fit either of them. She settled on the floor as he crouched nearby. Violet still felt the prickling sensation, as if hundreds of needles were on her back. Despite the pain, she yearned to feel more. She sensed warmth and wetness between her legs. 'I'm so embarrassed about this wetness,' she thought with despair.

"I know what you're thinking. That wetness coming between your legs is supposed to happen. Believe me, it's going to add pleasure to what we're going to do", he said, smiling as he crouched on top of her, his full weight of over two hundred pounds. He cupped her left breast and took it in his mouth. She felt his tongue circle and swirl over her hard nipple. She arched her back, wanting more of what he was doing. "This is your first time, and it will hurt for just a moment", he said, staring at her.

"I believe that after we go through this, we'll end up falling in love, and I want that with you. Is that what you want?" he asked.

"Yes," Violet said, nodding her head.

"Then keep your eyes on mine," he said as he arched his back.

Violet kept her eyes on him as he thrust his hips, sinking into the tight depths of her womanhood. A sharp pinch caused her to cry out, gripping Clarence's broad shoulders.

He's right; it hurts now, but it will be over, she thought.

Violet spread her legs wider and started to match the rhythmic thrusts that were speeding up.

Clarence admired Violet's curvaceous figure as he went deeper inside her. Her breasts, which were firm and tight, were magnificent as he captured her nipple between his lips. Violet's moans were growing louder.

"Come, Violet, come NOW!"

Violet let out a sharp cry, her back arched off the floor as she grasped Clarence tightly around the neck.

"I love you, Clarence!" she gasped.

"And I'm in love with you, Violet," he said through clenched teeth. Clarence's thrusts increased in speed until he felt the familiar pulsing that led to a release, causing him to cry out Violet's name once more. Then, it was over.

"I never expected that," Violet said, rolling onto her side and wrapping her arm around his chest as she rested her head on him. "You were right about one thing; it did hurt at first, but after a while, it began to feel wonderful. I didn't want you to stop, Clarence," she added, looking up at him.

"This feels right to me," he said, pulling her closer. "I never imagined this would happen to us. You're beautiful, smart, and I've been drawn to you ever since I started coming here to care for you and Mason," he said, kissing her deeply.

"I don't want to leave. What if I pass the exam? It's being announced at church tomorrow. If I pass, I won't leave you; I don't want to lose you," Violet said.

"You won't because you're mine now, and I've finally found the woman I'm meant to be with," he said huskily. He again ravished her mouth with deep, sweeping strokes of his tongue, and they made love once more.

It's three o'clock in the afternoon. Six hours have passed since Clarence went to pick up Violet from the teacher's exam. Where could he be? Maria wondered, pressing a lavender-soaked cloth against her forehead.

She thought, 'This baby always seems hungry,' as she made gentle circular motions on her belly with her palm. Mrs. Alice Wade, the midwife, had come to the house the day before and confirmed the pregnancy.

"Either you're going to have a big baby, or you might be carrying two like last time," she said during her exam of Maria. "Your belly is already quite round, and you're beginning to show a little. Are you prepared if it turns out to be twins again, Maria? If so, that would be such a wonderful blessing for you and Clarence!" she exclaimed, clapping her hands. Hearing this, Maria cried tears of joy at the prospect of having twins once more.

Her mind started racing as she nervously paced the kitchen floor. After fifteen minutes, she heard the familiar sound of a truck engine approaching from behind the house. Parting the kitchen curtain for a better look, she saw Clarence. Relieved, she smiled and exhaled deeply, but when he moved to the other side of the truck to open the door, he extended his hand to help Violet out. His children were down by the lake, so Clarence and Violet thought they were alone, or at least they did for a moment, because Clarence quickly glanced to his left and right as if to check if anyone was around. Then he pulled Violet into his arms and began to kiss her passionately. With his arm around her waist, they headed toward the lake.

Maria suddenly experienced a powerful wave of nausea. She rushed outside through the kitchen door, bent over, and vomited. After coughing and gagging, she looked toward the lake, where everyone was gathered, including her husband with his arm around Violet's waist, unaware that she was watching them.

CHAPTER TEN

The sound of a car horn startled Audine as she sat at the kitchen table, stirring her cold coffee. It was Sunday morning, and she had woken up at five-thirty, pacing around the kitchen before deciding to make coffee and a pan of cornbread for herself, Violet, and Mason. It had been weeks since her fallout with Wayne. Despite that, he still kindly picked her up in the mornings for work, even on his day off, so she wouldn't have to walk home. Aside from greeting each other, they rode in silence. On Sundays, Wayne, Audine, and her family rode together, but the only sounds were his conversations with Mason, who had come to love Wayne like a father, and Violet, with whom he discussed politics.

"I've heard many rumors about the Civil Conservation Corps that's supposed to employ a lot of people," Wayne said, glancing briefly in the rearview mirror while keeping his attention on the road.

Violet said flatly, "I've been hearing the same thing too, Mr. Wayne, but it's never going to help us, and we all know why."

"Due to the strong influence of the South, which is solidly behind segregation, these white Democrats in Congress historically insisted on racial segregation. Additionally, all Southern states had enacted laws enforcing segregation, and since the early 20th century, laws and constitutional provisions have marginalized Black people. Because of how these white individuals treat us, we are effectively excluded from politics, which is why we will never access the jobs offered by the Civil Conservation Corps."

"You're right," Wayne agreed with a nod. "That's why we need to stay united and support each other, no matter what. Clarence is a perfect example of someone we rely on for our smoked meats and vegetables, especially since some white shop owners treat us poorly. Yes, I tell you, I will spend all my money on Clarence's meats and vegetables for my home!"

The mention of Clarence's name made Violet smile broadly, especially about everything that happened yesterday. He wasn't shy about keeping his arm around her waist in full view of his children when they reached the lake. Clarence's children were so excited about seeing him that they didn't pay much attention to their father's overt sign of affection towards Violet. The memory of yesterday also made her reflect on their first kiss; how his lips felt, how, for the first time in her life, she was kissed and held passionately. The second time they made love, Clarence lay on his back and asked that she sit on top, facing him. Before she did, though, he took her hand and asked that she hold onto his manhood and start in on it in a slow and steady motion, sliding up and down his engorged flesh. When it was time, he told Violet to ease herself down on him, guiding himself inside her. It felt different, yet it was so pleasurable that it made Clarence grimace and call out her name. When it was over, they kissed passionately until they didn't realize how much time had elapsed and that it was time to leave. Before they left, Clarence held her close and told her that he was falling in love with her.

"We're here, everyone," Wayne announced as he parked the car on the side of the road. He went to the passenger side and opened the door for Audine, who remained silent during the ride. He offered her his hand to help her out, and she grasped it firmly as she swung her leg out of the seat. They looked at each other for a moment and held on.

"We should get inside quickly because it's crowded, and I don't want to sit at the back," Mason said as he closed the door.

"Here comes Mr. Clarence and his family," he exclaimed, excitedly waving at his friend Joseph as they greeted each other.

Clarence, who was driving the family car just to be driven on Sundays, honked his horn and waved through the open window. For a stolen moment, he and Violet locked eyes, and the corners of Violet's lips turned up.

"Come on, everyone, Mason's right. It's very crowded inside today because everyone's here to see who passed the teacher's exam. Are you excited about how you did, Violet?" Wayne asked.

"Yes, I am, but I'm also nervous," Violet replied, unable to take her eyes off Clarence's car as she watched him step out first and then hurried to open the passenger door for Maria. She got out slowly while Clarence helped her. After adjusting her beautiful, flowered dress, she took his arm as they headed to the church. Violet watched them, feeling disappointed and confused about what she saw: the affectionate exchange between Clarence and Maria, and how Maria was rubbing her belly. Their eyes met again. Maria looked at her with a fierce, death-like stare that made Violet so frightened she looked away, quickly taking Mason's arm to walk with him toward the church.

The service began fifteen minutes late because many church members had invited friends and relatives, some traveling from as far as Atlanta, Georgia, to support their family members who were taking the exam and awaiting the final results. The low whispers gradually grew into loud murmurs, but they were quickly silenced when the organist started playing. At the signal, everyone stood up.

"May the Lord Jesus bless all of you this morning!" Pastor Roy Coleman said as he stepped to the front of the century-old oakwood podium, which his father and grandfather had used for preaching since the time of slavery.

"Our sermon today will focus on disappointment. Saints of Christ, please take your seats," he announced. Many parishioners responded with enthusiastic Amens and nods of approval. "First, I want to share the results of the exams taken by twelve young women from our church who are present today. I have the results right here," he said, gesturing with a bunch of envelopes in his hand.

He said, "But my beloveds of God, only four passed the exam."

The murmurs grew louder as family members of the young woman who took the exam wrapped comforting arms around their daughter. Audine held Violet's hand firmly, offering reassurance. Wayne smiled and nodded at Violet. She looked across the church to catch Clarence's eye, but was met with Maria's cold glare. Sitting close to Clarence, Maria was holding his arm, and the room's circulating air couldn't keep them apart. She made circular motions on her belly with her palm, as if to remind Violet of her unborn child. Violet quickly looked away, a sense of dread washing over her, wondering if Maria had seen Clarence kiss her yesterday at the house. She told herself, "We were very careful, nobody saw us," then shifted her focus back to the pastor's words.

"This is exactly what I prayed for, that God would send a message to me to confront some of you who will be greatly disappointed after service today," Pastor Coleman said.

Audine thought to herself that this sermon would be just what she needed to hear. She subtly turned her head toward Wayne, who was looking straight ahead and avoiding her gaze.

"Saints, have you ever experienced a moment when your life felt completely broken, like the dust beneath your feet?" Pastor Coleman asked, peering over his gold-rimmed glasses. Murmurs of Amen and occasional handclaps responded.

"And when a misfortune struck you unexpectedly, how did you manage to trust the Lord's plan for your life? The devil is actively working right now, crafting his most wicked weapons against us and our loved ones! He uses seduction to lure you into loneliness with your thoughts, allowing his whispers to infiltrate your heart and ears, turning your disappointments into harmful choices! Oh, help me, Holy Spirit!" he yelled, stepping away from the podium. Several worshippers had already risen to their feet.

"If the devil can isolate you, especially when you're feeling down and alone, he will tempt you to act against your nature. You might find yourself doing things you wouldn't normally do, feeling like you've lost yourself. This can include jealousy, gossiping about neighbors who have been kind to you, lying, stealing, or even engaging in sins such as having an affair with someone else's spouse, knowing they are married. Such actions lead to spiritual death!"

From the congregation, loud shouts of "Amen!" and "Hallelujah, Jesus!" echoed, with some standing. Audine sat with her head bowed deeply, her eyes squeezed shut, rocking back and forth. Tears streamed down her face as she seemed to be in a state of shame and prayer, realizing the pain she caused Wayne, coveting Maria's possessions, and being ungrateful. She thought shamefully, maybe my sharp tongue is my punishment— losing Wayne because of what I said about Lena. Suddenly, she stood with her arms outstretched, weeping openly. Wayne then stood and embraced her around the waist, tears also flowing freely from his eyes. The church was filled with songs of thanksgiving, praise, and worship.

"Remember, beloved of the Lord, that dangerous desires formed within our unsettled disappointments are traps set to cause your downfall. You may rise quickly but then fall hard, straight into hell! Please help us, Holy Spirit! And saints, ask yourselves: what is the devil's plan? Be clear, his goal is to attack your mind until you submit to his lies and schemes. That's his strategy! Please help me,

Holy Spirit, and fight him every step of the way. Stamp him back to the fiery gates of hell where he belongs! The Bible says in James 4:7, "Submit yourselves then to the Lord and resist the devil, and he will flee from you!"

Loud shouts of "Glory Hallelujah!" from worshipers echoed until they gradually dimmed into murmurs.

Pastor Coleman loosened his tie, grabbed his white handkerchief, and wiped the sweat streaming down his forehead. He then returned to his podium and asked everyone to stand for the benediction prayer.

"Father God, we thank you for the blood of Jesus. As we prepare to leave your holy house, we ask for your blessing that we may have clear minds to grasp the truth of your word, which holds the power to transform us. Continue to help us pray for one another. When we depart today, Lord, grant us discernment to recognize when our minds are under attack by the enemy and to protect us from temptation that leads to sin. Keep us close to you, Lord, now and forever. Let the church say amen!"

The whole church responded with loud Amens and applause. The short service concluded.

Violet felt uneasy, thinking, 'Oh my God, if I didn't know better, this sermon seems to be about me and Clarence, especially considering what we did yesterday.' She looked toward Clarence, who had his arm around Maria's shoulders. Maria was repeatedly nodding and loudly praising God in French Creole. Clarence then looked up towards Violet's direction and gazed at her affectionately.

"Brothers and Sisters, I received the exam results yesterday. Out of twelve participants, only four passed, as I mentioned earlier. Let's head to the fellowship hall so everyone can see who passed. For those who didn't pass, we pray that the Lord will help you overcome this disappointment and emerge victorious. Can we all say amen?" Pastor Coleman said.

"Please come to the fellowship hall, all students who took the exam. I have the results and brief announcements to share." Everyone responded with enthusiastic applause and started heading toward the fellowship hall.

Pastor Coleman hurried down the center aisle, shaking hands with worshipers and pressing kisses on the women's cheeks.

"Audine, you should be very proud of Violet," Pastor Colman said quietly as he neared her. "I have a very special announcement about her. I'm so excited, I can barely hold it in!" he whispered into her ear, hugging her briefly. Then he moved away, pushing through the church crowd.

"Did you hear that, Violet? Pastor Coleman has an announcement about you! I bet it's about the exam you took!" Audine exclaimed, smiling and patting Violet on the shoulder.

Violet offered a faint smile. *If I pass the exam, what will Clarene and I do next?* she wondered anxiously, her heart racing.

"Come on, let's hurry into the fellowship hall," Audine said, brushing past Violet and Mason to stand beside Wayne. As she moved closer to Wayne, she noticed he was engaged in a deep conversation with Etta Pullman, one of the head ushers.

Humph! If Etta thinks she's going to sink her dirty fingernails into my Wayne, she'd better think it over! Audine thought as she glared hard at Etta. It worked because as soon as Etta glanced over Wayne's shoulder and made eye contact with Audine's hateful stare, she excused herself from their conversation and scurried away.

"Wayne, are you coming with us to the fellowship hall to hear the announcement about who passed the exams? Pastor Coleman already hinted that something wonderful is about to happen to Violet!" said Audine.

"Uh, yes, I do plan to go, but I was hoping Etta would join us. Suddenly, something seemed to spook her because she mentioned she needed to check on someone who left their Bible at church last Sunday," he said.

"Well, you know how she is, always skittish. Humph! I bet she's checking on William Wharton. Didn't his wife pass away two weeks ago?" Audine asked with a smile.

"Audine, stop it! We just finished a spirit-filled church service! Weren't you paying attention?" Wayne asked, disgusted with her accusation. "Come on, I'll escort all of you inside so we can get seated," he added.

Despite his scolding her, Audine slipped her arm into Wayne's crook, lifted her head confidently, and smiled cheerfully as if nothing had occurred.

Violet and Mason trailed behind as everyone entered the fellowship hall. The families of the examinees sat in the front rows. Pastor Coleman stepped up to the podium, took a sip of water, and cleared his throat loudly. Etta stood nearby, holding a bundle of envelopes containing the names and certificates of those who passed.

"Good afternoon once more, everyone. We are here today to celebrate those who passed the teacher's entrance exam. As I mentioned earlier, only four out of the twelve of you succeeded."

Low murmurs echoed through the hall. Many young women who took the exam clutched their parents' hands, some with defeated expressions, aware they might have failed. Violet grasped Audine's hand, squeezing it firmly. She craned her neck slightly, trying to catch a glimpse of Clarence sitting beside Maria. When their eyes met, he briefly nodded, prompting Violet to smile broadly and straighten her posture. Meanwhile, Maria shot her with an icy stare. Mason, observing the scene, looked confused by everyone's interactions. Frowning at Clarence, he began to glare at him. Why are Mr. Clarence and my sister constantly staring at each other like that? Mason wondered suspiciously. The booming voice of Pastor Coleman abruptly pulled Mason out of his thoughts.

Everyone, please quiet down. As mentioned, only four of you succeeded, and each of you has a spot reserved at the Teaching College in Virginia. You'll study there for two years and then take another exam. If you pass, you'll receive a teaching position in Washington, D.C., New York, New Jersey, and, according to the proctor I spoke with yesterday, an offer in Chicago. All four states urgently need Black teachers, and our goal is to ensure our children have the opportunity for an education that can lead them to colleges or universities, not just work in the fields or clean white men's toilets!" Pastor Coleman declared.

Thunderous applause and cheers erupted in the room as everyone stood in agreement with his statement.

"Please be seated, everyone. I want to remind you all of the message from this morning about disappointment and the dangers of temptation. Keep in mind that God has a divine plan for your life. He knows what's best and makes no mistakes. So, without further delay, let's begin, and may God's blessing and peace be with each of you." A loud chorus of amens filled the hall, then silence as Etta handed Pastor Coleman the first envelope.

"With a score of ninety-two, congratulations to Hattie Abbotts!"

Hattie stood, her mouth gaping open with surprise as she strived toward Pastor Coleman, who hugged and congratulated her. Etta rushed over to give her a tight hug and handed her a certificate of acceptance from the teacher's college, which was signed by the college president and the proctor who administered the exam.

"Congratulations, Essilou Bryant, on your score of ninety-six!"

Essielou squealed with joy as her family rose to their feet, clapping and cheering while she proudly approached to receive her certificate. Etta embraced her warmly for a long moment, reflecting their deep bond, since Essielou had been an usher since she was thirteen. Etta had guided her on how to walk, stand, meet, and greet everyone at the church. This moment was bittersweet for both—Etta preparing to say goodbye to her protégé, who was about to leave to learn more and eventually teach others.

"Jerlene Rogers, with a score of ninety-eight! Excellent work and well done!"

"Thank you, Jesus!" Jerlene's mother exclaimed loudly. Her father helped her out of her seat, overwhelmed with tears of happiness. Together, they went to collect her certificate. Jerlene's six siblings cheered loudly for her, the first in her family to complete her education. Her two older sisters eloped three years ago and have not been seen since. Jerlene was determined not to follow their path and wanted to serve as a positive example for her family, especially her three younger siblings, who also aspire to become teachers.

"There's only one more envelope left up there, and it's for you, Violet! I suppose the other young ladies who didn't pass might end up marrying or working at the hospital. Humph! Let's hope none of them meet the same fate as Maydell," Audine whispered loudly.

Several people within earshot turned and gave Audine dirty looks.

"Oh, I'm so sorry, I didn't mean to sound so rude. How un-Godly of me," Audine said sweetly as she crossed her legs at the ankles.

"You're not sorry." "My daughter worked hard for that exam, and if she doesn't pass, we won't know what to do!" said Phyllis Thomas, expressing her disgust at Audine's comment.

Phyllis's daughter, Carol, took out a handkerchief and dabbed her eyes. Phyllis then kissed and hugged her.

After clearing his throat and taking another sip of water, he kept the room silent.

"The last person to receive a certificate pass with a perfect score of one hundred!"

Murmurs and audience members were smiling, some already hugging their daughters who had just taken the exam. Phyllis Thomas continued to hold her daughter, who was gazing down at the crumpled handkerchief in her lap with her head bowed.

"The next award winner not only achieved the highest overall score on the exam but also exceeded expectations on the optional foreign language exam. The proctor remarked that he had never heard such perfect French Creole spoken by a Black student and recommended she take accelerated courses to complete two years in just over a year and a half. Brothers and sisters, the recipient is Violet Booker!"

"Oh, my goodness, thank you, Lord, praise God!" Audine exclaimed loudly. She jumped up with such enthusiasm that her chair fell to the floor. Wayne quickly picked up and replaced the chair. Audine hugged Violet tightly, took her hand, and navigated through the crowd, stepping on several people's feet, causing them to cry out in pain. She didn't look back or apologize. The crowd gave enthusiastic yet courteous applause for Violet, who was beaming with a wide smile.

As Violet made her way to the podium to accept her certificate, she looked into the audience to find Clarence, seated on the far left of the hall with his family. He was enthusiastically clapping, along with his sons and daughters. Maria sat nearby, her jaw clenched, and her eyes fixed disapprovingly on Violet when their gazes crossed. Violet paused briefly, momentarily frozen.

"Violet, come!" Audine grinned as she tugged at her arm.

Etta was the first to meet her as she walked down the aisle.

"Come here, dearest; we're all so proud of you!" she said, hugging her affectionately. She quickly nodded at Audine, who responded with a wry smile.

Pastor Coleman embraced Violet and gave her the certificate.

"Brothers and sisters, before we dismiss to enjoy the refreshments, especially those delicious cakes made by the choir and ushers, I have one last announcement. Violet, it is my honor to present you with a gift from your father. When he was called home to be with the Lord five years ago, he wanted to make sure you could continue your education beyond primary school. A week before he fell ill, your father, Rudell, visited me. He asked me to make sure you had what you needed to become a teacher if anything happened to him. As he spoke more about his passing, he handed me an envelope with your name on it".

Violet looked at the envelope, tears falling from her eyes as she gently touched it.

"I-I don't understand, what is in here?" she stammered.

"Inside that envelope is your path to a new life. It contains $800 for books, food, shelter, and clothing. Your father also asked me to tell you that any remaining money should be used for your future wedding or when you become a teacher. It's as if he's blessing you from heaven right now," Pastor Coleman said.

The audience was already in tears as they erupted into applause for Violet. Audine stood frozen, clutching her chest with her mouth agape. Mason quickly approached Violet, embracing her passionately, and openly wept.

"On behalf of the church, I invite the young ladies and their families to gather here with me so everyone can offer their congratulations and enjoy the refreshments. Thank you, and may God's peace be with you all."

Everyone stood up from their seats, many heading to the front to share congratulatory hugs. Some immediately went to the tables with sliced cakes and pies to feed hungry children before they ran out, despite there being over twenty cakes, ten sweet potato pies, and eight large pans of cornbread. The women's remaining families, who didn't pass the exam, quietly and discreetly left through the side door to hide their disappointment.

"Violet, I'm so happy for you!" Jerlene exclaimed, hugging her. Perhaps we could share a room and travel by train to college. My mother and father don't want me to go to Virginia alone," said Jerlene.

"I think that's a good idea because I was wondering how I'd get there, but not alone. It's just too dangerous. But let's talk about that after church next Sunday," said Violet.

"I will, and maybe our mothers and my father can talk about it some more with us," said Jerlene.

"Now that's a fine idea, Jerlene!" said Audine, excited by the suggestion.

"Tell your mother and father that I'd love to talk more about this after service next Sunday. Oh, and by the way, congratulations, honey," said Audine.

"Thank you, Mrs. Booker, I will. I'm going to get some cake because I'm very hungry right now! I want to get some of Miss Franklin's jelly cake before it's all gone!" she said as she hurried to the already crowded table.

"I can't begin to tell you how proud I am of you, Violet!" said Audine, hugging her.

"The biggest surprise of all is what your father did for you, honey. That was the most wonderful and kindest thing he could ever do for you. Even though we were very poor, it was worth it for him to set aside money to save up for you. Ooh my God, Violet, you're going to be a teacher and the first one in this family to go to college!" said Audine.

"Thank you, Ma," Violet said with a broad smile. Glancing away, she noticed Clarence engaged in a deep conversation with Maria, with his arm draped over her shoulders.

She wondered enviously what they were talking about and why he had to have his arm around her that way.

"Bonjour, Violet!"

Violet quickly spun around after feeling someone tap her on the shoulder. She recognized the voices of Izelle and Rosetta.

"Bonjour mes beaux amis!" said Violet as they took turns hugging and kissing each other on each cheek.

"Congratulations, Violet! We're so happy for you, especially for passing the French exam!" they said together.

"You're going to be a wonderful teacher, and your students will learn so much from you!" Rosetta said.

"Will you teach your class how to speak French, Mademoiselle Violet?" Izelle said as she took a bite of the cake.

"Oh, my goodness, I don't know!" said Violet, beaming.

"I would love to teach my future students the basics first, such as reading, writing, arithmetic, and language, depending on what grade I'll be teaching. Thanks to both of you, I'll also get extra lessons to speak even more French! Soon, I'll be able to talk to you both in French and French Creole! She joked, making the twins laugh.

"Excuse me, Violet."

Violet turned to see Carol Thomas, who appeared disheveled and sorrowful, standing next to her mother, who was holding Carol's hand tightly.

"Hi Carol," Violet said, hugging her. Suddenly, Izelle and Rosetta joined in the hug. Carol sniffled, fighting back tears. Her eyes were swollen and red, clearly distraught from not hearing her name called.

"I wanted to come over here to congratulate you and say that you'll make a fine teacher," said Carol.

"Thank you, Carol. Perhaps we could meet after church next Sunday to discuss. I also want us to visit Pastor Coleman and ask if you'd be willing to teach the children's Sunday school classes and assist students who need extra help with their schoolwork. After I leave, someone needs to help these children, and who knows, there might be openings next year for new teachers. You'll have the chance to retake the exam and pass it. I know you can do it, Carol!" said Violet.

"And Rosetta and I will begin teaching you French Creole, and our father can help you with the science part of the exam because it's mostly about agriculture," said Izelle, excited about the idea of a new friend coming to the farm for lessons in French Creole.

Carol's eyes lit up as she smiled at the thought of having a second chance to take the exam again and pass!

"I think that's a fine idea and a Christian way of thinking!" exclaimed Phyllis, who was excited that they wanted to encourage her daughter.

"I think that's wonderful!" Audine said, smiling as she placed her hand on Phyllis's shoulder. "And Carol, if they have to retake the exam and you don't pass, the hospital where I work is looking for about six women to do cleaning jobs. They need women to scrub floors, wash patients who soil themselves, empty bedpans, and scrub toilets. It's tough work, but you'd be well-suited for it. If you fail, it probably means teaching isn't your calling. However, you can always pretend to be a teacher here at the church. In terms of daily work at the hospital, scrubbing toilets might be what you're best suited for," Audine said with a smirk.

Phyllis snatched her shoulder away from Audine and glared at her, enraged at what she dared to say about Carol. Everyone in the small group circle looked at Audine with hate. Carol sprinted out the door, running away. The twins hurried after her.

"I want you to understand that my daughter doesn't need to scrub floors or toilets, Audine Booker," Phyllis said, leaning closer to Audine, who started to step back. "Let me remind you that we are in the Lord's house, and He wants us to encourage each other in love, not say hurtful or discouraging words. Your daughter was kind enough to say some very nice things to Carol to make her happy and to soothe her disappointment – didn't you hear the sermon this morning? Maria's daughters were also willing to lend a hand. But you? You speak words that hurt others, Audine. You should be ashamed of yourself! 'He who guards his lips guards his life, but he who speaks rashly will come to ruin. A wicked messenger falls into trouble, but a trustworthy envoy brings healing!" Phyllis said, nodding at Violet.

"You don't pay attention to what's being preached here at this church. Instead of gossiping, why not take the time to read God's Holy Word, Audine?" said Phyllis as she slipped on her gloves, prepared to leave. She then paused, turned around, and addressed Audine, who was still standing there.

"Oh, and one more thing, Audine," Phyllis called out. "Reckless words can hurt, but the tongue of the wise brings healing." Then she slammed the door and left. Everyone, including Violet, looked at Audine, who was embarrassed to be scolded by someone she considered insignificant.

Humph! I was trying to help her! At the very least, Carol could have shown gratitude and thanked me! Audine thought to herself, oblivious to the hurtful things she said to Carol.

"Uh, please excuse me. I need to grab a few slices of jelly cake and sweet potato pie. They might run out if I don't hurry to that table. Come on, Mason, let's find Wayne. Maybe he saved me some cake and slices of pie," she said, walking away and leaving Violet alone.

She finally saw Wayne sitting at a table, chatting with Etta once more! Audine scurried in a huff across the room, upset, to where Wayne and Etta were seated and laughing.

Soon after, Rosetta and Izelle reappeared inside the fellowship hall, but without Carol. They walked toward Violet.

"We couldn't find Carol. It's as if she disappeared. We want her to be okay," said Izelle.

'We saw her mother, and she was pretty mad about something,' said Rosetta.

Violet said, "I'll be back soon. I want to find Carol and say sorry for what my mother said. She made some really mean remarks, and her mother had every right to be upset. If it were my daughter, I'd be angry as well."

"Go ahead, we'll be here when you come back," said Rosetta.

Violet hurried through the crowded room, but was repeatedly stopped for more congratulations, making it harder for her to catch up to Carol, who was probably already gone.

Outside, Violet scanned the roadside to spot Carol and her mother. The only figures she saw were church members either entering their cars or walking home.

Several of them waved and offered congratulations, but Carol and Phyllis had already left. That suited Violet fine.

Hopefully, I'll see her next Sunday, she thought to herself. Turning around to go back into the church, she froze when she saw Maria standing there, her piercing green eyes glaring at her with hate and disgust.

'Hello, Mrs. Margaret," Violet greeted.

Maria remained silent, standing still and eyeing Violet intently. After what felt like an eternity of silence, she finally spoke.

"I saw you and Clarence kissing. Stay away from my husband, or you'll face serious trouble!" she said coldly.

CHAPTER ELEVEN

"Mrs. Margaret, you must be mistaken. I didn't kiss your husband! Oh my God, I would never do something so vile. He was the one helping me study for the exam. I swear, even out of gratitude, I would never kiss him like a wife kisses her husband. I'm telling you the truth!" Violet said in a choking voice.

"You must think I'm a fool! I saw you yesterday when my husband came home. I was out of my mind with worry when he said he'd be back soon after going to get you, then return to take you and Mason home because your mother was still at work. My husband was out nearly six hours! When he finally came home, I saw him get out first, then go to the other side of the truck to open the door for you. As you got out, he looked around to make sure no one was watching, since our children were down by the lake fishing and playing. He pressed you against the side of the truck and kissed you, Violet! Then, as you both headed towards the lake, he put his arm around your waist. Seeing this made me so sick that I had to go outside to vomit. I was unwell for the rest of the day. Thanks to your behavior with my husband, I almost couldn't make it to church, but I knew I had to get up this morning and tell you, you filthy whore, to stay away from my husband, or I promise you will face lifelong consequences! Keep your disgusting lips away from my husband, you wicked woman," Maria said, spitting on the tip of Violet's shoes before storming back inside the church.

Oh my God, she knows! She saw Clarence and me kissing! What should we do now? Clarence, I won't give you up! Even if she found out, we'll act as if we don't see each other and just be cautious to avoid getting caught again. I also need to consider whether to attend a teacher's college seriously. Two years is a long time to be apart from him! Violet pondered, feeling confused.

"I don't care what you just said, Maria. I will be with Clarence!" Violet declared loudly.

When the coast was clear, she returned to the church fellowship hall, her eyes scanning for Clarence, but he, Maria, and their family had already left. The only others there were the people sitting at a table engaged in conversation, and Audine, who was sitting near Wayne, eating her third slice of cake.

Mason was sitting outside the church on a large rock behind a thicket of bushes, which concealed him among wild pink and red roses. He was alone, enjoying a large slice of yellow cake with fluffy chocolate frosting, which had been given to him by his Sunday school teacher. While eating and peering through the bushes, he saw Maria slip out the door, looking noticeably agitated as she paced around. Then he noticed Violet rushing out as if searching for someone, probably Carol and her mother, who had left quickly. Carol was crying hysterically, with her mother, Phyllis, trying to comfort her. With her back turned to Maria, Maria approached Violet, who seemed surprised but then started talking loudly and getting angrier, as if upset at something Violet had done. Mason got up from the rock, moved closer, and listened to their conversation.

"I saw you kissing my husband, Violet!" The words Mason heard resonated with panic and disgust. My sister was kissing Mr. Clarence? No wonder Violet seemed so happy at the lake, and when we returned home! Mr. Clarence had his arm around her, but we all ignored it because we were having such a good time! Mason thought in shock. He covered his mouth, backed away

slowly, grabbed his plate of unfinished cake, and tossed it aside. Nausea twisted his stomach, and his heart thumped wildly. Taking a deep breath, he quietly returned the plate to the church, then sat alone at a corner table, glaring hatefully at Violet until it was time to go home.

CHAPTER TWELVE

Wayne was driving everyone home. Violet was lively and enthusiastic about the day's events, while Mason suddenly fell unusually quiet. Audine, meanwhile, was sulking, looking out the window now and then, wiping her eyes, and letting out deep sighs.

"Violet, I know you've heard this before, but congratulations on scoring the highest on that exam, doing exceptionally well in the French language part, and on that surprise your father left for you. I'm sure Rudell is smiling down from heaven," said Wayne.

"Yes, I know he is," said Audine, who was staring out the window while Wayne drove them home.

"I'm very happy, but I'm also so scared," Violet said. "I now have everything I need to become a teacher. I've been accepted into a two-year college program, I have a place to stay at the rooming house for Black women, and I have money for books, clothes, and food. Still, I'm unsure because part of me wants to stay here in New Orleans."

"Yes, I bet you'd like to stay here in New Orleans," Mason said, gazing out the window and avoiding eye contact with Violet.

"Huh?" Audine asked, turning to look at Mason, who had remained silent during the ride home. "Why would you say something like that, Mason? And Violet, why would you even have second thoughts about staying here after everything that's been done for you, especially Maria's daughters teaching you to speak French and Clarence? I mean, my God, Violet, I heard that many of those girls failed because they knew nothing about the agriculture part of the exam. You were very lucky to have Clarence help you with that. I know his wife and I don't get along, but you should definitely thank him before you leave. What do you think about that, Wayne?" she asked, searching his face for approval.

"I believe that's a wonderful idea. I also have some wildflowers in the yard that I can gather for Maria's daughters, so you can thank them for teaching you French so quickly. Violet, you can bunch them nicely, and I'll cut some twine long enough to hold the stems. I'm sure Mason will help you. What do you think, son?" Wayne asked.

Mason kept staring out the car window, ignoring Wayne's words. Wayne frowned, puzzled that Mason wasn't responding.

"Boy, Mr. Wayne just asked you a question!" Audine snapped, giving Mason a disapproving look. "Answer him!" she said loudly.

"Yes, sir, I think that's a fine idea. That's mighty nice of you," Mason replied flatly, continuing to look out the window.

Audine kept staring at Mason before shifting her focus back to Wayne, who gently patted her hand.

"We're all very tired, everyone. It's been a very exciting day, so when we arrive at your mother's house, let's all go in and rest," Wayne said. As he drove the next twelve miles away from the church, everyone remained silent, watching the afternoon sun set until they finally arrived at Audine's house.

"Violet and Mason, I was wondering if you could go inside the house first. I need to speak with your mother alone," Wayne said, turning off the ignition. Violet nodded, and Mason didn't respond as he got out of the car first and hurried into the house, slamming the door behind him. Wayne helped Violet out of the car, hugged her, and again congratulated her on a job well done. She then went into the house.

Why does he need to speak with me alone again? The last time, he pretty much left me. Humph! After today, he'll probably say he won't take me to work or church. Etta must have gotten into his unzipped pants, Audine thought bitterly. Before she could think of anything else to say, Wayne was back inside the car.

"Audine, I need to talk to you," Wayne said.

Audine remained frozen, unable to move or speak, dreading more bad news from him.

"I've spent a lot of time thinking about many things, about you, Mason, and, after today, Violet. She has grown into a very smart and beautiful woman. I remember her as a little girl who adored her father, and I know you're proud of her; we all are," he said.

"Yes, Rudell certainly loved Violet and her brother. His death upset her so deeply that she was bedridden for a week. After that, she always kept busy reading, doing well in school, and making me proud. Becoming a teacher is truly a miracle. But what do you want to talk to me about, Wayne? You've already broken my heart before. What's next? Will you say you won't drive me to work, take me, Violet, and Mason to church, or tell me you want Etta?"

"The answer to your question is no, Audine," Wayne replied, exhaling slowly. "I wouldn't dare put your life or those of Violet and Mason, especially with how the Klan might react to a Black woman walking home alone on these roads. No! I love Violet and Mason as if they were my own children. If anything were to happen to them, I could never forgive myself. I know what loss feels like," he said, grimacing.

"And as far as Etta is concerned, she's a friend I've known for years. We were discussing a man at work I want to introduce her to because she's never been married, and neither has Howard Dotts, the man I have in mind."

"Wait a minute, Howard Dotts, who works at the hospital? The ambulance driver?" Audine said, relief evident in her voice upon hearing about Etta.

"Yes, he's very interested in meeting her, and that's what she and I were talking about," said Wayne.

"I believe he would be a good match for her, especially since they were never married. I'm glad for them! But why are we here, sitting in your car and talking?" she asked.

"Because I need to say a few things to you," Wayne said, clearing his throat. "Since Lena's funeral, I've felt like my life was finished. She left me and then died in some godforsaken place. But through it all, you stayed with me. Now, I want to tell you something, Audine. You were partly right about Lena running off with a ruthless man. However, you had no right to say such cruel words about her. She was, after all, my wife."

"Wayne, I truly apologize for the terrible things I said about Lena. I feel ashamed, especially while you're still sorrowing for her. Please forgive me for my unkind words. Sometimes I accidentally hurt others with what I say. I hope you'll forgive me, Wayne," Audine said, looking down in remorse.

"Audine, look at me," Wayne said, gently lifting her chin so they could meet eyes. "I forgave you this morning in church. That sermon about disappointment and how it can tempt us in the worst ways made me realize I was disappointed in Lena. After all these years of marriage, we still had no children. My disappointment must have tempted her, which she gave in to, and it ultimately led to her death. I accept responsibility for that. It's as if I led an innocent lamb to slaughter," he said, voice trembling.

"No, no, no, Wayne! Lena, leaving you wasn't your fault. You must accept that things didn't work out between you two, and, sadly, she got involved with the man she was staying with. Stop blaming yourself! I sincerely believe that someday you'll meet someone who will make you very happy, and you'll build the family you've always wanted. I believe this with all my heart," Audine said.

"Do you mean that, about what you said just now, me meeting a woman who'll make me happy and the promise of a family?" he asked.

"Yes, I do, Wayne. You are a kind and deserving man who deserves a second chance at life and love. I believe you will find that woman. Just look at what's happening to Etta and Howard," she said.

"Suppose I've already met that special woman," he said.

So, he's already moved on. Well, good for him. I hope Wayne finds happiness, but I suppose I should start figuring out how to get myself to work each day and how my family and I will get to church on Sundays. She felt her stomach tighten as she gazed at Wayne intently.

"Oh, so you've met someone already?" she asked.

"No, I already know this woman. I've known her for years. She lives right here in New Orleans," he said with a broad smile.

Audine sat, staring at Wayne with wide eyes, unable to find words due to shock upon hearing this news.

He said, "She's someone who speaks her mind, even if she can be sharp-tongued at times. She's aware of it, and I believe she'll try harder to control it. What truly made me fall in love with her is how she stayed by my side and supported me after Lena died. She changed my thinking, making me realize it's time to move on from sadness to someone who completes my life. I need to tell her I love her and ask if she'll be my wife."

"So, does that mean we're done forever, Wayne? Does that mean you'll never see me or my children again? Who is this woman?" Audine asked tearfully.

Wayne smiled and said, "The woman I'm talking about is you," feeling relieved to leave the past behind. He was optimistic about the future, knowing he had something to look forward to, and believed that Audine, despite her sometimes-brash nature, would be good for him. He loved Mason and Violet as if they were his own children, and perhaps soon, Audine would want to start their own family.

"What?!" Audine exclaimed.

"Say yes, you'll marry me, and we'll start a new life together with you, me, Violet, Mason, and our future children," then he pulled out a small box from his lapel pocket and opened it.

"Oh my God, Wayne!" she exclaimed. Inside the box was a gold-banded ring with a sapphire, and even as dusk approached, it continued to sparkle.

"Does that mean yes, Audine?" he asked with a smile.

"Yes, Wayne, I'd be happy to be your wife! I've loved you for so long, but I was afraid you'd leave me forever. Oh, how much I love you!"

A wide smile appeared on his face as he took the ring from the box, held her left hand, and carefully placed the ring on her finger.

"Audine, the ring I just placed on your finger belonged to my mother. My father gave it to her, but never revealed its origin. He only told her that when she was to join him in heaven, she should ensure the ring came to me. When the right woman appeared to be my wife, I was to give her the ring,' he said.

"But what about Lena?" asked Audine. Wayne silenced her by placing his finger on her lips, closing his eyes tightly, and shaking his head.

"I know what you're thinking," he said slowly, opening his eyes. "When the veil was placed over Lena's face and the lid sealed her, that marked the end. At the cemetery, as her casket was lowered and the minister spoke those final words, she and I were no longer connected. She's gone forever, but I'm still here, and I want to live. That ring was meant for the right woman, and you are that woman, my only one," he said. Wayne leaned in and kissed Audine. She wrapped her arms around his shoulders. His open mouth pressed against hers, and after five years following Rudell's death, she responded to Wayne's passionate kiss with an urgency that took his breath away. He gently moved her right hand to his crotch; his arousal brought back many fond memories of her long-ago marriage with Rudell.

Unzipping his pants, Audine found the spot where she fumbled and pulled out his hard, bulging erection. Looking down, she felt a thrill at how long and thick Wayne was. What she was seeing made her smile a little wickedly.

"That will be yours for the rest of your life. It's meant to bring you pleasure and to fill our future home with children. I want them as soon as we're married, Audine. I can't wait for you to be my wife and the mother of our children," he said, his eyes fixed on her as she started to fondle him more quickly.

He threw back his head, closed his eyes, and grimaced as Audine started to pleasure her future husband. His breathing became short and heavy. She quickly reached into her purse and pulled out a pink lace handkerchief.

"Ahh, Audine, got-dammit!" he groaned through clenched teeth. She held the handkerchief over his throbbing erection, catching the emission as it expelled. After it was over, she carefully placed the crumpled, wet handkerchief into her purse and snapped it shut.

"Come here," Wayne said, holding his hand out to Audine.

Audine slid next to him and claimed his lips again. As they kissed, she felt his hand brush over the top of her dress, squeezing her left, aroused breast until she moaned.

"Audine, I think we should stop now before we wind up in the back of my car. Besides, we're in front of your house, and your children are inside," Wayne said, grinning as he zipped his pants.

"I love you, but we must wait until we're married. I want us to do this properly, and once we're pronounced husband and wife, I expect us to do this every night. However, I need to warn you, Audine, *I will want you every night*, even after we have children. Okay?"

A smile spread across her face as she looked at him. *The man sitting next to her was going to be her husband! Hah! At last, my children and I can move out of that shit-hole we've been stuck in and move into Wayne's house! I can't wait for that day! Audine thought, giddy with anticipation.*

"You don't even need to think twice about that," she said, admiring the ring Wayne gave her. "I plan to be a loving wife and mother to all our children—both the two we have now and the ones to come. Once we set our wedding date, I want to begin planning for our family immediately. It's a new beginning for both of us."

He asked, "You promise to be a God-fearing wife who will take care of me, our children, and our home?"

"Yes, I will," she said, nodding. "Your house needs the sound of new life, and I plan to be that vessel. Right now, I love you so deeply that I will do anything to ensure your happiness."

Wayne said, "Let's choose a date to get married in two weeks. If possible, Pastor Coleman might agree to perform the wedding after the service!"

"But we should be going now", Audine said, straightening her dress and patting her hair in place.

He said, "Before I leave, I want to come in so we can tell Violet and Mason that we're getting married."

"Oh, my goodness, yes! We've been out here so long that they're probably wondering what happened to us," said Audine.

"Believe me, I'll never tell what just happened in the front seat of this car," Wayne said with a wicked smile.

"You'd better not!" Audine said, snickering.

They both exited the car and entered Audine's house, holding hands. The aroma of baked chicken, green beans, gravy, biscuits, and peach cobbler filled the house immediately after they stepped inside.

"Violet and Mason, come here, please!" Audine called. Wayne had his arm wrapped around her waist. "You might as well stay for dinner; there's no use going back to that empty house," she added.

"Why, thank you. I'm hungry, and it looks like Violet has prepared a wonderful dinner. I'm looking forward to being your husband, father to your children, and sharing more family dinners like this," he said, kissing her cheek.

Violet exited her room and joined her mother and Wayne.

"Where's Mason?" Audine asked.

Violet described her observations: "As soon as we entered the house, he headed straight to his room. When I checked on him, he told me to leave and slammed the door in my face! I don't understand what's changed, but he's been acting very strangely since we returned from church. At the reception, he sat alone at the table, glaring at me as if he was upset."

Audine glanced at Wayne, who was just as puzzled as she was.

"Let me check if he's okay. It was a big day for all of us, and he's probably tired. I'll be right back," Wayne said, squeezing Audine's hand.

Wayne knocked twice at Mason's door.

"Mason, it's me," Wayne said. "Can I come in so we can talk? Your mother and I have some news to share with you and your sister," he added.

After a brief pause of silence, Mason eventually opened the door, and Wayne entered.

"What do you think they're talking about, Ma?" Violet asked while pulling out a chair and sitting down.

"I don't know," she said, pulling out a chair and sitting across from her. "You mentioned Mason was acting quite strange?" Audine asked, frowning.

"Yes, it seemed like only a minute he was with us after I received the award, smiling and so happy that he nearly cried, especially when they mentioned what daddy did for me. I saw Mr. Wayne put his arm around Mason's shoulders. Soon after, Mason took a slice of cake, went to talk with Joseph, and then stepped outside to eat. All of this occurred while we were busy congratulating everyone, including me and the other girls," said Violet.

"Well then, I think Wayne can talk to him about whatever is troubling him. He cares for Mason as if he were his own son and speaks very highly of you, too, Violet. The look on his face when you received that award was like a father's pride honoring his daughter,' said Audine, smiling brightly.

"What's going on between you and Mr. Wayne? I saw how happy you both looked when you walked in. Does that mean you're friends again?" Violet asked.

"Once Wayne and Mason come out, we'll tell you both what's happening," said Audine.

After about ten minutes, Wayne and Mason emerged. *Mason appears very tired; as soon as we eat, he needs to go to bed early, Audine thought anxiously, watching him closely.*

"Mason, how are you feeling? You seem very tired," said Audine. She took him by the shoulders and looked into his distant-looking eyes.

"I'm fine, just hungry and tired. Mr. Wayne said you have something you want to talk about?" said Mason.

"We do," said Wayne as he wrapped his arm around Audine's waist.

"Your mother has been a wonderful friend to me, especially after Lena left me. That day, I went home to a household of loneliness. But your mother helped me through it all. She cooked enough food for a week, washed and ironed my clothes, and made my home joyful again. When I learned Lena was murdered, I felt sad all over again, but your mother was there for me, even traveling to New York to ensure I was okay. I know she can be a handful at times because of some things she says, but she's trying to work on that, right, sweetheart?" Wayne said, smiling at Audine, who nodded and rested her head on his shoulder.

"This made me realize I need her in my life. Violet, you are like a daughter to me, and Mason is the son I've always wanted. I need all of you because you're my family. I love your mother, asked her to marry me, and she accepted to be my wife".

Mason hurried over to Wayne, embracing him as Audine wiped tears of joy from her eyes.

Oh my God! I have to leave here to go to the teacher's college in Virginia, and I might never see Clarence again! No, no, no! This can't be happening! Violet thought, tears filling her eyes.

"I'm so happy for you, Ma," Violet said, wiping her tears before hugging Audine. Audine embraced her daughter tightly.

"I realize this is sudden, but Violet, Wayne is a good man, and I love him. He'll make a wonderful husband and loving father to you and Mason," she said, wiping away tears. "When you're at college in Virginia studying to become a teacher, it'll just be Wayne, Mason, and me. Then, it will be another two years before Mason leaves for college. He wants to study agriculture or science with Joseph. That's why, right after Wayne and I get married, we're going to start a new family. He wants to have children right away, so you can meet your new sister or brother when you come home for the summer next year! And after the first child, Wayne doesn't know this yet, but I plan to have another in six months, and two more in two years. By then, you'll be married and starting your own family! We're both building new families! My God, everything is finally falling into place for me!" exclaimed Audine, feeling excited.

"Hey, everyone, let's eat!" Wayne called out as he and Mason waited at the dinner table for Audine and Violet to join. Wayne sat at the head of the table, a spot rarely used since Rudell's passing. Audine sat opposite Wayne, while Violet and Mason sat facing each other, though Mason avoided direct eye contact with her.

"Wayne, as the future head of this family, could you bless the food?" Audine asked, proudly gazing at him.

He smiled and nodded in agreement. Extending his hand to Violet and Mason, everyone linked hands to bless the food. After the blessing, dinner plates were circulated as lively conversation continued. Earlier, while Audine and Wayne talked, he remained silent when she and Mason were in the house. He went directly to his bedroom, slammed the door, and refused to answer Violet when she asked what was bothering him.

Now he was sitting at the dinner table, eating, smiling, laughing, and even joking with Wayne and Audine. Violet sat silently.

"Everyone, I'm very tired and I'm going to bed now. The last two weeks of studying have finally caught up with me, and I'm saying goodnight. Congratulations once again, Mr. Wayne," she said, walking toward Wayne, who stood up from his seat to hug her.

"There's no need to call me Mr. Wayne anymore, Violet. Mason already calls me dad, so you can too if you'd like."

"Is that okay with Ma?" Violet asked, looking at Audine, who smiled and nodded in agreement.

"Goodnight, Mason," Violet said with a smile to her brother.

He didn't respond. Instead, he turned to Audine and inquired about ways to earn extra credit at school starting the next day, aiming to stay at the top of his class alongside Joseph.

"Good night, everyone," said Violet, feeling hurt by her brother's sudden snub as she walked toward her room.

Violet removed her clothes, slipped into her nightgown, turned off the small table lamp, and went to bed. She still felt sore between her legs from her encounter with Clarence the previous day. As she closed her eyes, she replayed every detail of that afternoon: how he stroked her breasts, kissed her, and felt inside her. Their kiss was long and passionate, leaving her lips swollen and her breasts tender where he had touched them. She also thought about his wife, Maria, and their confrontation earlier that day.

How did she find out? She claims she saw Clarence and me kissing! How can I stay away from him? I can't, unless he says it must come to an end. She wondered as she drifted into a deep sleep and started having nightmares.

The nightmare started with her wearing a pink dress with tiny blue dots. She sat alone at a large, splintered wooden table. Before her was a big plate of salted fish, which she despised because the salt made her throat dry and triggered her cough. In the dream, however, she was starving and ate the fish eagerly. Each bite made her cough, and when she finished the fish down to the bones, her coughing became uncontrollable. She got up from the table, gasping at the sight of her inflated belly. Her pink dress with blue dots seemed too tight, making it hard to breathe. Her cough worsened, and she noticed the room filling with thick gray smoke, causing her to gasp for air. She called out for Clarence to help her, but he was not there. Suddenly, she collapsed, clutching her huge belly. She felt something slide out from between her legs, first a gush of water, then an intense urge to push. Then everything sank into nothingness.

Maria. At one o'clock in the morning, the cauldron was simmering gently in the toolshed. Earlier that afternoon, after church, the ride home was chaotic, with the children loudly discussing various events from that day. The argument between Maria and Clarence on Sunday was so intense and heated that Clarence left Maria's bedside in the middle of the night and slept in the barn. He lied and denied any kiss with Violet, even when questioned about the exact time he was caught. When Maria brought it up again before bedtime,

Clarence accused her of being crazy. This so angered her that she slapped him twice.

She grabbed a handful of cedarwood chips and dried tobacco leaves, throwing them into the cauldron. As smoke slowly rose, she took the doll she had crafted from a pink and blue lace handkerchief Violet had left in Clarence's truck, and marked an "X" over its eyes and three "X" s across its mouth. With her eyes closed, she held the doll above the smoldering herbs in the cauldron and recited her petition.

"I ask that you join me and listen. I respect your capacity for love and generosity. Please listen to my plea. I am asking you to intervene with a woman named Violet, whose lips and tongue were on my husband's mouth. This has caused him to lie, and she must be stopped. Enter her mind as she sleeps and fill her dreams with smoke and pain. Send her away to a place where she will never live or die, and curse any of her descendants to be born with both male and female parts. Please remove Violet Booker from this place, and let her never return."

Maria removed the doll from the cauldron, placed it on the ground, turned it upside down, and ran a rusted nail through the doll's mouth, belly, hands, and feet to secure it.

After slicing a lemon in half, she sprinkled red and black pepper on each side and petitioned the spirit to make Violet's throat, mouth, and belly burn as if they were on fire. She placed the doll between the two lemon halves and took long pins to secure the doll and the lemons. Petitioning three more times, Maria smeared the lemons across the doll's mouth and threw them all inside the cauldron. After adding more wood chips inside the cauldron, it began to smolder as Maria stood and chanted the petition until the contents were reduced to ashes.

Maria quietly took the cauldron out of the shed and hurried toward the road. At the corner, she carefully looked both ways for cars, wary of being seen by a white driver who might harass or harm her. She poured the ashes from the cauldron where the cars paused to let others pass. "May you leave and never return here, you pute," she muttered as she fled the scene. She gathered the tools used for crossing and stored them away. After a quick outdoor bath with rainwater from a barrel, she dried off and felt the baby move. Holding her belly, she looked toward the barn, knowing Clarence was inside sleeping, but also that he would return to Audine's house to watch Mason and Violet. This would end soon, she thought bitterly, as she quietly entered the house and went to bed. Sleep came quickly for Maria, but in the

dark barn, Clarence lay awake, thinking about Violet.

CHAPTER THIRTEEN

Violet thought her throat felt dry and rough as she slowly got out of bed, but she ended up falling back down with a thud.

As she took a deep breath to get some air, a sudden bout of coughing began. She tried to stand again, but her legs were weak, and the coughing grew worse, causing her to spit up thick, yellow, foul-tasting phlegm into her hand. The coughing only got worse.

"Help me, I feel sick!" Violet shouted, wheezing. She saw her purse on the floor beside the bed, picked it up, and opened it, recalling the handfuls of peppermints she had taken from the bowl at church yesterday. She ate one, placing it in her mouth. The cool mint soothed her throat, and the extract immediately stopped her coughing. Sitting on the edge of the bed, Violet's breathing was heavy and loud. After about ten minutes of sitting still, she started to feel better. She reopened her purse, looked inside, and counted thirty-five pieces of the hard candies that had stopped her cough. She swallowed, feeling her throat dry but also experiencing a tightness as if another cough was imminent. Struggling to stand from her bed, Violet was sweating heavily. She noticed her bed was soaked with sweat. Absentmindedly, she made her bed as best as she could.

The house was utterly silent. Mason left early for school, while Audine headed out early for work with Wayne so they could show off Audine's engagement ring to her colleagues.

No more coughing! I need to get better so I can see Clarence tonight. Who knows when we'll be together again, especially with my mother marrying Wayne. I've fallen in love with Clarence, and I need him! Violet thought, holding back tears. After washing up, she went to the kitchen and found a note from Audine.

Good morning, Violet. I hope you're feeling better. I heard you coughing all night and checked on you, but you were asleep, so I didn't wake you. There's still coffee on the stove and some biscuits from yesterday. Please don't do too much today; rest up. Later, I'll be at Maria's to apologize, show her my engagement ring, and let her know that we're getting married in November. I'm so excited I hardly know what to do!

Love,

Your Mother

Oh my God! Are they really getting married in November? That's only two months away! Depending on when she chooses a firm date, it could be just weeks! Violet felt panic-stricken at this sudden news. Then, she *started coughing again. Violet grabbed another peppermint and put it in her mouth, which helped her cough fade away.*

The morning sun and voices heard outside from the open bedroom window woke up Maria. Her eyes fluttered as she slowly sat up in bed. At around two in the morning, she experienced a horrible nightmare of Clarence lying on the ground, dead, and a red snake slithering back inside its den. Blood and foam spilled out of Clarence's mouth, and his eyes were open and motionless. Then everything went black, and she woke up in a daze. Sitting up in bed, she felt nauseated. The baby inside of her was growing, but the morning nausea and vomiting grew so intense that some days had her bedridden until late afternoons. But today was Monday, with much to do. It was washday, dinner had to be prepped by two o'clock, and another visit by the midwife would confirm how the baby was doing.

Maria thought that having another baby a year after this one was impossible, especially after seeing Clarence kiss Violet. She believed the coughing would only stop when she left, as she slowly got out of bed.

After making the bed and fluffing the pillows, she thought about Clarence sleeping inside the barn, which she kept at a distance due to the foul odors that increased her nausea. She placed her hand on her stomach.

« Je vais m'assurer que vous arrivez ici en toute sécurité », chuchota-t-elle *en créole français en caressant son ventre.*

Maria went to the large porcelain bowl on the dresser and washed her face and body with the water she poured into the bowl on Sunday evening. The subtle scent of lavender and rose made her feel better. She changed into a loose, floral house dress that was comfortable enough to move around in and that accommodated her expanding belly. Her thoughts were interrupted by the distinct aroma of coffee and freshly baked cornbread.

Tying her head up in her tignon, she put on her shoes and hurried to the kitchen. A chill ran down her spine. Once again in her kitchen, she found Audine sitting at the table, sipping coffee and spreading a generous amount of butter on a hot piece of cornbread.

"Oh my, you're finally awake! I was a bit concerned about you, Maria. I've been here for over an hour because Wayne wanted to speak with Clarence. I called out to let you know I was here, but I didn't get any response. So, I quietly checked your children's bedrooms, but they had already left for school. I then opened your door and saw you asleep. I didn't have breakfast, so I made a fresh pot of coffee and some cornbread. By the way, you'll need more butter because I used it all," said Audine as she took a bite of the hot, buttered bread, licked her fingers, and sipped her coffee.

Maria stared in disbelief as a cold shiver ran through her body.

"Audine, what are you doing here?" said Maria.

"Please, Maria, don't get mad. It's not good for your baby. Come over here and sit next to me. I have some news to share!" she said, excitedly, as he patted the chair beside her.

Who the hell does this woman think she is, coming into my home uninvited, looking around, and again, eating my family's food! Maria thought, furious.

"Audine, I appreciate that you made coffee and cornbread, but this is my house, and it's out of place for you to help yourself to anything without asking. Next time, please wait until I invite you in. Do you understand?" Maria said, clearly upset with Audine's unawareness.

"Come sit next to me so we can talk, okay?" said Audine, ignoring what Maria just articulated.

Maria shot an angry look at Audine and sat down. Smiling brightly as if nothing had happened, Audine immediately fussed over Maria.

"Cream and sugar in your coffee, right?" Audine asked as she poured the steaming hot coffee into the cup.

Maria nodded silently, observing Audine scoop a heaping teaspoon of sugar and add cream to the black coffee, transforming it into a smooth café au lait. She then spread a generous portion of her remaining butter on two pieces of freshly baked cornbread and handed the plate to Maria.

"I figured you'd be hungry, so I also brought some of that sausage you like to go with the cornbread. Besides, you want to ensure your baby eats too!" she said, pushing a platter of skillet-fried sausages toward Maria.

"Audine, what are you doing here? You haven't explained why you're in my house at this time. I have a lot to do and an appointment at one o'clock," Maria said, sipping her coffee quickly.

"Oh! Sorry to take up your time, but if I hadn't come here with Wayne, you'd still be sleeping until noon. It's almost ten o'clock now. I guess the same thing will happen to me next year when Wayne and I start a family," she said, her eyes sparkling and a smile lighting up her face.

Maria asked, with mild amusement, "Starting a family?"

"Look!" Audine said, holding out her left hand to Maria. On her finger was a ring with a thin gold band and a blue sapphire. It was old but valuable. Maria looked at the ring.

"Wayne gave it to me yesterday after church. We had a long talk about a lot of things, especially my behavior towards others. He forgave me for saying hurtful things about Lena, then told me he loved me and asked me to be his wife. It feels like the sun is shining on me, hah! On the way home, we discussed ideas for expanding his house, as Wayne and I plan to have children immediately after we get married. After our first, we'll aim for another next year. By then, Mason will have finished school and be headed to college. Wayne and I will wait two more years before having another child. This way, we both get what we want! For me, it means a new house, thanks to your husband helping Wayne expand it for our four children. My two will be grown, and I'll have what you and Clarence have, hah! And to think that Lena left him because she was bored. Stupid woman! I'll tell you what, Maria, Lena did me a wonderful favor by leaving because I ended up with exactly who I wanted: Wayne! No one told her to leave and then get herself killed. She did it to herself! Wayne felt very guilty about Lena's early death, but I reassured him he wasn't to blame, and that Lena could make her own choices. It's clear she didn't think things through because she got herself killed. Her mistake became my gain, and this will keep us all happy for many years to come. By the way, we've set our wedding for the Saturday before Thanksgiving, planning to have it in the afternoon with lunch afterward. I'll need Clarence to take care of Violet and Mason for another month; then I plan to leave my job at the hospital to care for my family."

Maria tapped her foot loudly with anger and impatience as she sat across from Audine, who was likely eating her second slice of cornbread. Audine swayed in her seat, licking her fingers and murmuring, "umph, umph, umph!"

"Audine, you have no right to freely enter my house, browse my kitchen, cook, and help yourself to my family's food. This is yet another instance of meddling, first spying on my husband and me when we shared love in the barn, and now this! What is wrong with you? Didn't anyone in your family teach you manners?" Maria said sharply.

Audine's piece of cornbread slipped from her fingers onto her plate, and she looked at Maria in disbelief at what she had just heard her say.

"I came here with the hope of sharing some wonderful news with you," she said, dabbing the corners of her lips with a napkin.

"I could have just come here to check on you, let you sleep all day, and then leave. Instead, I chose to be kind to you, mainly because I promised Wayne I would change, especially after Lena died, I- "

Maria sharply interrupted Audine, shouting, "And that's another thing with you! You always speak horribly about Lena. Lena was a kind person who didn't have many friends, partly because of you and that foul mouth of yours. She just wanted to be a good wife and mother for Wayne. We talked often about her marriage, and I tried to comfort her many times. She confided in me that she couldn't endure it anymore and planned to leave Wayne. I begged her not to go, especially with that gambler from New York. I warned her that if she left, bad things might happen to her. So, I can't and won't be happy for you. Wayne deserves someone better; a woman who will make him happy into old age, *not you!*"

Audine stood up, feeling mortified by Maria's rant and her admission. She considered that she and Lena were friends, *and Maria knew Lena was leaving Wayne?* Audine wondered to herself.

"You knew Lena was leaving Wayne and that you and she were friends without me knowing?" Audine stammered.

Maria looked at Audine with hatred and refused to respond.

"I can't believe you, of all people, would hide something like that from me! I really thought we were the best of friends!" she exclaimed loudly.

Maria turned her eyes away from Audine with a look of disgust.

Audine bitterly expressed, "All I ever wanted was a home like yours. I longed for a husband who would adore, love, and care for me. I wish to be like you and Clarence, with more children to grow older with everything you have, including a new child to complete my family. As I said, Lena's loss is my gain. Once I become Mrs. Wayne Collins, I'll have what you have: a husband, more children, a bigger house, and a happier marriage!"

"What do you mean by saying that?" snapped Maria.

"Oh my God!" Audine said, roaring with laughter. "You didn't think I could piece together that Clarence was sound asleep in the barn among those nasty-smelling animals you all got up there? Hah! I guess things aren't as perfect with you two as you think! The one thing I've learned in all this is to keep Wayne excited about me because even after he puts a baby inside me, I still plan to do everything I can to keep him in our bed. Hah! At least he won't be sleeping in a barn, waking up smelling worse than any yard dog I've seen on this side of New Orleans!" She laughed unapologetically.

Maria swallowed the lump in her throat. Everything in the kitchen began to spin, and Maria had to grip the edge of the table.

This woman's presence is a harmful power in my home and must be removed! The venomous words she hurls are soiled and hateful, much like her daughter! Maria thought, recoiling from Audine's fiery outburst.

"Get your things and leave my house," Maria snapped, her face twisted with disgust. "I can't even stand to look at you."

"Oh, please, Maria! How many times have you said that? I'll just be here, sitting in the kitchen, eating your food. When Wayne's house, sorry, our house, is finished, I might invite you over for coffee, or maybe not, humph! By then, I'll have new friends visiting with their children to play with mine. I'll be so busy that I won't have time for you!" said Audine.

Audine wiped her lips, grabbed two pieces of cornbread, and wrapped them in Maria's napkin.

"I'll be leaving now. This is the last time you'll see me—until the wedding next month. Wayne has already asked Clarence to be his best man. Since we're not friends, I suppose Violet will be my maid of honor. I'll see you at the wedding, but it will be the final time we meet and the last you see of Violet. A year from now, I'll be just like you, Maria—ready to give birth!"

Then she walked out of the kitchen, slamming the door so hard it made the house shake.

Maria sat, staring at the door.

"I don't think so, Audine. You will never have a husband or children," she whispered, her throat tight with disdain.

As she rose to clear the mess Audine had left, she noticed Audine's handbag on the table. Inside the small black bag, she found a crumpled handkerchief, a list of food, and familiar names from the New Orleans Creole community, like Mrs. Chaperouix, a seamstress known for her wedding dresses.

Audine is planning a wedding similar to her first, which will happen but ultimately fail. Maria thought that Violet would face a major downfall if she didn't keep her distance from my husband.

Maria gently retrieved the crumpled handkerchief from her purse and tucked it into her apron pocket. Almost immediately, the kitchen door swung open to reveal Clarence.

"Good morning," Clarence said tersely, moving awkwardly around the kitchen as if searching for something.

"Good morning," she said. Maria finished the remaining coffee in her cup and then began clearing the table, not even glancing at Clarence.

"Audine said she was having coffee with you, but had to leave so she and Wayne could return to work. They're getting married next month, and Wayne asked me to be his best man, which I happily accepted, making him very happy. I also agreed to help with some work on his house, as Audine plans to add a few extra rooms while they prepare to start a family soon after the wedding. Before the ceremony, she plans to sell her house to pay for the construction. Wayne, Mason, and Kempton can help me, especially on weekends, which should help us finish faster. If all goes well, everything should be done by early next year. Wayne mentioned they hope to have their first child in October, the same month Lena passed away," said Clarence.

"Audine should be ashamed of her deeds! The timing is just wrong, just like your judgment! Do you really think I haven't seen you and Audine's daughter together? You're all wrong! What you've done to me, what Audine plans to do, and her daughter Violet's behaving like a common whore, kissing a married man with children and another one on the way—is shameful. Get out, Clarence! The item you're searching for is on the table. Remove Audine's purse from my sight and get it out of this house!" said Maria.

A sudden wave of shame flashed across Clarence's embarrassed face, reminding him once again of his reckless mistake. He silently approached the table, grabbed the purse, and then left.

CHAPTER FOURTEEN

Since Audine left, Clarence remained outside working. The only times he entered the house were to drink water and sponge off his sweat before returning to work. Meanwhile, the morning quarrel with Audine and Clarence exhausted Maria so much that she lay down on her bed and fell asleep again.

The loud, relentless knocking on the door woke her up.

"Maria, are you home?" a female voice called. "It's me, Alice Wade. I brought a surprise with me. Are you there?"

Maria sat at the edge of the bed, exhausted.

"I'm coming, Mrs. Wade. I'll be right there!" she called out as she swiftly tied her shoes and rushed to answer the door.

Mrs. Alice Wade, the midwife for the Black women in the community, was well known and had been delivering babies since she was twenty-two. Now, at seventy-four, she still attended to many women, now in their early thirties, many of whom were having additional children as long as it was safe.

"Good afternoon, Mrs. Wade! I apologize for missing your call earlier; I dozed off after cleaning up this morning. Please come in," she said, opening the door.

"Oh, my dear, don't worry about it. You need to rest, and it's good that you were able to do your chores before we came to check on you. And I have a surprise for you," she exclaimed as the two hugged.

An elderly Creole woman in a tan dress stood in the corner of her eye view. Her hair was pulled back into a tight bun, and she had a shawl draped casually over her shoulders. Maria quickly recognized her.

"Madame Frère Eucharista Birch! Oh, mon Dieu, c'est merveilleux de vous voir après toutes ces années ! Oh, Madame Birch!"

"Maria St. Laurent, do come to me!" she said, opening her arms to welcome Maria. She dropped her bag to the floor as the two women shared a warm embrace. Tears of joy streamed down Maria's cheeks. Eucharista Birch was the closest thing she had to a mother, whom she hadn't heard from in many years. Mrs. Birch and her mother often attended the infamous Octoroon Balls. Maria was supposed to marry a French navy officer, whom she danced with all night under her mother's watch. After discussions, the officer agreed to marry Maria and accompany her to France, as requested by her mother. Instead, nineteen-year-old Maria secretly left her mother's house and eloped with Clarence Margaret, whom she had been secretly seeing since meeting him on the docks. They were married in secret by their young Baptist preacher, now the senior pastor of their church. The next morning, she and Clarence visited her mother to announce their marriage and to inform her that it had been consummated.

Maria's mother told her that her marriage would be cursed and that her husband, Clarence, was a no-good man who would cause her nothing but pain and sorrow. Her mother made the sign of the cross on herself, then spat at Maria's feet and slammed the door on both of them. Maria would never see or hear from her mother again.

"Ladies, please come into the kitchen. I have coffee," Maria said, guiding Mrs. Birch by the arm into the kitchen.

"It's been many years since I last saw you, mon plus cher. You were just nineteen then, and now you are a wife and mother of five. Your husband has done a wonderful job caring for you," she said with a smile, but suddenly her smile faded as she fell into a distant gaze.

She knew something was wrong, Maria thought to herself. Turning away, she spoke to Mrs. Wade, who was patiently waiting to examine Maria and why she was showing symptoms so quickly.

"Before you start fussing over coffee and other things for us to enjoy, I want to check on you, as I feel you're under a lot of strain. Do you mind if Mrs. Birch comes with us?" Mrs. Wade asked, noticing Maria's unease from her fidgeting at her apron since arriving and her apparent exhaustion. Even during her pregnancy with the twins, she hadn't been this tired.

Maria expressed her desire for her to be with her, saying, "I'd love for her to be with me." She then extended her arms toward Mrs. Birch, who responded with a warm embrace. "Come this way, we'll go into my bedroom. It's quiet, and my children won't be coming home until three o'clock."

The two women waited outside the door as Maria undressed, only keeping her undergarment on, which was already fitting very snug around her swollen belly.

"Maria, are you ready? Can we come in?" Mrs. Wade asked softly as she gently knocked on the door.

"Yes, please come in", she said.

Both women entered quietly and closed the door behind them. Mrs. Wade approached the bed, pulling back the coverlet that Maria had draped over herself, revealing her belly. Mrs. Birch then took a soft blue towel to cover Maria's swollen, large breast.

"Your baby will have plenty of milk to feed on. He's going to grow up to be a very handsome and brilliant young man," she said, smiling broadly.

"I had a clear vision of him," Maria said, giving her a weak smile. "All I want for him is to grow up happy, and not turn out like his father, Clarence."

Mrs. Wade and Mrs. Birch exchanged wide-eyed glances. Mrs. Birch's skin tingled intensely, prompting her to pull her shawl closer to her neck. The sudden coldness struck her to her core.

"Uh, let me start this examination so we can see what's happening, shall we?' Mrs. Wade said, clearing her throat.

She carefully inserted the earpieces of her stethoscope into her ears and placed the cone, attached to a long black rubber cord, on Maria's belly. Fascinated, Maria watched closely as Mrs. Wade slowly moved the cone over different areas of her swollen belly. Afterward, she jotted down notes on her scratch pad. She then examined her breasts, one at a time. They appeared noticeably larger than during the last check-up. Maria winced in pain as Mrs. Wade pressed each breast gently between her palms.

"Does that hurt when I press on them, Maria?" Mrs. Wade asked with concern.

"Just a little. I don't wear anything to support my breasts anymore because it hurts. I'm also exhausted; I eat constantly, but not today. I cry so much," Maria's voice was thick with tears, and she sobbed uncontrollably.

"Let's get you up first, then we'll all talk, because I felt something wasn't quite right on the way here," Mrs. Birch said softly as she and Mrs. Wade carefully helped Maria to her feet and helped her into a blue-flowered nightgown. After fluffing the pillows, Maria managed to sit up straight.

"Maria, I have some chamomile tea leaves in my bag. I'm going to the kitchen to boil water for tea, and I'll be right in to see you," said Mrs. Wade.

Mrs. Wade opened her black leather bag, which was designed for midwives who still relied on herbs and tinctures in their practice. She retrieved a glass jar of tea leaves and hurried into the kitchen to prepare everything.

Mrs. Birch approached Maria, who was inconsolable. Her shoulders trembled as she fidgeted with her gold cross, tracing its surface for comfort.

"It's going to be alright, mon Cheri. Shhh," she cooed, holding her firmly in her arms.

"Both of you hurt," she said, placing her palm on Maria's belly. Suddenly, Mrs. Birch began praying in French-Creole. She held Maria close, wrapping her arms around her to protect her from any harm, seen or unseen. Maria shut her eyes tightly and prayed along with Mrs. Birch, who was praying so intensely that she started shouting. When she finished, she removed her shawl and draped it on Maria's shoulders. After several more minutes of fervent prayer, she reached into her dark tan leather bag and took out a vial of holy water. She sprinkled some on Maria's head, belly, feet, and hands. Once done, she blessed and prayed over the four corners of the bedroom. As if on cue, Mrs. Wade entered with two cups of steaming hot tea.

"I'll set the cups of tea on your table near the bed. After I talk to you about your exam, I'm going to start dinner for your family because it's clear you're not in any condition to do it yourself. You're tired, upset, and you need to sleep. While I prepare dinner, Mrs. Birch will sit with you. Do you understand me, Maria?" Mrs. Wade said firmly.

"Yes, and thank you," Maria said, relieved, nodding in agreement.

Mrs. Wade pulled out her notepad and pencil as she sat beside her bed. She adjusted her gold spectacles and took Maria's hand. Mrs. Birch moved to the other side of the bed, slipped off her shoes, and reached into her bag, pulling out a pair of thick socks she put on, along with a wooden box she cradled. She then climbed into bed with Maria.

It feels truly right that these two women are here to help me at the worst time of my life. Mrs. Wade cares for me and my baby, while Mrs. Birch feels like a mother to me. I wish my mother were here with me, Maria thought regretfully.

Maria's mind drifted to the night she and Clarence eloped and how they told her mother. The true sign of their marital curse was when her mother cursed in

French-Creole and then spat on Maria and Clarence's shoes. The look of humiliation and disgust on the naval officer Maria was supposed to marry was too much to bear. After Maria's mother slammed the door, the officer was loudly ranting expletives behind the closed door.

"Madame, comment avez-vous pu laisser votre fille s'enfuir avec ce nègre sale" he was heard yelling.

Mrs. Birch murmured, "You were better off without that naval officer," as if she instinctively understood Maria's thoughts. "Two weeks after he and your mother moved to France, he was killed. It appears he already had a fiancée, and her father discovered he was planning to make his new wife humiliate her. In response, her father shot him in the head with a pistol."

Maria gasped in shock at what she heard. Mrs. Birch looked straight ahead as she tightened her grip on Maria's hand.

Mrs. Wade said, "Maria, there's no doubt that the child growing inside you will be a large one." She added, "This explains why your belly is so round and swollen. The baby's heartbeat is also very strong, which is a good sign. I know you and Clarence hope to have one more child after this one is born. If you were expecting twins again, that would have been a wonderful blessing. If you still wish to have one more child, you-"

"No, no more children for us, Mrs. Wade. After this baby, there will be no more," interrupted Maria.

Sensing the bitterness in her tone, Mrs. Wade nodded and readjusted her spectacles. She rose and went to the table where the steaming hot cups of tea were steeping. Grabbing two cups, she handed one to Maria and the other to Mrs. Birch. Before sitting down, she went to the kitchen and picked up the remaining cup. The three of them sipped their tea in silence.

"Maria, you're experiencing something that's causing you so much distress that it's affecting your health. Your skin appears very dry, so try to drink more water. You will have a large baby, but I also notice you're losing weight. I recommend eating more vegetables and soups. For breakfast, have porridge, and for lunch, enjoy a hearty soup loaded with vegetables and meat. Adding a biscuit to your bowl will make it thicker and beneficial for the baby," Mrs. Wade said.

"What can I add to the porridge? I don't like how it tastes, it's terrible," Maria said bluntly.

"Humph!" Mrs. Birch grunted loudly.

"If you have nutmeg and an apple that you can cut into small pieces, add them on top of the porridge. It tastes Magnifique!"

"And you'll need to improve your strength to breastfeed this child," Mrs. Wade said as she sipped her tea. "Make tea with fennel, because it can increase your breast milk. Several new mothers, whose babies I delivered a month ago, told me that my special blend helps soothe their babies' constant crying and aids digestion. I'll leave you some jars to start drinking, along with a jar of blessed thistle. Don't brew too much, as it's very bitter—add a little sugar. The new mothers mentioned it makes their milk taste sweet."

"Mrs. Wade, sometimes I feel a pinch in my lower back," she said, placing her hand on that area.

She instructed, "Turn over to your side and draw your knees up."

Mrs. Wade carefully rolled Maria onto her side and helped lift her knees, then gently pressed on Maria's lower back. She identified a sensitive spot when she saw Maria's painful wince in response to her touch.

"Is it here?" she asked, applying a little more pressure.

"Yes, yes, right there! OUCH!" Maria exclaimed, wincing in pain once again.

"You seem to share a common trait with many women who develop this condition, but usually not until much later, close to their due date. I'm concerned because you're not that close yet," Mrs. Wade said as she helped Maria settle back onto the pillows.

"Alice, she's in a lot of trouble. I have a salve made from mint, eucalyptus, holy water, and peppermint," Mrs. Birch said, shifting to her side to get out of bed. She opened her bag and retrieved a glass jar containing a white cream with green herbs. "Help me roll her onto her side again," she requested.

Mrs. Wade and Mrs. Birch helped Maria slowly roll onto her side. Mrs. Birch lifted Maria's nightgown without hesitation to expose her lower back. When she twisted open the jar, a mint scent filled the room. Mrs. Birch dipped two fingers into the salve and applied it to Maria's sore area. Gently kneading the salve in deep, rhythmic motions, the coolness began to take effect immediately. After five minutes, the tightness and throbbing pain subsided.

"Feeling better now?" Mrs. Birch asked as she gently pulled Maria's nightgown back in its place.

"Yes, I feel so much better. Whatever you put inside the jar was like a miracle; the pain is all gone. *Merci, Madame Birch, depuis que je suis venue m'aider, c'est comme si vous étais ma mère, je vous aime pour avoir fait cela pour moi*". Maria said, hugging her.

"Alice, could you leave Maria and me alone? I need to talk to her, and some of our conversation will be in our French-Creole language."

"I was about to mention that I'll clean the dishes and start preparing dinner for Maria's family. I plan to bring some biscuits, ham, and water to Clarence, who has been working in the fields and barn since we arrived. While I'm there, I'll ask him to pick some sweet potatoes so I can make enough pies for a few days. You can rest for a bit, Maria." She quickly collected the teacups and closed the door, leaving the two women to talk.

"Maria, it's clear to me you're going through a tough time right now. I can feel it, and the whole house seems tense. I also notice it through my senses-when Clarence welcomed Alice and me, I could smell the scent of another woman on him, and his lips looked strangely like snakeskin. I'm sorry to have to tell you this," Mrs. Birch said.

Maria said, angrily, "I saw them kissing right here in our yard! When I confronted Clarence, he claimed I was mistaken and that I was tired and imagined it. So, you're telling the truth; he was with another woman and keeps lying about it!"

"You've also been having nightmares, haven't you?" Mrs. Birch inquired as she pulled out what looked like a deck of cards Maria hadn't seen before.

"Yes, and they're horrible! They're so real that one night I screamed, and my husband wasn't even here beside me in bed to comfort and protect me," Maria said.

I'll provide your answers. My cards, though unusual, always reveal the truth. They were gifted to my family by a slave from Congo, a place in Africa known for its secrets. He was born with a veil and told my grandmother that her future child would also have one:

me. To honor the three of us born with veils, he crafted these cards, infusing them with life. My grandmother has passed them down to my mother, and now they are with me. The cards and I will now communicate with you, she said as she shuffled them.

Mrs. Birch said, "I'm going to divide the cards into three piles of eight. They are called houses, mon Cheri. All of them will be faced down. I want you to choose which house you will visit first, and the houses you choose to visit will speak to you."

Maria felt a flutter of nerves in her stomach, her hand trembling as she reached across the table to pick the first house on her right. She handed the cards to Mrs. Birch, who nodded and wrapped them in a white cloth, folding it into thirds to separate the remaining piles. Maria then spread the cards out on the table, slowly turning each one face up while whispering in French-

Creole, as if speaking to them. After a brief pause, she shook her head fiercely.

"Non! S'il vous plaît dites-moi quelque chose de différent, oh non s'il vous plaît!" she murmured as she twisted her head away from the cards. After another long pause, she finally spoke.

"The cards have spoken to me, Maria," she said. A worried frown creased her brow.

"The three of knives have appeared," she said, pointing to a card featuring a roughly drawn image of a small tree. Instead of leaves, it had sharp, bloody, jagged knives. In front of the tree on the ground was a heart with a knife stabbed through it and another heart tied with twine, with a disheveled doll pulling at it. "This card indicates that a female spirit who has passed away is very angry about your disobedience regarding your marriage to a man who isn't the right fit for you. Your union was not approved, and thus it was cursed by her," Mrs. Birch explained.

Oh my God, my mother is gone, and she's angry with me even after death, Maria thought as tears flowed down her face.

"You were right, I should've never married Clarence. Please forgive my disobedience, mother, forgive me!" Maria wailed breathlessly. Mrs. Birch went on with the reading, oblivious to Maria's muffled wails of anguish.

"The large basket containing gold coins symbolizes that a mother figure is beside you to guide and support you now, during the birth of our child, and through what lies ahead. You will benefit from her presence and lean on her during your time of loss. You will feel safe in her company. That mother figure is me, Ma plus chère," she said, grasping Maria's hand but never taking her eyes off the cards. She pointed to the next card.

"This card features six coins. Your children will all receive education and make us proud, especially the one growing in your belly". Six coins are also symbolically warning of a woman nearby whom you dislike. She pretends to be your friend but is actually a jealous gossip and a deceitful woman. She has spoken evil of the wife of the man she plans to marry—a kind but naive woman," said Mrs. Birch, closing her eyes and making the sign of the cross.

"She loved you, Maria, and saw you as her only friend. She didn't want to leave this world the way she did, but she's now in heaven, where no one can hurt her anymore. The woman who continues to be a thorn in your side will marry the man she's engaged to, but that marriage won't last even a year. The six coins on this card tell me there's a suitcase outside their front door, which usually indicates a quick departure. The third coin suggests she will wander without a permanent place to stay. Wherever she goes, it won't be for long because of her wicked tongue. She will face worry, misery, despair, disgrace, and failure as she moves from town to town. By the end of her journey, she'll lose something dear to her and suffer from poor health. The first house has spoken," said Mrs. Birch. She carefully collected the first set of cards and set them aside.

"Two more houses to choose from," she said, placing the two decks on the tray. After studying them briefly, Maria pointed to the deck of cards on her left. Mrs. Birch nodded, reshuffling the cards. She then arranged them face down in an order that reflected what the cards were telling her. Once done, she turned them face up to unveil their secrets. Her eyes remained focused on the cards, and she sighed deeply. "Non, pas encore! Pourquoi son esprit véridique ? Je vous en implore, s'il vous plaît ne lui faites pas ça, elle a assez souffert," Mrs. Birch said in French Creole. She then began to interpret the message conveyed by the cards.

"The loudest speaking card is this one," she said, tapping her finger on a card with a drawing of a heart that was cut in half. Another doll on this card had a black cord wrapped around its body several times. The doll, which looked grotesque, seemed unhappy, and a gold wedding band was on its left toe. "It's telling me about your husband and another woman. Clarence is involved with the daughter of the woman I mentioned earlier. What happened between them went beyond just a kiss. The card indicates that their involvement has become so intense that it's uncontrollable. It's warning you that his attraction to her will bring pain and suffering to both families, yours and hers. It's more serious than you can imagine," Mrs. Birch paused briefly. After a few moments, she softly began to speak in French-Creole.

"Oh no," she whispered. Carefully, she pointed to a card showing a baby wrapped in a blanket, pink on top and blue on the bottom. At the baby's feet was a bloody straight-edged razor. "The woman he is with is going to have his child, mon plus cher. The baby will be born two months after your son, in mid-August. When grown, this child will hold many secrets and will deceive others, just like the woman's mother. What is most troubling is that your son will be the one deeply involved in the deception."

This bit of news made Maria sob uncontrollably.

Mrs. Birch tried her best to stay composed and felt sorrowful about having to bear the news to Maria. She wiped away her tears several times. She went on with the rest of the reading.

"This is the card that speaks the loudest of all, representing your destiny," she said, pointing to a card showing a large, beautiful house. In front of the house, a man with a suitcase and a woman at the door looked to be in deep distress. The man's hand was wrapped with a red snake.

This card indicates that you need to prepare for a rapidly approaching change. When it arrives, you should seek out the support of everyone at your church and all your friends, as you'll need us to stay close and keep your mind focused. The clouds above the house symbolize strong winds that will uproot and blow away things that once seemed destined to stay with you forever. Your plans will shift in ways you can't fully understand. In the coming weeks, you will receive news that won't be favorable. This is when your anger might lead you to your workroom, next to this house, the shed where you do your petitions. There, you'll discover that the truth has caused pain and broken your heart," she said, her eyes suddenly moist with tears. Taking a deep breath, Mrs. Birch pointed to another card depicting a child's hand holding a rose.

This indicates that relief from your pain and despair is on the horizon. Hope is on its way, along with repairs to your home and money being safe for many years, even long after you've passed away at an advanced age. Your patience through this mess will ultimately bring a blessing so immense that you will find it hard to believe it's yours. From now on, you will never need to worry about money again. Maria stayed quiet, and her crying subsided.

"Two more cards to read from this house," said Mrs. Birch. She fixed her gaze intently on the last two cards in the deck.

"An old woman leaning on a cane and a child," she said, picking up the card that depicted a slightly bent old woman using a cane and holding the hand of a cheerful young girl. The card also featured several groups of beautiful flowers, along with some that were withered, dying, or dead.

"The old woman is saying that you saw the truth that had been intentionally veiled by darkness. Humph!" Mrs. Birch said. Maria leaned in to get a better look at the image.

"See here?" she said, pointing to two clusters of flowers. One cluster consisted of dead roses located on the bottom left of the card, while to the right was a cluster of shriveled honeysuckles, still alive but fading.

"Maydell, I knew it! He was with that filthy whore all along! And the other one is Violet. I saw him kiss her last week, and oh my God, he's been with her too! Clarence is a worthless liar!" Maria said angrily, her nostrils flaring.

I'm genuinely sorry, Maria. The cards show that even without concrete proof of the double deception, you sensed something was wrong. Today, that intuition proved to be correct. My God, Maria, your husband is a deceiver and a wicked man who tries to appear loving and caring, but he harbors darkness within. His secrets will come to light, and the final card for this house reveals that once Clarence is gone, you must trust your instincts and the gifts you've been given, as you'll need to rely on your strength," she said, shaking her head in disgust.

"After all, your children will need you. Trust those dreams you've been having and call on me, your second mother, for help because, during this dark time, the sun's light will eventually shine in your favor," Mrs. Birch said. As she picked up the next bundle of cards and shuffled them, she laid the cards on the table, gazed at them, and murmured words in French Creole. "Oh no, not again. She's suffering enough!" she said firmly, shutting her eyes tightly. After about a minute, Mrs. Birch opened her eyes and looked at Maria. "My dear, this house is not safe at all. I need you to be very strong and prepared. The outcome will be painful and filled with grief. But as your second mother, I will be with you. Are you ready to hear this final message?" she asked, gripping Maria's wrist.

'Yes, I have no other choice but to be brave and move forward for my children and their future,' Maria said, her eyes dropped, and her hand gently circling her belly.

"The top card shows the loudest message," she said, pointing to a card depicting a young man in a military uniform, as if prepared for battle. He holds a rifle but looks morbidly wounded. In the background, twenty graves are marked with wooden crosses.

This young man is your eldest son, Kempton. He's battling numerous enemies but is severely wounded. The crosses mark his fallen comrades who fought alongside him. Your son will endure severe bruising, be beaten, and face torture. He will fight until his final breath. Kempton will be a courageous soldier who ultimately makes the ultimate sacrifice: his life".

"Are you certain about this? No, no, Mrs. Birch, it can't be my son! Please God, not my Kempton!" Maria shouted despairingly, shielding her face from the sight.

"I'm so sorry, Maria. These cards prepare you for what's ahead, and the work is needed to bring peace to yourself and your household. Over the coming months, your worst fears about your eldest son will start to materialize; nightmares will increase, bringing despair and sleepless nights. But when Kempton is returned to you, you'll find renewed hope and relief from suffering. Those who caused you pain will be gone, allowing you to move on. Here is a card that signifies good news, she said, placing her hand on a card depicting a slice of cake with a gold coin on top. The cake rested on a worn blue wooden table with jagged splinters, and a broken matchstick lay next to it. A nearby teacup held two gold rings inside.

"Yes, yes. This card speaks of happiness that will finally come to your life. The gold coin on top of the cake will symbolize prosperity. You're going to be in danger of losing everything: your house, the land, and the farm. However, you're going to be presented with money in the most unlikely way. It's a blessing that will be presented to you. There will be abundance, money, food on the table, workers working on your land, and no sickness. The broken matchstick symbolizes discord, not about your marriage, but of the son that you're carrying inside your belly. This card is telling me things about your son as a man. He's going to meet someone whom he'll fall in love with, but this person has a very shameful secret that will reveal itself. Your son isn't going to accept it very well, not at all. In the end, there will be a loss of life", said Mrs. Birch, sighing deeply. Then she turned up another card. "But the final card that is coming through says this", she said, urgently tapping on a card that had a picture of four knives plunged into each corner of a heart. The heart appeared to be jagged in the center, but not splitting in half. It stayed intact.

"The card states: Throughout your life, you'll endure all sorts of ruthless challenges-hard times, a friend who gossips behind your back, betrayal, and distress, all of which will eventually leave you. After facing these trials, you'll gain the ability to discern whom to trust and learn from your mistakes. Ultimately, you'll instill in your children and grandchildren a respect for our traditions, and most importantly, family. This marks the conclusion of the messages I have conveyed to you. Mrs. Birch then gathered the cards, tied them with twine, and placed them in her bag. "Les cartes ont dit la vérité," she said.

"Wait," Maria said softly, gently touching Mrs. Birch on the elbow before she got up to leave the bedroom. "Am I going to have grandchildren? Which of my children will be starting a family?"

"Izelle. She suffered the loss of her first love, but she's going to meet a man who looks exactly like the one she lost, except he's grown. He's wearing a uniform, and they'll be married the year after they meet. Rosetta will become a bride two years after Izelle gets married.

That's when Izelle finds out she's expecting a child. Rosetta's children will come later in her life, which is fine with her because she's in no rush," said Mrs. Birch.

Maria closed her eyes and exhaled deeply.

Thank you, Madame Birch. The ancestors who communicated through the cards conveyed some difficult truths, but they were honest. The only solace I find is in knowing that Izelle will marry someone who looks just like Jonathan, the young boy who was murdered. My son Joseph had visions about him, and it was revealed that Izelle would marry a man resembling Jonathan as a grown man. This brings me great relief, knowing my daughters will be married and raising their children," Maria said.

'You are welcome, my dear Maria. Things won't be easy for you. You'll face a long period of uncertainty. I also must tell you that you and your husband will have a major argument soon, before the season changes. Family secrets will come out unexpectedly, and it will be heartbreaking for you and your children. However, remember that I will be here to support you. The ancestors have spoken, my daughter,' said Mrs. Birch as she closed her bag. 'Your family is home; I can hear them. Mrs. Wade has prepared a wonderful dinner — I smell red beans, rice, ham, and those sweet potatoes she mentioned,' she said, taking a deep breath.

"I'll finish helping her feed your family, and then we'll leave. We have one more patient to visit, after which she and I are going home."

"Thank you, Madame Birch," Maria said. Today began terribly, and even though I received some bad news during the reading, knowing you'll be there provides some comfort. But please tell me, when did my mother pass away?"

"In France, two years ago, I received a letter from your sister Adele, in which she told me your mother died peacefully in her sleep shortly after the morning church service. She said your mother was exhausted and went back to bed. When Adele and her husband tried to wake her, she didn't respond, and they realized she had passed away. After her funeral, your sister and her husband cleaned her room and found the money the officer paid your mother when you were just nineteen, at the Quadroon Ball. This payment secured your marriage so you wouldn't have to go through a placage like the other young women at the ball. Your mother was steadfast in ensuring that you married first before having children with that man. That's why they hurried to get you married early that morning and then boarded the next boat to France. Anyway, your sister kept the money and told me that you were dead to her," Mrs. Birch said.

Maria froze, stunned and hurt by the revelation of her sister Adele's feelings.

Not only did my mother disown me, but my sister hates me, too! I have no family now, and so my mother was right after all. If I had married the officer, I wouldn't be in this mess with Clarence, she thought bitterly. " Ce qui est fait est fait ", Maria whispered, her throat thick with heartache.

Mrs. Birch went to Maria and embraced her. She felt Maria's tears on the shoulder of her dress as she wept softly.

"It's the past, and you can't change it, Maria. You have more important things to worry about, which is why I'm here to help. I'm going to greet your family and get some food for you. Rest now, I'll be right back," she said, kissing her on the forehead. Gently, she closed the door to enter the kitchen.

She held back tears as today's events overwhelmed her. But the news of what was to come was about to change her life forever.

"Merè?" Izelle and Rosetta peered in from the doorway.

"Oui. Come here so I can see you," said Maria as she wiped away her tears.

Izelle, holding a tray with a steaming bowl of broth and two biscuits, and Rosetta, carrying a tall glass of water with lemon slices, followed closely. Maria sat up and assisted in guiding the wooden tray of food onto the small table. Rosetta placed the glass of water beside the broth, and they embraced Maria warmly.

"Come, sit with me," Maria said, gesturing for them to come closer so they could talk.

"Mère, what's going on? Are you alright? Are you sick?" Rosetta asked, worried.

"When we came home, we were surprised to find Mrs. Wade cooking in the kitchen", Izelle said.

"We asked if we could visit and see how you were doing. She said everything was fine and that Mrs. Birch was with you, discussing private matters we didn't need to worry about. We then helped Mrs. Wade prepare dinner. She showed us how to add a sweet potato to the biscuits. She already had some boiled and cooled sweet potatoes. When we added the flour, she told us to cut the sweet potato into small pieces and mix them into the dough. We rolled the dough and shaped the biscuits just like the ones you bake. That's why they're orange; the sweet potatoes give them that color. Then she had us taste one. They were wonderful, Merè!" Izelle said with a smile.

"They look delicious! I was wondering why the biscuits are orange," Maira said. She reached over to the tray and eagerly took a bite of the warm biscuit, which had a hidden dollop of homemade blackberry jam inside. Maria then took a second biscuit and bit into it again. She licked her fingers after finishing the second one. Izelle and Rosetta watched with relief as Maria started eating again.

"Mère, what's happening? We're all scared," Rosetta asked, moving closer to her mother. Her bottom lip was trembling.

"I don't want either you or your brothers to worry about me or the baby. I had a busy day, and Mrs. Wade thought it would be best for me to rest, that's all. You have nothing to be concerned about," Maria said.

Rosetta and Izelle looked at each other, their eyes showing confusion.

"I understand what both of you are thinking. I'm being honest about how I feel. I had a tough day and needed to talk to Mrs. Wade and Mrs. Birch about some things that have been bothering me. After our talk, things started to make more sense. I need to rest for the rest of the day, and I believe tomorrow will be better. I'm tired and need some rest," she said, taking a sip of cold water. "I've been drinking the tea I had earlier, and it's made me quite sleepy. Please take everything back to the kitchen for me and ask Mrs. Wade and Mrs. Birch to come in before they leave."

"Oui, Merè", Izelle answered as she rose from the bed and took the tray.

"May I ask you something, Merè, and please don't be angry. All of us-me, Izelle, Kempton, Joseph, and Sampson-are very upset," said Rosetta.

"What about? What's going on?" Maria asked, alarmed by Rosetta's forthright question.

"It's Dad, isn't it? We all hear you fighting, and this morning, when Kempton and Joseph visited the barn, they found him asleep inside. They had to wake him up in case anyone came to buy something from the smokehouse. Is he planning to leave you?"

Oh my God, they know! There's no hiding what's happening in this house. I can't let them find out what I saw and what Clarence is lying about, Maria thought, a cold tremor running through her body.

"Your father and I often disagree about the farm and when he will finally stay home at night to care for us. It won't be for much longer because Audine and Wayne are getting married soon, so we won't have to worry about that anymore," Maria said with a smile.

"Oh, I see," Rosetta said as she moved to follow Izelle into the kitchen. She embraced Maria tightly and whispered in her ear, "I don't believe you, Merè. You and

I know the truth. I'm not stupid. Sleep well. I'll send in Mrs. Wade and Mrs. Birch. Then she left.

Maria sat stunned after her daughter admitted she knew the truth. But how did she find out?

"Maria, we're about to leave now," Mrs. Wade said as she and Mrs. Birch quietly entered her bedroom. Kempton, Joseph, and Sampson waited outside the door, while Clarence was nowhere in sight.

"You have a beautiful family. I enjoyed talking with your children, and you taught your daughters to speak French Creole perfectly! Your sons are wonderful young men; you should be proud of all of them, Mon Cheri," as she bent down to embrace Maria.

"I enjoyed myself too. As I was cooking dinner, Izelle and Rosetta were surprised to see me in the kitchen, but after I explained what was happening, they immediately started helping me. I showed them how to make biscuits with mashed sweet potatoes mixed into the dough. It's a good thing I made extra because everyone had two helpings. Hump! Clarence ate three!" Mrs. Wade said, smiling broadly.

Mrs. Birch cleared her throat loudly to get Mrs. Wade's attention and eyed her cautiously.

"Oh, and just to let you know, the kitchen is clean, and everything has been tidied up. You don't need to worry about cleaning. I also prepared extra food to last until next week, including a special soup for you to enjoy later. It should last for a few days and will be good for both you and the baby," Mrs. Wade said, leaning in to hug Maria.

"Thank you both for what you did for me today. I believe I'll feel better tomorrow after a restful night. I appreciate you taking the extra time to make the soup because my appetite is returning, but I'll wait until later to eat. Do you have far to go? It's getting late,"

"Clarence will give us a ride to Lillian Butler's house. She's aware we'll arrive a bit late to see her. Her husband will be home in time to look after their four daughters. He wishes for a son, but Mrs. Birch told his wife she's expecting another girl. When they all grow up and marry, that will mean five weddings his husband will need to pay for," Mrs. Wade explained.

"Tell Lillian I said hello and that I wish her the best," Maria said.

"Take good care. We'll be back next month. If you need us, you know where to find me or Mrs. Birch. Good evening, Maria," said Mrs. Wade.

Then they all departed, but not before each of Maria's sons went inside to hug her. Maria listened to the chatter and laughter outside until she heard the truck doors close and the engine start. Everyone exchanged goodbyes.

Maria thought bitterly to herself that Clarence didn't come to check on how I was doing.

Sleep came swiftly that night. She didn't have any nightmares this time. Later, when she woke for a glass of water, the house was silent, and everyone was asleep. The only sound was the rustling leaves in the wind on this sultry-cool night. Looking out the window, she fixed her gaze on the dark, empty barn, mirroring her marriage.

CHAPTER FIFTEEN

Violet quickly moved to the window at the familiar rumble of the truck, drawing in deep breaths to steady herself. Her thoughts were consumed all day with Clarence, dreaming of seeing him and feeling his tight embrace once more. As the headlights dimmed and the engine stopped, Clarence stepped out of the truck and headed toward Violet's house. Unable to hold back any longer, Violet threw open the door and dashed toward him so swiftly that Clarence could only stand still with his arms wide open to catch her. She kissed him passionately, leaving him breathless.

"I love you so much, Clarence. I can't wait to see you tonight. I have so much to tell you about what's going on with my mother and Wayne. Let's go inside and talk. I've got coffee ready for us," she said, gripping his hand. She then paused and went into another coughing fit.

"Violet, are you okay? You don't look well," Clarence said, pulling her close to his chest with concern in his voice.

"I woke up coughing, and it's been a bother all day unless I take some of these peppermints. They help for a few hours. Drinking hot tea helps some, but then the coughing comes right back again", she said.

Let's go inside because it's been getting cooler at night, and I don't want you to get sick. I love you too much to lose you; you're everything to me."

His voice was thick with emotion as he pulled her into his arms again and kissed her more passionately, his tongue deeply dipping and curling. Then, taking her by the hand, he led her into the house and shut the door.

"Where's Mason?" he asked, taking his shoes off as he made his way into the kitchen to sit at the table.

"He's in his room sleeping when I checked, but I'm worried about him. He's been acting strangely around me, like he's angry. I tried to talk to him earlier, asking if something was wrong, but he wouldn't respond. Instead, he went straight into his room and slammed the door. Two hours later, he turned off his light and went to sleep," she said as she placed the hot coffee on the table in front of Clarence.

"That doesn't sound like Mason at all. Is he doing okay with his schoolwork, or is someone bothering him at school?" Clarence asked while taking a sip of his steaming hot coffee.

"He's doing very well in school. From what my mother has said, he's at the top of his class, passed all of his tests, and his teachers believe he'll go much further in his studies," said Violet. She poured herself a cup of coffee and stirred in sugar and a splash of milk.

"Don't worry about Mason; he'll be fine. He's just busy with his studies. Still, keep an eye on him until you leave," he said, motioning for her to sit on his lap. Violet approached, sat down, wrapped her arms around his neck, and kissed him passionately. "Mmm," he sighed, letting out a slow, steady breath. His firm touch caused her to exhale sharply, making her forget the coughing fit she had before he arrived. Fortunately, the peppermints helped.

"Clarence, what should we do about us? How do we truly feel about each other? I'm about to leave for teacher's college. What worries me most is that my mother and Wayne will be getting married in a few weeks. Once they are married, she plans to quit her job and stay home with Mason. She also mentioned her resolve to give Wayne the family Lena couldn't provide. Clarence, we may never be together again. What are we going to do? I've fallen in love with you," she said, her face showing her pain.

Clarence's expression shifted from bewilderment to agony at the thought of never seeing this young, beautiful, and smart woman he was holding in his arms. For the first time in many years, finally, a woman to be with who was going to be a teacher and teach the next generation of Black children that would promise to fight for the rights and justice due to many that fought and died violently for this country, as his grandfather did in the civil war and how his great-grandfather tried to escape a plantation during slavery.

Clarence thought with a frown, I love Violet, and I need her. He then asked, "Do you want to end this, Violet?"

Violet vigorously shook her head no and silently began to unbutton the front of her dress. Taking his hand, she guided it onto her bare breast. Clarence cupped her swollen breast and caressed it until he teased the bud of her nipple between his fingers. She closed her eyes and moaned softly.

Recognizing she was ready, he took her dark brown areola into his mouth and pulled gently. Violet arched her neck and let out a loud moan; Clarence continued with even more intensity until he felt his own arousal grow.

"Take me to your room; I can't wait any longer. You're mine, and I'll find a way for us to be together," he said in a raspy voice.

Without saying anything, Violet smoothly slipped off his lap and stood before him, offering her hand. As he grasped it, his café noir eyes gleamed with admiration for her daring and mischievousness. To everyone else, she appeared intelligent and beautiful. But at this moment, she was entirely his. She smiled and trailed her fingers down his unbuttoned trousers, revealing his arousal. Clarence shivered and, in a swift motion, stood up and lifted her from her feet. She clutched his neck as he lifted her hips, allowing her long legs to wrap around his waist. Violet buried her face in his shoulder, and he carried her to the dimly lit bedroom. Once inside, he used his foot to push the door closed.

"Violet, are you sure you want this, because if not, I'll leave after your mother and Wayne marry. I'll return to my wife and try to repair things with her. If we keep going this way, stopping isn't an option. I'm willing to leave my wife, children, and home to start a new life with you. We could move to Virginia, where you can work as a teacher. I won't let you give that up. So, are you ready?"

"I will never give you up, Clarence. If you're willing to leave everything behind for me, I'll stay with you forever. So, yes, I want to be with you," she said.

Clarence smiled and began to undress her. Unbuttoning her dress, she allowed it to fall to the floor, where it pooled around her ankles. Clarence's eyes widened when he saw that Violet wasn't wearing anything. He looked at her, his eyes appraising with need. He took off his shirt and unzipped his trousers. Taking her hand, he guided it to his erection. Violet's hand tightened even more around his straining shaft, and she continued the slow and steady motion, sliding her hand up and down his swollen flesh. Feeling that he was going to explode, he took Violet to her bed.

"I love you, Clarence," she murmured, raising her arms to him. He climbed over her and soon entered her. He recalled their first time—how eager they were, but they had to hurry because of the limited time that afternoon. Now, he had all night with her until early morning. As he went deeper, Violet moaned more loudly, wrapping her strong legs around his waist.

"Faster, Clarence!" she snarled through her clenched teeth, holding on to him desperately.

Clarence's arousal grew more intense as he thrust deeper into Violet, sweat dripping down his forehead. He sensed he was close to climax and tried to withdraw, but it was too late. "Violet!" he called out, his movements increasing in rhythm and depth.

His breathing became faster, and then an uncontrollable, explosive warmth came rushing out from his throbbing erection. He continued thrusting deeper until one last powerful orgasm made them both climax. Not to wake Mason, Clarence claimed her soft lips, kissing her deeply, stifling her loud moans.

"Are you alright?" Clarence whispered as he carefully pulled himself out.

"Yes, but I didn't want you to stop. Promise me that you'll always do this whenever we're finally together," she said.

"We can, but there'll be times when we can't," he said, smiling as he rolled onto his side and pulled her to his chest.

"Why wouldn't we? We love each other," Violet said, nestling herself closer to him.

"There are moments when we must be extra careful, Violet. I have five children and am expecting another baby. When I leave my family, I must ensure they are taken care of. If we're not careful, we could end up with a baby being born when we're not prepared for it, at least not at this time."

"I wish I could have one for you, Clarence, because that would make me so happy," she said.

"Shhh," he said, placing his finger on her lips.

"One day, we will have our family, but only after you complete your studies and become a teacher. There's a lot I must think about, especially when I leave my wife and family behind. When I tell Maria, she might never allow me to see my children again. Let me handle a few things first," he said.

"I see," Violet said. Her eyes were downcast and disappointed.

"Violet, look at me," Clarence said earnestly, lifting her chin so she would meet his gaze. "While you're in Virginia settling into the teacher's college, I need to stay here to handle several matters, like asking Maria for a divorce, making sure my family and the farm are taken care of, and ensuring I have enough money to support us all. Once I've divorced Maria, I'll come to Virginia to be with you. When you graduate, start teaching, and we get married, we can begin our family and have as many children as you want," he said with a broad smile. He kissed her forehead.

"If you do it that way, I'll wait as long as we're together. That's going to make me study even harder to reach the top of my class. I'll wait, but when will you tell Maria the truth about us, Clarence?" Violet asked.

"After the wedding. As soon as your mother and Wayne are married, I will tell Maria the truth about us," he said.

"I'm scared of what my mother will say and what Maria might do. They no longer get along, and I suspect that once I tell my mother about us, she might throw me out. If that happens, at least I have the money my father left for me to rent a room in a house for Black women training to become teachers.

"There's nothing they can do to us except get very angry. No matter what, you're mine and I'm only in love with you," he said as he rolled on top of Violet.

Using his knees to spread her legs apart, he penetrated her deeply once more. When he climaxed inside her again, Violet silently wished to conceive a child tonight with Clarence.

CHAPTER SIXTEEN

November 1933

The Wedding

Today is the day I will be called Mrs. Wayne Collins, Audine thought, smiling as she looked at herself in the mirror. A radiant glow lit her face as she turned to the side for a final look at her simple ivory satin and chiffon wedding dress, which reached her ankles. Her shoes, matching the dress in color, were ivory Oxfords, not her preferred style but practical for the cool November afternoon. The dress's beauty was enhanced by a cascading veil secured with a crown of small flowers. The veil extended to the nape of her neck, drawing attention to the forty buttons running down the back of the dress.

"So, how do I look?" Audine asked with a big smile.

"You look fine, Ma. Let me straighten your necklace before we leave," Violet said, adjusting the pearl necklace Wayne gave her as a wedding gift. As she carefully fixed the pearls, her mind kept drifting to Clarence since she woke up. With Wayne and Audine heading on a week-long trip to New York, funded by Wayne's inheritance from Lena's funeral, this would be their last time together.

When my mother and Wayne return home, Clarence plans to tell Maria the truth about us, and I will tell my mother and Wayne. She thought this to herself while watching Audine, who was still in front of the mirror, smiling and admiring herself.

"Let me take one more look at myself and then we're leaving," Audine said. Taking one more glance, she nodded in satisfaction. "Get your flowers and let's go because I'm getting married today!" she squealed in happiness.

Mason, dressed in a gray suit, white shirt, and striped tie, looked dapper. The suspenders holding his trousers upright, along with the new black Oxfords, gave him a resemblance to a young Black businessman. Wayne took him to the local barbershop, where he received a short, clean, and sophisticated hairstyle. Audine paused and looked at her son, who at this moment wasn't a boy but stood before her as a young man.

"Your father would be so proud of you, Mason. You look every bit of him standing there," she said, dabbing her tear-filled eyes.

"Thank you. I miss Dad, but Wayne is here now and will take care of us. He said he's going to teach me many things as I get older," Mason said, hugging his mother and kissing her on the cheek. They heard a car pulling up in front of the house.

"Come on, they're all waiting for us", he said, taking her hand to help her out the door.

"After Wayne and I return from our trip to New York, we're moving to his house. Trust me, I won't miss this place," she said, casting one last glance at the rundown shack they had called home for years. She let out a heavy sigh at the memories before they headed out the door.

"Ma, go on ahead, I forgot my gloves!" Violet said as she rushed back to her bedroom.

The gloves rested on the bed where she had left them. As she looked at the bed, memories flooded back. This was where she and Clarence first made love over a month ago, and just two weeks prior, they had fallen asleep in each other's arms. Tears gathered in her eyes as she wrapped her arms around herself.

I can't cry right now. Tonight, I'll see Clarence again, and we'll make our final plans to be together after everything is settled. As for Maria, Humph! She has no choice but to accept that Clarence loves me. Once I finish my studies and become a teacher, we will have our own home where his children can visit us. He will keep the farm running, and eventually, we can get married and start our family. Everything will be perfect for us, she thought, smiling as she wiped away the tears streaming down her face.

Just as Violet scooped up the gloves from the bed and started to walk out of her room, a sudden wave of nausea, followed by dizziness, took over her. Fearing she would vomit all over her custom-made blue silk dress, Violet sprinted to the kitchen sink and threw up. The cramping in her stomach was so intense that she began to shake, and her knees felt like they would buckle. She heard the car horn honk a few more times, but she could only hold onto the sink until the wave passed. The vomit in the sink reeked of her stomach contents. She grabbed a glass, filled it with water, rinsed her mouth, and spat out the foul-tasting water. Then she filled the glass again and poured water into the remaining contents in the sink. Once everything was clean, she opened her small purse, popped a peppermint into her mouth, and started to feel better. As she reached for her small bouquet of roses and nosegays, she turned around. Mason stood at the door, his face showing contempt, shaking his head.

"Sorry for making everyone wait. I wasn't feeling well. I'm better now, but still a bit weak. Could you help me, Mason?" Violet asked nervously.

"Help yourself, Violet. You're no longer my sister. And by the way, I'm not a stupid kid; you're ruining everything for our family!" he said, slamming the door shut and walking out.

Violet stood in the kitchen, dumbfounded at what she had just heard her brother say. Running her hand through her long braid, her heartbeat raced. Feelings of hurt and confusion were taking center now. As she began to walk towards the door, another violent wave of nausea and stomach cramps came. Dropping her bouquet and her purse, she ran back to the kitchen sink again and vomited.

The church was filled, and guests were beginning to grow restless. Audine, Violet, and Mason were already forty-five minutes late. Wayne, wearing a new brown tweed wool suit, an ivory Oxford shirt, and a matching beige and brown-striped tie, fiddled nervously with his gold pocket watch, a family heirloom from his grandfather. The church pastor kept glancing at the door, hoping that Deacon Moss and his wife would arrive soon so her son could escort her down the aisle.

"What's going on here? Is Audine about to arrive?" Wayne whispered nervously to Clarence.

"She's coming, I'm sure of it. She's probably fixing her dress and hair to look beautiful for you. Plus, you paid for the food, the photographer for two pictures, and that two-day train trip to New York to visit her sister," Clarence said.

No sooner than he said those words, Mason rushed in, heading straight towards Wayne.

"Mason, thank God you're here, son! What's going on? Why did it take so long, and are your mother and sister okay?" Wayne asked nervously.

"Hi, Dad," Mason said, bending at his waist to catch his breath.

"What's wrong, son? Is your mother and sister alright?" Pastor Coleman asked, his eyebrows raised with concern.

"My mother is fine, sir. It was Violet. She's been throwing up and coughing. We had to sit her down for a while. Deaconess Moss gave her some medicine and water. That seems to have helped her a lot. Deacon Moss is outside helping my mother get out of the car," said Mason.

"Praise God! Everyone, please listen. Audine is here, and we will begin once she steps out of the car and enters the church," Pastor Coleman announced.

"Mason, is Violet doing better? Does she need anything from me?" Clarence asked, his stomach tightening as he twisted his gold wedding band.

Mason, avoiding eye contact with Clarence, straightened his shoulders and stormed away.

"What just happened with Mason storming off like that? Is everything okay?" Wayne asked directly.

"I'm sure he's just concerned about Violet and Audine. That's fine, but let's go ahead and get you married," Clarence said with a grin.

Looking toward the back of the church, Clarence saw Maria, who appeared stunning. She wore a burgundy drop-waist dress that accommodated her growing belly. She seemed absorbed in thoughts about their children, their education, chores, and being the loving mother she always was. Clarence, still sleeping in the barn, only communicated with her about the children and farm concerns. Their marriage seemed to have faded into the background.

Their eyes met as the pianist played the chords of Here Comes the Bride. Maria's expression was one of disgust, and her eyes looked cold. Clarence quickly looked away from her icy gaze and focused on the back of the church.

Violet, wearing a blue dress and matching Oxford shoes, slowly walked down the aisle, smiling brightly. The audience murmured in admiration at her beauty. Several young men, along with their mothers and Audine's friends, watched proudly. The young men, dressed in suits or army uniforms, looked at Violet with approval, hoping to have a chance to talk to her briefly after the wedding.

Clarence, unable to think of anything else, smiled widely at Violet as if she were the only woman present. Their eyes connected, and Violet showed a hint of longing through her smile. Maria, noticing their eye contact, confirmed what Mrs. Birch had told her days earlier: that Clarence and Violet's lies and deception were happening openly, even within their place of worship.

Although we may not sleep in the same bed, he remains the father of our children. Maria thought with disgust, furious at what she was witnessing.

After Violet positioned herself opposite Clarence, they stared at each other, unaware of their surroundings, while Maria looked at them with disgust.

Pastor Coleman moved to the center aisle between the first two rows of pews.

He announced, "Everyone, please rise for the bride."

Everyone rose and faced the center of the aisle. Audine, guided by Mason, walked slowly in sync with the music. Many guests gasped at her stunning appearance. Wayne, among the wedding crowd, strained his neck and finally caught sight of his future wife.

When their eyes met, Audine felt tears of happiness well up as she saw her future husband, Wayne. That day, she was filled with love for him, the man who took her to work every day, loved her children as if they were his own, and was about to become their father, her husband, and the father of their future children. Audine was overjoyed. As she reached the front of the church where Wayne was waiting, she took her place beside him, while Mason sat in the second row to watch the ceremony.

Maria thought to herself, shaking her head, that this marriage wouldn't last. Although Audine appears beautiful, her heart is wicked and deceptive.

"In faith, Audine Booker, do you take Wayne to be your husband, in sickness and health, for better or worse, for richer or poorer, in the sight of God and his people, until death separates you? If so, please say I do," said Pastor Coleman to Audine.

"I do," Audine whispered, as she squeezed Wayne's hand.

"In faith, do you, Wayne Collins, take Audine to be your wife, through sickness and health, for better or worse, for richer or poorer, in the presence of God and his people, until death separates you? If so, please say I do," said Pastor Coleman to Wayne, who was smiling warmly at Audine.

"I do," Wayne replied in a bubbly voice, causing Audine to respond with joyful tears.

"Wayne, please give Audine her gift to seal your marriage."

After placing her ring on, Wayne kissed her hand, making her close her eyes and sigh deeply.

"Audine, present your gift to seal your marriage to Wayne." Taking the ring carefully from her daughter's hand, Audine placed it on Wayne's finger, and then they clasped their hands together firmly.

"Everyone, please bow your heads in prayer," Pastor Coleman said.

Everyone in the church bowed their heads and closed their eyes. Audine and Wayne also closed their eyes, holding hands tightly as their Pastor prayed.

However, Clarence and Violet kept their eyes open and looked at each other.

"I-love-you," Clarence mouthed silently to Violet.

"I-love-you too," Violet mouthed back in the same manner.

Maria watched in horror, her eyes and mouth agape as she witnessed the scene unfold. She swiftly raised her gloved hand to her mouth to suppress a gasp of disgust.

It was appalling that they behaved so shamelessly in front of everyone they admired. Her husband's and that woman's intimate exchange was downright revolting, making her feel ill. She anxiously wondered what would happen if someone were to see this disgraceful act.

Maria felt deeply betrayed by this act. She reached into her purse, took out her handkerchief, and gently dabbed her tears as they started to fall. She quietly blew her nose and exhaled slowly. After placing her handkerchief back in her purse, she snapped it shut softly. Throughout the rest of the ceremony, her cold green eyes and pinched lips remained fixed on Clarence and Violet.

"By the authority granted to me by God's church and my office, I now declare this man and woman of God to be husband and wife on this day in November 1933. Wayne, you may now kiss your bride!"

Pulling Audine close, they wrapped their arms around each other and shared a passionate kiss. She slipped her arm into the crook of Wayne's elbow as they faced the congregation. Violet handed Audine her bridal bouquet.

The guests cheered enthusiastically with "Amens!" as Wayne and Audine walked down the aisle while the pianist played the bridal recessional music. As they made their way, guests offered congratulations. Clarence and Violet then followed, with Violet's arm resting in the crook of Clarence's elbow, and Mason walking behind, accompanied by Pastor Coleman.

Audine and Wayne were filled with happiness. As they reached the end of the church aisle, just before turning into the fellowship hall, they shared a passionate kiss, unaware of anyone watching.

"I love you, Wayne," Audine said, squeezing his hand.

"And I love you too, Mrs. Collins. This is the happiest day of my life. I want to thank you for loving me. I'm looking forward to spending the rest of my life with you," said Wayne, kissing her hand. They entered the fellowship hall and took their seats at the designated table before a stream of guests filed in. "Tell me, though, why were you so late? Mason said something about Violet coughing and throwing up? Is she feeling better?" asked Wayne, leaning in to inquire. His forehead was raised with concern for Violet, who was now his daughter.

"This is why I love you so much, Wayne. You love my children as if they're your own, and now we are truly a family. Violet is feeling much better. Honestly, I think between studying, preparing to become a teacher, and planning our wedding, it must have been too much for her and made her sick. She's doing fine now. When we return from visiting in New York, I plan to take her to see the Black doctor in the city. Don't worry, she'll be okay. But doesn't all this food look delicious? When we leave, I'll make sure it's all sent to our new home, so our family will have plenty to eat. I can't wait to try everything!" Audine said as she kissed Wayne.

Maria observed Clarence and Violet as they proceeded down the aisle. Violet briefly looked at Maria with a sudden expression of alarm. Clarence noticed the exchanged glances between the women, which made him feel uncomfortable.

All we're here for is to celebrate Audine and my friend Wayne's wedding day. Maria doesn't know anything about Violet or me. I'll tell her everything once they return, Clarence thought to himself.

Seated at tables for twelve, Audine, Wayne, Violet, and Mason sat together at a special table to demonstrate that they were now a family within the church. Clarence welcomed guests at other tables, while Maria found comfort engaging in lively talks with Ricks, his wife, and several of Rick's friends and their wives. Despite this, she would quickly look away whenever Clarence met her gaze, returning to her conversations. When Pastor Coleman reached the center of the floor, everyone returned to their seats, and Clarence moved to join Maria at her table.

He smiled at Maria as he pulled out his chair to sit next to her. Maria, without looking at Clarence, moved her chair closer to Cornelia, Rick's wife, so she could better hear Pastor Coleman and also keep an eye on Violet to ensure she stayed away from Clarence.

"Guests, could I kindly have your attention?" Pastor Coles announced.

"Today, we celebrate the wonderful union of Wayne and Audine. They are not only married, but Audine's children are also embraced in this union. God has blessed them with many wonderful blessings. Two individuals who lost their spouses have come together, initially as friends, now as husband and wife. We are also grateful that Brother Wayne is stepping in to serve as a father figure to Violet and Mason. As a special gift, Wayne, a good man, arranged for documents through the state of Louisiana, his attorney, and this church to legally adopt Violet and Mason!"

Audine's mouth drops open as she clutches her chest, watching Wayne retrieve two signed and sealed documents from his jacket pocket—one from the city's courthouse and one from his attorney, displayed for everyone. Thunderous applause erupts from the wedding guests. Unable to hold back any longer, Audine jumps out of her chair, hugging Wayne, who then extends his arm to include Violet and Mason in the embrace. Tears of joy flow freely as everyone celebrates the heartwarming family surprise.

Pastor Coleman lifted his hands to quiet the chatter.

"Dear guests, today has been a remarkable day to witness God's goodness and love for this family. Let us bow our heads to bless the food, nourishing our minds and bodies. Amen!"

After the blessing, guests were guided in an orderly fashion to the abundant food tables by the church's head usher, Etta. Audine told Wayne that it didn't matter if Etta was there to help at the wedding because they'd be married now. She also told Wayne that inviting Etta's suitor to the wedding was fine, and if he wanted to help

Etta on their wedding day, that was okay too. He happily agreed to assist Etta.

"Did you enjoy the wedding, and wasn't Audine a stunning bride? I thought Wayne's gesture for Violet and Mason was truly wonderful, wasn't it, Maria?" Clarence asked.

"You must think I'm stupid, Clarence! I saw what you and that two-bit whore were doing up there! Do the words I Love You " and I Love You Too " sound familiar? Huh!?! This is the second time I've seen you do dirty things with that whore, and this time it's right in church!" Maria hissed.

"Shhh, lower your voice, Maria-we're in church, for God's sake!" Clarence exclaimed, gripping Maria's arm.

"No, you be quiet! You both can go to hell!" Maria shouted, standing abruptly and causing her chair to fall to the floor. She then stormed off, leaving the guests at their table in stunned silence.

"Is she okay?" Cornelia, Rick's wife, asked with a worried frown etched on her forehead.

"She'll be fine. She's been moody and acting strangely due to the upcoming new baby. She gets tired easily and, honestly, she wants another one after this. Then all three of them will drive me crazy!" he said, trying to hide his embarrassment with humor. It worked, as everyone, including Ricks, was smiling and holding Cornelia's hand.

"Everyone, the food is ready. The plates are placed on the left and right sides of the table," Etta announced.

Everyone stood up from their seats at the table where Clarence was sitting. They let their wives go first, with the husbands following in a single file. Before heading to the food table, they all approached the table of Wayne and Audine.

"Thanks for being my friend and best man today, Clarence," Wayne said as he stood and reached across the table to shake Clarence's hand warmly. "Audine and I truly appreciate what you're doing with our house, making it bigger for our family. But soon, this beautiful woman here, whom I'm proud to call my daughter, will be leaving us to become a teacher. And in another two years, my son Mason will be gone too," he said, gesturing toward Violet. She looked up from her plate, filled with hot, fresh food, and smiled sweetly at Clarence, who nodded in response. Mason, ignoring Clarence, continued eating a mound of potato salad.

The extra rooms are necessary because we plan to expand our family soon. After we return from New York in a week, you won't need to stop by to care for Violet and Mason anymore, as I won't be going back to work. Violet is leaving soon, and then it'll just be my husband, Mason, and me. Before you leave, is everything okay, Clarence?" she asked after shoving a forkful of baked ham.

"What do you mean?" Clarence asked, confused by her question.

"Well, we saw Maria storm out of here, and she looked quite upset. Is everything okay? Is there a problem with the baby? I must admit, she's already showing quite a bit. Humph! Do you think you all might be expecting another set of twins, perhaps boys this time? That would be something, Violet," said Audine, chuckling as she dabbed the corners of her mouth with a grease-stained napkin.

"Well, I'm sure Maria will be fine," said Violet, clearing her throat as she took a long sip of lemonade.

"Well, after you finish teacher's college, you'll be on your way to a wonderful job and may meet a kind man you'll marry and start a family with. Perhaps you'll end up like Maria with twins! But before having children, remember getting married, just as I did. Wayne and I are already excited to start our family," Audine said, smiling up at Wayne.

"So, that means you'll be the older brother to your mother and Wayne's new children when they arrive, right, Mason?" Clarence asked, leaning forward toward Mason.

Mason fixed Clarence with an intense, fevered glare that made Clarence step back; his clenched jaw signaled hostility, as if he was ready to leap over the table and lash out.

Clarence thought, confused by Mason's gesture, 'Get away from this table right now. Something's got this boy looking to fight.' But why? He and my son are best friends.

"Well, I'm going to grab some of that food before it's all gone. I see some of those young men in uniform already going for a second plate," Clarence said, walking away.

"Will you be coming by this week? Audine and I are leaving for New York City on the train tonight at eight. Deacon Chester and Deacon Vance will drive us to the station. I also spoke with Ricks, who said he and about six of his men will follow us in their cars, while the rest will take the wives home. We need you to watch our son and daughter for one more week; then it will be done. You've been a wonderful friend, Clarence," said Wayne.

"I'll be there after the reception ends and cleanup begins. I do not doubt that you'll want the leftovers, so I'll ask them to pack everything into my truck. Violet,

Mason, and I will bring it all inside when we arrive at your house."

"Thank you, Clarence. You know, Maria is very blessed to have you, but I'm the lucky one today, way luckier," Audine said, squeezing Wayne's thigh. Wayne felt Audine's hand travel further up his thigh, getting noticeably close to his crotch.

"Ahem," Wayne said as he cleared his throat and dabbed the corner of his mouth with his dinner napkin. "Don't forget where we are, Mrs. Collins. We'll have all week at that Harlem hotel and other plans I've made for us." He whispered into her ear with a mischievous smile and a glint in his eyes.

"Violet, right?" the handsome six-foot-tall young Black man in his army uniform asked, smiling at her.

"Yes, I'm Violet, and you are?" Violet asked, curious about who this man was.

"Good afternoon, Violet. My name is Harold Clark. My mother and father used to attend church here, and I wanted to come by to say hello and congratulate your parents," he said.

"Wait, you're Harold Clark, Nelson and Dorothy Clark's son?" Wayne asked as he stood up from his chair.

"Yes sir, that's correct, I am their son, Lieutenant Harold Clark. I enlisted in the army immediately after finishing school seven years ago, when I was eighteen. I'm currently home on a visit until I go back to the base in Georgia in two weeks," he said, stepping forward to shake Wayne's hand.

"I can't believe what a fine young man you've become! Audine, do you remember Harold? My God, you were just a child the last time we saw you and your family, when my former wife and I were here. Well, you've probably heard what happened to Lena," Wayne said awkwardly.

"Yes, sir, and I'm very sorry about what happened to her," said Harold.

"Oh my!" Audine exclaimed as Wayne assisted her out of her seat. "Harold Clark, I remember you as a baby! How are your parents, and where are they? I'm so glad you could come to see Wayne and I get married today!"

"Over there," he said, pointing at a couple sitting at the corner table on the other side, who waved and blew kisses at Wayne and Audine.

"Wayne, come on. Let's go over there to say hello and also greet everyone else who came to wish us well," said Audine as she waved back to Nelson and Dorothy.

"Excuse me, ma'am, sir. May I have permission to talk to your daughter for a moment?" asked Harold.

"You may, son," Wayne said as he and Audine moved away from the table. Audine then approached Harold and hugged him.

"She's leaving for college in a few weeks to study to become a teacher. However, you have our permission to court her properly. We'll return in a week so that you can ask her father then. I'm confident he'll say yes," Audine whispered, briskly tapping his shoulder. She smiled and nodded as she and Wayne headed to see Harold's parents, who were delighted to see the newly married couple. Imagine that: Violet will be a teacher, and if all goes well with Harold, she'll become the wife of a Black army officer! His parents are well-off with a beautiful home. Humph! Maria will go crazy, especially when we host one of the biggest weddings in New Orleans!" Audine thought to herself,

"Hey, Mason, how have you been?" Harold asked as he stepped forward to shake Mason's hand.

"Hi, Harold, glad to see you," said Mason as he and Harold shook hands.

"You got taller, Mason!" Harold exclaimed, stepping back and admiring how tall he had become.

"And you got older!" Mason said as they both burst into laughter.

"Hello, Soldier," Clarence said, balancing two dinner plates, each overflowing with hot food and bread.

"Good afternoon, Mr. Margaret. It's a pleasure to see you after all these years, sir. How are things on your farm, and how is your family?" asked Harold, standing straight. Violet watched Harold with admiration, impressed by his display as a young, handsome Black soldier with perfect manners. However, she was quickly brought back to reality when she heard Clarence's voice, as both men engaged in a brief yet deep conversation.

Harold is such a handsome man, yet among all the unmarried women here at this reception, he chooses to talk to me. But my heart belongs to Clarence, Violet thought to herself, smiling.

"Violet, would it be okay if we sat at the front of the church to talk for a while? Your father and mother said it was fine," Harold asked.

"Oh, yes. If they said it was fine with them, then certainly, we can talk. Let me gather up my gloves and flowers," she said. She quickly gathered her belongings from the edge of the table. As she stepped away from the table, she and Clarence briefly exchanged glances.

He smiled and moved to the table, placing the two plates of food in front of him. Ricks was engaged in a lively discussion, making everyone at the table burst into laughter. Clarence, sitting alone, tried to appear cheerful, but he watched as Harold offered his arm to Violet, and then they exited the fellowship hall. Harold and Violet sat inside the church vestibule on a single wooden pew. Harold held her flowers as he helped her sit, then took his seat.

"I understand that congratulations are for you, Violet. My mother mentioned that she received a letter from your mother, informing her that you earned a certificate and an award for speaking French-Creole, along with a gift that your father left for you. That's wonderful, and I'm very happy for you! Your mother also said you're leaving for Virginia in a few weeks to begin at Teachers College?" he asked.

"Thank you. I'll leave for Virginia right after my parents return from their trip to New York, which is the week after Thanksgiving. I plan to depart on Sunday, right after church. The letter I received on Friday stated that classes will start on Tuesday because some of the women attending will be traveling and need rest, and we also need to collect our books. Additionally, we'll have lunch tea with the college President after the early morning classes on Tuesday," Violet said, trying to be gracious.

"That seems like a busy week ahead once you're settled in. Luckily, it's not too far from where I am stationed. If you're okay with it, I'd love to visit and maybe take you out for coffee. I can also stop by to take you to church on Sundays. Would that be alright, Violet?" He raised his eyebrows and smiled, hoping she would say yes.

"Well, I should talk to my parents first because I'll be attending an all-Black women's college. I need to find out the rules, especially if I won't be properly chaperoned. Can I get back to you later?" she asked.

"Yes, of course. I understand completely because you'll be there alone, and I wouldn't want anyone to hurt you. How about we go back inside for some cake and coffee? I'll ask your parents if it's okay to visit you, and then I'll give you my address, where I'm stationed. When you get to Virginia, write to me and let me know your decision," he said.

Harold rose from the pew and offered his arm to Violet as he escorted her back into the fellowship hall. Maria stepped out of the shadows, peering from behind the wall where Violet and Harold had been sitting just moments before. *Humph! If only he knew what I saw, he wouldn't want that unclean whore who kissed my husband!* Maria thought bitterly. After the walk outside, it was getting quite cold, and since she had stormed out of the fellowship hall without a coat, she felt the November chill. *All I want is a hot meal, coffee, and to go home to my precious children. I don't want to be around Audine, her daughter—who's a real whore— and my poor excuse of a husband, Clarence.*

"The three hypocrites!" she muttered quietly. As she passed the pew to enter the fellowship hall, Maria noticed Violet's crumpled white gloves from the wedding lying near her bouquet. She quickly grabbed the gloves, slipped them into her cloth purse, and snapped it shut. Straightening her shoulders and posture, Maria strode back into the reception, which was in full swing. She went directly to the table, sat down, and eagerly ate the food Clarence had prepared. Acting as if nothing had happened earlier, she joined the conversation with Rick's wife, Cornelia, laughing along with everyone at the table and completely ignoring

Clarence, who was glancing repeatedly at Violet, who was deep in conversation with Harold Clark.

At six o'clock, Wayne and Audine Collins left the fellowship hall to catch the eight o'clock train for their two-day ride to New York.

CHAPTER SEVENTEEN

Harlem, New York

The Teresa Hotel

"We finally made it! After two days on the train, we're back in New York. I can't believe how cold it is, it's freezing!" Audine exclaimed, shivering as Wayne helped her out of her coat, which was too light for the cold evening. They walked over a mile to find a Black taxi driver who took Black passengers from the train station to the Teresa Hotel, Harlem's premier hotel.

"I'm glad we're off that train, sweetheart. As soon as we boarded, I knew we had to make the best of it. The train was chilly, and I had to squeeze our suitcases around our uncomfortable feet, which was especially tough for someone like me with long legs. Honestly, sitting in that Pullman Palace Passenger car was no palace; it was just the truth, humph! It was Southern Railway car number twelve hundred," Wayne said as he hung up his hat and coat.

"The so-called bathroom was terrible. "I'd heard about that railway car, but actually riding in it was something else. It was tiny, had no toilet paper, and after using it, everything would fall onto the tracks as the train moved!" Audine said, sinking into the plush corner chair, its backrest pressing against her neck.

"Well, all I can say is thank God Etta packed a nice basket of food and some jars of water and lemonade because by the time we reached Washington, D.C., we still had enough to continue to New York. Now, we're here, Mrs. Audine Collins," said Wayne.

"Ummm! I love the sound of that name, Mrs. Audine Collins. That means I'm yours for the rest of our lives. I'm never going to stray away from you, not like Lena did."

Audine said, rising from her chair to wrap her arms around Wayne's neck. Audine stopped short and detected the look of irritation on Wayne's face. His jaw tightened and his body stiffened.

"Oh no, Wayne, I'm so sorry! I let my big mouth get the better of me; I didn't mean to say that, especially now. Please forgive me," said Audine, covering her mouth and wincing.

"You know, Audine, I came to New York hoping we could start anew because our last visit here was during a very sad time. I arrived crying and left even more upset. Despite everything we went through back home, I took you back with the promise that you'd never mention Lena's name again. Yet, now we're married, and you still bring her up. Why? You can go straight to hell!" Wayne shouted, furious at her comment.

Audine, stunned by her husband's explosion, slowly stepped back.

"Wayne, I didn't mean what I just said. I would never say anything to hurt you. Please forgive me. I'd like us to work this out, and my sister, Cee-Cee, and her husband, Hubert, are excited to see us tomorrow for dinner. Oh, please, let's not fight. We just got married, and I love you," she said.

Wayne, feeling disgusted by Audine's mention of Lena's indiscretion, felt confused and hurt. He wondered why she couldn't just leave that part of his life alone since it was over.

"Audine, come here," Wayne said, gesturing for Audine to sit next to him on the large, soft bed.

Audine walked slowly to the bed, sat beside Wayne, and looked down, feeling ashamed.

"Listen to me," he said, pulling her closer and cupping her chin to make her gaze meet his. "I'm really sorry for what I just said, telling you to go to hell. That was a terrible thing for me to say, especially to you; you're my wife. Please forgive me."

"Of course, I forgive you, Wayne. You're my husband, and I should have never mentioned Lena," she said.

"Then promise me you'll never mention her name again. Lena is dead and gone forever. Please show some respect for what I endured. I never brought up your husband, Rudell, did I?" he asked.

"Yes, you're right," Audine replied, visibly shaken.

Wayne said, "Let's agree not to mention Lena or Rudell. We are here, married, and have declared before God, family, and friends that we will love and cherish each other until death. I intend to honor that promise, and I expect you to do the same."

"You're right, Wayne, and I promise I won't mention Lena again," Audine said earnestly.

Wayne drew her closer and claimed her lips. Their kisses deepened as the warmth of his tongue twirled inside Audine. In one motion, Audine positioned herself and straddled his lap. Pulling up her wool skirt, she revealed only the garters holding up her stockings. Noticing her daring choice to go without the panties she typically wore, and which he had removed during their lovemaking, he was surprised. Watching his facial expression, Audine grinned wickedly at him. Unable to wait any longer, Wayne unzipped his trousers, eager for Audine. Pulling out his erection aggressively with both hands, Wayne tilted his head back and waited as he finally felt Audine using the tip of her tongue to make circular motions up and down his length before she took it all in.

"Ohhh, Audine!" he groaned aloud, overwhelmed by the mix of pleasure and pain as she nibbled and twirled her tongue over his large erection. Audine, pleased with her view, anticipated what her husband would do next. She paused briefly to stand and remove her clothing. Wayne then followed her lead until they were both completely naked.

"God, you're beautiful," Wayne said, gazing lustfully at his wife. Suddenly, he grabbed her waist, wrapped his arm around her knee, and scooped her up. Audine let out a joyful squeal, showing she trusted his strength to lift her five-foot-two, 185-pound frame.

Wayne grinned and said, "Bet you didn't know I was this strong," as he effortlessly laid her on the bed.

"Come here, Wayne. I'm waiting for you to take care of me," said Audine.

Wayne went to Audine and parted her thighs wide open to receive his thrusting heat. Audine had massive breasts, but he noticed that they were a lot fuller than they were before, as he took one and nursed on it until she began to moan loudly. Then, using his knees to spread her thighs further, he could feel her womanly warmth. As Audine held onto his shoulders, Wayne penetrated, sinking deeper inside with fast and powerful thrusts. Audine's moans grew louder, making Wayne thrust faster and deeper.

Wayne cried out uncontrollably as a wave of pleasure surged through him, spilling inside Audine from his throbbing erection. Audine started to experience intense orgasmic contractions, causing her to breathe in convulsive gasps. However, she didn't want Wayne to stop. After attempting to keep their secret from everyone during their after-work activities, she now relished the freedom to express their love as husband and wife openly.

"Are you alright?" he asked, smiling as he turned onto his side and pulled Audine closer. He gave her generous, rounded buttocks a firm slap and an affectionate squeeze.

"I know you want me to do that whenever we finish. I was initially worried it might hurt you, but it seems you do like it".

"I don't like it; I love it, and I expect you to do it for me whenever we're finished," she said, pausing with a wicked gleam in her eyes.

"It'll be my pleasure to do that for you again and again," he said.

Audine said, "There's something I need to tell you, but I wanted to wait until after the wedding."

Her tone captured his attention, causing his eyes to widen. "What's wrong? Is everything all right? Are our children safe?" He sat up, frowning, and focused entirely on Audine.

"Do you remember back in October when we started going to your house after work to be together? It was when we realized that we were more than friends. We broke the rules by waiting until we got married. We couldn't wait; at least I couldn't. I was falling in love with you, especially after I saw how wonderful you are with our children," she said.

"So, what's wrong, Audine? You're not making much sense," Wayne said.

"After spending a lot of time at your house, I noticed my monthly flow was twelve days late. My breasts began to hurt and swell. Do you remember the day I asked you to go to work and let me stay at your place because I wasn't feeling well?"

Wayne said, "Yes, I remember that day. You mentioned you felt sick and stayed at my house all day until I finished work to take you home."

"While you were working, I called Mrs. Wade to come over to your house because she was nearby visiting another patient. When she arrived, she seemed quite surprised to see me answer your door, and I think she realized I had been over. I begged her not to tell anyone, especially our Pastor. She agreed but was very reserved. She examined me, looked at my breasts, feet, and belly, and asked if I was eating more, feeling hungry all the time, or in the mornings when I felt like vomiting. I confirmed she asked about my late monthly flow, and when I said it was late, she told me I was going to have a baby! I asked her when, and she replied that it would be early July. Mrs. Wade suggested we set up a time for her to visit again soon, since everything was happening so quickly. She congratulated me and advised that it would be best for us to get married, as having a baby outside marriage wouldn't look good. That's why I wanted to wait until we were alone after the wedding. I'm having your first child, Wayne," she said. Wayne was silent, staring intently at Audine before speaking.

"You're having our child?" he asked softly. "Oh my God, Audine, I'm going to be a father! This is the second-best day of my life!" Then he wept softly.

"Then tell me, what was your first best day?" she asked, gently wiping his tears. "The day we said I do," he replied. He then got up, turned off the lights, and made love to Audine again until dawn.

CHAPTER EIGHTEEN

New Orleans, Louisiana

Saturday Evening

"I placed the final wedding gifts in your parents' bedroom, and the cash was hidden under their mattress. The food has also been stored. Based on what we've put away, you and Mason have enough for Sunday dinner through the end of next week," Clarence announced to Violet and Mason. They were now in their new bedrooms at Wayne's house. After organizing everything, Mason went directly to his room and slammed the door, ignoring Clarence's calls to help carry in more food and gifts.

As Violet undressed, her thoughts drifted back to the wedding reception. She looked at the paper with Harold Clark's address, where he was stationed. Harold, his father Nelson, and Wayne were engaged in conversation, and Wayne's hearty laughter would have made him lean on Nelson's shoulder to support himself.

"Violet, Harold would like to see you when you have some free time from your studies. He's becoming quite fond of you, especially after some of your conversations. He thinks you're a very intelligent and thoughtful woman," Dorothy, Harold's mother, said while holding hands with Audine. Both women were smiling warmly at Violet.

"I have already discussed with my husband, and he agrees that Harold is a good young man to court Violet. Therefore, we're comfortable with them beginning to see each other once Violet has settled in," said Audine. Without hesitation, Violet watched as Audine and Dorothy quickly approached Harold and whispered to him. Harold looked at Violet, smiled, and appeared delighted by what was said.

"Violet!"

Hearing her name called jarred her out of her thoughts about the events at the wedding reception hours earlier. She turned to see Clarence standing at the doorway of her new bedroom. Since relocating to Wayne's house, which has a second floor, her bedroom has become much larger. Mason's room is just down the hall.

"I've been calling you for the past minute. Didn't you hear me?" Clarence asked, frowning as he approached Violet and hugged her.

"I'm sorry, Clarence. I've been lost in deep thought," she said, hugging him tightly.

"About what? Come, sit down because you've been quiet and well, not looking quite like yourself," said

Clarence as he gestured for her to sit beside him on her new bed. They sat, their arms wrapped tightly around each other.

"Clarence, I'm frightened. I'm very anxious about leaving in two weeks for college, and both my mother and Harold's mother are urging him and me to begin courting. He even shared the address where he's stationed and is urging me to write to him as soon as I arrive in Virginia because he told me something in confidence during our conversation," said Violet.

"What did he say to you?" Clarence asked, alarmed by Violet's admission that Harold would overwhelm her.

She whispered, her gaze lowered, 'You must not tell anyone what I'm about to say because Harold told me that only people in the army are supposed to know this.'

"Harold told me about a crazy man in Germany named Hitler. I can't recall his first name, but Harold mentioned he's been hearing rumors that this man is unstable and causes trouble in Germany by holding meetings in beer halls. He gets the attendees excited by shouting and waving his arms, to the point that they leave crying and shouting due to their happiness with what they hear. Harold fears that if this isn't stopped, it could lead to a war worldwide," she whispered, her eyes wide with fear. Clarence listened carefully, paying close attention to her face after she finished speaking.

"I've heard enough," he snapped. "The Got-damned nerve of that young man, coming here and spreading lies to you in our church! I should go tell Audine, his mother, and our pastor what he said. Don't you see these lies just to make himself look good, probably because he's an army officer? Humph! If people here find out about this, it'll scare them more than the Klan!" Clarence said with anger, then abruptly stood up and paced around her room.

This was a side of Clarence she had never seen before—a man on the verge of losing control, which frightened her. She stood up, approached Clarence from behind, and wrapped her arms around his tight waist.

"I'm not going to write or see him, so you don't need to worry about that," Violet said softly.

"There's something else that scares me more than anything else, and I don't know how to tell you," Violet looked down at her feet, avoiding his gaze.

"Violet, please tell me what's wrong. Are you unwell, or did Harold say something to upset you? If he did, I feel I have no choice but to confront him in front of his family and tell him he's spreading false rumors about a man elsewhere in the world. I swear, if he- "

"Clarence, no! That's not it at all!" she said, shaking her head at him. "Sit down, because the room feels like it's spinning," she added, trudging back to her bed and collapsing in exhaustion.

"What's the matter? I could tell something was wrong just by the way you've been acting," Clarence said, sitting beside her.

Over the past few weeks, I've been feeling very unwell. Almost daily, especially in the mornings, I feel nauseous and sometimes vomit. I have stomach pain, and my woman's monthly flow hasn't come for a month. My breasts are sore all the time, and I've been coughing a lot. That's why we arrived late at the wedding, because I threw up and felt dizzy. My mother thought it was because I had been studying too hard, then taking the exam, and afterward attending the wedding.

However, I didn't tell her about my monthly flow not coming through because I didn't want to worry her."

Clarence suddenly felt a chill run through his body.

This can't be, we only spent a few times together! Clarence thought, stunned, recalling the similar experience Maria had when she was pregnant with the child she's now carrying.

He whispered in astonishment, "Are you sure?"

"Yes, I'm very sure. I'll even show you. Close the door," she said, gesturing toward the open door. Then, she undressed.

Clarence's heart pounded as he shut the door behind him. Turning around, he saw Violet standing, facing him, her upper body exposed. Clearly, her breasts had significantly increased in size since he last saw her, now twice as large and no longer firm.

"You're expecting my child. I can see it in your face and from what you've told me. I need to make this right and do my duty by my wife, my children, you, and our baby."

"What are you going to do, Clarence?" Violet asked.

A sudden sigh left his lips. "I'm going to tell Maria about us and that you're carrying my child. Then I will tell her that I plan to marry you."

CHAPTER NINETEEN

"Thank you, Deacon and Mrs. Moss, for going out of your way to drive me and my family home. My husband, Ricks, and his men will be at the church for some time, packing up all the food from the reception as well as the wedding gifts. I must admit, I was quite surprised by the number of gifts they received," Maria said as Deacon Moss moved around to let Maria and her family out of the back seat.

"You're welcome, Maria. We noticed how quickly your husband and Ricks began tidying up right after Audine and Wayne left. I'm also pleased that Ricks had enough men to escort a car full of their wives and enough to follow Audine and Wayne to the train station until they boarded. I must say, Ricks and his men really know how to look out for all of us." He said.

Deaconess Moss expressed her confusion about why Audine wouldn't allow guests to take food home. She emphasized that Audine, as a woman of faith and charity, should have been more generous. Some Sisters of Charity, who had helped set up, whispered that Audine had told Etta to pack all the food for her new house, forgetting that it was no longer her house or her food, but theirs.

"The house is in Wayne's name. The Sisters felt disappointed, especially during tough times when families hoped to gather some food."

Moss added that Audine married a wonderful man who welcomed Violet and Mason as his own, yet believes she won't change, because she remains a deceitful gossip and unkind.

"Berline, that's enough talk about Audine," Deacon Moss said, raising his voice to interrupt his wife. "I'm sure

Maria wants to get inside to be with her family and rest, especially with that new baby on the way," he added.

"Oh, I'm doing just fine, and so is my child," Maria said with a smile, gently resting a protective hand on her belly.

"Oh, please forgive my rudeness. I shouldn't have been gossiping or speaking unkindly about Audine. I'm so embarrassed," Berline said, pleading with Maria.

"You have nothing to worry about; you were simply sharing your feelings. Thank you both again for the ride home. Are you picking up Violet and Mason for church tomorrow? My husband will come to get me and our family. Wayne informed Clarence that Violet and Mason will stay with you until Sunday evening, after which Clarence will pick them up and take them home," said Maria.

"Yes, that is the plan. When Wayne and Audine come back home, she'll be staying home all the time, according to what Wayne told my wife and me. Won't that be something? Well, you have a good evening, and God bless you all," Deacon Moss said, tipping his hat to Maria. Maria leaned over the window to Berline as the two women hugged and waved farewell. Then she went into the house to join her family.

"So, what did you think about that wedding?" Berline asked as she scooted closer to her husband.

"I'm very happy for them, but something's just not right, honey, especially with Clarence, Maria, and Violet. Mason seemed completely out of it. He acted like he didn't even want to be at the church once he arrived," he said as he started the car.

She asked, astonished, "What do you mean?"

"Well, when we were all asked to bow our heads for prayer, not everyone had their eyes closed up there where they were standing," Deacon Moss said candidly. "I watched something unfold right before my eyes, Berline. Clarence looked at Violet and mouthed the words "*I love you*". And she mouthed back to him, "I love you too". Then they bowed their heads, as if in prayer, alongside everyone else. I'm telling you; I was so taken aback by what I saw! I couldn't believe what I was seeing! There was one more person who also saw the whole thing happen up there."

Berline, seated in unnaturally still silence, went numb upon hearing Clarence declare his love for Violet.

"Oh, my Goodness, who else saw this happen?" she asked.

"Clarence's wife," he said, and then they drove home.

CHAPTER TWENTY

This must have been one of the worst days of my life. I wasn't the only one who saw what my husband and Violet did. I noticed the disgusted look on Deacon Moss's face; when he looked at me, it was clear he knew I was watching. He shook his head and took Berline's hand, as if praying for Wayne and Audine. Maria thought as she quietly wept.

"So, how was the wedding?" Kempton asked as he took her shoulder wrap and handed her a hot cup of coffee. They moved to the kitchen and sat down.

"The food was wonderful. Everyone contributed something to the wedding dinner. There was so much food that everyone expected Audine to tell the Sisters of Charity to let us take some home, especially given the current depression. Of course, the group would set aside enough for her and Wayne. However, Audine refused. She instructed Etta to pack everything and told Ricks, his men, and your father to load up the food and deliver it to her new house. When Etta asked about the plates, pans, and pots used for cooking or given back, Audine looked at her as if the question was crazy and said they were all hers, explaining that if the guests had given her food, it was a gift for her. Therefore, she claimed all the pots, pans, platters, and food as her own," Maria said, shaking her head in disgust.

"That's pretty awful, Ma. I can see why you and Deaconess Moss only prepared a small pie for the wedding dinner while making larger ones for us and her family. I overheard your conversation about it in the kitchen while you were baking," Kempton said, taking a sip of coffee. "Is Dad at Audine and Wayne's new house?" he asked.

"Yes," Maria replied, her spine involuntarily stiffening.

If you only knew what kind of man your father has become, Maria thought, her eyes darkening with pain.

"What's the matter, Ma?" Kempton said. It seems that whenever Dad is brought up here, everyone falls silent. Things have gotten strange around here, especially between Joseph and Mason.

"Your father and I are having some differences that don't involve you. It's something only he and I can fix.", she said.

Kempton asked, without glancing at Maria, "Is that why he's sleeping in the barn?"

Maria couldn't look away from his face, marked by sadness. My God, Clarence is tearing this family apart! she thought angrily.

"Kempton, look at me," she said, her eyes wide with astonishment at what he knew.

Kempton looked up with a detached expression. "Something is happening between your father and me. Will it work itself out? I don't know because we don't have all the answers. What I can tell you is: let your father and me handle what's happening between us. No matter what, this family will get through it. You also said something about Joseph and Mason? What's going on with them?"

"Mason's behavior has been very unusual. He used to be close friends with Joseph, studying and chatting regularly. But that's no longer the case. Mason now isolates himself, no longer walks to school with us, and appears constantly angry. Joseph mentioned that he's afraid of Mason, so he's been spending time with some of the older, very intelligent boys at school. These older boys talk about either going to college or joining the army," said Kempton.

"The army? What's that all about?" asked Maria.

"Oh, I forgot to tell you. Just before you returned home, Harold Clark came by to say hello. I haven't seen him since we were kids. He looks very different now, especially in his army uniform. We talked for a long time about a lot of things".

"About what?" Maria asked, setting her coffee cup aside to focus entirely on Kempton.

"We mainly discussed the army, especially on how Black soldiers are treated and how he became a Lieutenant. His attention to loading a gun, obeying his commanding officer, and studying hard in college helped him stand out among others in his barracks. He also mentioned a wild man named Adolf Hitler, who is causing trouble in Germany. Harold believes we might go to war, but it isn't certain. He suggests I should join the army before any conflict arises, preferably right after I finish school, because I- "

"War? Army?" Maria interrupted before he could finish. She shouted, leaping up so quickly that her chair tipped over and hit the floor with a loud crash. "If you sign up, you'll just be cooking for those white soldiers and cleaning their filthy toilets! Don't listen to Harold! You're not joining any army. There's no need for you to fight for freedom; we don't even have it! Let the white boys fight if there's a war. They're the ones with freedom, not us!" Kempton stood up, picked up the fallen chair, and set it back at the table so Maria could sit down again. Maria widened her eyes at Kempton.

"You listen to me. You're going to college, and as far as the army is concerned, you're not going. And another thing, Harold Clark isn't to come over here unless either I or your father is here. The nerve of that young man coming here without even asking! He saw me and your father at the wedding, so why didn't he ask us if he could visit, especially when we weren't at home?" she demanded.

Kempton explained, "He said he looked for you, but you weren't at the table where you were sitting, and Dad was busy helping Mr. Ricks, and his men pack up all the food. Harold mentioned that everyone was busy, so his father and mother stopped by here briefly to visit, then he had to leave."

"I'm tired and I have something I need to take care of, then I'll return," Maria said. As she got up from her chair, she turned around and was shocked to see her sons and daughters gathered at the door. She clutched her stomach due to the sudden shock. "How long have you been standing here, and what did you hear?"

"When we heard a crash in the kitchen, it scared all of us," Izelle said, her eyes wide with fright.

"Excuse me," Maria said, pushing past her children as she hurried to her bedroom, slamming the door so hard that the entire house shook. Izelle held onto Rosetta, who was crying.

"You didn't tell Ma what you're planning to do?" Izelle whispered to Kempton. Kempton got up from his chair and walked to the sink after finishing his last sip of coffee.

"Nope," he said as he washed and dried the coffee cup.

"Tell Ma what?" Sampson asked, frowning.

Joseph said, "Kempton is joining the army after he finishes school."

CHAPTER TWENTY-ONE

The only light emanating from the wood shack was the dimly lit candle, which gently flickered in the breeze. The window was partially cracked open. Maria was sitting on a three-legged stool in a dark faze.

Maria was furious about the last twenty-four hours; she refused to be humiliated in front of her children and friends. Clarence was unaware that his actions were tearing the family apart, and she felt she needed to act to protect her children and preserve her sanity.

Rising slowly from the stool, she stumbled and grabbed the splintered wood wall, closing her eyes to wait for the dizziness to pass. She rubbed her belly.

She whispered, "Don't worry if it takes the rest of my life; I'll protect and watch over you, though I may end up doing it alone."

She went to the deep corner of the shack and pulled out the wooden box that contained her affirmation tools. After whispering a quick prayer for guidance, she opened the box and selected the tools she'd need to work with: black pins, twine, four pumpkin seeds, a small mound of hog manure, the small black cauldron, matches, dry twigs, and molasses. From her apron pocket, she took the handkerchief she found inside Audine's purse when it fell to the floor. Looking deeper into the box, she discovered a bundle of short sticks held together with twine. She hand-picked these sticks from the woods based on their appearance and scent, then carefully cut them all to an even length and width, smoothing away any stubble. Untying the small bundle of twenty sticks, she returned them to the box. Taking the first two sticks, she shaped them into a semi-crooked "X" with her fingers. Using pre-cut twine, she wrapped the center until the figure was sturdy. She then placed a pumpkin seed at the top of the sticks to represent a head, ensuring its position was just right. She scooped a small amount of pig excrement and coated the top of one stick with it, quickly working to avoid the rancid smell. She placed the seed atop the excrement. After setting it aside, she pulled out Audine's crumpled, stained, and sticky handkerchief. Upon examining it closely, Maria smiled and whooped in delight.

Audine had even fooled me into believing that she was a sacred widow, preserving her chastity until she remarried, hah! My God, she had Wayne's seed spill onto her handkerchief after taking his manhood into her filthy mouth! The water in the swamp is cleaner than inside hers! Maria thought, disgusted.

After carefully prying it apart, she cut a slit in the center and slipped it over the spirit doll's head. Then she named it Audine Booker Collins and set it aside. Taking the second set of sticks, she created the second spirit doll in the same way, naming this one after Wayne. She attached the seed to the stick with molasses to resemble his head.

"I put molasses on your seed face because you have a kind soul. Audine doesn't deserve a man like you. So, to make Audine go away from you, she will stink just like the hog shit that is smeared on her face and body," said Maria.

After reciting her petition, she tied the two-spirit dolls together, facing away from each other. Maria then unfolded a second handkerchief, which Audine had previously used to wipe up spilled coffee months ago, ·and laid it on the ground. From the box, she took a smaller cloth containing a mixture: ground walnut to make Wayne fall out of love with Audine, slippery elm to silence her from speaking hurtful words, gossip, and lies, red pepper to stir confusion and fights in her marriage with Wayne, dried lemon peels to break their union, and small cedarwood pieces to make Audine move away. To add an extra piece of joy, Maria added a generous smear of the hog excrement on the handkerchief that held Audine's spirit doll. She then placed the two dolls on the coffee-stained cloth and tied them securely with two knots. Lastly, she inserted a black pin into the bottom center of Audine's doll.

"Accomplished, done," said Maira.

The cedarwood chips inside the cauldron began to smolder. Adding one fresher cedarwood chip, she threw the spirit dolls into the cauldron and watched as they disintegrated into ashes. The smell from the excrement permeated the shack so much that Marai had to open the window wider to let the cool night air in to filter out the stench. She hurriedly pulled up the bottom of her apron to her face to take deep breaths of the sweet smell of pies baked earlier in the week.

Maria tugged inside her apron pocket and retrieved the delicate white gloves Violet had left in the church pew. She then looked into the wooden box once more and chose two ribbons: one blue and the other pink.

"You're merely a reckless, ordinary whore seeking my husband's affection, and you are the result of your mother's wicked pride. She will remain barren forever. Meanwhile, you will be cursed with a child possessing both male and female private parts," she said.

Taking the gloves, she grabbed a stick, scooped out some excrement, and smeared it on the palms until they were no longer white.

"Violet Booker, as I pour this shit on you, your life will inevitably fall into ruin. Throughout your journey, you'll find yourself in a circle of darkness alongside others who are just as lost, if not worse. I hope your life deteriorates, and the same goes for the seed in your womb. May it dry up like a raisin under the sun. You are a wicked, foul-smelling woman, and I wish for you never to find happiness. Your health will decline into suffering; no doctor will be able to help you later. Your hair will fall out, and pus-filled boils will appear on your face, causing people to turn away. This comes from the depths of my heartbroken soul," she recited.

She carefully pressed the gloves together, tied the ribbons nine times, then threw the gloves into the hot cauldron, watching as the contents turned to ashes. She added the remaining sticks and cedar chips to the cauldron. From her apron pocket, she pulled out a stubbed cigar, lit it, closed her eyes, and took a long inhale of the sweet-smelling smoke. In each corner of the small shed, Maria blew two long clouds of smoke until the air was thick with it. She then moved to the window, pushed it open further, feeling the cool breeze coming through.

"Que *les esprits font ce qu'ils doivent* - Let the spirits do what they must", she proclaimed.

Once she announced her proclamation, the smoke vanished from the window. She then carefully packed away the tools she had used into her wooden box, except for the vial of goofer dust, which she tucked into her apron pocket. Although the cauldron remained warm to the touch, she was able to lift it. She carried it a few yards to the lake behind her house, reaching as close to the water as possible, and poured the contents into the lake. Standing back, a shiver ran through her body from the cold November air. Her eyes burned with despair.

"You truly don't care, do you, Clarence?" she yelled, devastated by his betrayal and insensitivity. Turning to walk away, Maria clutched her stomach and wiped away her tears.

After a quick cleaning and returning the cauldron to its place, she silently went back to the house and headed to her bedroom. She removed her garments, which carried a strong scent of cedarwood, folded them carefully, and placed them on the floor to be washed the next morning. The large water basin she prepared earlier was still warm. She used a lavender-scented washcloth to wash herself, filling the room with a sweet aroma. She then massaged a few drops of lavender and rainwater into her skin. Satisfied, she put on a clean nightgown. She climbed into bed, lying on her back, gazing into the darkness of her quiet house. Sleep did not come.

CHAPTER TWENTY-TWO

Harlem, New York

The Saturday Evening Supper Club

"Can we order another round of drinks, please?" Wayne had to shout to the waitress over the loud music from the band. The dance floor was crowded with patrons dancing, and laughter echoed at every table. The Saturday Evening Supper Club was one of Harlem's most popular venues, renowned for its live music, delectable food, and fine drinks. On weekends, guests arriving at 7:00 a.m. enjoyed breakfast, music, and live entertainment. Audine, Wayne, her sister Cee-Cee, and her husband Hubert had been visiting the club every night since Audine and Wayne arrived, even catching a breakfast show there.

"Bet they don't have this back home in New Orleans, Audine," Cee-Cee said, as she flung her head back in laughter.

"I know one thing; this has to be the best time I've ever had in my life!" Audine said, laughing jovially. "I wish we could stay here for another week! We've been here every night, even coming for breakfast to see a show, hah! We'd never see something like this happen back home in New Orleans! I feel like I am the happiest woman in the world." Audine said, nestling closer to Wayne.

"I'm happy for you both," Hubert said. "A toast," he added, raising his glass. "May you both find happiness for the rest of your lives, grow old together, and be blessed with a new family."

"To Wayne and Audine!" Cee-Cee said.

They all raised their glasses and sipped the sweet wine when, suddenly, a sharp pain and wave of nausea struck Audine, causing her to drop her glass, which shattered on the floor.

"Audine, what's wrong with you?" Cee-Cee asked, looking alarmed.

Feeling another wave of nausea, Audine hurriedly bolted from her chair, causing it to topple onto the floor. Wayne stood up to go after Audine, but Cee-Cee stopped him.

"Stay here, Wayne. I'm sure she'll be fine, but let me see what's wrong with my sister," she said as she rushed toward the ladies' room.

"Cee-Cee, please check on my wife and see what's wrong!" he shouted. Wayne sank into his seat, covering his face. Hubert and other patrons who witnessed the incident approached the table to offer comfort.

"Audine, Audine! Where are you?" Cee-Cee yelled, rushing into the bathroom. Thank God there's nobody in here, Cee-Cee thought with relief.

Loud groaning echoed from the last stall. As Cee-Cee hurried over, she heard a sudden, high-pitched scream that made her freeze in place.

"Audine, this is Cee-Cee. What's happening inside?"

"I-I need help," Audine faltered. "Please help me, Cee-Cee."

Cee-Cee pushed open the stall door and gasped at the scene before her. Audine, sitting on the toilet, was bent so far forward that only the crown of her curls was visible. What shocked her most was the bloodstained underwear and a large, gelatinous mass that looked like bloody fecal matter. The odor was overwhelming, prompting her to take out a handkerchief to cover her nose.

"I-I didn't arrive in time, Cee-Cee. I made a big mess here," Audine said, voice trembling.

"Was it all that food you've been eating since you got here?" Cee-Cee asked.

"No," Audine answered, slowly raising her head. "Wayne and I just lost our baby." Then she broke down crying uncontrollably.

CHAPTER TWENTY-THREE

New Orleans

Monday

The sun shone brightly through the window. Violet was awake early. After an intense night of intimacy with Clarence, she felt elated upon waking. He left her bed while she slept to rest on the pallet in the spare room being renovated, so Mason wouldn't catch him if he needed anything. She rose and looked in the mirror, noticing her breasts were sore and swollen, not only from Clarence's rough fondling and pinching but also because, upon grasping and examining them, it was confirmed she was carrying his child.

"Your breasts are going to get much bigger, and your belly too. But before I tell my wife, we need to see Mrs. Wade, the midwife, to confirm that you are carrying my child," she recalled Clarence saying to her earlier that evening.

The sudden wave of nausea struck, and she barely had time to grab her nightgown and slip it over her head. She carried the garment in her hand and rushed to the kitchen, where she vomited into the sink. Turning on the faucet, she took a cup, filled it with hot water, and poured it into the sink to help wash away the residue. She then slipped her nightgown back on. When she turned around, Mason was standing behind her.

"Oh, my goodness, Mason, you scared me!" she said, alarmed. "How long have you been standing there?"

"Long enough to see that you do this every morning," he said with a look of disgust.

"I've been awake all night. At first, I thought I was dreaming because I heard sounds that seemed like someone was hurt. I got out of bed to check what was happening. As I moved closer to your room, the noises grew louder. I turned the doorknob to look inside. When I peeked in, I saw you and Mr. Clarence. He wasn't wearing any clothes, and neither were you! He was touching you all over with his hands; your legs were apart, and the more you called his name, the faster he went inside your private parts! He's my best friend's father, and Mr. Clarence is supposed to be watching over us! You know what? When Ma and Dad find out, it's going to be terrible, not just for you but for Mr. Clarence, too. Right now, I hate both of you!" Shoving her aside, he grabbed his lunch sack and bolted out the door, slamming it behind him.

Violet stood in the middle of the kitchen, silent and stunned. *Oh no, he knows! she thought, blinking back tears of shame. She pulled out a chair, cradled her head in her hands, and rocked slowly. Is he going to tell Ma? Oh my God, she thought frantically. She'll beat me, and Maria will kill us!*

"Nobody is going to hurt you, I promise", Violet whispered, looking down at her belly.

Feeling another wave coming, she grasped the edge of the table to steady herself and let the dizziness pass. Her heart was pounding uncontrollably as she quietly moved toward the front door and stepped outside. There was no sign of Mason. It's as if he disappeared into thin air. The only person she saw outside in the front yard was Clarence, who was hammering on a wooden plank. Looking up, he stared at Violet with a furrowed brow.

"Did you sleep well?" he asked, setting the hammer aside and walking to the doorway where Violet was waiting. He spread his arms wide, and she went to him. Clarence lifted her, making her squeal and laugh.

"I slept very well, thanks to you, Mr. Margaret," she whispered into his ear, tightening her embrace around his neck.

Clarence wondered about Mason's unusual behavior, noticing he slammed the door and hurried away as if fleeing from someone. Despite greeting him, Mason ignored him entirely. Clarence questioned whether something was bothering Mason and considered whether he should speak to him.

"No, there's nothing wrong with Mason. He's just nervous about school and the talk going around that he might graduate early due to his grades. When my mother and Wayne return, the schoolmaster and Mason's teachers have asked to meet about his future," she brushed her soft hair away from her eye.

"As long as he remains unaware of us, since you were quite loud last night, young lady," he said with a wink, giving her a playful pat on her backside.

"It's nearly eight o'clock. Can you wash up and get dressed so I can take you to see Mrs. Wade? I need to know if you're having a child. If Mrs. Wade confirms it, I'll inform my wife, and you'll need to let your mother and Wayne know when they come back. After everyone is informed, I will plan for us."

Maria will finally learn the truth about Clarence and that I am the woman he's in love with! Violet thought, feeling grateful that Clarence was brave enough to tell his wife that he had finally fallen in love.

"What are you so happy about?" Clarence asked.

Violet said, taking a deep breath, "I'm worried about what will happen after I tell my mother and Wayne about us and the baby. Mason knows about us, too; he saw us last night, Clarence."

"Oh no, how did that happen? How did he even spot us?" said Clarence.

"Do you remember last night when you told me that I'm having your child because you saw how this happened with your wife?" she asked.

Clarence nodded.

"I felt so happy knowing this could happen. Last night, when we were together, I couldn't help but call out your name loudly, and you cried out loudly before it was over. The noise woke Mason, who came to my room, thinking I was in danger. When he opened the door, he saw us without clothes, with you on top of me," she explained.

"That explains why he rushed out of the house so quickly. If he's aware, we should hurry to visit Mrs. Wade before her day begins. You go ahead and get ready. I'll put the tools away and start the truck, so we're prepared to leave," said Clarence.

"I'll get ready as fast as I can," said Violet. She quickly kissed Clarence and went inside to change into her clothes.

Clarence thought he needed to either talk to Mason about the situation with Violet or wait until Audine and Wayne returned. No matter what, chaos was inevitable, he reasoned as he climbed into the truck and started it.

It looks like Mrs. Wade is still here, as I see the same brown leather bag she always carries when she visits. See it over there?" Clarence said, pointing to a large bag resting on a wooden chair. Clarence eased the truck to a stop and turned off the engine.

Violet sat staring at Mrs. Wade's lovely small home. Most of the black midwives lived in squalor, and the conditions of their homes were quite unpleasant. Mrs. Wade's home was neat, clean, and pleasing to the eye. She also had a well to draw fresh water and a large vegetable and herb garden.

"Are you ready?" Clarence asked as he opened the truck door for her. Violet stepped out, and they headed toward Mrs. Wade's house. She was already looking out from behind the lace curtains. Before Clarence could raise his hand to knock, Mrs. Wade suddenly flung open the door.

"Well, good morning, Clarence. How are you?" she said, smiling as she greeted him. However, internally, she was puzzled about why Maria's husband was at her door, accompanied by Audine's daughter.

"Good morning, Mrs. Wade. It's nice to see you again. Do you know Violet Booker, Audine's daughter?" he asked.

"Why yes, of course, I do. Good morning, young lady. How are you?" Mrs. Wade asked, peering over her gold-rimmed glasses that balanced on the bridge of her nose.

"Good morning, ma'am. It's very nice to see you," said Violet.

"So, what brings you here, Clarence? I would have expected you to be with your wife. Is Maria okay?" she inquired.

"Well, uh, Violet and I were wondering if we could come in to talk to you? Are you getting ready to make visits?" Clarence asked.

"No visits until tomorrow morning. I was very busy yesterday," she said, motioning for them to come in. "Please sit down. As I mentioned, I had a hectic day delivering four babies. Mrs. Wallison had twin girls, and her husband was so overjoyed that he cried when he saw them, holding the tiny ones in his wife's arms. I also delivered two more babies. Mrs. Leatherbond, in the fourth ward, had her first child, a boy, and eight houses down, Mrs. Dicole had her third, a girl. Since all deliveries went smoothly, I don't need to visit today. Your wife is scheduled for next week, though. So, what brings you both here?" she asked, looking curious.

"Well, Violet needs an examination. She might be expecting, and we want you to check on her," Clarence said directly.

"You're what?" Mrs. Wade asked, alarmed, as she looked directly at Violet.

"But you're planning to attend that all-Black women's college in Virginia to become a teacher, right?" she asked, her voice tinged with confusion as she pushed her glasses up. Mrs. Wade sat upright in her chair, giving Violet her full focus.

"Yes, ma'am. I haven't had my monthly blood flow for two months, so Clarence, I mean Mr. Clarence, brought me here to see you and have you examine me," said Violet.

"I'm surprised by this news, Violet," Mrs. Wade said, shaking her head. "I have many questions for you. First, do your mother and Wayne know about this?"

"No, ma'am, they don't know anything," Violet replied, her eyes fixed on her clasped hands.

"I see. They're in for a big surprise and disappointment when they return. No doubt Audine is especially shocked because she's expecting a baby too".

"What?" Violet gasped.

Oh my, didn't your mother tell you she's expecting a baby late next summer? I guess that explains her rush to get married. But you're not even married yet. I'm curious—why isn't the father of your child here? If you haven't had your monthly flow since September and it's now November, then you're definitely going to have a baby. So, who is the father?"

"I am," Clarence responded. "I'm the father of our child. Violet and I are deeply in love. We found that out months ago, but I already knew, even before she told me how she felt. My wife and I have not been getting along for over a year now, and to be honest, if it hadn't been for her having our child, I would've left Maria and gone on to be with Violet. Things just got a little mixed up, but I am going to do right by Violet. I'm leaving Maria to marry Violet," he said.

Mrs. Wade sat in stunned silence, her eyes wide, as she watched Clarence rise from his chair and stride toward Violet. He extended a beckoning hand, pulling her from the seat and lifting her into his arms.

"Dear God! What's happening here?" she exclaimed sharply. "I've never seen or heard anything so sinful in my life! You're a married man with five children and expecting another with your wife! And now you're having another child with this woman? This is shameful, both of you are disgraceful!"

Clarence pulled away from Violet's embrace and spun around to face his accuser, who sat in her chair with her lips twisted in anger and disgust.

"Mrs. Wade, Violet, and I were wrong, very wrong about what we both did. I'll be the first to say that I shouldn't have let this go on. Once I touched her, we couldn't stop it; we fell in love, and now she's going to have my child. All we want to know is if she's definitely going to have our baby and when. After that, you'll never see us again.

Mrs. Wade sat gripping the arms of her chair and tapping her foot loudly.

"You're both very wicked, and God will not show mercy. Come on, get up and follow me to the back," she said sharply, rising and quickly pulling herself away from Violet, who was quietly crying.

"Everything will be fine, just follow her and we'll be out of here soon", Clarence whispered as he brushed away her tears.

"She hates us, Clarence," said Violet. "But my mother, is she having a baby too?"

"Violet, hurry up! I don't want either of you here in my home with this sinful nature!" Mrs. Wade snapped angrily.

"Yes, ma'am, I'm coming," Violet called out as she hurried toward Mrs. Wade, standing at the doorway.

Violet entered the small, sparse room that held a cot, a dresser for towels, a water basin, and a three-legged wooden stool. Mrs. Wade slammed the door, causing Violet to jump. As she approached the dresser, Mrs. Wade grabbed a large blue cloth and threw it at her.

"Put this on," Mrs. Wade said sharply. "Then undress, but only keep your panties on. I'll step out to give you privacy." She left, slamming the door behind her. Violet unbuttoned her dress and followed Mrs. Wade's instructions.

Mrs. Wade is displeased, and I'm scared. Clarence loves me, not Maria, so I don't understand why Mrs. Wade can't see that. Meanwhile, my mother is expecting a baby, which explains why she rushed the wedding. Violet thought as she took off her shoes and draped the large blue cloth over herself.

Mrs. Wade knocked loudly on the door and, without waiting for a reply, burst into the room. She was wearing her apron and carrying her large leather midwife bag. Sitting on the stool beside the bed, she opened the bag and retrieved a peculiar-looking device. This device had two long, narrow rubber hoses with small earplugs. At the bottom, it featured another long, narrow hose linked to a small, silver-shaped object resembling a bell.

"May I ask what that is?" Violet asked, frightened, as Mrs. Wade inserted the unusual-looking device into her ears.

"It's called a stethoscope so I can listen to your heart, lungs, and the baby. While I examine you, please don't talk unless I ask you to, OK?" she said sharply.

"Yes, ma'am," Violet replied. She then coughed so violently that she had to sit up. Mrs. Wade's gaze sharpened as she examined Violet's face, showing no sympathy for her coughing fit and continuing with the check-up. She quickly pulled the cloth aside to reveal Violet's bare breasts, then placed the cold stethoscope's small metal disc on her chest. The cold metal made Violet flinch. Mrs. Wade kept her eyes squeezed shut as she moved the stethoscope around her breasts, quietly counting to herself up to twenty. Once she finished, she moved it again until she completed her check. She then hung the stethoscope around her neck, took a notepad, and jotted down her observations of Violet's heartbeat. She snapped the notepad and set it aside. Finally, she cupped Violet's breasts, pressing firmly and prodding to examine them.

"Ouch!" Violet groaned in pain. Mrs. Wade paid no attention, showing no sympathy or apology for her discomfort. After thoroughly examining Violet's breasts, Mrs. Wade noted down additional information on her pad of paper. Once finished, she lifted the cloth to inspect her abdomen and immediately noticed signs of early pregnancy, reacting with visible disgust. She then used a stethoscope, moving its cold steel bell across Violet's abdomen to listen for sounds. Shaking her head in disgust, she removed the stethoscope and tucked it into her apron pocket. Rising from the stool, she pressed her cupped hands firmly on Violet's abdomen, moving in circles and causing Violet to wince further. She then took a measuring tape from her apron pocket to measure the top, bottom, and sides of Violet's slightly protruding belly. After jotting down her final notes and closing her notepad, she stored it in her bag. She stared at Violet with a look of disdain and contempt.

"You're having a baby. Your heart is strong, but there are a lot of crackles in your chest, which makes you cough, something I've never heard before. Your breasts are already swollen, meaning they'll be sore and feel heavy. They're going to get fuller with milk to feed the baby, and based on my hand and tape measurements, as well as the timing of your missing your monthly flow, you'll be about three months along in two weeks. The baby will arrive around June or early July," she said in a cold voice.

Draping the cloth around herself, Violet sat up.

"So, is my baby expected to arrive in June or July?"

"Yes, that's right. Under better circumstances, if you were a married teacher, I'd be happy for you and your husband. But instead, you have the nerve to show up at my door with Clarence Margaret, a married man with children! For heaven's sake, Violet, he's expecting another baby, which, if all goes well, his wife Maria will give birth to in May, just a month before your child is due. And we shouldn't forget your mother, who will have her baby in August! Imagine the three of you all with a child: Clarence's wife, you, his mistress, and you being Audine's daughter, with a child of your own. That would make Audine a grandmother, and you, her daughter, the older sister to Audine's baby! This has to be the biggest mess I've ever seen in my entire life! One thing is certain, though: when the news about this mess comes out, it's going to break Maria's heart, and your mother will be outraged. A young lady like you should be ashamed. You and Clarence are wicked and disgraceful. Mark my words: God will punish both of you and that baby in your belly. Get dressed and leave, because you both disgust me!" Mrs. Wade said bitterly. She quickly gathered her medical belongings, hurried to the door, and slammed it shut again.

Dazed, Violet sat on the edge of the cot, feeling attacked and numb by Mrs. Wade's outbursts and her malicious comments.

She doesn't understand! If she knew what Clarence was going through at home with Maria, she wouldn't say such horrible things to me. But everything will be okay because once my mother and Wayne return, Clarence and I plan to leave, she thought as she started getting dressed.

Violet opened the door and approached the parlor, immediately startled to find Mrs. Birch standing next to Mrs. Wade. Clarence was standing at the front door with his hand on the handle. The atmosphere in the room was tense beyond words.

"Good morning, Mrs. Birch. How are you?" said Violet.

Mrs. Birch, who had her arms folded defiantly across her chest, looked straight ahead at Clarence, refusing to respond to the greeting.

Mrs. Wade said, "This is for you," as she pressed several crumpled, scribbled notes into Violet's chest.

Mrs. Wade explained, "These are the notes from today's examination, showing the date, day, and time of the visit. I recorded your breast and belly measurements and noted that you missed your monthly flow. The notes also mention that this will be your first baby and that you have a bad cough. I signed the notes with my certificate number for Black midwives in Louisiana."

She moved away from Violet and approached Clarence.

"I want both of you out of my home," she said in a low voice.

"You should be ashamed of yourselves!" Mrs. Birch said, looking at Clarence, then fixing her gaze on Violet. "You know this man is married and his wife is expecting another baby. How could you do such a shameful thing, laying with a married man, humph! Clarence, you're worse than she is! I heard what you did, kissing Violet when you came home after six hours away, while your wife was beside herself with fear, worried that the Klan or some bad white men might do what was done to Jonathan when he was murdered! And another thing, during Audine and Wayne's wedding, you both mouthed 'I love you' to Violet, and she said it back. Maria saw it all! But let me tell you, Clarence, as sure as I am standing here, you will never see that baby inside Violet's belly!" she declared. "That child is cursed. It will be a confused soul, unable to tell the difference between being a man or a woman, and neither of you will be granted mercy or forgiveness!"

Pushing Clarence's hand off the door handle, Mrs. Wade flung the door open.

"I won't care for you or the baby out of respect for Maria and what she will experience once she learns all of this. Now, both of you get out!" she declared.

"Violet, come on. We're leaving," Clarence said, holding out his hand to her.

Violet, surprisingly holding her head high, approached Clarence with her hand trembling as she reached for his. Just before leaving, Clarence took a wad of bills, counted out twenty dollars, and placed the money on the small wooden entry table near the front door. They intertwined their arms and left. Mrs. Wade slammed the door behind them. From behind the curtains, Mrs. Wade and Mrs. Birch watched, disgusted, as Clarence led Violet into his truck. After Clarence got in, Violet moved close and rested her head on his shoulder. He lifted her chin, and they kissed deeply. He started the truck, and then they drove away.

Mrs. Wade and Mrs. Birch looked up at each other, horrified by what they saw.

Mrs. Wade expressed her shock, saying, "In all my thirty years delivering babies here and in New Orleans, I've never seen anything like this—Clarence's nerve to do something under Audine and Wayne's roof. I feel so sorry for Maria, her baby, and the children. My God, what a mess. And I can't imagine what Audine and Wayne will say, especially with her expecting their first child!"

Stepping away from the window, Mrs. Wade sank into the chair and slipped off her shoes. Mrs. Birch sat in the chair opposite her.

"When the time comes, Alice, we need to be with Maria and help her in every possible way, especially since she's been like a daughter to me. A mother would never leave her daughter, especially at a time like this," Mrs. Birch said.

"Humph!" Mrs. Wade grumbled loudly. "That money on the table, which Clarence left, will be given to Maria since she needs it for the baby. I certainly don't want it."

Mrs. Birch nodded in agreement.

"Eucharista, I apologize for not offering you coffee or a piece of the pound cake I baked last night that I wanted you to try. So, what brings you here? I don't have any deliveries, and I won't need to see the ladies for a few weeks," said Mrs. Wade as she got up from her chair and headed to the kitchen.

Don't worry, Alice, it's okay. But before you fetch me some coffee and that cake, I have something to tell you, this is why I'm here. You might want to sit down, especially after hearing what I have to say.

Mrs. Wade went into the parlor and sat down.

Mrs. Birch said, "Etta from our church called my son last night. It seems Wayne called Etta from New York with some very dreadful news."

Mrs. Wade asked, confused, "What did Etta say?"

Mrs. Birch took a deep breath, then removed her spectacles and rubbed her eyes.

"Audine lost the baby, and she and Wayne will be arriving home on Wednesday".

CHAPTER TWENTY-FOUR

"Don't cry, there's nothing to worry about. I'm sorry you had to hear those awful things Mrs. Wade and Mrs. Birch said about us," Clarence whispered, his voice laced with sorrow. "They had no right to speak such words about the woman I love, who will soon be the mother of my child."

Heartbroken, Violet sobbed and hacked as she gripped Clarence's hand tightly.

"Why did they say such terrible things to us, Clarence?" she asked. "Mrs. Birch's judgment about our child being cursed was unkind, and she also said we would never receive mercy, calling us sinners who will suffer forever. You know what? She might be right, Clarence. Now I'm worried for us and our baby."

Clarence, fed up with hearing all the lamentations that started swirling in his mind, swerved the truck onto the right shoulder of the dirt road, nearly hitting a tree head-on. Violet screamed, cradling her belly with one hand and holding onto the bottom of the open window. Clarence pressed the brakes, causing the truck to screech to a stop and narrowly missing the tree.

"Oh my God, are you okay?" he yelled to Violet. Although he missed the tree, the impact caused Violet to hit her head on the dashboard with a loud thud. "This is my fault! I let what those two women said distract me from driving. I vow never to let anyone say such terrible things to you again, like at Mrs. Wade's house. I also promise always to be here to protect and care for you and our baby. And I will tell Maria that I'm leaving as soon as your mother and Wayne return," he said.

"Clarence, today has been terrible. I want to get home," Violet said, gripping Clarence's arm tightly.

Holding her in a firm embrace, he nodded. Turning on the ignition, Clarence sped onto the road without bothering to check for oncoming cars.

"Slow down!" she cried out.

"It's okay, I'm driving slowly so I can get you home and into bed. You need to rest, and I need you, as our child does," he said quickly, glancing at Violet, who suddenly seemed to be dozing. He then pulled her closer with his free arm.

"I'm not ever going to leave you," he whispered, placing his hand on her belly.

The drive back to Audine and Wayne's home could have been quicker, but after the near-fatal incident that could have gone badly, Clarence took precautions, even keeping his eyes on the dirt road and letting another truck driven by a white driver have the right of way.

"We're here," Clarence whispered. Violet was asleep on his shoulder. His eyes watched her peaceful face. Her hand rested across her belly as if shielding their child. Violet stirred and woke up.

She asked sleepily, "Are we already here?"

"Yes, we're here," he said.

As Violet sat up, she touched her forehead and winced in pain. Although Clarence didn't hit the tree, she had slammed her forehead against the dashboard, creating a large, throbbing bump the size of a half-dollar that made her head feel like it was going to burst. After being helped out of the truck, they hesitated at the house, stopping abruptly. A white piece of paper was taped to the outside of the door. Clarence slipped his hand into his trouser pocket and gripped his pistol firmly, which he always carried when driving alone.

"Clarence, what's that on the door?" Violet asked, her voice filled with concern.

"Don't move, stay right where you are", he said.

Walking carefully up the two stairs to avoid an ambush, he grabbed the paper from the door and read it aloud:

Dear Violet and Mason,

Something terrible happened to your mother, but she's okay now. The Harlem doctor advised that she should return home to rest, so she and Wayne have already left New York and are heading home. They're expected to be back tomorrow. Where are you and Clarence? We knocked and waited for half an hour, but no one was there.

God Bless,

Deacon and Mrs. Moss

Clarence folded the note and slipped it into his pocket.

"What is it?" asked Violet.

"Your mother and Wayne are coming home. It seems like your mother fell ill, but the doctor who treated her said she should go back home and rest," Clarence said, placing his arm around her waist. He opened the door and guided her inside. Violet gradually sank into the small, overstuffed chair.

"So, what does this mean?" Violet asked, taking a deep breath. "Because now that Mrs. Wade has told us that I'm having your child, everyone will find out, especially Mrs. Birch, who'll tell Maria."

Clarence approached her and gently pulled her out of the chair she was sitting in. He sat down and pulled her onto his lap, wrapping his arms around her. Her head lolled drowsily against his shoulder.

"I'm going to personally tell my wife that our marriage is ending because I want her to hear it from me directly. I'll explain that I am now in love with you and that I plan to ask for a divorce. She can keep the farm, and my sons can look after it. I'll also talk to Ricks to see if he and his men can lend a hand temporarily. I will visit my children regularly, especially the one expecting. Any earnings from the farm and smokehouse will be theirs after division, as I will care for our baby and you once you become my wife".

Violet lifted her head and looked at Clarence; a smile creased his face.

"I'm asking you to be my wife. I know the timing of all this may be off, and when we tell your mother and Wayne when they come home, I'll tell them we're getting married as soon as Maria and I are divorced," he said.

"Do you mean it, about making me your wife?" she asked, her voice husky with tears of joy streaming down her face.

"Yes, I mean it, Violet. "Will you marry me?" he asked.

Despite her throbbing headache, a faint, breathless whisper escaped her lips.

"Yes."

His gentle, warm breath hovered just above her swollen lips. He brushed her face with his finger, then claimed her lips with a tongue-thrusting kiss that rekindled memories of their first kiss, which caused him to thrust his tongue deeper.

"I can't wait until we're married, Clarence," she said.

I understand, but remember that your mother and Wayne won't be happy about this, especially right after you marry. I know one person who'll be especially upset—my wife. I'm expecting two babies; one was conceived when I was with my wife, and the other is with the woman I need to be with: you. Here's the plan: I'll leave tomorrow morning after Mason goes to school. You start packing as much as you can. I'll come over tomorrow night at eight. Both of us will tell them you're having a child and that I am the father. I'll tell Wayne that I'm getting divorced and that you and I are getting married. Then, we'll head to Virginia."

Despite a dull headache, Violet managed to smile and wrap her arms around Clarence's neck and hug him.

"How's your head feeling?" he asked, touching the bump on her head.

"It's not hurting as much as before. I need to clean up and start making dinner since Mason will be home soon. Will you go back home today?" she asked.

"Yes, I need to go back home to check on the farm, my children, and Maria," he said.

Violet flinched when she heard him mention her name. "I see. You should head home soon; it's going to get dark," she said. As she tried to stand, the door suddenly swung open. Mason remained standing in the doorway.

"What are you doing here?" he asked, glaring at Clarence.

Clarence rose and confidently approached Mason. He seized Mason by his shirt collar, pressing him against the wall, which made the books in Mason's arms fall to the floor, prompting Violet to scream. She started to step back.

"Boy, I need to tell you this, I might not be your father, but I won't tolerate you speaking to me like that!" Clarence said fiercely through clenched teeth. "I've spoken to you several times, and you either ignore me or give me short, abrupt answers. If any of my sons ever responded to me this way, I'd punish them with a leather strap to their ass! You're no different! So, you better straighten up and behave when you're around me. Do you hear me, boy? Answer me!"

"Yeah," Mason muttered, avoiding eye contact with Clarence.

"Yeah, what? You answer me correctly, boy," he admonished, tightening his grip around Mason's neck.

"Ye-yes, sir," Mason replied, sputtering and coughing.

Clarence eased his hold. Mason ducked, grabbed his books, and hurried to his room, nearly knocking Violet over. He then slammed his door shut.

"Clarence, why'd you do that to him? You didn't have to smash him against the wall like that!" said Violet.

"He's the same age as my son Joseph, and he's not gonna speak to me like that! I am here, watching over and ensuring the safety of you two, now three, if I include myself. It's better that I am the one telling him rather than a white man who might harm him. I am heading out now to check on my family. Tonight, I plan to talk to Maria about us. I will return later with my belongings, so when your mother and Wayne arrive, we can tell them everything".

"This is all happening so quickly, and I'm starting to worry, Clarence. What if your wife says you can't leave?"

"She has no choice. You are the person I love and intend to marry. I will take responsibility for all of you. The most important thing is to tell your mother and Wayne, and then we will leave for Virginia," Clarence said, embracing her.

"I'll be back later, but don't wait for me. Lock the door and pull down the shades, keep the lights off; you don't want any strangers coming in here."

"I will. I'll make a plate of some red beans and rice with sausage and leave a plate out for you and Mason," she said.

"Thank you," he said as they walked toward the door. They embraced and shared a passionate kiss one last time before he left. She stayed at the door, watching him get into the truck and start the engine. He honked twice and waved goodbye.

After closing the door, Violet headed to the kitchen, grabbed a pot from the cupboard, and filled it with water. She placed it on the stove to heat while she changed in her bedroom. When she glimpsed herself in the mirror, she gasped at her reflection. Her forehead bore a large, grotesque purple and blue bump. She covered her mouth in horror. Her once beautiful face was now a distorted mess, making her cringe. She slipped off her shoes and slowly removed her dress, leaving only her slip. She then returned to the kitchen, found a washbasin, and filled it with tepid water from the stove, adding cold water to reach the right temperature. Because Wayne's modern bathroom was still under construction, he and Clarence planned to work on it once he returned from New York; the washbasin would have to do for now. Carefully, she carried the basin to her bedroom, shut the door, and began to undress. The crumpled notes Mrs. Wade had scribbled during the examination spilled out from the top of her slip. She unfolded the notes and read her handwritten scribbles.

November 20, 1933 – Time of examination: Ten o'clock (Morning hour)

Name: Violet Coral Booker   Born on February 12, 1911, Age: 21

Husband's name-Miss Booker is <u>Not Married</u>

Note: Miss Booker came to me to confirm if she is expecting. I asked when her last monthly flow was. She said it stopped in September. Conception may have occurred two weeks before her monthly period, meaning the baby will be born sometime in June. There is proof of tenderness and the widening of her breasts. Miss Booker will be able to breastfeed the baby. After examining her lower belly, it appears that Miss Booker is expecting. She says that she has been throwing up every morning. Miss Booker is not married, and the father of her child is Mr. Clarence Margaret, who is married.

As a midwife with strong morals and church beliefs, I cannot provide care for Miss Booker's needs because I am already caring for Mr. Margaret's wife.

Respectfully Yours,

Mrs. Alice Teresa Wade, Midwife, New Orleans, Louisiana -Certificate Number: 8397

November 20, 1933

Violet examined the notes and read them twice more before understanding she was going to have a child with Clarence, who was already married. She carefully folded the papers and tucked them into her purse, which also held the envelope containing eight hundred dollars her father had left her. Tears flowed down her face as she recalled that Sunday, overwhelmed with grief for disappointing her father.

I'm so ashamed right now! Clarence and I love each other deeply, and he's even leaving Maria and their children. He promised to do the right thing and marry me, but he'll still take care of his family. I want everything to work out for all of us! she thought as she started to bathe.

After drying off and slipping into a fresh nightgown, she quietly went through the front door, poured the water from the basin onto the ground, and left it to dry outside. The cool, crisp November air made her shiver, and dusk was already settling in. Inside the icebox, a modern appliance Wayne had added to the house, the leftovers from the wedding dinner still looked fresh and abundant. She took out a plate of sliced ham, potato salad, biscuits, and sliced tomatoes, then arranged everything on the table to prepare dinner instead of making the red beans with andouille sausage. After plating the meal, she filled a glass with water and grabbed a plate for Mason. She balanced the plate of food in one hand and the glass in the other.

She stood at Mason's door.

"Mason, it's Violet. Could you please open the door? I have dinner for you, and there are cakes and pies in the kitchen if you'd like more. Could you open the door?" she asked.

Mason didn't answer. She knocked on his door again more urgently.

"Mason, open the door!" she pleaded. Then she heard his footsteps stomp heavily toward the door, and he violently swung it open. Mason stood in front of her, his face showing clear disgust. His shirt was soaked in sweat, and from what she could see over his shoulder, his room was a disaster, with books and papers scattered all over the floor and on his bed. Violet was stunned by what she saw.

"Hi, I have some food for you and- "

Mason interrupted her before she could finish, grabbing the plate and glass of water. Without a word, he forcefully kicked the door shut, slamming it in her face.

Violet trembled as she stood there, instinctively stepping back while a hollow sensation gripped her stomach. In that instant, she realized she no longer had a brother who loved her; all their love and bond vanished instantaneously. She accepted that they would never be close again, leaving her heartbroken and lonely. Slowly, she moved back into the kitchen, pulled out a chair, and sat alone, eating in silence.

CHAPTER TWENTY-FIVE

Clarence eased the truck to a stop in front of his house. There were three large baskets of sweet potatoes on the front steps. Each basket had a handwritten sign that read: Twenty-five sweets for 25¢.

He stepped out of the truck to get a closer look at what he was seeing. There were two barrels, one on each side, with a thick piece of reclaimed wood on top, serving as a makeshift table.

This is what Joseph and Sampson did. Who else would come up with such an idea? Clarence wondered to himself, smiling.

Clarence felt a hand on his shoulder, causing him to spin around and see it was Ricks.

"You're more scared than a fox who's met his match!" Ricks said with a smile, revealing his bone-white teeth. "Where have you been?"

"Whew! You damned near scared me to death! I thought you were a white man looking for trouble. Damn, I would've been ready to defend my family," Clarence said, patting his pocket where his pistol was kept.

"No need to worry, because my men and I will be watching your home and family until Wayne and Audine return. After that, everything can return to normal. I'm sure you'll be happy to be with your family again, especially your wife, who misses you," Ricks said as he exhaled a puff of smoke from his pipe.

"I don't know, Ricks," Clarence said. "I've known you for years, and you've been more than a friend to my family; you've been like a father to me. Maria and I have been going through a lot of deep pits in our marriage. We've been fighting all the time, and well, I'm in love with someone else."

"You what?" Ricks asked, leaning against Clarence's truck.

Clarence said, "I'm in love with Audine's daughter, Violet, and I plan to tell Maria that I'm leaving her to be with Violet."

Ricks stood speechless.

"Son, what trouble have you gotten into? You have a wife expecting your child, and your other children will need you. What about the farm and the smokehouse? You're the only Black farmer we trust and rely on because of your honesty. Clarence, are you really going to leave all this for some young woman? Jesus, you're in a serious mess! And how will you tell Audine and Wayne?

You know they won't be happy about this, no, sir! What are you going to do now?"

"I thought it all through after Violet and I discovered today that she's expecting my child. That's where I'll need your help. But first, I need to talk with my wife inside, to tell her the truth about myself, Violet, and the child I fathered with her. After that, I plan to pack my things and leave. I want us to discuss what happens after I go to Virginia with Violet," Clarence said. "Before I go inside, I've written down instructions on how to care for the farm and smokehouse while I'm away. You can read it while I talk to my wife. It covers everything you need to do to support my family after I leave. I plan to visit twice a month in the warmer months and once a month during winter. Please read everything I've written, and will you promise to help me?" Clarence pleaded, handing Ricks a folded note with his handwriting. "I'll be back as soon as I finish talking with Maria," he added, rushing toward

his house and going inside. Ricks took the paper, looked

it over, and shook his head in disbelief.

CHAPTER TWENTY-SIX

Clarence walked into his house and immediately caught the aroma of onions, fried fish, sweet potatoes, and greens. Behind the closed bedroom doors, faint voices of Kempton, Joseph, and Sampson chatted softly. He gave a warm smile and approached their door, a wave of heaviness suddenly sinking over him.

Clarence reflected that he would never again hear his sons' voices coming through the door. A year from now, he would be married to Violet, be a parent to their new child, and live somewhere else. Although everything would change, he was determined to do right by Violet, their baby, and his family here.

"What are you doing here, Clarence?"

Clarence's thoughts were interrupted when he quickly turned around to see Maria standing nearby. She remained in her blue short-sleeved dress, apron, with her curly dark hair neatly pinned up in a tight bun, a few loose strands framing her round face. Her green eyes pierced through him.

Kempton opened the door to see who was outside his room.

"Hi, Dad," he said.

"Hi, Kempton, I was just about to surprise all of you," he nodded.

"Dad, I need to talk to you about something. Can we find a moment to talk alone?" asked Kempton.

"Of course, we can talk, son, but first I need to speak with your mother alone. After that, we can talk, okay?" said Clarence.

"Yes, sir, I'll be here. Joseph, Sampson, and I were discussing our earnings from selling sweet potatoes to Mr. Ricks and about thirty of his men we haven't met before.

We sold twenty-eight baskets and four hams. During fishing, we caught around twenty catfish, and one of his men bought six for two dollars. Today, we earned thirty-two dollars because Joseph sold bacon to Mr. Ricks's men,' he said proudly.

"What? Kempton, that's wonderful! Yes, you and I will discuss what you and your brothers did today, selling all those items. I'm sure the wives of Rick's men will be pleased with what they're bringing home. This farm will be busy over the next few days, with Thanksgiving and Christmas approaching, so we have a lot to talk about. But first, let me speak to your mother," said Clarence as he hugged his son.

Kempton nodded and closed the door. Immediately, lively conversations could be heard among Kempton and his brothers.

"Maria, can we go to our room? I need to talk to you," Clarence said.

Maria's brows furrowed as she turned around and headed toward their bedroom. Clarence followed and walked in, closing the door behind him.

"What do you want, Clarence?" she asked.

"We've been having a lot of problems between us, and it's affecting our family," he said, in a deliberate voice. "I'm sleeping in the barn with the animals; we're always fighting and-"

"Shut up, Clarence!" Maria hissed. "You're only sleeping in the barn because of that young woman you're caring for. That's why you're not in our bed. I saw you kissing her and heard you say 'I-Love-You' at Audine and Wayne's wedding! Did you think I didn't notice? I'm not stupid! How dare you act this way in front of me, showing such disrespect to me, our baby, our children, our home, and our marriage! Until you end things with her, you'll keep sleeping in the barn, just like the yard dog you are!"

Clarence bowed his head and stared at the floor, wishing he could escape the room. He stayed perfectly still.

"So, what exactly are you here for, Clarence? What do you want?" she said.

"Violet is having my child," he blurted out. "We went to see Mrs. Wade this morning, and she said the baby will arrive sometime in June. I love Violet, and I'm only here to collect my belongings before returning to be with her, so we can tell her mother and Wayne that I want to marry her. We're leaving for Virginia tomorrow to start fresh. You, our baby, and the children can keep everything-the house, the farm, the smokehouse-everything. Kempton will start college next year and will help out as much as possible, while Ricks and his men will manage the farm work. Violet, our child, and I will visit twice a month to check on our children. I'll work with Ricks on the farm, and Violet can visit Audine and Wayne. It will be good for our children to have another brother or sister. And Maria, I want a divorce," he said. He grabbed his gold wedding band, twisted it off, and placed it at Maria's feet.

"I never intended for any of this to happen, nor did I expect Violet and me to fall in love. I will handle everything and- "

The sudden closed fist that struck his jaw made him fall backward, hitting the floor with a loud thud. Maria stood above him, her hands still clenched into fists.

"Get out!" she shrieked. "Get your things and get the hell out of this house! You and that whore you slept with will be cursed forever! But you will not live to see that bastard child you made! All three of you will die and rot in hell with the devil! You've betrayed me and our children, you blaspheming son-of-a-bitch! Get out!" Then she delivered one last swift kick to his head. Clarence screamed in pain, cradling his head.

The bedroom door swung open suddenly. Their children gathered at the doorway: Izelle and Rosetta, weeping uncontrollably while holding each other, and Sampson and Joseph, trembling and hiding around the corner.

"So, it really is true!" said Kempton. "Mason told me he saw you and Violet in her bed, and you were on top of her, and- "

"Stop it, shut up!" Rosetta screamed, holding her hands to her ears. She wept uncontrollably as Izelle tried to hoist her sister up to keep her from sinking to the floor. Sampson and Joseph followed their sisters to their room and slammed the door. The wails and screeching could be heard from their closed door.

Clarence stood up. His jaw was red and swollen. He blinked his eyes in disbelief that Maria blindsided him with a swift kick. The revelation of everything unraveled, and now his family was destroyed.

"You're everything Mason said you are," Kempton said, his voice firm and sharp like his look. "I'm leaving in two weeks to join the army," he continued, handing an envelope to Clarence. "I wanted to talk to you about whether to enlist now or wait until I finish school. But after hearing all of this and seeing how low you went with Ma; I've definitely decided that joining the army is the best choice for me. I can't believe you're having a baby with Violet—what kind of man are you!" He then stormed into his room and slammed the door.

Looking down at the envelope bearing the United States Army stamp, Clarence unfolded the letter. His hands trembled as he started to read.

Kempton Pierre Margaret

12 Old Moss Road

New Orleans, Louisiana

November 11, 1933

Kempton P. Margaret:

You are hereby accepted into service in the United States Army. You are expected to go to the enlistment office, where you will undergo a physical, receive inoculations, and have measurements taken for your uniform. You will then be sworn in. Please arrive at the office by 8:00 a.m. for further processing.

Respectfully,

The United States Army

The letter slipped from Clarence's fingers as he sank to the floor.

"Look what you've done to our family!" Maria burst out in anger. "Kempton is leaving, and he might never come back home, especially to this mess you caused! I want you gone right now! Leave and never return! You will never see this family again, especially not the baby inside me!"

Clarence slowly stood up and boldly strode towards Maria, who was visibly shaking and cradling her belly.

"That's where you're wrong", he said angrily. "This family and the baby inside you mean everything to me. I made a mistake, starting with kissing Violet, wanting her instead of you, then being with her, and now she's carrying our child. I fell in love with her, and now I want to do right by her and our baby. That's why I'm divorcing you to marry the woman I love. I'm truly sorry for what

I've done, but one thing is certain: I will come to see my children. You won't be able to stop me, especially when our child is born in a few months. I have my rights," he declared.

"Rights, what rights? You gave up all your got-damn rights the moment you placed yourself between her legs!" she shrieked.

Then, going under the bed, she lifted the coverlet, grabbed a large suitcase from beneath, and threw it, narrowly missing Clarence's head.

"Get out, Clarence! You'll never see any of us again, and I swear that the moment your foot touches the third stair outside this house, you will die. You should have never slept with that two-cent-whore." Maria said tearfully as she shoved him aside to leave the house.

After she left, Clarence started packing his belongings. Looking out the window, he saw it was already dark. His suitcase was large and deep enough to hold clothes, shoes, and the tools necessary for beginning work once he and Violet arrived in Virginia.

Once Violet and I are married and settled, I will ensure Ricks sends the farm's profit split. Maria will receive her half, and the remaining will be for me and my new family, he thought to himself.

After twenty-five minutes, the suitcase was filled. He patted his overall pocket, took out his pistol for protection, and quickly counted a stack of three hundred dollars earned from selling meat at the smokehouse. He slipped the cash wad into the sole of his shoe and tied it securely. After putting on his light wool jacket and lifting the heavy suitcase, he took a final glance at the bedroom he shared with Maria.

We made all our children in this room. He shook his head sorrowfully, closed the door, and left.

The house was quiet and dark. As he walked past his daughters' room, he faintly heard their muffled sobs, with one comforting the other. He raised his hand to knock, but quickly withdrew it, thinking it would be unwise to discuss his indiscretion with the woman they tutored in French-Creole. Instead, he placed two fingers to his lips and gently pressed them against the door.

He whispered, "Goodbye, my beautiful angels. I'll be back soon."

He stood outside his son's door, gradually moving closer and pressing his ear to listen. He overheard Kempton whispering loudly to his brothers, filled with curse words and anger. Kempton was telling them that he planned to ask Mr. Crowns, the school principal, for early graduation because he had passed all his exams.

"I passed all my tests with A's and one B-plus," Kempton said proudly. Mr. Crayman, the science teacher, urged me not to join the army because they mistreat Black soldiers. He explained that all the army would allow Black men like me to do is cook, clean toilets, or dig trenches. Well, I'm going to show them all a thing or two, especially how smart I am in science and arithmetic. Mr. Crayman also mentioned wanting to discuss with Ma and Dad my attending Meharry to study and become a doctor. Humph, we can forget about all that, thanks to Dad and Violet".

"Why?" Sampson could be heard asking heartbreakingly as he sniffed back tears.

"Because dad put a baby inside Violet's belly!" said Joseph with disapproval. "He's leaving Ma and all of us to marry Violet, which means both Ma and Violet are having a baby by Dad. I hate him!" Sampson could be heard punching the wall before breaking down into sobs.

Oh no, he thought in distress, now his sons despised every part of him.

"Goodbye, sons. Take care of one another. I'm very proud of you, Kempton. Show those white army boys how clever you are," he whispered.

He then left the house and quietly closed the door. The night air was brisk and cold as he looked up at the star-filled sky. His thoughts drifted to the future: two children would be born a month apart. Beyond the yard, he gazed at the barn and smokehouse, structures that not only fed and clothed his family, thanks to the income they provided, but also supported the entire community, which relied on him to keep their families fed during the depression.

Ricks, his men, and my sons will maintain this place, Clarence thought as he paused to put on his jacket to protect against the cool night air. As he descended the stairs, he noticed a fine layer of dust on each step. He shrugged and brushed the dust off with his foot. After stepping down from the last step, he approached his 1930 brown Ford. He opened the rear door, lifted the suitcase, and slid it inside.

The house felt cold, and there were no logs next to the wood stove for tomorrow morning, Clarence realized. The large firewood storage box, filled with bundled logs stored along the house, was complete. He moved towards it, opened the lid, and reached inside to lift eight logs. He planned to place them by the front door as a reminder for one of his sons to take the logs into the house near the woodstove.

"The last log," Clarence said as he reached into the crate. "Ouch-shit!" he shouted in pain. He quickly withdrew his hand, but despite the cold, the red pygmy rattlesnake had burrowed deep inside the crate and was still coiled around his hand, its fangs so long they had penetrated and clamped onto the other side of his hand. He yanked it free and threw it into the yard. Drawing his pistol, he fired two blind shots at the snake, but it was too fast and had already vanished. The pain in his hand was sharp and unbearable.

Staggering toward the house, Clarence only made it to the third set of stairs, which were covered with goofer dust that Maria had sprinkled. The venom was rapidly spreading. His hand swelled, looking grotesque and unnatural.

"Clarence, Clarence! What happened?" Ricks yelped.

"Snake bit me," Clarence said as he collapsed.

Eight of Rick's men, armed with rifles, encircled the backyard.

"He's over here! But stay in your positions and keep those rifles raised and loaded!" Ricks shouted.

"Pygmy rattler got to me, Ricks. I shot it, it's over there on the grass," said Clarence through labored breathing.

Looking over at the grass, Ricks clicked on the button of his USA Lite Miner's flashlight.

"Everyone, point your rifles to the ground and be careful. A pygmy rattler just bit Clarence, and those snakes are quick and dangerous!" Ricks shouted.

All of Rick's men cocked their rifles and pointed them at the ground, eager to shoot the snake. However, after a quick search, there was no sign of the snake.

"Ain't nothing here, boss!" shouted all the men. Ricks turned his attention back to Clarence, who was slumped on the stairs. As Ricks moved closer, Clarence's eyes drooped, and he was no longer breathing. Ricks shook Clarence's shoulder to wake him, but his body was already rigid. Ricks took off his hat and placed it over Clarence's chest. Facing the men, who were beginning to crowd closer, Ricks shook his head.

"Clarence is gone," he announced. Out of respect for their friend, they all removed their hats, held them over their chests, and bowed their heads.

With his head bowed low but cocking his head just enough to look intently at the side of the house in the direction of the toolshed, stood Maria, who was watching everything. She appeared to be holding the bloody remains of the severed head of the snake that had just killed her husband.

CHAPTER TWENTY-SEVEN

Since midnight, Clarence never appeared, and Violet paced in her room in half-circles. She glanced at the two packed suitcases, which held her belongings and a shirt Clarence had left behind. She gently took the shirt, held it to her chest, and, as she fell asleep, inhaled his scent with a smile, dreaming of their future as his wife and the mother of his child. During the night, she opened her eyes and sat up, expecting Clarence to be sleeping beside her. Feeling alarmed, she quietly slipped out of bed, tiptoed past Mason's room, and headed to the unfinished room where Clarence was supposed to be. The pallet and covers were untouched, and Clarence was not there.

Maybe he's on his way. He's probably struggling with telling Maria about us. His children will also learn they have a new brother or sister on the way with their mother's baby, she thought, feeling worried.

"It's a mess, but we have to move forward for our baby," she said aloud before returning to sleep.

Eight o'clock. It was morning, and the sun was shining brightly. The nausea, although having subsided, still struck unexpectedly at times. Violet sat up, looked around, and glanced at the side of the bed. The only thing that belonged to Clarence was his crumpled shirt on her pillow. She hoisted herself out of bed and went toward the room where he might be sleeping. When she opened the door, it was the same as last night. She stepped back, holding her hand over her belly, as a sudden wave of nausea hit her, making her feel that something was wrong.

"Clarence, are you here?" she called out. There was only silence. Running to Mason's room, she knocked on his door.

"Mason, open the door! Where's Clarence? He's not here!" she cried out desperately. She pounded on his door and jiggled the doorknob, but it was locked. "Where are you, Clarence?" she whimpered in fear. She backed against the wall and sank to the floor, crying.

"Why are my suitcases here at the door?" a familiar female voice boomed through the now dark house, waking Violet, who had been sleeping on the floor all day in front of Mason's locked door. Suddenly, the lights flicked on, forcing Violet to shield her eyes from the glare.

"Violet, why are you on the floor?" Audine asked, alarmed to see her daughter leaning against the wall opposite Mason's bedroom.

"What's going on here? Are you hurt?" Wayne asked as he hurried over to help Violet stand up.

"I-I must've fallen asleep on the floor," she stammered. "Where's Clarence? Is he here?"

Audine looked at Wayne, baffled at what she had just heard.

"Well, that's a mighty good question, Violet. Where in God's name *is* Clarence? He's supposed to be here watching you and Mason. As a matter of fact, where is Mason?" she asked.

Suddenly, the door swung open, revealing Mason, who looked like he had been at school all day.

"Hi, Ma, hi, Dad. I'm so glad y'all are back home," he said, rushing past Violet to hug Wayne and Audine.

Audine snapped, 'What's been happening here?' and I repeat, "Where's Clarence?'

"Ask Violet, Ma. I'm sure she can tell you exactly where he is. Isn't that right, Violet?" said Mason.

"What is he talking about, Violet? And why are my suitcases and two sacks of food by the door? You're not supposed to leave until Sunday after Thanksgiving. So why are the suitcases over there? Answer me!" she demanded.

"Audine, please come to the kitchen and sit down. I believe we can discuss this as a family now that I am the father to both of you. Regarding Clarence, I'm confident we will resolve this issue. When he arrives, I'll speak with him privately," Wayne said, signaling everyone to follow him into the kitchen.

Wayne supported Audine, who was grimacing as if in severe pain. He steadied her by the waist and led her to the chair, where she collapsed onto it with a grunt of discomfort. Once everyone was seated, Audine started to speak.

"Wayne and I had to cut our New York trip short because I became very ill. I had a surprise to share with both of you when we returned," she said, holding Wayne's hand.

"We were about to tell you both that Wayne and I were expecting a baby, but I lost it. The baby didn't have a chance to live, and the doctor says I won't be able to have children for Wayne ever again!" she sobbed. "This isn't fair. Why can't I start a new family? I wanted more children to complete ours!"

Wayne slid his chair next to Audine and embraced her as she sobbed.

"I am so sorry, Ma," Violet whispered, softly dabbing tears from her eyes. "I didn't realize you and Wayne were beginning a new family so soon. I would have loved to help take care of our new brother or sister."

"Oh my God, Violet! You know you won't have time to care for a new sister or brother! Soon, you'll be busy taking care of your own child. Come on, tell them, Violet!" said Mason.

"Tell us what?" Wayne asked.

"Oh-ho! Violet has some news to share with the whole family!" Mason exclaimed with laughter.

"Why's Mason laughing like that? What's going on here? Answer me, Violet!" Audine admonished loudly.

Violet remained seated, her gaze lowered. Her heart pounded wildly, almost bursting from her chest.

This isn't how it's supposed to happen! Clarence should be here with me so we can share this news. Oh my God, Mason and his big mouth! Why did he have to come out with it? Damn you, Mason! She thought anxiously as she suddenly felt her bladder weaken.

"I'm expecting a baby, Ma. I visited Mrs. Wade yesterday, and she told me the baby will arrive in June. That's why I have the suitcase by the door because Clarence- "

"What-what did you just say? You-you are having a baby?" Audine asked, alarmed.

"Yes, Ma, I'm having a baby and Clarence is the father".

Suddenly, Audine leapt from her chair, rushing forward to slap Violet, who was knocked back, causing her chair to fall and break. The women then fell to the floor in a fierce struggle, with Audine hitting and slapping Violet.

"Ma, stop it!" Violet screamed as Audine delivered a fierce punch right on Violet's mouth, causing her lip to split.

"Audine, stop! You're hurting her! Mason, help me with your mother!" Wayne shouted.

As the two lifted Audine away from Violet, Violet was curled on the floor, bleeding and crying loudly, clutching her face with her hands.

"Clarence Margaret is having a baby with you! During all the time I was working, that man was lying in bed with you, making a baby, right in my house?" shrieked Audine, who Wayne and Mason were holding back.

"He's a married man with children, and oh my God, he's expecting another baby with his wife! Get out! Leave this house now, you filthy whore! How dare you and he be here doing nasty things, and he putting a baby inside you? Get out of this place!" Audine sank to the floor, covering her face and crying loudly.

"Mason, I need you to call your Aunt Cee-Cee in New York. When she answers, let me know so I can talk to her," said Wayne.

Mason went inside Audine's purse and fished out a crumpled piece of paper that had Cee-Cee's telephone number scribbled on it. Stepping aloofly over Violet's crumpled body, Mason made the call to his aunt.

"Audine, listen to me, honey. I'll find out what happened because, legally, Violet was taken advantage of, and I will make sure Clarence goes to jail," Wayne said angrily.

"No," Violet sputtered as she stood up, bloodied and weak. "Clarence and I are getting married. He's leaving

Maria and, on his way, here to talk to you before we leave."

"Over my dead body!" Audine shrieked. "You're leaving tonight to stay with your aunt and uncle in New York until we can get Clarence arrested for what he's done! You dirty, nasty whore, you've disgraced me! What will people in this town think of me? You are up here with a baby in your got-damned belly, and here I am being told I can never have a baby for my husband! What about me, huh? What about *me!*" Audine cried and wailed so loud that all Wayne could do was hold her close as he silently rocked her back and forth.

"Wayne, I mean, Dad, Auntie Cee-Cee is on the telephone", said Mason.

"Mason, come over here and stay with your mother while I speak to your aunt," said Wayne, as he slowly lifted himself from Audine's tight embrace.

"Honey, listen to me. Mason is right here, and I'm about to be on the phone with your sister, so stay right there".

Wayne motioned to Mason, who quickly sat on the floor to console Audine, who was weeping hysterically.

Where is Clarence? Oh God, please let Clarence come through that door now, God! Violet prayed silently.

"Okay, she'll arrive on Friday afternoon. Yes, she can stay until she has the baby? Thank you, Cee-Cee, and God bless you and Hubert for doing this. Yes, uh-huh. Once Clarence is arrested, we'll see what we can do regarding money to send to you. She'll need many things for the baby. Yes, I know. It's not the time for trouble. No, Audine can't come to the phone right now; she's in pretty bad shape. But as soon as we get things sorted here, I'll call you. "Yes, thank you," Wayne said grimly as he hung up the new telephone he bought for the household.

"Violet, come here, please", said Wayne.

Violet moved silently to stand beside Wayne. She looked at him, but he was staring straight ahead without making eye contact. His forehead was wrinkled with concern, and his jaw was clenched.

"I just spoke with your aunt in New York," he said hoarsely. "Your bags were already packed, and luckily, a train to New York leaves within the next two hours. I'll take your mother's suitcases — the ones you didn't even ask her permission to take — and put them in the car. I don't have time to contact Ricks and his men to follow us to the train station, so we're leaving right now. After I leave you at the train station, I'll go to Clarence's house and tell him, in front of his family, what you both did. First thing tomorrow morning, I'll call my lawyer to have Clarence arrested and jailed."

"You don't know the whole story," Violet muttered, distressed. "I let Clarence touch me, kiss me, and he said he loved me and that he was going home to ask Maria for a divorce so he could marry me. We, we're going to be a family, and-"

"Violet, stop it!" Wayne said sharply. "Clarence is married with children and another on the way! He's not going to marry you, and you're not the first woman he's told this to! He was involved with Maydell Scott for years! And do you really think he loves you? Humph! What he did was lie to you, sweetheart! His lies have brought heartbreak and shame to our family. You won't be able to go to college to become a teacher either. So, what now, Violet? What are you going to do after the baby's born and as the child grows? No, no, no. I'll pack up the car now so we can get you out of here," said Wayne.

He walked over to where two large suitcases and three sacks of food that Violet had packed were against the doorway and gathered them in his hands.

"Mason, please help me open the door", he said.

"Yes, sir," he said, rising from the floor where he sat with Audine. He strode past Violet, brushing against her shoulder and nearly causing her to fall again. Without a word or glance back, he helped Wayne lift and load the baggage into the car.

Violet was stunned and confused by the terrible things Wayne said about Clarence.

How could that be? Clarence was with that woman, Maydell? Not true! Clarence told me he loves me and wants me to be his wife! He'll tell everyone the truth that we are getting married as soon as he arrives any minute now! She thought to herself.

Suddenly, Violet experienced a strong, intentional tug as her small purse was yanked from her hand. She spun around and saw Audine rummaging through her purse.

"What are you doing looking inside of my purse?" Violet asked, startled.

Audine didn't answer as she rummaged through her purse, determined to find what she was looking for. Impatiently, she tossed the purse upside down, causing all the contents to spill onto the table and floor. Then, a broad smile spread across her face when she saw the canary blue knotted handkerchief on the table.

"Ma, please leave that alone. That's the money daddy left for me. Oh, please leave it alone, it's mine!"

Violet said, trying her best to hold back the tears building in her throat.

Audine untied the handkerchief, took out the eight-hundred-dollar cash wad, removed a ten-dollar bill, folded the remaining money, and tucked it into her bosom.

"Before you leave, clean up this got-damn mess," she said coldly. "The ten dollars is yours. Don't foolishly spend it all, because you're gonna need it. Standing here isn't my daughter but a low, ten-cent whore with a bastard in her belly, conceived by a worthless, married man. We all had high hopes for you, and now look at yourself, humph! No man will ever want to marry you, Violet! You ruined my good name and reputation in town and at my church. I'm so ashamed that it ain't even funny. Well, that's all over now. Clear this mess from my floor and table. When you're finished, never come back to my house again," Audine said, hobbling to her bedroom to escape the chaos in the kitchen. She slammed the door behind her.

Collapsing to her knees in desperation, Violet wept bitterly as she gathered up the remnants of her purse that lay strewn on the floor. With trembling hands, Violet took the ten-dollar bill and slipped it inside her shoe. Knowing that she'd be traveling alone, she made sure that the money would be safe from a thief who would maybe hold her at knifepoint and run off with her purse. Wiping her tears, Violet went over to the box on the floor and grabbed a small sack. Filling it with several peaches and a few apples, she reminded herself that the trip would be for two days. Luckily, the other sacks in the suitcases had additional sandwiches and cake slices.

"Let's go, Violet", said Wayne, peering from the door. "We've not much time".

"I'll be right there. I need to grab my Bible," Violet said. She quickly entered her room again, gathering a few essentials: her Bible, some handkerchiefs, and Clarence's plaid shirt. She brought the shirt close, inhaling the subtle scent of sandalwood mixed with his sweat. Carefully folding it, she tucked his shirt into the sack. She surveyed the room one last time before lowering her gaze and placing her hand on her belly.

"Your father will come with us to New York, you'll see! Afterwards, he'll marry me, and we'll all move to Virginia, where there's peace," she whispered.

"Hurry up, Dad's waiting!"

Violet spun around and saw Mason standing at the door. His voice reflected the sternness of his gaze.

"I'm coming," Violet said as she slowly walked toward the door to leave. "Mason, I'm sorry," she whispered, her eyes looking down. "You're my brother, and I love you-"

"Shut up, Violet!" he snapped, his voice trembling with anger. "You don't love me, Ma, or Dad. If you did, you wouldn't have gone near Clarence! But honestly, the best part of all this is that you're both finally gone for good. If I were bigger, I'd have killed him after he slammed me against the wall, like he did. I'm glad he's gone, and I hope he ends up in jail." A look of contempt flickered across his face as he turned away from her, headed to his room, and slammed the door.

Violet experienced a sudden shiver as she hurried forward. With no time left to debate, she quickly made her way down the short corridor and paused at Audine's door.

"Goodbye, Ma," she said softly, her voice trembling. She received no response. Violet then left, stepped outside, and sat in Wayne's car. Without saying anything, he started the engine and drove into the night.

After driving in silence for half an hour, they arrived at the train station. Wayne got out, took her bags, and gestured for her to follow him into the small station. While standing in the line marked "For Colored," Wayne bought a one-way ticket to New York for Violet.

"Follow me," he said. He walked briskly out of the station and onto the platform, where several other Black men and women waited for the same train. "This is as far as I will go, Violet. The man who sold this ticket told me the train to New York will arrive in ten minutes, without a moment to spare," Wayne added, pressing the ticket into Violet's trembling hand. I also placed twenty dollars inside the ticket sleeve. Where did you put the money that your father left you?"

"Ma took everything, except ten dollars she let me keep," Violet replied, her voice trembling more and more.

"She what?" he asked.

"I only have ten dollars, sir," she said.

Wayne shut his eyes and let out a heavy sigh.

"Put the money that I gave you inside your shoe right now," he said, glancing around to make sure no one was watching, as Violet did as she was told.

"I'll write to you once everything is figured out. I need to leave now. I am upset by what this family has endured in such a brief period. We all believed in you and hoped for better.

Take care, and may the Lord protect you," he said, hugging her tightly. Then he departed. Violet stood on the platform, watching Wayne leave the station door.

After ten minutes, the train horn sounded as it approached. She decided there was no more time for tears and gathered her belongings. She followed the Black passengers into the last car. Sitting alone, she watched longingly as the Black men carried their wives' suitcases and neatly placed them under their seats. The couple then sat together, holding hands and sitting close to each other. She silently vowed to herself that she would be like them someday, closing her eyes.

As the train started to pull away, she took one last look at New Orleans.

CHAPTER TWENTY-EIGHT

"That low son-of-a-bitch, I trusted Clarence, he was supposed to be our friend! He's about to pay dearly for what he's done to my family!" Wayne yelled angrily, pounding his fist on the steering wheel of his car.

Wayne made a sharp left onto the dirt road leading to Clarence and Maria's home, hitting the brakes so his car screeched to a stop. Over twenty cars, small trucks, and two horse-drawn wagons lined the road, along with an unmistakable funeral hearse from the city parked backward right in front of Clarence and Maria's house.

"What the heck happened here?" Wayne whispered to himself.

He pulled the clutch to shift into park, turned off the ignition, and stepped out. He quickly moved toward the funeral coach, peering inside to see a pine coffin long enough to accommodate a tall man.

Wayne thought, 'Oh no, not Kempton,' as a sudden wave of panic arose in his stomach.

"Good evening, Wayne." A sudden heavy hand on his shoulder startled him, making him spin around so quickly he almost lost his balance.

"Jesus, Ricks. You nearly scared me to death", Wayne said, shaken.

Sorry about that. I heard footsteps right after I heard a car door close. With everything that's happened here tonight, I wanted to make sure no outsiders were coming up to do something foolish, especially now," said Ricks, taking a long puff from his pipe.

Wayne asked, "I'm here to see Clarence because we have a lot to discuss. But I noticed something's wrong. Why is the funeral coach here? Who died?"

"You won't be talking to Clarence anymore," Ricks answered quietly. "He's dead."

"What? What happened?" Wayne exclaimed, covering his mouth.

"A lot has happened. I've been told it involves Audine's daughter, Violet," Ricks whispered.

"Jesus, Ricks. Who else knows about it?" Wayne asked.

"Me, Maria, and Clarence's kids. When he was preparing to leave, he gave me instructions on managing his farm business and house," Ricks said, gazing into the distance as he took a long draw from his pipe. "See, he told his wife everything about his relationship with Violet and how they'd been seeing each other. Well, they ended up being together in her bedroom, and that's when they went to see the midwife, Alice Wade, the other day. Clarence told Alice he was the father of the baby. Upon hearing this, she got so angry that she told Violet never to come back, because Maria was also having a baby, and what they did, Clarence putting a baby in Violet's belly, was a disgrace before God."

Wayne's face was grim with rage as he rubbed his head.

"You should've been here to hear the screaming and crying going on," said Ricks. "I saw Maria running outta the house, shouting in Creole. Before she entered the shed, I saw her take a jar from her apron pocket, open it, and sprinkle what appeared to be dust. She then ran into the shed and stayed inside for a long time, until Clarence came out of the house. I was talking to my men with my back turned when I suddenly heard Clarence screaming near the woodpile he uses for the stove. I rushed over to see what was wrong, and that's when he showed me his hand."

"What happened?" Wayne asked, his eyes showing a flicker of shock.

"A snake bit him, a red pygmy rattler. Clarence said that son-of-a-bitch clamped onto his hand and wouldn't let go! Said he snatched it off and threw it onto the grass. But as soon as I looked at his face, I knew he wasn't gonna make it. He started twitching, and then his eyes rolled to the back of his head. Then, foam mixed with blood started coming out of his mouth. When he heaved his last breath, he was gone," said Ricks.

"Jesus", Wayne replied. He shifted his eyes to the funeral coach that held Clarence's body.

"Funny thing is, none of us could find that snake. I had my men search the entire yard. What's strange is that those kinds of snakes don't appear here at this time of year. So, why did it come around?" Ricks asked, his face showing a somber expression.

"I-I gotta go back home and tell Audine about what happened here tonight," Wayne said, his voice devoid of emotion.

"What about Violet? Guess she won't be coming to Clarence's funeral", said Ricks.

"No, she won't be attending. Neither will my wife, my son, nor I," Wayne said flatly.

Ricks watched as Wayne got into his car and drove off.

On a sunny yet brisk Friday morning, Ricks and his men helped pull out the pine casket containing the remains of Clarence Margaret from the funeral coach. As they approached the grave, Maria was supported by Kempton, Alice Wade, and Eucharista Birch. Following quietly behind were Maria's children, Joseph, Sampson, Izelle, and Rosetta. No members of their church attended the private service. Maria, overwhelmed with grief, chose to avoid the potential gossip and inquiries about Clarence's affair with Violet. During the final prayer by Pastor Coleman, some of Rick's men lingered to tip their hats and pay respects. Clarence's children quickly left, still shaken and angry about their father's relationship with Violet, eager to return home and process their grief as a family.

Kempton, who walked tall and proud, stayed with Ricks and his men; all thirty-five were present. Seven of his men walked in front, seven behind, and the rest formed a surrounding perimeter to the left and right of the Margaret family. The remaining members of Ricks's group stayed near the cars and the funeral coach.

"Maria, how are you doing?" Mrs. Wade asked, her voice laced with concern.

"I could be better, but this all feels like a terrible dream. My husband is gone forever, along with his secrets," Maria said in a strained voice.

"I know, daughter," Mrs. Birch said, hugging Maria. "My dearest, we can't be sure what secrets Clarence took to the grave. He had many, many things hidden inside of him, namely deceit."

Mrs. Wade stopped and peered at her friend and shook her head vigorously as if to tell her to cease her chatter and opinions about Clarence.

"I'm so sorry, mon Cheri, I certainly meant no harm in what I was saying. I'm just very angry about what Clarence was going to do to his family. And as for Violet, humph! I heard Audine sent her away. Good riddance!" said Mrs. Birch.

"Ahem!" Mrs. Wade cleared her throat loudly.

"Ladies, I need a moment alone with my husband before he's laid to rest. I'll return shortly," Maria whispered. She gently moved away and started walking back toward Clarence's coffin.

"Of course, dear," Mrs. Wade said, suddenly gripping Maria's arm firmly. "We'll join everyone else, but we especially want to stay close to your children. Your eldest appears comfortable talking with Ricks and his men," she added. "Come, Eucharista, let's go."

The two women departed, walking arm in arm and speaking in quiet voices. She glanced over her shoulder, ensuring they were far enough away as she moved closer to Clarence's casket.

"You betrayed me, our family, and our friends," Maria said coldly. "You lied, went behind my back, and betrayed me with a woman I despise deeply. Not only were you with her, but you also put your seed inside her, and now a part of you grows like a weed. That child that latched inside Violet's belly will be cursed and won't understand what it is when it enters this world. But let me tell you, Clarence, you and that woman will both rot in hell. I release you forever," Maria declared.

Unsnapping her purse, Maria pulled out a white, bloodstained handkerchief. With black-gloved hands, she unfolded it and revealed the severed head of the pygmy rattlesnake that bit Clarence. Slowly lifting the upper half of the casket, she gazed at the remains of her husband. He appeared darker and stiffer. His eyes were sunken in, and his once full lips were now twisted and tightly contorted downwards. Taking the remains of the snake's head and bloodied handkerchief, she placed them on his chest, directly over his heart, and took two bloodied coins that were dipped in the snake's blood and pressed them on top of Clarence's closed eyelids.

Maria whispered, "Both of you go straight to hell," then spat on Clarence's face. After slamming the casket's lid, she straightened up, quickly snapped her purse shut, and hurried toward her waiting family and friends.

CHAPTER TWENTY-NINE

Harlem, New York

Friday Late Afternoon

"New York! This is the final stop, New York City!" the conductor called out loudly from the train doorway.

Violet took another bite of the sweet apple until she reached the core. She finished the last of her lunch, which was a small ham-filled biscuit. The sacks that once held multiple ham sandwiches, thick slices of pound cake, and a jar of potato salad were now empty. Over the past two days, the trip from New Orleans to New York had been lonely, exhausting, and marked by numerous trips to the tiny, narrow bathroom designated for Black passengers. The bathroom was so cramped that sitting on the toilet made it hard to stand up, especially when the train was moving quickly. Days and nights were filled with anxiety and sleep deprivation. Thoughts of Clarence made her tear up from sadness. Her only comfort was clutching his plaid shirt close and using it as a blanket when she felt cold.

Your father probably received an earful from Audine and Wayne when he came to pick us up, but don't worry, he'll be here next week once he learns where we're staying. I'm sure of that! Maybe we can get married in New York, and when we leave, I'll be his wife, she whispered, looking down at her belly.

"This is the last stop, get out!" The angry-looking conductor shouted directly at her.

"Yes, Suh, I'm so sorry, Suh!" she said, startled.

The train was almost empty of Black passengers, except for a Black woman seated ahead, struggling with a heavy suitcase. Violet hurriedly gathered her suitcases, along with four empty food sacks and her purse. She tucked Clarence's shirt into one of the sacks. Wiggling her toes inside her shoe, she ensured the unspent money was safe. The memory of Audine's assault replayed painfully in her mind. Taking such a large amount of money made her chest ache. She shook off the thought and continued struggling with her belongings. When she finally got off, the train station was overwhelming and seemed to move slowly.

Violet thought that this must have been what her mother and Wayne saw when they arrived here, as she bent down to adjust the weight of the suitcases.

"Need any help with your things?"

Violet spun around to catch sight of a smiling; young, handsome Black boy dressed in tweed knickers.

But before she could respond, she felt herself being pushed from behind, causing her to lose balance and fall to the dirt ground. The grinning boy seized one of her suitcases and ran away.

"Help! Help me!" she shrieked as she lay injured on the ground. "That boy ran off with my bag, stop him!"

Not a soul came to her aid. As Violet lay on the ground, clutching her belly, she was stunned to see how everyone ignored her cries for help and kept walking by.

"I don't want to live here; I want to go home to Clarence!" she wailed in anguish.

"Violet!" a man's voice shouted.

Gazing up, she saw her aunt Cee-Cee and her husband Hubert running and bumping into people to reach her.

"Oh my God, Violet, what happened?" Cee-Cee cried out.

"That, that boy ran away with my suitcase!" said Violet, pointing at the boy wearing knickers who was running and bumping into passersby.

"Cee-Cee, stay with her. I see him running! C'mon, fellas!" Hubert shouted to the four men with him. The five of them sprinted, disappearing into the crowd as people moved aside.

"Violet, oh, honey, I'm so sorry this all happened to you! Here, let me help you up; easy now, get up slowly", said Cee-Cee.

Taking hold of Cee-Cee's arm, Violet winced in pain but managed to stand.

"I gotcha," said Cee-Cee, as she firmly wrapped her arm around Violet's waist to steady her.

"Well, this may not be the warmest way to welcome you to New York, but I have to admit you're certainly bringing a lot of things worth conversation. Speaking of which, is the baby okay? I saw you grabbing onto your belly," she said.

"I'm okay, just a little sore and scared", said Violet.

"Come on, let's get everything inside the car. We'll wait for your uncle and his friends to get back. Grab those food sacks while I carry your suitcase to the car", said Cee-Cee.

Violet nodded and grabbed the sacks while Cee-Cee took the suitcase. Holding the sack with Clarence's shirt close to her chest, she hobbled over to Cee-Cee.

"This is our car right here," she said proudly as they neared the 1931 Chevrolet Eagle Sedan.

"Is this your car?" Violet asked, eyes wide as she gazed at the black vehicle, which could comfortably seat four to five people.

"Yes, it is. Your uncle and I saved money for two years to buy this car from the man he works for. The man he drives for is a wealthy, tough lawyer. His wife, a beautiful woman, wanted to take their baby girl to Paris. He said no, the baby should stay in New York and be cared for by their housekeeper, who would take care of the baby. Humph, his wife never returned; he divorced her and took their daughter. Your uncle was always at that man's beck and call, driving him everywhere. The day before Christmas, he said he was tired of the car and offered it to us for three hundred dollars. Your uncle's no fool, and neither am I. We worked every day, except on the Lord's Day. When I earned the first one hundred and fifty dollars, your uncle came to dinner on New Year's Eve with an extra two hundred and fifty, totaling four hundred dollars. The next day, your uncle paid the man three hundred dollars. Two days later, that man bought a bigger car and handed the keys over to your uncle. One thing's for sure, just like in New Orleans, he keeps two black chauffeur's hats in each car, one in the car he drives the lawyer around in, and the other always stays here," she said, pointing to a black, unassuming cap with a silver monogrammed "H," hanging near the driver's side window.

"Why does Uncle Hubert have to ride around with a cap in his own car?" Violet asked as she opened the door and got into the back seat of the most luxurious car she had ever been in. Cee-Cee signaled Violet to slide closer to the open window and spoke softly.

"It's put there because it's used as a prop. Your uncle has been stopped by the police so often that they all recognize him. If he told the police he owns this car, they would refuse to believe him, thinking it had been stolen. Even if they believed him, they would likely react violently due to their prejudice, especially considering his race and the car's beauty. Fortunately, the lawyer had a clever solution: he drafted a document stating that the police should contact him if they had any doubts. This approach always worked because, after reading the paper, the police usually left him alone. There are three copies: one your uncle carries whenever he drives, one at our home, and another inside the family Bible".

As soon as Cee-Cee opened the passenger door of the car, a burst of angry shouts erupted, and a loud thud against the side where Violet was sitting made her yelp in alarm at the sudden impact.

"You apologize to my niece for what you did, you piece of gutter shit, you hear me?" Hubert demanded.

The young man's lip was split and bloody, his nose looked broken, and his left eye was turning a grotesque purple and swollen shut.

"I said to apologize to her now!" he shouted, slamming the young man's face against the car window. The other men who accompanied Hubert had the car surrounded. Cee-Cee, who seemed completely unfazed, took out a lipstick tube and applied the bright red color onto her lips.

"I-I'm sorry for stealing your suitcase," he sputtered.

Hubert struck the young man on the head, making him cry out in pain.

"If I ever see you here again, I'm gonna give you one of the worst ass-whopping you've ever had in your life! Now get the hell outta here!" Hubert yelled. He loosened his grip from the young man's neck, then took off.

"You ladies, okay?" Hubert asked.

"We're fine, honey, but how's the suitcase? Did he take anything?" said Cee-Cee.

"Nope!" he replied with a rough laugh as she pushed the suitcase beside Violet and closed the door. "Thanks, boys, for helping me chase that piece of shit. If you see him or his greasy friend, kick both their asses, because they're known around here for stealing women's purses!" said Hubert.

"No worries, we'll look out for `em. We know what to do," said the younger man wearing a tweed hat. He took a long puff from the cigarette dangling from his lips. After tipping his hat to Violet, he and the other men walked away.

"Are you okay, Violet?" Hubert asked.

"Yes, sir," Violet replied in a soft, trembling voice.

"Violet, listen to me. You're now in New York. It can be a fun and exciting place, but it can also be a dangerous one. Your mother and Wayne have entrusted you to our care, and we plan to keep you safe from any harm. Moving forward, you'll need to be attentive and extra careful, especially with you uh, being with child", said Hubert.

"Yes, sir, I'll be careful, and thank you for getting my suitcase," she said, lowering her eyes.

"Let's go home," said Cee-Cee, her arm around his neck as they kissed. Hubert started the car and drove to Harlem.

During the ride, Violet felt both excitement and fear. She looked out the window at the busy street, filled with people, various cars, buses, and shops. Then, suddenly, the scene changed. They arrived at a place bustling with hundreds of Black people, shops, and restaurants. Everyone appeared engaged in their activities; some paused to smile and chat, while women pushed baby carriages. Confused, Violet finally spoke.

"Aunt Cee-Cee, where are we?"

"Harlem! Everything we need is right here for us. The church we go to is just over there, the store I shop at is down the street, and there are so many restaurants nearby that choosing is tough!" she said excitedly.

"And this is where we live," said Hubert as he gently steered the car closer to the curb. A group of children playing on the sidewalk paused their activities and looked at Hubert's car. Several men passing by smiled and nodded at the vehicle, while Hubert honked the horn and waved in response.

"Okay, ladies, we're home. Violet, I'll come around the back to get your belongings, and Cee-Cee will open the door on the other side for you to slide out", said Hubert.

"So, are you ready to begin a new chapter? Harlem isn't like New Orleans, where life is quiet and rural. You'll notice many differences here. The Black community in Harlem is also different; you'll notice the difference. But first, let's get you settled, fed, and then your uncle and I need to discuss a lot of things with you," Cee-Cee said, looking directly at Violet.

Violet thought, 'This isn't going to be good, oh God, Clarence, please come get me!' as she felt her stomach cramp in pain.

Hubert opened the door and grabbed the suitcases and food sacks. Alarmed, Violet quickly snatched the sack with Clarence's plaid work shirt from the car seat.

"I'll take this," she said quietly as she pressed the sack close to her chest.

He asked in a curious tone, "Is there something personal in there?"

"Yes, sir," she replied.

"Come on, Violet, let's go inside and get comfortable," said Cee-Cee.

Violet stepped out of the car and took Cee-Cee's hand firmly. Together, they followed Hubert up the stairs into a two-story tenement. As Violet held Cee-Cee's hand, she noticed piles of broken bottles scattered about and rats scurrying around old, splintered crates that served as trash. Several men were tossing what appeared to be dice against a brick wall. One man, stocky and dressed in a suit, his hat pulled low to conceal his face, seemed indifferent as he counted the cash, cursed, and grinned loudly.

"C'mon, Violet, stop just staring at those men, especially the one in the suit. Keep away from him; he's dangerous," Cee-Cee said, lifting her chin to point at the heavy-set man counting his cash.

"That's right", Hubert said, nodding in agreement. "He's not just a gambler, but there's a rumor he murdered the laundry woman who lived right here a few months ago," he added, pointing to the first-floor window. "According to a friend of mine named Evans, when she was discovered, half of her nose had been cut off. Poor woman, she was so tiny, she stood only this high," Hubert said, mimicking a height with his hand.

Violet tightened her grip on Cee-Cee's hand after hearing the gruesome account of the murder. Her thoughts raced, recalling Jonathan's murder back in New Orleans and her mother's words when he was brought to the hospital, even though he was gone. Violet's legs felt weak as she ascended the stairs into the building.

"Aunt Cee-Cee, what's the name of the man you told me to stay away from?" Violet asked quietly and nervously.

"He goes by the name of High Roller-Gunn," she said, keeping her voice very low. "Stay away from him".

Though the outside of the building looked run-down with an adjacent alley, Cee-Cee and Hubert's home was spotless the moment Hubert unlocked and opened the door.

"Ladies, after you," he said, holding the door open for Cee-Cee and Violet.

The small flat was tidy and inviting. The living room featured two large brown chairs, a small two-seater couch, two lamps, and a central table holding a photo of Cee-Cee and Hubert on their wedding day. Two Bibles, stacked on Top of Each Other, rested on the table.

"Follow me, Violet," Hubert said as he led her into a small, beige-painted bedroom with a bed, dresser, lamp, and a single window obscured by white lace curtains.

"Make yourself comfortable, Violet," Cee-Cee said, peering from the doorway. "Dinner will be ready in fifteen minutes. I've already cooked everything, so all I need to do is cut up the eggs for the potato salad, and we'll be ready to eat," she added. Hubert closed the door behind them.

Standing in the middle of the bedroom, Violet looked around but chose to sit on the bed's edge to rest. On the floor, a new pair of slippers with a note attached caught her attention. She picked up the folded note and started reading it.

Violet,

Make yourself comfortable and feel at home. It's simple, but Hubert and I consider it our home. Please wear the slippers when you're inside, especially as your baby grows.

Love,

Aunt Cee-Cee

Violet thought it was kind of her Aunt Cee-Cee, but she figured she wouldn't need the items once Clarence arrived to pick them up, as she massaged her belly.

She took off her shoes and socks, then slipped her swollen feet into the slippers, which fit perfectly. She got up from the bed and walked around to check that they didn't pinch her toes. From the corner of her eye, she noticed the sack containing Clarence's shirt. She opened it, took out the shirt, and gently pressed it to her cheek. Smiling, she closed her eyes, brought his shirt to her nose, and took a deep breath.

"Violet?" It was Cee-Cee, knocking softly on the door, which startled her.

"Yes?" Violet responded as she pushed Clarence's shirt under the pillow.

"Dinner is ready. Your uncle and I are waiting for you", she said.

"Thank you, Aunt Cee-Cee," said Violet.

Violet tidied her dress and adjusted her hair before heading to dinner with her aunt and uncle. As she stepped into the kitchen, the comforting aroma of New Orleans cuisine filled the air. She looked at the table and couldn't help but smile at the spread before her: pan-fried fish on a small platter, sliced tomatoes, a bowl of creamy potato salad, cornbread, and jambalaya.

"Have a seat over here," Hubert said, rising from his chair to help Violet sit.

"Everything looks delicious!" Violet exclaimed.

"I know you'll enjoy a taste of home. Let's bless the food so we can eat. Hubert, please say the blessing," Cee-Cee said with a smile.

"Father God, we thank You for nourishing us with this food. Please extend mercy to comfort the soul that has departed and the loved ones remaining behind. We pray all this in His blessed name, Amen".

Violet opened her eyes wide and looked at Cee-Cee and Hubert, appearing confused as she stared at Hubert.

"Uncle Hubert, I'm confused about what you just said during the blessing. Who's departed?" her voice trembled as she spoke. "Did something happen back home?" she asked quietly.

Cee-Cee looked down at her lap and said nothing.

Violet looked over at Hubert, who was sitting nearby. He then reached out and took her hand. Filled with terror, she quickly stood up from her seat.

"What happened back home? Did something happen to my mother?" she asked in a strained voice.

"Violet honey, sit down," Hubert said gently. She yanked her hand away, stood at the table, and shook her head wildly. "Okay, very well then," Hubert replied, rubbing his forehead. "We were late to the train station because Wayne called with some news. Your mother and brother are both fine. The call was about Clarence."

"What about him? He was supposed to come to my house so we could tell my mother and Wayne about us, and I'm having a baby. He was supposed to marry me-" Hubert interrupted her.

"Violet, Clarence is never coming back," Hubert said, gazing into her eyes. "He was bitten by a red pygmy rattlesnake when he reached into the woodpile near his house for firewood. Clarence has died, honey. Wayne told me he was buried this morning."

Violet froze in place, then a tremor ran through her, causing her to start collapsing to the floor.

"Hubert, catch her! She's falling!" Cee-Cee shouted.

Hubert quickly got up from his seat, but it was too late. Violet was sprawled on the floor, gasping for air. She tried to scream, but no sound came out.

Outside, the noise of men gambling against a filthy, piss-stained wall echoed with curses. Drunken men, lost and stumbling, tried to find their way home to wives and kids who had long abandoned them, as distant thunder and lightning accompanied heavy rain.

These sounds were drowned out by Violet's tears and her anguished screams.

CHAPTER THIRTY

New Orleans

Sunday morning church service

"I can't go inside, Wayne. I feel so ashamed, and I know everyone will laugh at me and talk about me behind my back! I'm so embarrassed to have to do this," Audine admitted with shame. "To think I have to give up the certificate and money Violet received to Carol Thomas-humph! I bet her mother, Phyllis, will be the first to gossip about me having to hand over that damned money. I suppose she'll have Carol packed and ready to leave for Virginia, humph! But I'm not worried at all because she'll probably fail at college anyway; she didn't even pass the entrance exam, that stupid girl, hah!"

"Be quiet, Audine. Since you told Violet to leave, all you do is argue with me, fight, cry, and leave the house a mess. Additionally, the leftover food from our wedding has spoiled. Mason saw eight mice eating the food you stored in the kitchen boxes. My God, Audine, there's a depression here, and we can't afford to waste food like this! Are you crazy or what?" Wayne said, annoyed, gripping the steering wheel as he drove to church.

Mason, sitting quietly in the back seat behind Wayne, gazed out the car window, seemingly unaware of their ongoing arguments, which were sometimes so loud and heated that he would retreat into Wayne's car to focus on his school lessons.

"What do you expect me to do with all that food, huh, Wayne? There are only three of us living here now, and I'm too tired to do all that cleaning in such a big house. Right now, I'm just more worried about who will start talking about me, especially after the mess Violet made for this family," said Audine.

"One thing that's sure a blessing for me is that I'm so glad she's gone from this town and away from me, humph! The got-damned nerve of her and Clarence staying in my house, doing all sorts of nasty things to get a baby inside her belly, and then I end up losing my own baby. It's not fair that she's having a baby and I can't! Oh my God, Wayne, the best thing that could've happened is Clarence dropping dead from that snake bite, hah! It's a shame he left behind all those kids he had with Maria, but for God's sake, he left behind a bastard child inside Violet, and another thing, who's going to take care of them? I'll tell you something else, Violet is most likely gonna end up like Lena, lying up in bed with a bunch of men who'll pay her money and then end up killing her like the two-cent whore she's become!" snorted Audine.

Wayne gently eased the car to a stop at the church, but before he could fully brake, Mason threw open the door and hurried out, loudly rambling. He then sprinted up the stairs, flung the door open, and rushed inside.

"I didn't raise my son to behave this way!" Audine exclaimed with disgust. "Honestly, I might have to discipline him until he apologizes for his recent behavior. I'm sure everyone in their cars saw him! I know people will be talking about me after today. First Violet, now Mason. What am I doing wrong to deserve such punishment?"

Wayne turned off the ignition and swiftly grabbed Audine's wrist with a firm hold.

"Ouch! You're hurting my wrist, Wayne, let me go!" she yelled loudly.

"Enough, Audine! Since we got in the car, all you've done is make everything about yourself. This affects all of us! You're the meanest, most selfish, hateful, jealous, and biggest liar I've ever encountered," he said firmly.

"Mason is behaving this way because of our ongoing fights. I can't believe how we went from being so happy on our wedding day to where we are now. We should let everyone at the church know about the sensitive family issue that has come up, and that Violet had to withdraw from college. The certificate and funds will then be handed over to Mrs. Thomas's daughter, Carol. Regarding your comments about Lena, I've given you many chances to stop talking about her, forgiven you numerous times, yet you continue to speak unkindly about her. After today, I want you out of my house. Yes, Audine, my home!"

His voice echoed the severity of his gaze as he forcefully released Audine's arm. She sat there speechless, her mouth agape and eyes wide as saucers. She flinched when Wayne opened his door.

"Oh, and another thing you need to know is that Mason stays with me. I won't allow our son to be with you, dragging a suitcase and moving from town to town, staying in flop-houses filled with drunks, thieves, and wayward women. While he's in my care, I'll work early shifts at the hospital so I'm home when he gets out of school. He'll keep going to church with me, study his Bible lessons with me, and next year, after finishing school, he'll visit colleges with me by his side. One more thing, Audine, you're a thief!" he said with disdain.

"What did you just call me?" Audine asked angrily.

"I watched you, Audine!" he shouted.

"Shhh, lower your voice! People passing by can hear you!" she hissed.

"Good! Maybe they'll realize the kind of woman you are and recognize the mistake I made in marrying you! You thought I didn't see you, didn't you? I could hear you getting out of bed in the middle of the night and quietly opening the drawer with all the money that the stranger had put inside a card addressed to me, not you, after Lena died. After you took all my money, at least what was left after the wedding and our trip to New York, you counted every last dollar, then stuffed it into your purse along with the money Violet's father gave for her college savings. But guess what, Audine? On Friday morning, while you were in the bathroom, I went into your purse, took out all the money, and deposited it into my savings at the bank," he said.

"You only gave Violet ten dollars of the money her father intended for her. Yes, she told me what you did. How was that poor girl supposed to live on that, huh, Audine? I sent her forty dollars and called Hubert, instructing him not to touch Violet's money until she opened the envelope. I told Violet to keep twenty dollars for herself and to give the other half to Hubert for food and other expenses while Violet stays with them. And as for you, you have ten dollars for a ride and a train ticket to leave tonight. After church, we'll go home, and you're to pack your suitcase and leave. Also, I've spoken to our Pastor and told him I want our marriage annulled."

Wayne rushed out of the car, slammed the door, and hurried toward the church to escape the vileness of the woman he used to love.

Audine unzipped her purse and rummaged through it until she found a crinkled, grease-stained envelope with a wad of cash, one five-dollar bill, four singles, and four quarters. She hurled the envelope onto the dashboard, ignoring the coins spilling onto the floor of the car. Overcome with shame, she bowed her head, winced her eyes, and began to sob, trembling as she realized she had not only been caught stealing but also feared her marriage might end by day's end.

Maria St. Laurent, standing a few yards away on a gentle slope, observed the entire scene with a slight smile on her lips.

CHAPTER THIRTY-ONE

New Orleans

Monday morning

"Ma, I'll be leaving in fifteen minutes. Harold said he was going to drive me to the army building where Black recruits will be sworn in," Kempton said softly as he knocked gently on Maria's bedroom door.

Last Friday, Kempton had an early graduation ceremony. Maria and Ricks, along with his wife, Alice Wade, Eucharista Birch, and Kempton's siblings, gathered in a small auditorium to watch Kempton and ten other boys, who were about to join the army, receive their high school diplomas. Instead of graduating in June, they were set to start basic training immediately. The crowd was filled with pride and happiness as they watched Kempton walk proudly across the stage to shake hands with his teachers, the schoolmaster, and the principal. Kempton looked handsome in Clarence's gray suit, which fit him perfectly. Maria intentionally kept the suit hidden in a corner of her closet, choosing instead to bury Clarence in his dirty, soil-stained shirt, overalls, and worn-out shoes from the day he died.

As everyone cheered loudly when Kempton's name was announced for the agriculture award, Maria smiled at him, but a wave of fear gripped her heart.

"Ma, are you up?" Kempon asked, knocking repeatedly on the door.

"Yes, I'll be there in a moment", Maria replied as she finished tying her Oxford shoes.

Kempton is leaving me today to serve in an army that has long despised Black men and treated them as mere trash. All we can do is keep him in our daily prayers, Maria thought bitterly. After one last look in the mirror,

Maria adjusted the tight bun at the nape of her neck and brushed away delicate wisps of hair from her face. The apron strings now felt tighter as her belly began to protrude. There was no denying that in five months, a new member would join the family. She stared at the bed where she and Clarence had lain and conceived their child. At first, she marveled at their plans to try for another, hoping that the baby born in five months wouldn't grow up alone. But her happiness quickly faded when she thought of Violet, who was also pregnant by Clarence, only a month apart. Her joy was replaced with disgust at Clarence's betrayal, for Violet had deceived everyone with her innocence.

Maria quickly brushed away a tear spilling from the corner of her eye and went out to join the small group of well-wishers who came to bid farewell to Kempton.

Ricks and eight of his men, along with their wives, were all engaged in a deep conversation with Kempton. Mrs. Wade and Mrs. Birch were having a lively discussion with Izelle, Rosetta, Joseph, and Sampson. Deacon and Deaconess Moss sat in chairs opposite each other, reading scriptures from their Bibles.

"Bonjour Mère", Izelle said in a strained voice.

"Bonjour, Izelle, and good morning, everyone. Thank you all for coming to witness my eldest son's departure," Maria said, but her voice quivered as she struggled to hold back tears and then broke down in deep sobs.

Kempton excused himself to go to Maria, who was weeping uncontrollably.

"Don't cry, Ma. I'm right here," he said, as he gently wrapped his arms around her trembling shoulders.

Everyone in the tiny room moved in unison to console Maria. Rosetta rushed into the kitchen to get herself a glass of cold water, but as she filled the glass, she, too, was overwhelmed by tears.

"Ma, please don't cry," Kempton whispered. "This is my calling. I excelled in school and can follow instructions after hearing them once. I'm going to make a damn good soldier,"

Maria looked up at Kempton, who was already over six feet tall. She had never heard him curse before, but on this day, she permitted herself to do so. A faint smile flickered in her eyes.

"What's got you tickled?" he queried, his hazel eyes twinkling.

"You just cursed," she said, dabbing at her nose with a handkerchief. "If you were younger and shorter, I'd have taken a switch to your behind."

He said with a smile, kissing her forehead, "Well, I suppose when I return to see you, I'll pick a switch from the tree to fulfill my punishment."

There was a loud knock at the front door.

"I'll answer the door, Mère," Izelle said, swiftly heading toward the door.

Izelle took a moment to straighten her dress before opening the door, surprised to see a six-foot-tall soldier with bronze skin who resembled Jonathan, though older.

"Good morning, Ma'am. My name is Lieutenant Harold Clark," he said, removing his hat and extending his hand in greeting.

Izelle remained still, gazing at the handsome soldier who grinned at her, showing his perfect white teeth.

"Uh, may I come in? I'm from the U.S. Army here to pick up Kempton."

"Yes, of course! I'm sorry, but you look like someone I knew a long time ago. My name is Izelle, Kempton's sister. Please come inside," she said politely.

"Thank you", he said.

"Hi, Harold, it's good to see you again," Kempton said as he eased himself away from Ricks and his men.

"Good to see you too, soldier. Or at least, you'll become one in a few hours," Harold said with a smile.

"Yes, I know, but before we leave, this is my family, and they all wanted to be here before I go," said Kempton, gesturing to everyone.

He said, "I'm going to start here with my mother."

Maria stepped forward, attempting to appear brave, but all she could manage was a nod. Harold approached her and took her hand.

"I promise, Mrs. Margaret, that I'll look after Kempton. He's like a brother to me, so don't worry," he whispered.

After all the introductions, Harold was surprised not only to see Izelle again but also to learn she had an identical twin sister. Both sisters looked at him, but Harold felt a special connection to Izelle.

Following a series of probing questions from Maria and Ricks, Harold and Kempton prepared to depart. Deacon Moss requested that everyone form a circle with Kempton and Harold in the middle and lay hands on his head. He then started to pray.

"Heavenly Father, we come to you in Jesus' name. Our son, brother, and young friends, Kempton Pierre Margaret, and Harold Anthony Clark, will soon leave to serve our country. We pray for your protection over Kempton and Harold, and ask that you send angels to surround and stay with them daily, from morning until night. Grant Kempton and Harold courageously faced challenges, even without violence. If lives must be taken in defense, please forgive them. May they serve only you as their eternal God. Let us all say Amen".

When the prayer ended, everyone was crying, even Ricks had to take out his handkerchief to wipe his reddened eyes and blow his nose. Harold, who was also moved by emotion, quietly asked to be excused.

"Izelle, may I please use the bathroom?" Harold asked. Kempton and I have a long drive ahead, and then he needs to report to the army officers for processing, so we won't have time to stop.

"Yes, please follow me," Izelle said as she walked ahead and gestured toward the bathroom.

"Thank you," he said, smiling. "Your home is very nice, the first farmstead I've seen with a bathroom instead of an outhouse."

"Thank you, my father wanted to make sure that we had a proper bathroom instead of an outhouse. The only thing missing is a bathtub," she said, holding his gaze.

"Uh, I'll be right out, excuse me," he said softly as he closed the door.

Izelle closed her eyes, puffed out her cheeks, then spun around and went to the kitchen to prepare a food sack with freshly baked cornbread, sausages, and thick slices of coconut pound cake made by Rick's wife.

Maria said, "I already made two sacks for each of them and two jars of lemon water."

"Oh, I was going to make Kempton and Harold sacks of food," she stammered.

"Izelle, come here," said Maria.

Maria's eyes were tear-filled, and she looked worn out. It was clear she was scared for Kempton, who had never been anywhere outside New Orleans. The idea of him in the army, confronting the dangers of being mistreated as a Black man, filled her with fear for his safety.

"He reminds you of Jonathan, doesn't he?" Maria said with a smile, lifting the corners of her lips.

"I thought I was the only one!" she exclaimed. "He resembles Jonathan, but older. How did you realize this?"

"I saw him at Wayne and Audine's wedding," she said with a sigh. "He was talking to Violet, but we all know what happened with that".

"Oui, Mère, but don't ever speak about them again," said Izelle.

"Listen, take the sack I made for Harold. I prepared something special inside it. If he gives you a wad of paper with his address so you can write to each other, accept it. You have my blessing to write to one another," Maria said.

She asked, "How do you know he's going to give me a piece of paper with his army address on it so we can send letters to each other?"

"I just know he will," Maria said, her voice tinged with optimism. "Besides, it shouldn't take this long for a soldier to pee."

"Mère!" Izelle exclaimed, giggling.

After everyone bid farewell, Maria and Izelle accompanied Kempton and Harold to the covered army jeep marked "United States Army".

"Kempton, come here, son," Maria called, leading him to the back of the jeep for a last word.

"Uh, this is for you, Harold," Izelle said as she handed him the food sack.

"Whatever is in it smells wonderful. I didn't have time to eat anything before I left, and I'm really hungry. Thank you, that's very thoughtful," he said.

"So, I suppose this is goodbye, and it was a pleasure meeting you, Harold. Please look after my brother; we will miss him, and take care of yourself as well," she said.

Harold reached out to shake her hand but unexpectedly bent down and kissed her cheek instead. His gaze remained fixed on her face as he held her hand, pressing something into her open palm. He quietly folded her fingers to keep the exchange discreet. After closing his eyes, kissing her hand, and tipping his hat to her, he stepped into the car. When he started the engine, it was apparent it was time to go. Kempton gave Maria a final hug and then joined Harold in the front seat.

"I'll be back soon, Izelle. Take good care of Ma. I love you," said Kempton.

"I love you too, Kempton," she said, her voice husky with tears.

Harold honked twice, sped the jeep toward the road, and then they disappeared. Maria went to Izelle and hugged her.

"Be sure to pray for your brother and Harold every night, my dearest. I'm going inside now to check that Mrs. Birch and Mrs. Wade have enough coffee and pie," Maria said as she went up the stairs to the house, pausing briefly to watch Izelle open the piece of paper with Harold's army address.

Izelle turned around smiling, and at that moment, Maria realized Izelle's heartbreak over Jonathan's death would heal forever.

CHAPTER THIRTY-TWO

Everyone else had left except Ricks, his wife, Eucharista, and Alice. After more than four hours of conversation, Ricks excused himself and took Joseph and Sampson for a relaxed walk around the barn, smokehouse, and the fields that Clarence had cultivated all his life.

"With Kempton now in the army and your father gone, you boys need to learn how to work hard on this farm that your father dedicated his whole life to. I know he made some mistakes with y'all, but listen, you're like family. My wife, my men, and I are here to help. You boys will continue your schooling, but on Fridays and Saturdays, you'll be working instead of playing. When spring arrives, we'll go fishing and sell whatever we catch. Do you understand?" said Ricks.

"Yes, sir, Mr. Ricks, we understand," said Joseph.

"Yes, Mr. Ricks," Sampson replied, looking down and wiping his wet eyes. Ricks then embraced Joseph and Sampson.

"Listen to me," Ricks said. "As long as I'm alive, I'll be here to watch over all of you, especially you boys. I promised your father that I would do this, particularly if anything happened to him. If you have any problems or questions, come to me, do you hear?"

"Yes, sir," they both said.

C'mon, let's see if we can catch any fish by the lake," said Ricks.

"I'll fetch the poles, Mr. Ricks," Sampson said, running toward the barn to grab the fishing poles.

Rick's watched Sampson run and smiled.

"Mr. Ricks, may I ask you something?" Joseph inquired.

"Of course, you can, son. What's your question?" he asked.

"It's December, and folks have been saying it's rare to see a red pygmy rattlesnake around here. So how come one was in that wood pile the night my father got bitten? Earlier that night, Sampson and I stacked ten logs beside the woodstove. We knew it was going to be cold, so I don't understand why my father would add more to the ten logs we already laid out. It doesn't make any sense to us," said Joseph.

Ricks asked, baffled, "Wait a minute, you and Sampson pulled ten logs earlier that evening?"

"Yes, sir, we did", Joseph said.

Ricks turned around and looked at the shed with Clarence's tools, recalling seeing a shadowy woman resembling Maria nearby, holding what appeared to be a large, decapitated snake.

As he approached for a closer view, the woman disappeared, and the snake that bit Clarence was never located.

CHAPTER THIRTY-THREE

"Maria, please sit down; you've done enough today," Eucharista urged gently as she took the coffee pot from Maria's hand and put it back on the stove to keep it hot.

"I agree with Eucharista," Alice said as she led Maria to the kitchen chair where they all sat. Earlier in the morning, friends visited and stayed until three in the afternoon. Fortunately, everyone contributed food, including platters of biscuits, sausage, salad, fish, green beans, tomatoes, and various cakes and pies. After all the running, cleaning, and making sure guests were comfortable, Maria felt overwhelmed and exhausted. The baby growing inside her was developing well, and with her appetite returning, Maria started to glow.

"I've been feeling a lot better, I've been eating a lot more, and my dresses are starting to get a little tighter around the middle over here," she said, rubbing her belly.

"I feel much happier now. I realize things will be tougher for us, especially with Clarence gone, but Ricks mentioned he and his men will stay to support us. Some of his men with older sons are willing to help in return for four-bushel baskets of vegetables and a quarter pound of meat from our smokehouse. I believe that's fair because we need the help." Maria said, rubbing her forehead.

"You're doing very well. Honestly, I was worried the last time I visited because I thought you might have lost the baby after everything Clarence did to you. But let me say this: you have definitely come out of this whole affliction blessed," Alice said, sipping her coffee.

"Humph, if you ask me, he deserved it," said Eucharista. "I don't mean to speak badly of the dead, but after everything that man did to you, the baby growing inside of you, your children, and then showing up to see Alice and examine Violet, it was just perverted, in my opinion."

"Well, speaking of Violet and her big-mouthed mother, it seems they are both gone," said Alice, biting eagerly into a forkful of cake.

Maria was captivated by what she was about to hear from Mrs. Wade, a half-smile lingering as she remembered the events that took place in the tool shed weeks before Clarence's death, Violet's abrupt departure, and the end of Audine and Wayne's marriage.

"You know Etta, the head usher at our church?" Alice asked.

Mrs. Birch and Maria nodded silently.

"Well, Wayne invited Etta for breakfast after Mason went to school and confided in her everything. That night, your husband was meant to visit Violet's house to inform Audine and Wayne that he was leaving you to marry Violet, as she was carrying his child," Alice said, disgusted.

Eucharista shifted her chair closer to Maria, who appeared visibly repulsed by what she was hearing. The two women clasped hands.

"So then, what happened, Alice?" Eucharista asked.

" Well, as we all know, Clarence didn't make it, leaving Violet to fend for herself."

"So, who told Audine and Wayne about the baby?" Eucharista asked.

"Wayne told Etta that it was Mason.

"Mason?" Maria blurted out.

"Yes, indeed," said Alice. "It seems that when Clarence stayed at Audine and Wayne's house, he wasn't sleeping in the extra room they had prepared for him. Mason told them that, while he was sleeping, he heard loud thumping noises that woke him up. After getting out of bed, he quietly went to Violet's room, where the noises were coming from."

"So, what happened then?" Maria asked hesitantly.

"Humph, do you want to know what I'm about to tell you? Because, from what Etta told me, it's pretty straightforward," said Alice, pushing her spectacles to the bridge of her nose.

"Tell me everything," said Maria as she gripped Eucharista's hands more tightly.

"Mason approached Violet's room and, upon hearing high-pitched groans and heavy breathing, realized she was calling Clarence's name. The noises from her bed grew louder and more frantic. Curious, Mason noticed her door was slightly open and pushed it open further. He saw Clarence on top of Violet, with her legs wrapped around him. Shocked by what he saw, Mason hurried back to his room and stayed there until morning," Alice revealed.

"This was happening every night Clarence stayed over".

"Have mercy, Jesus," pleaded Eucharista, lowering her head. Maria also bowed her head, looking defiant.

After Wayne and Audine received that news, Audine finally realized why Violet was ill on her wedding morning. Etta told her that Audine was beating Violet so badly that Wayne and Mason had to step in to stop her. Additionally, Audine had kept almost all of Violet's father's money for herself, leaving only ten dollars, taking every dollar that girl had. Wayne then called Audine's sister in New York to inform her that Violet would arrive in two days. After Wayne saw Violet off at the train station and left, he came here looking for Clarence to confront him. But after Ricks told him Clarence had died, he hurried back home to tell Audine. He learned about her mistreatment of Violet and uncovered another of her wicked deeds, revealing what kind of woman she truly was."

"And what was that?" asked Eucharista.

"Audine ain't nothing but a low-down, dirty gutter rat who's a thief. Wayne caught her stealing money from the drawer where he kept his shirts! But listen, there's much more to this," said Alice

Maria held back the tears rising in her throat by taking a long sip of hot coffee. Clarence, Violet, and Audine had only brought her pain, humiliation, and betrayal. In the end, they each received what they deserved.

"Good riddance to all of them," Maria said, holding her head up high as tears spilled from the corners of her eyes.

CHAPTER THIRTY-FOUR

Harlem, New York

January 1934

"Be careful, Violet. The narrow roads and alley just before you turn left are the quickest routes to the hairdresser. Mrs. Marcel is expecting you within the next forty-five minutes. By the way, Wayne has sent you money. Hubert divided the cash so we each have our half, yours being out of eighty dollars. Hubert also went to the bank to exchange your money into smaller bills so that you can stop at The Southern Pot for coffee and a sandwich for lunch. Don't forget to wear the boots I got for you because it's already snowing," Cee-Cee said, looking out the window.

Violet glanced at her dresser clock; it was going on 7:30 a.m. Thanks to Wayne, who has been sending her forty dollars every month since Audine forced her out, she now had eighty dollars in the wooden box beneath her bed. The extra forty dollars she received today brought her total to $120. She planned to spend five dollars this week on coffee, sandwiches, and sometimes a slice of vanilla cake or sweet-potato pie from The Southern Pot, a popular Harlem restaurant.

Today, until the baby comes, I'll be working at a hairdresser. Back home, we'd go to someone's house to get our hair done for only ten cents. Not here! It costs a dollar! Violet thought to herself as she slipped her feet into the boots Cee-Cee bought for her.

"The boots feel strange on my feet," Violet said softly as she entered the small, glowing kitchen. The room was filled with the aroma of fresh coffee, biscuits, and pieces of diced sausage and bacon, which the maid had brought to Hubert from the attorney they served. Hubert told Cee-Cee that the attorney was always throwing out food, but the maid would wrap and divide it into two bags—one for herself and one for Hubert. With the ongoing depression in the country, she dared not throw away leftovers.

"The boots fit your feet well," said Cee-Cee as she handed Violet a warm biscuit with a slice of bacon tucked inside. Violet took a bite and savored the flavor.

"It's going to be very cold, Violet. Remember to bring your gloves, wear your hat, and tuck a handkerchief in your coat pocket," Cee-Cee said as she handed Violet an envelope with a letter and extra cash from Wayne.

"Read it when you get home," said Cee-Cee. "Put the envelope and money in your wooden box. So, how's your savings been?"

"It's been going well, Aunt Cee-Cee. Thanks for telling me what I'll need for the baby and Uncle Hubert's advice after the baby is born. I've saved one hundred and twenty dollars," she said, rushing back to her room and stuffing the envelope under her pillow.

"That's very good. We're proud of how you're saving your money and your plans for after your baby is born. We'll talk more about it as your due date gets closer, but for now, make sure you have enough time to buy lunch and walk through the alley to the hairdresser," said Cee-Cee.

"I'll see you when I get home and tell you all about my first day at work," Violet said after finishing her biscuit and bacon. After exchanging hugs, Violet left.

Walking down the stairs, she briefly glanced at the door marked 101. She listened to Cee-Cee and Hubert talk about the woman who used to live there, described as a God-fearing, wonderful woman. She was the laundress whom everyone loved, Miss Paula.

"Poor woman, she was found murdered. Folks who live here said that when she was discovered, half of her face was beaten in, and even her nose was hacked off," said Hubert, shaking his head after hearing the details from his friend Evans.

Soon after the murder, cleaning was completed, and two men and a woman moved in: Simeon, Thomas, and his wife, Murielle. They began offering laundry services to residents, including ironing, which became especially popular on weekends. Several tenants who worked as chauffeurs took advantage of a bundled deal, adding a whitening agent to their white shirts and requesting crisp ironing. Even Hubert and his friend Evans regularly dropped off their white shirts every Friday evening, picking them up after the Sunday church service.

"I'll get that for you, beautiful young lady," a deep voice said from behind Violet. She turned quickly to see who was speaking, her eyes settling on the large hand gripping the doorknob.

"Morning, pretty lady," said the stocky man with a chocolate complexion, tipping his hat. He smiled, and a touch of arrogance flickered in his acorn-colored eyes.

"Good morning, sir," Violet greeted as she stepped outside and hurried down the stairs. Unused to the icy, falling snow, she lost her footing on the slick stairs, slipping and tumbling down the first few steps. She yelled out in alarm, but the stocky, well-dressed stranger quickly descended the stairs and caught her by the arm, preventing her from hitting her head on the stairs.

"Are you okay? Jesus, you could have fallen and hurt yourself," he said, showing concern as he helped her to her feet.

Violet's new coat was covered in snow, and she felt a dull pain in her rump. She was grateful that this man was there to save her.

"I'm okay, just a little ruffled, but I'm fine, sir. Thank you for helping me up," Violet said, dusting snow off her coat.

"You ain't from around here, I can tell just by the way you talk to me. Where are you from, young lady?" he asked, adjusting his derby against the cold wind.

"New Orleans, sir. But I have to leave now; today is my first day of work, and I need to get a sandwich from a place called the Southern Pot," said Violet.

"That place is three blocks away, and it's already gonna be crowded. How about you get in my car? I'll take you to the Southern Pot. By the way, where's your new job?" he asked.

"Marcel's Hairdresser. I should be there by eight-thirty, but I can skip the Southern Pot and walk," said Violet.

"Bessie Marcel, I know her! I've known her for years. And as far as the Southern Pot is concerned, they all know me and always have three ham sandwiches and a slice of pie. If you walk, I guarantee you'll slip and fall again, especially when you go through the alley. I'ma take you. Get inside my car, please," he said.

Before Violet could protest, the stranger already had her arm and was cautiously guiding her toward the black, shiny Cadillac. He opened the door and helped her inside. Violet scanned the interior of the car and couldn't believe how spacious it was. The inside was spotless but carried a faint smell of stale perfume. The sudden sound of the car door opening startled her, causing her to flinch.

The man she had just met was so stout he had to lift his right leg to get it inside and then straddle himself on the seat to move quickly into a comfortable position. She watched him start the car. After a brief moment, he shifted the car into gear and drove toward traffic.

"Are you comfortable, pretty lady?" he asked, still focused on his driving.

"Yes, sir, I am," Violet replied. The car was cold, and he seemed to sense her thoughts as he handed her a blanket.

"Put it across your lap to keep warm," he said, keeping his eyes on the road.

Violet felt safe and grateful sitting beside the very kind stranger. Thinking back to what Cee-Cee said, she was right about the winters in New York; it was freezing.

Imagine having to walk to get lunch, go through the alley, and around the corner to be on time for work, Violet thought to herself.

"So, what brings you up here to New York? Are you visiting?" he asked.

"I'm from New Orleans and have been here for two months. I'm staying with my aunt and uncle, and I'm also going to work at the hairdresser's every day except Sundays," she said.

"New Orleans?" he asked with a raised eyebrow. He gently slowed the car to a stop to let a group of people cross the street.

"A few months ago, I visited there and enjoyed some of the best food I've ever tasted, including gumbo, beans with rice, pork chops with onions, cornbread, biscuits, and sweet potatoes! He said, clapping his hands happily. When I left, I brought some people with me, hoping for a better life. I took in a woman to live with me, but it didn't work out, so I had to let her go", he added as he sped up the car.

The snow was falling more heavily, and the wind was howling fiercely, forcing him to drive very slowly.

"Oh, so you know about New Orleans and the delicious food we cook?" Violet said, her voice tinged with nostalgia as she remembered New Orleans, the wonderful food, the hot summer heat, and Clarence.

"What happened to the woman staying with you? Did she go back to New Orleans?" she asked.

"Uh, something like that," he replied. "Let's just say she ain't coming back to Harlem ever again."

"Oh, I'm so sorry, and I beg your pardon if I was intruding on your affairs, sir," Violet said, feeling embarrassed by her question.

"Don't worry about it. She wasn't grateful for the things I was doing for her, so she had to leave. I insisted because I can't keep anyone here who isn't grateful or obedient," he muttered. "Anyway, we're at the Southern Pot," he said, stopping the car in front of the busy restaurant. It was filled with Black men in chauffeur uniforms, some in factory work clothes, and Black women wearing wool coats, hats, boots, and gloves over their maid uniforms. They all huddled against the wall, waiting to grab their food, pay, and leave.

"I'll be right back," he said, as he put the car in park. It was just as difficult for him to get out of the car. He opened the door and slowly wiggled out until both feet touched the snow-covered road. Bending at his sturdy waist, he stood up straight. After closing the door, he hurried into the restaurant. Violet noticed how the customers at the counter gave way when he entered.

Several men tipped their hats to him but quickly moved aside to join others waiting against the wall. The busy cashiers paused their work to gather three bags of baked ham on biscuits, the day's dessert special, a hefty slice of chocolate cake, and a slice of sweet potato pie. They also carefully filled three jars with hot coffee sweetened with brown sugar and milk. Violet watched in awe as this man received respect from both customers and clerks. It seemed everyone knew him, yet he didn't pay for the three bags. He left without saying thank you, which Violet found strange.

Back home, we'd say thank you, Violet thought to herself.

Violet was startled when a loud knock on the passenger side window caught her attention. The stranger, carrying three bags, gestured for her to roll down the window.

"Here you go, only the best for my lovely lady!" he said with a grin as he handed over the bags. The aroma of freshly baked biscuits and thick slices of ham, still warm from the stove, made Violet's mouth water, and she could feel the baby moving inside her belly.

"Thank you, sir," said Violet as she took the bags he handed to her. She held the bags close to her chest, which made her feel warmer against the freezing blast of air when he climbed back into the car.

"You're very welcome," he said with a grin. "Are you still cold? Since you've just come in from New Orleans, you're not used to this kind of weather. Let me give you this," he added, reaching for another blanket that was folded in a corner on the back seat. "Lift the bags," he instructed.

Following his instructions, Violet lifted the bags. He then unrolled the second wool blanket and spread it over her lap. She pressed the warm bags against her chest, feeling more secure and warmer.

"Okay, let's get you to work," he said as he started the car and resumed their trip. "You still have around ten minutes. If I hadn't driven you, you'd still be waiting in that long line, then you'd have to walk another twelve blocks on the icy, slippery sidewalks, and you'd be late on your first day. Look over there," he said, pointing at the passenger-side window. Violet turned to see, and sure enough, two women without hats or boots slipped on the icy walkway and fell to the ground.

"Oh, my goodness!" Violet exclaimed, horrified by what she had just witnessed. *That could have been me!* She thought

"Humph, that could've been you lying on that walkway if you had walked to Bessie's place. In fact, here we are," he said.

Violet peered out the window and spotted a modest but sprawling building that had a sign in the window that read *Marcel's Hairdresser."*

A sign was posted on the window indicating the days and hours of operation. The place was already open. A woman in a white, starched cotton long-sleeved dress and white Oxfords was busy straightening the chairs in the waiting area.

"That's Miss Bessie Marcel, one of Harlem's top hairdressers. Many singers, ministers' wives, and other women come here to get their hair styled," he said.

Before Violet could ask any more questions, the stranger was already out of the car, walking slowly on purpose. The snow was blowing in all directions, worsened by the wind, making visibility nearly impossible. The only bright spot was the brightly lit salon.

"Hand me the bags, except for one—the larger one, which is my lunch," he said, winking at her.

"Yes, sir", Violet said, handing him the two bags as he instructed. She put his bag on the driver's side, slid off the blankets, and was surprised to see his outstretched hand.

"I got you, pretty lady," he said.

"It's gotten worse out here, I'm afraid," she said, distressed.

"You'll be fine. Grab my hand so you won't fall again. I'll make sure you get to the other side. C'mon, you can trust me," he said.

Violet grasped his hand tightly, holding on as he effortlessly pulled her out of the car and shut the door. He carried food and coffee in his left hand, while his right arm wrapped securely around Violet's waist, her notice of his almost possessive grip. Violet instinctively placed her hand on her belly to shield her baby. Suddenly, a car sped toward them from nowhere, narrowly missing them. Violet cried out as the driver skidded, honking loudly. The stranger reacted swiftly and with strength, lifting Violet off the ground and carrying her across the street to the salon. Watching this from the window, Bessie quickly opened the door to let them in.

"My God, that car nearly hit both of you!" exclaimed the small but lively Bessie Marcel. "Come inside; it's freezing out here!" After pulling Violet inside, she embraced her warmly.

"Welcome to Marcel's! The weather isn't ideal today, but we'll get through it. She indicated a long hallway and said, "The coat closet is just there. We have a new uniform, a white over smock to protect your clothes, white shoes, and some brushes to style your hair. Take your time, dear. We've already had two customers call to say they can't make it because of the snow."

"Thank you, Miss. Marcel. It's a pleasure to meet you at last. My Aunt Cee-Cee mentioned that you're the best hairdresser in Harlem, and I'm grateful that you're letting me work here until it's my time. Um, may I use the bathroom?" Violet asked politely.

"Yes, of course, you may. It's across from the closet," said Bessie.

"And sir, I can't begin to tell you how grateful I am to you for helping me. Thank you and God bless you," said Violet as she hurried to the bathroom.

"So, Bessie, how's everything?" he asked, placing the damp sacks on the small round table next to one of the hair dryers. "By the way, I bought you some coffee, biscuits with ham, cake, and Essie might have slipped in an extra slice of pie."

"Business is doing better than ever, thanks to many new customers coming through. Even with this depression going on, Black women still find ways to save up to two dollars for their hair done. The new customers are the dancers at Smalls, who are paid well, as long as they keep their legs closed," said Bessie, as she rummaged through a sack and pulled out a jar of coffee that was hot to the touch.

"Uh, so I gotta question for you, Bessie," he said as he strained his neck to see if Violet was close enough to hear their conversation.

"What's your question? Make it quick, because I have a lot to show Violet today," said Bessie as she carefully sipped her piping hot coffee. She took a hungry bite of the warm biscuit, which had a thick slice of ham inside.

"Who exactly is that young lady? Why is she working here with you?" he started, but Bessie cut him off suddenly, flicking her hand with a look of irritation and impatience.

"Her name is Violet Booker, and she lives with her aunt and uncle, who are honest, diligent, and God-fearing. She just moved to Harlem from New Orleans about a month ago. She has a sad story; she was supposed to be a schoolteacher," said Bessie.

"She was supposed to be a schoolteacher?" he asked, bewildered.

"Yes, and she's a very smart young woman. She speaks French Creole fluently and also taught Sunday school, helping children of all ages with their studies. From what I hear, if Violet hadn't been there, many Black children at that church might have failed in school. Humph, to think that this young woman had so much to offer," said Bessie.

He was speechless. "She knows how to speak French and understands how things grow in the dirt, too?" he finally asked.

"Yes, she does," Bessie replied, taking another bite of her biscuit and brushing off the fine crumbs from her white starched uniform. "She scored the highest on the teacher's exam and received an award for the French exam. Her aunt said the white man who gave her the test couldn't believe what he was hearing, umph! Imagine that, a Black woman who could speak perfect French Creole!"

His heart fluttered wildly as he heard the details of this young woman, unlike any he had ever known. She was not only beautiful but also intelligent.

"Just as things seemed to be going well for her, she opens her legs wide for the first man she falls in love with. Unfortunately, that did not end well at all, because she has a baby growing in her belly. When her mother found out, she told Violet to leave and live with her aunt and uncle, warning her never to return to New Orleans."

"Damn," he said. "So, where's the father of Violet's baby?" he asked, baffled.

"Dead. The night he was about to inform Violet's parents about the baby, a snake bit him. An hour later, he was dead, and the day she reached Harlem was also the day of his funeral. Here's what I'll tell you: leave her alone. She'll work for me, earn her keep, save money for her baby, and maybe get a flat when the baby is older. She had to learn a very hard lesson, but she doesn't need a man, or you. So, leave her be," Bessie said, taking another sip of coffee.

After hearing about Violet's sorrowful story, compassion sparkled in his eyes. He quietly stood up and sighed.

"So, what time will she be done today?" he asked.

"Looking at how fast the snow is falling, I'd say it's around one o'clock. My loyal customer, Mrs. Loomis, will come for her press and curl regardless of the weather. After her appointment, I'll close up and send Violet home. So, why do you need to know when she finishes?" said Bessie.

"I'm coming back to get her and take her home. It's too dangerous out there for her to be walking out there," he said. He finished his coffee in one last gulp, and before Bessie could object, he was already out the door.

"Miss Marcel," Violet said.

Bessie quickly turned to see Violet dressed in a snug uniform that highlighted her prominent belly. She adhered to the salon's protocol by tying her hair into a tight bun with bobby pins, wearing a pink smock that reached below her hips, white work shoes, and carrying a small notepad with a pencil for any patrons needing to schedule another hair appointment.

"Don't you look lovely and ready to work!" Bessie exclaimed.

"Thank you, Ma'am," said Violet.

"Please call me Bessie when we're alone, but as a worker, you should address me as Miss Bessie or Miss Marcel."

"Yes, Ma'am", Violet said, smiling.

We've had two cancellations so far, but that's okay because it gives us more time to discuss your job duties, answering the phone, cleaning the bathroom, sweeping the floors, and doing a wet floor scrub just before closing on Saturday, so the salon is ready for Tuesday morning.

You'll also make sure that the stations are well-stocked with shampoos, pomade, fresh towels, clean combs, and brushes. Additionally, you need to clean the sinks after each client has their hair washed. You're supposed to have your lunch from 1:00 to 1:30 in the back room; I've set up a box on the shelves for each worker to store her handbag and lunch. Our salon closes at 3 p.m. every day; however, we may stay open later by appointment. We are closed on Sundays and Mondays. Do you have any questions for me, dear?" Bessie asked.

"No, Ma'am, I don't have any questions for you except: after my baby comes, will I be able to come back to work for you?"

"Yes, you certainly may. I expect you to take a few weeks off, and then we'll discuss your return date. Is that alright with you?" Bessie asked.

"Yes, it is, and thank you, Miss Bessie. I have one more question. Who was the man who brought me here? He lives in the same building where I stay with my aunt and uncle. He was very kind, buying me lunch, coffee, and giving me a ride. Without him, I might not have arrived on time," Violet said.

A sudden flicker of alarm crossed Bessie's mature hazel eyes.

"Violet, sit down," Bessie said, motioning for Violet to sit in the chair next to her. Violet obeyed.

"He goes by the name of High Roller-Gunn," she said, letting out a heavy sigh. "He can be charming at first, but for your sake and his, don't make that man angry. Several of his female acquaintances would come here on Saturday mornings to get prettied up for an evening with him. After two weeks, they'd return for hair appointments and be covered in bruises. Some had black eyes and split lips. They always lie, saying they fell or tripped over shoelaces. One woman, like you, from New Orleans, came here nervous, asking to get her hair done quickly. I told her it was fine because my regular was unavailable. When she sat down, I knew Gunn had bruised her; she had bruises around her neck and arms. She spoke while looking down, missing a tooth. I never saw her again until I got a call from Mr. Wainwright at E.W. Wainwright's funeral parlor, asking me to style a murdered woman's hair for her funeral the next day. Mr. Wainwright paid me fifty dollars. After closing the salon, I rushed to the funeral home. He took me upstairs, where the deceased waited to look presentable. When he opened the casket, I nearly fainted; it was that woman with bruises and a missing tooth! I asked Mr. Wainwright what happened. He said she was found by her hosts, a couple from her church, and she also worked at their restaurant. Her throat was slit, and there was so much blood it took weeks to clean. She was from New Orleans, and her husband and another woman traveled by train to bury her. The minister said her husband was inconsolable." Bessie shook her head.

"He cried so much that the funeral service started fifteen minutes late. However, the woman accompanying him, hmm! When she turned her head to the side, pretending to be crying, the minister watched her face closely. Surprisingly, he said she was actually laughing but was somehow making crying sounds! Oh, my Gawd! Later, the minister told me he hoped that man would never marry her because all she cares about is his money. He described her as a desperately wicked woman."

Violet sat with her mouth wide open and eyes wide, feeling a sense of familiarity from the story she had just heard.

It can't be, oh my God, no—Wayne, Lena, and my mother are the ones Miss Bessie mentioned! she thought, panic rising in her. Still, she felt compelled to ask Bessie one more question.

"Miss Bessie, since I'm from New Orleans, what was the name of the woman who died?" said Violet.

Bessie's eyebrows knit into a thoughtful frown, then she clapped her hands, remembering.

"I recall now! Her name was Lena Collins, as indicated by the tag on her toe just before her shoes were put on. Her husband's name was Wayne, yes, Wayne Collins, because he asked Mr. Wainwright if they could hide the deep gash on her neck with a strand of pearls. The woman he was with kept asking Mr.

Wainwright, before Lena's casket was lowered, if she could remove the pearl necklace and keep the pearls, arguing it made no sense to have real pearls in the grave when she could wear and show them off. How pathetic is that?" Bessie said, her face a mask of disgust.

"May I ask you something else?" Violet inquired softly and nervously. Bessie nodded in response.

"What was the woman's name who was with Wayne Collins?"

"Humph! That's an easy one, since after she left, everyone, including the minister, was talking about her."

"Her name was Audine Booker," Bessie said.

CHAPTER THIRTY-FIVE

Marcel's Hairdresser

Late Afternoon

"Miss Bessie, I've finished mopping the floor and cleaning the bathroom," Violet called out.

"That's fine, leave the mop and pail outside the back door so it won't smell. Also, empty the dirty water. The snow might freeze the mop, but that's alright, it won't make the salon smell," Bessie said, patting the freshly curled and perfectly styled waved hair of Mrs. Loomis, who squealed with delight when Bessie handed her the mirror to see herself.

"Bessie, as usual, you've outdone yourself! Thanks for always making me look better than those other women constantly eyeing my husband, hah! They don't realize he's only got eyes for me, and since he's one of eight

Black police officers patrolling to keep us safe, humph, they figure it's okay to target him as well as the other officers! And what's funny, Bessie, is that they're all married! Well, here you go," Mrs. Loomis said, opening her purse, pulling out a stack of six one-dollar bills, and handing them to Bessie.

"There are two dollars today and another two dollars for my next visit in two weeks. One dollar is for you, and the other is for your new helper. I like her because as soon as I arrived, she took my coat, hung it up, and helped me into your chair. She even took my boots to the backroom to keep the floor clean and dry. She's a lovely young lady, but I have a question for you," Mrs. Loomis whispered. She nodded for Bessie to come closer.

"Thank you for the payment, Mrs. Loomis, and I'll make sure Violet receives the dollar," Bessie said as she untied the protective smock Mrs. Loomis had on while getting her hair done. "So, what's your question?"

"Well, I noticed that she's, uh, showing a little bit," said Mrs. Loomis softly. "I also saw that she's not wearing a wedding ring. Is she in trouble?"

Bessie quickly snapped the smock off to brush away the excess hair. The loud sound startled Mrs. Loomis.

"The man that Violet was with died suddenly, and that's all I know. For now, she needs a job to care for herself and the baby she'll be having this summer." She said, folding the smock and placing it on her station table.

"Tsk, tsk, tsk," Mrs. Loomis muttered through her teeth. "That poor young woman. I believe she and her husband had some moments of happiness, but certainly not enough to see their baby born. Such a shame," she said, shaking her head as she stood up and admired herself again in the mirror.

Mrs. Loomis expressed her satisfaction about visiting to get her hair done and meeting the new helper. She gave Bessie seventy-five cents extra to add to the dollar tip, saying it was for her baby's future. Mrs. Loomis announced that she was finished for the day, noting that her husband would return in about four hours. He'd be cold and hungry after being out in the snow since morning. She mentioned how perfect this day is for hot soup and appreciated how easy it is for her to come down, as they live directly above the salon, and Bessie lives across the street. She ended with well wishes, asking Bessie to be careful and pass her regards to Violet.

"I certainly will, Mrs. Loomis, and we appreciate your ongoing loyalty to this salon," said Bessie.

After putting on her boots and coat, Mrs. Loomis left. Bessie locked the door and placed the 'closed' sign in the window.

"Violet, would you please come here?' Bessie called.

"Yes, Ma'am," Violet replied, shutting and locking the back door after placing the mop and pail outside.

"Have a seat, dear," Bessie said, motioning Violet to sit.

"It seems you've left a great impression on Mrs. Loomis. She appreciated your hospitality and felt very welcome today. And she gave you this," said Bessie. She reached into her smock pocket and pulled out the dollar and seventy-five cents.

"This is for you," she said, handing her the money.

Violet's eyes flashed with shock at the money she had just received. She couldn't believe the amount she was given simply for being polite to the only customer who had come in all day. The gesture moved her almost to tears.

"Thank you, Miss Bessie," she said.

"You're welcome. And just so you know, she noticed your belly and asked about—well, your husband," Bessie said uncomfortably. "I told her that the man you were with for a short time died suddenly and left it at that. But between you and me, we know the truth, and that's where it'll stay, between you and me. Besides, it's none of her damned business."

Violet looked down slightly, feeling ashamed, and wondered what would happen as her belly grew. What would come next? She wiped away a tear that slipped from her eye. Bessie reached into her smock pocket and gave her a handkerchief.

"Thank you, Miss Bessie," Violet said softly as she blew her nose.

"Listen, you're not the first or the last to be involved with a married man and have his child. Many young women like you get pregnant here in Harlem, often coming from the South after their parents disown them. Some are alone, but you were fortunate to be taken in by your aunt and uncle. You've made a mistake, but at least you have a roof over your head, a job, and food. Life can be hard, especially with many Black people out of work, but you're lucky, Violet, because some girls have nothing. Next time someone asks about your baby, say it's fine. If they inquire about your husband or ask too many questions, tell them he died and walk away, pretending you're busy," said Bessie.

"Yes, Miss Bessie, thank you," Violet said.

"I'm closing the salon now because it's getting worse out there, and besides, nobody is coming. Why don't you go get your coat and boots now? I'm going to open the salon at nine o'clock tomorrow morning. You can plan to arrive here at eight-thirty to help set up, count the towels, and make sure everything is ready. I have a feeling that we're going to be very busy tomorrow because so many who didn't come today will show up then," said Bessie. "Then you'll also meet Peaches and Clarissa."

"That's fine with me, and I'll be here tomorrow morning. I'll get my coat and boots on, then we can go home," Violet said as she hurried to the backroom to fetch her coat and boots. *It's so bad outside, and I'm worried for me and the baby. How will I see where I'm going?* She wondered, feeling anxious.

After placing her earnings for the day into her purse, she snapped it shut, collected her untouched lunch and an empty coffee jar, and returned to the salon's reception area. She paused, surprised to see the stranger who had driven her to the salon, now known as High Roller-Gunn, standing there. He stood and greeted her.

"Good afternoon, Violet. I'm here to drive you home since it's too dangerous for you to walk outside. Are you ready?" he asked.

"Good afternoon, Mr. Gunn. I think I'm ready to head home," Violet said. "Miss Bessie, do you need me to do anything else?"

"Yes, please visit the gentleman in your building before coming here in the morning. Their door is number 101. Hand them this," she said, handing Violet an envelope.

"There is one dollar and ten cents for ten towels washed and dried for the salon. Since only one customer came today, no exchange is needed, but please inform whoever you see there that you're picking up towels for Marcel's and give them the envelope. Tomorrow, you'll receive a fresh batch of towels to bring along," said Bessie.

"Yes, Miss Bessie, I will do this as soon as I get home," Violet said, taking the envelope.

"If that's everything, I suggest we leave. The snow is coming down quickly, and it's icy outside," Gunn said as he approached Violet and took her untouched lunch sack.

"Have a good day, Bessie," said Gunn as he tipped his derby to her.

He opened the door, allowing Violet to go in first. Holding Violet's arm by the crook, Bessie watched as

Gunn helped her into his car. After Violet was inside, he walked to the passenger side and got in with some effort. He started the car and drove away.

Looking once more in the salon, Bessie put on her coat, hat, gloves, and boots. She snapped off the lights, propped up the closed sign, locked the door, and hurried across the street to her home.

CHAPTER THIRTY-SIX

"So, how was work today, pretty lady? Did you get a chance to eat your lunch?" Gunn asked while looking straight ahead as he drove.

Violet sat in the passenger seat, observing his acorn-brown eyes, which were the most unusual color she had ever seen.

'Many customers didn't come because of the snow, but Mrs. Loomis did. She lives above the salon with her husband, so it's easy for her to attend her appointments. I enjoy talking with her about politics, cooking, and the struggles Black people face in the South, especially New Orleans. We also discussed Brooklyn, Black-owned restaurants in Harlem, churches, and parts of New York I haven't visited yet. She even shared some good shopping spots for dresses and shoes, just in case I need them," said Violet.

"And what else did you do today? Did Bessie teach you anything?" Gunn inquired, his gaze remaining fixed on the road.

"Yes, Miss Bessie had me do a lot of things in the salon, such as mopping the floor, collecting the money, and counting the towels for the day, including which towels need to be sent out for laundering every other day. Where we live, I'm supposed to go to the laundry people who live in flat number 101 to give them the money to pay for clean towels and hand over the sack of dirty ones to be laundered. She said every Tuesday morning, I am to take a count of all the supplies needed for the salon for the week," she said.

"I know the washermen, and one of them is married to the woman staying there. They're very nice people and do a swell job washing my bed sheets and shirts. But you didn't answer my question, Violet. Did you eat?" he asked, never taking his eyes off the road, which made it impossible to see ahead.

"I took a few bites of that ham sandwich during the first few minutes we had, just before Mrs. Loomis left. I was so hungry, and the coffee was still piping hot! I didn't get a chance to finish eating the cake, but I'll bring it tomorrow when I go to the Southern Pot".

Why is he asking me if I ate the food he bought for me? That's the second time he asked. Violet wondered.

"I'm glad to hear you had a good day and that you were able to eat some of the food. Bring the leftovers with you tomorrow. What about that ham? Did you leave any?" he asked.

"Uh, let me check", said Violet as she poked inside the food sack. "Yes, I left a chunk of ham in the sack with my piece of cake".

"Why don't you go ahead and eat it when you get home, because there's no sense in wasting food, especially during a depression. Food can become very scarce, believe me on that," he said.

"How did you know my name, Mr. Gunn?" Violet asked softly. Gunn eased the car to a stop as he approached the curb of the tenement building where they lived.

The entire street was blanketed in snow; many of the cars were clearly buried, only visible by the fresh layer of snow on them. Carefully parking his car in the usual spot, Gunn put the car in park and took the key out of the ignition.

He said frankly, "The same way you discovered my name and who I am here." "Bessie and I have known each other for years. I respect her honesty and truth — she never lied to me. That's why she told me about you, a smart young woman who was meant to be a schoolteacher and knows French-Creole. Do you know how many of our people speak other languages? Some can't even speak English well. But you? According to Bessie, you even help young children and older children with their schoolwork, and they improve because of it. She also mentioned that you're expecting a child, but the father has died. I'm truly sorry about that, Violet. She told me your mother kicked you out of her home. That's terrible, kicking out a young woman like you to be alone in an unfamiliar place? That's simply cruel. You made a mistake, but I'm not here to judge what you and that man did. I want to be your friend," he said.

Violet sat listening, captivated by every word he said, yet she was surprised that Bessie told this stranger about her business. But Bessie warned her not to make this complicated man angry, or else suffer the consequences.

"I'd like to get to know more about you, Mr. Gunn, and, besides, I've only just arrived here from New Orleans, so I'm in no condition to even go out socially", she said.

"No, I'm not asking you to go out with me, Violet," he said, gazing into her eyes. "All I'm asking is to be your friend. I can drive you to your job at Bessie's, especially with all this snow and ice. And another thing that would worry me is you walking home when it gets dark outside."

"Walking in the dark?" she asked. Why would I be scared to walk home at night? I finish work at five, and in New Orleans, it's bright as day. It doesn't get dark until eight, and by then, Black people are supposed to be inside because of the Klan- "

She was interrupted by Gunn's fist pounding the steering wheel several times, silencing her.

"You ain't in New Orleans!" he shouted, removing his derby hat and pushing his hand through his bald head impatiently. "Here in Harlem, time and weather change. It gets dark by four. If you walk from Bessie's place to here, you'd have to enter the alley, which is full of drunks, robbers, women sucking on men's dicks, and if it's really cold, you could slip on ice and hurt yourself. That's why, as your friend, I'll come in the morning to pick you up for work and take you home. That's all, nothing more," he said.

Violet couldn't stop staring at his acorn-colored eyes, which were beautiful, yet she felt an uneasy sense of darkness that lay just beneath the surface of his spirit. It was downright terrifying if Gunn was crossed.

"I had no idea about everything you just told me, especially how dark it gets up here at that time," she said. "As for being your friend, I'll accept that, but nothing more. I have a lot to do and learn here in Harlem for my sake and my baby's," Violet said, looking down at her belly.

Delight flickered in Gunn's eyes. He wanted to hug her close just because she had accepted being friends.

"Good," he said. "Let's get inside because the wind is so strong that it's making the car shake."

Violet nodded in agreement as she observed him struggling to exit the car. He had to trudge through the snow, which was so deep it covered his ankles. Gunn opened the side of the car door and took her hand.

"Take your time; it's slippery and deep", he said.

She thought to herself that he was right, and she was grateful he brought her home, knowing she might have fallen otherwise, as she firmly grasped his hand to prevent slipping.

"Take my arm to keep yourself steady," he said.

Violet intertwined her arm in the crook of his elbow, and they slowly climbed the stairs into the tenement building. Gunn opened the door to let her inside. The warmth was welcoming as Violet tried to stop shivering. All she wanted was to take off her coat, boots, and hat and enjoy a hot bath. Hubert was lucky enough to get a flat in this building that had a bathroom, two bedrooms, a small kitchen, and a parlor, much to Cee-Cee's delight.

"Hand me your coat," said Gunn.

Violet swiftly took off her coat and handed it to him. He then went to the front door and opened it. Grasping her coat by the shoulders, he snapped it several times to remove the excess snow and to freshen it with the blowing air. Violet watched him, amazed by this courteous gesture of shaking off the snow and refreshing her coat. After closing the door against the howling wind, he returned her coat, which looked as if no snow had ever touched it.

"Here you go," he said, handing it to her. "Don't forget to collect Bessie's towels for tomorrow," he added, gesturing toward door number 101. "I'll take your belongings and place them by your door, so they won't get the towels wet," Gunn explained.

"Thank you, I truly appreciate all you've done for me today," Violet said.

"You're welcome. One more thing, when you get home, place your belongings beside the radiator to dry for at least an hour. Afterward, hang your coat in the closet, and keep your boots, hat, and gloves near the radiator. This way, they'll be dry and warm for the next morning," he tipped his derby hat to her. "Good evening." Then, he quickly went upstairs.

Violet wondered how he knew about the radiator in her room as she watched him hurry up the stairs. She reached into her purse to find the two dollars Bessie had given her to pay for the fresh towels the next day.

Violet knocked on the door of flat number 101.

"Yes, who is it?" a female voice asked.

"It's Violet, ma'am. I work for Miss Bessie, and I'm here to pick up the towels for her salon," she said.

Violet heard a few more muffled voices. Then, she heard the sound of two locks being unlocked from inside, followed by the door opening.

"Good afternoon, Miss-?" the chestnut-haired man asked as he stood at the door. He was about five feet ten inches tall, likely in his forties, with gold-rimmed glasses, a light blue Oxford shirt rolled up to his elbows, blue overalls, and black shoes. He carried a bag with a week's supply of fresh towels. Beside him was a slightly taller, well-built woman wearing an apron, a flowered dress, and slippers.

"My name is Violet Booker, and I work for Miss Bessie," she said. "I'm staying upstairs in flat number 208 with my aunt Cee-Cee and Uncle Hubert."

"It's very nice to meet you, Violet. My name is Simeon Johnson, and this here is my wife, Gloria," he said, extending his hand to Violet.

"Hello, Violet, pleased to meet you," she said. Her discolored and jagged teeth flashed in a friendly smile.

"We have Miss Bessie's towels ready for you. We took them off the clothesline last night, and it's a good thing we did, because look at what it's still doing outside!" said Gloria.

"It's pretty bad out there", said Violet, nodding in agreement. "It's also very windy now. I just arrived from New Orleans, and I'm not used to this kind of weather, especially the cold and the wind."

"The ice," another man said, who looked exactly like Simeon, but a little older. He stood behind Simeon at the door with a lit cigarette between his teeth. He reached out to shake Violet's hand, but Gloria playfully slapped his hand away.

"Your hands smell like cigarettes! Don't touch her hands!" Gloria said, grinning.

"Excuse me, miss, I'm Clyde, Simeon's older brother. I wouldn't want your lovely hands to smell like the cigarette I just smoked or the hot sauce I shook onto my fish and potato salad," he said, winking at her. "But oh, my Gawd, we definitely wouldn't want this beautiful woman to smell like she just stepped out of a cheap, smoke-filled dance hall that serves fish and potato salad!"

Everyone burst into laughter. Violet was laughing so intensely that she had to clutch her stomach. Ever since Clarence's death and her departure from New Orleans, laughter had been absent from her life, so this silly joke was precisely what she needed. Once everyone regained their composure, the attention shifted back to Violet.

"Anyway, Simeon, I've come to pick up Miss Bessie's towels. Here's the two dollars she owes. She mentioned that her receipt would be inside the bag marked 'paid,'" Violet said.

"Yes, all the towels are folded, and I always slip the receipt inside the third folded towel inside the bag marked paid", Simeon said, handing her the brown paper bag. "If she has any questions, she can call me now that we have a telephone. I wrote the number on the receipt", said Simeon.

"Thank you," Violet said. "I'll make sure to inform Miss Bessie that you have a telephone and that the number is listed on the receipt. Is there anything else I need to know?"

"Yes, tell Miss Bessie that because of the snow, ice, and cold, we're a little behind on the laundry. We'll take in towels on Wednesday and have them ready by Friday," said Gloria.

"I'll be sure to inform her. Thank you all, and it was a pleasure meeting you," Violet said.

"It was a pleasure meeting you. Have a nice afternoon," said Gloria. Simeon and Clyde also said their goodbyes. Violet turned and walked up the stairs to the second floor. When she reached the top, she turned left and saw her coat and hat, neatly folded and stacked in front of the door. She unsnapped her purse, took out the key, and opened the door.

She pushed the key into the lock and turned it to the right to open the door. Stepping over her belongings, she set her bag on the floor, then grabbed her coat and hat before shutting and locking the door from the inside. Hubert told her and Cee-Cee that, no matter what, they should always lock the door after coming in, as many tenants forget this simple task.

"They were the ones who got robbed," Hubert said firmly. Violet grimaced at the idea.

Finally! I am inside a warm place I am getting used to, she thought as she went to her room. Remembering Gunn's advice, she quickly draped her coat over the radiator just enough to dry it, and later, she'd hang it up.

She placed her boots apart to dry and avoid creating a puddle of melted snow on the wood floor, which would not make Cee-Cee happy. Going into the bathroom, she relieved herself and turned on the bathtub faucet. A cloud of steam from the scalding hot water filled the tiny bathroom. Cee-Ce was kind enough to share her toiletries, especially the Yardley's English Lavender Soap bars given by the maid Hubert worked with, who said the wife of the lawyer he works for sends him twenty bars of soap from England, but he throws them away because he hates her so much. The maid would save the soap bars from the trash, keeping ten for herself and giving the rest to Hubert to give to Cee-Cee. The smell would linger for up to three days after a hot bath with the soap.

Violet turned the faucet to a trickle, then went back to her room. She undressed from her uniform and hung it up for the next day. After removing all her undergarments, she approached the mirror. Her belly was growing larger, and her sore breasts reminded her constantly of what had happened with Clarence. She closed her eyes, reminiscing about their first kiss, their declaration of love, and their first night together. He had put a baby inside her, but he was gone forever. Tears welled up, fulfilling her with disappointment not only because she couldn't see the man she loved but also because he would never know about his child. There was no point crying; instead, she focused on the coming June, when a new life would arrive. Much-needed preparations, especially finding a midwife, lie ahead. Suddenly, a strong lavender scent from the steam-filled bathroom startled her, blurring her vision.

Violet fanned the steam with her hand, then bent down and reached for the spigot at the front of the tub to turn off the hot water. The smell of lavender soap evoked the scent of wild lavender that grew deep in the woods back in New Orleans. Clarence had surprised her one day with two lavender flowers when he stayed overnight two days before he died. She shook her head tiredly, haunted by that not-so-long-ago memory. Clarence is gone now, and I can't even cry anymore, she thought bitterly. She dipped her finger into the scalding water to check its temperature, winced, and quickly pulled her hand back.

"Too hot," she whispered. She got up, left the bathroom, closed the door, and wandered into the kitchen. On the table was a note from Cee-Cee.

Dear Violet,

My friend Lessie Walker came over and asked me to go to the hospital with her to work because about four people quit due to the snow, and the hospital needed Black nurses. Since we live just two blocks from the hospital, I agreed to work. It looks like I'll start early at 6:00 a.m. and return home by 5:00 p.m. We need the money, and the pay for Black nurses during this depression is quite good. Hubert won't be home until ten tonight, but I should be back by 5:30 after walking home through the snow. Please use the pieces of chicken and sausage Hubert brought home yesterday to make gumbo. There are seasonings from back home. You also received mail this morning; please open and read it. Uncle Hubert and I hope you had a good day at work. Remember to eat and put your money away.

Love,

Aunt Cee-Cee

Violet folded the note and smiled, feeling happy that Cee-Cee would be working, and that more money would come into the household now that all three of them had jobs. She set the note aside and began preparing a rich yet quick gumbo, perfect for such a day. Since arriving home, it had been snowing heavily, and the fierce wind made the building sway. Violet looked inside the refrigerator and gathered the necessary ingredients to make the gumbo.

Cee-Cee had all the spices she needed. The rice was cooked first, then the gumbo, and soon, the entire flat was filled with the smell of New Orleans. While the gumbo simmered, Violet went into the bathroom, which was filled with the scent of lavender. After retesting the water, she found it perfect. She slipped off her robe and stepped into the deep tub, sitting down.

Closing her eyes, she felt a rush of heat flow through her body, banishing the cold that had settled inside her bones. She rested against the towel draped over the edge of the tub and drifted into a deep sleep.

The scent was what jolted her up. She quickly grabbed the sides of the tub, hoisted herself out, rinsed herself, removed the stopper, and dried off. After applying lotion, especially on her belly, she ensured every part of her was coated with the sweet-smelling lotion. Then, wrapping her head in a tignon, she slipped into her robe and slippers and went to the kitchen. She removed the cover from the simmering pot, and the fragrant steam hit her face.

Stirring the hearty gumbo, she turned off the stove and let it cool. She hurried back to the bathroom, cleaned the tub, turned off the light, and hung up her towel to dry.

The flat was quiet except for the howling wind. Finally, she had a warm bowl of homemade food, a cool glass of water, and a leftover slice of cake for herself. Sitting at the table, she said grace before beginning to eat. She took out the letter she had left on the table to read. As she opened and turned over the envelope, money spilled out: forty dollars in five and one-dollar bills. Inside the envelope was a folded, handwritten letter.

January 19, 1934

Dear Violet,

I hope this letter finds you well. Things have been so busy here since you left. So, I'll go ahead and tell you everything.

Your mother and I are no longer married. I realize this may come as a surprise to you. The reason is that one evening, while I was asleep, I heard noises as if someone was rummaging through the clothes drawers in our bedroom.

When I say I was scared to death, my heart was pounding! I opened my eyes, and who do I see? Your mother is going into the drawer where I kept the money from Lena's funeral. I stayed still and watched her open the envelope, count the money, and then put it into another greasy envelope she had saved from our wedding. She snapped her purse shut, and I heard her say:

"Humph! Wayne is so damn stupid! He won't realize any of this money is gone. If he asks me about it, I'll just say a robber broke in while we were asleep and stole everything. Like a fool, he'll believe every word I say, hah!"

When she turned around to go back to bed, I acted as if I were still asleep until morning. When I woke up to get ready for work, she was already taking a bath, so I hurried outside to wash, then returned to get dressed. After breakfast, I told her I was leaving. But guess what? Hah! I fooled her! Just before heading to work, I visited the bank and transferred all the money into my savings.

I also moved your father's money, which he left you, into my account so it would be safe. On Sunday, your mother was very upset because she had to give your certificate and award to Carol Thomas, the young lady who missed out by two points.

Once again, your mother suggested to Carol's mother, Phyllis, that perhaps Carol could work as a toilet scrubber at the hospital because they were still looking for people to do that and clean up their loose bowel movements when they soiled themselves in bed. Well, everything turned on your mother because Carol left right away for Virginia, and I heard that she's the one doing better than everyone else!

The ending wasn't ideal because, as we were in the car preparing to go into the church, she made another terrible comment about Lena. I then told her what I saw-her stealing money given to me by Lena's Minister, and the money your father gave you, which she took the night she threw you out of our home. I explained that I now have all of it in a safe place where she can't get it. I also told her that after church, she should pack her bags and leave. Additionally, I informed her that the papers she signed made Mason my legal son, so he stays with me; I wasn't going to have him chasing after her, living out of suitcases, no! After she left, I went to the courthouse with our marriage papers and had our marriage annulled. I am very sorry that things didn't work out between me and your mother. And I hate to say this, but it was for the best that we didn't have a baby. Nonetheless, I will always think of you as if you were my real daughter.

Violet, you did a very sinful thing, lying with another woman's husband and then letting him put a baby inside you. But it's all over now, and it's time for you to look ahead so you can take care of the baby and yourself. I'll make sure to send money until it's almost gone, but listen to me, Violet: save your money, find a bank to put it in so nothing will happen to it. Also, start buying things you'll need for the baby.

Ask your Aunt Cee-Cee to list what you'll need, and finally, save money if you're working to buy a flat. This way, when the baby cries at night, it won't disturb anyone you're staying with. Take care, and I'll write again when I send you the money next month. God bless and keep you.

Your Father Forever,

Wayne

Violet carefully folded the letter again and slid it back into the envelope. Tears blurred her vision as she thought about her mother's true nature: self-centered, vindictive, judgmental, and jealous. Besides, she was a thief, stealing from those who loved her, including me and Mason. Look at what you've done! Despite everything, I will forgive you, but you will never be a mother to me. Violet thought, sniffling as she fought back tears.

Wayne was the saving grace, indirectly rescuing Mason from a life of drifting. Only God knows what could have happened if he had traveled with Audine, living out of a suitcase.

"I'll be a good mother to you," Violet whispered to her belly.

After she finished her meal and cleaned the kitchen, she went to her room and snuggled under the warm blankets. The wind outside howled relentlessly, but it only helped Violet drift to sleep.

Gunn stood just outside flat 208, leaning heavily against the door with his eyes tightly shut as he took a deep breath. The aroma of the gumbo filled the entire building, evoking memories of his time in New Orleans, when he won money and lost Lena.

This woman is different. She's intelligent, beautiful, and capable in the kitchen. However, she made a careless mistake. With the child's father gone, if she has a boy, he will need a man to guide him, especially on what it means to be a Black man. If she has a girl, she will need protection from men who might take advantage of her, and eventually, Violet will need a husband to help raise her.

Gunn decided that Violet and the baby needed him, so he went back to his flat, number 313, and shut the door.

CHAPTER THIRTY-SEVEN

The snow had ceased, and Harlem was beginning to stir. Outside, it was cold and dark, with only the sounds of honking cars, a few people cautiously navigating the knee-deep snow, and a group of men loudly cursing as their snow-logged cars refused to start, threatening to make them late for their morning shift.

Violet removed the covers and promptly knelt beside her bed for morning prayer.

Father in heaven, please forgive my mother, as she is unaware of her actions, and kindly pardon her indiscretions. I am thankful for the roof over my head, my aunt Cee-Cee, Uncle Hubert, and the job I have been blessed with. Bless Miss Bessie, and thank you for providing me with a ride from my upstairs neighbor, Mr. Gunn. I sense something about him that makes me uneasy, and I ask for your divine protection. I also thank you for my neighbors in flat number 101. Please bless me today to reach work safely and return home safely. Forgive my sin with Clarence, but watch over me and the child I am carrying. Bless this day, amen.

After finishing her prayer, she rose, made her bed, and wrapped herself in her robe. Tiptoeing toward the window, she was surprised to see people heading to work. She then opened the door to find the lights on, but the flat was completely silent.

"Aunt Cee-Cee, Uncle Hubert?" she called. Silence. She then went to the kitchen, where she saw a yellow note written by Cee-Cee.

Violet,

Because of the snow, I had to stay late at my new job. Many people were coming in sick or had bad falls on the street. I didn't get home until ten o'clock, and your Uncle Hubert had to stay overnight at his workplace because the roads were so bad. Thank you for the gumbo and for leaving the pot on the stove to keep it warm. As soon as I arrived at the door, I could smell the spices of New Orleans! Don't worry if I'm not home again today, because I'm pretty sure more people will be visiting the hospital. Just remember to lock the door when you leave for work and again when you come home.

Love,

Aunt Cee-Cee

Violet smiled after reading the note. She thought to herself how different she was from her mother. Aunt Cee-Cee is always kind, thoughtful, and caring. She's firm yet shows me lots of love and understands everything. She quickly hurried into the bathroom to get ready for work.

After bathing and putting on her uniform, shoes, boots, and her coat, which she laid close to the radiator, everything felt warm and toasty. She tucked her hair under her hat and slipped on her gloves. Gathering her purse and the bag of towels, she remembered to take a dollar for a sack of food when she went to the Southern Pot. Turning off the lights, she left, remembering to lock the door to the flat.

Violet grabbed the stair rail and hurried down the stairs, eager to reach the hairdressing salon. She dreaded the idea of tripping over heavy snowdrifts, so she took a deep breath and stepped outside, preparing for the long and potentially risky journey to her job.

"Morning, pretty lady," said the familiar voice. She looked up and saw High Roller-Gunn leaning against his car, a faint smile playing on his lips.

Violet froze on the final step of the building, clutching the iron rail to avoid falling. Her eyes sparkled with surprise upon seeing him there, as if he had woken up solely to see her.

"What are you doing here?' she asked.

"Well, just take a look out here," he said, gesturing at the snow-covered walkways.

Violet observed several people already stumbling over the snow, while others attempting to cross the road slipped and fell on hidden ice patches.

'Are you sure you want to walk through all this?' he asked. "Your arms will be full with that large towel bag for Miss Bessie's salon, and you might not notice where you're stepping or icy spots. You could fall and get hurt, which wouldn't be good for your baby, especially if you slip on the ice and fall backwards on your head. Shit, you think anyone would help you then? Humph! Thieves are always looking for someone to take advantage of. As soon as you're on the ground, hurt, they'll rob you! If I see that happen, let's say you won't see their fucked-up faces ever again," he said.

Violet's eyes blazed with fear at the idea of harm to herself and the baby.

"Yep, just as I suspected, beautiful lady. Allow me to help you in my car. We'll stop at the Southern Pot again, just like yesterday, to pick up coffee and food sacks. Then, we'll head to Bessie's. Hand me the bag of towels," he said, extending his hand.

Violet gradually released the stair rail and staggered toward Gunn, who held his arm out. Suddenly, she slipped on an ice patch and nearly fell forward.

"Gotcha!" Gunn exclaimed, holding her tightly. Violet froze, unable to move. The few seconds between walking toward him and nearly falling to the ground were terrifying.

"Are you alright?" he asked.

Violet nodded, too shaken to answer.

"Come on, let's get out of here. Hold onto me and don't be afraid. I've got you, and I ain't letting you go," he said, gently guiding her into his car.

"You okay now?" he asked again after Violet was settled.

"Yes, she said in a strained voice. She clutched her purse close to her chest and closed her eyes, grateful for the decision to be driven once again to work.

He's right. If I'd walked to Miss Bessie's, I wouldn't have reached the first block. He saved me and my baby, she thought as she massaged her belly, unaware that Gunn was watching her. Grabbing the blanket from the back seat, he handed it to her, and she draped it across her knees. He started the car and drove off.

"As you can see, it's dangerous outside after a snowfall," he said. "You really shouldn't walk to work during winter, especially with ice and snow on the sidewalks. Until Spring, I want to drive you to work and pick you up after your salon shifts. It would reassure me that you and the baby are safe."

Violet turned to look at him while he kept his gaze straight ahead, concentrating on driving as if the road were clear of snow and ice.

"Okay," Violet said, with a hint of apprehension. "You can drive me to work and pick me up, but only if you agree to do this for the entire winter. Once my baby is born, I'll be walking to work."

Gunn didn't reply. He smiled with his lips, but his acorn-colored eyes stayed focused on the road. When they arrived at The Southern Pot, he eased the car to a stop, leaving the engine running.

"Be right back with the coffee and three sacks of food, pretty lady," he said.

Getting out of the car, he carefully trudged through the snow and entered the crowded restaurant. Violet watched the same scene from yesterday: patrons moving in unison against the wall to make way for him. Behind the counter, the register clerk efficiently handed him three sacks and three Mason jars of steaming coffee, pre-mixed with milk and brown sugar.

"Will that be all, Mr. Gunn?" the clerk asked pleasantly.

"Uh, can I have an extra piece of that cake?" Gunn said, gesturing toward the large slice of freshly baked lemon pound cake.

"Yes, sir," the clerk said. After slicing a thick piece and wrapping it in wax paper, he placed it in a bag and handed it to Gunn. Snatching the bag from the clerk, he tossed the clerk a nickel, left the restaurant, got in his car, and drove Violet to work while chatting with her until they arrived at Marcel's.

CHAPTER THIRTY-EIGHT

Peering out the car window, Violet saw that the salon was already open. Inside, three unfamiliar workers dressed in hairdressing attire sat at their stations, laughing and sipping from mason jars of hot coffee, with split brown paper bags on their laps that held buttered cornbread or hot biscuits with chopped ham; no doubt, they had all stopped at the Southern Pot earlier before it got crowded. Gunn eased the car to a stop as close to the curb as he could. A shovel path led from the curb directly to the salon door. Violet let out a sigh of relief.

"Looks like someone was kind enough to do this for Miss Bessie," Violet said as she looked out the car window.

Gunn said, "I made a few calls to some of my men who live nearby. Whatever I ask, they'll do for me without question. They did a great job, so I'll pay them all after I drop you off. Are you ready for another day of work?" Then, opening the door to step outside.

"As ready as I will be," said Violet.

Scooting to the car door, he opened it and took the large bag of towels while she gripped the sacks holding all the food he had bought for herself and Bessie for the day. As he helped Violet out of the car, she could see that the hairdressers had almost stopped what they were doing because all their attention was on her and Gunn.

"Watch yourself, pretty lady," he cooed, offering the crook of his elbow. Violet linked her arm with his. He shut the door with his snow-covered shoe and led her to the salon. He reached for the doorknob, opened it, and gestured for Violet to walk through.

"Morning, ladies!" Gunn announced loudly.

"Good morning, Mr. Gunn," each hairdresser said, some with mouths full of breakfast. All greeted Gunn except the one in the middle chair, who stared at Violet with hateful eyes.

Bessie, who was inside the supply room, strode out to greet everyone.

"Good morning, Mr. Gunn," Bessie greeted. "Thanks for telling your uh, acquaintances to clear away all that snow and ice from the salon. I watched them clear everything from eleven o'clock last night until I was ready to open. They worked all night without stopping. God bless them. I told them to bring their wives on Saturday morning, and I'll charge only twenty-five cents each for a press and curl or finger wave. It's the least I can do to thank them because our salon has the only clean walkway from the street to the door."

"Uh-huh," the hairdressers all said, nodding in agreement.

"I'll make sure to tell them everything you said," Gunn said, handing Bessie the bag of towels he took from Violet. "I know their wives will appreciate what you're doing for them. I stopped by the Southern Pot and picked up your usual," he added, handing her the bag with her breakfast. "I need to head out to pay my men and handle other businesses in Brooklyn. Take good care, ladies."

Gunn quickly left the salon, got into his car, and drove away.

"Everyone, we have a new worker with us. This is Violet Booker from New Orleans. She will be responsible for cleaning the salon, sweeping, keeping the bathroom clean, emptying trash, organizing your stations, and managing the stockroom inventory," Bessie announced happily.

One of the hairdressers asked sharply, "Can she make appointments?"

"In due time, maybe in a month," Bessie said. "But before we discuss what she'll do next, let's introduce ourselves."

"I'll go first," said a short, fair-complexioned, curvaceous woman with medium-dark hair styled in tight curls. Her green eyes sparkled as she approached Violet.

"My name is Nettie Wharton. Folks here call me Peach. Nice to meet you and welcome," she said, extending her hand to shake hands with Violet.

"It's so nice to meet you, Peach," said Violet with a smile.

"I'm Clarissa Myron, and it's a pleasure to meet you, Violet," said the gray-haired Clarissa, who looked older than all the hairdressers, including Bessie. "I usually work with women a bit older than those coming in for fancy hairstyles," she explained, taking a bite of her biscuit. "Most of them attend the church just down the street, and they still want their hair to look beautiful."

"It's also nice to meet you, Miss Clarissa. I look forward to greeting your customers when they arrive," said Violet.

"I like you already, young lady," said Clarissa, cautiously sipping her piping hot coffee from a Mason jar with both hands.

"Thank you, ma'am," said Violet.

The last hairdresser, a tall, wiry woman with almond-shaped brown eyes, looked disheveled. She was the one who asked if Violet could set up appointments. Her uniform was stained with old, oily hair pomade, especially the deep pockets, and her smock was dirty, with yellow-stained underarm seams. Sitting in her operator's chair, she constantly nibbled on her cornbread, spilling crumbs on the clean floor, while making loud slurping sounds as she drank hot black coffee. Her hairdressing station was in poor condition: the once-clean cotton towels used to blot her straightening combs were burnt, some with holes, and all her pomade tins were left open. A noticeable musty odor emanated from her soiled uniform.

"Good morning, my name is Violet," she said politely.

The hairdresser didn't answer.

"Excuse me, Williana," snapped Bessie. "In my salon, we greet each other. Violet said good morning to you. If you can't bother to respond, you can leave and be replaced. There are plenty of women in Harlem eager for work."

Williana's eyes narrowed at the words. She stood up and slammed her coffee jar down on her disorganized station. The noise made Clarissa flinch.

"Morning, I'm Williana," she snapped at Violet. With a hostile stare, she spun around to her workstation and began slamming tins of hair pomade, pretending to work.

Bessie shook her head in disgust and turned her attention back to the group.

"Everyone, we'll be very busy today because of the heavy snowfall yesterday. Many customers avoided coming yesterday but might come today, and several housekeepers who have the day off will be coming in again. Some of these women haven't been here since Christmas, so they'll need extra hair care, especially for itchy scalps. Be sure to use the smaller combs to remove dandruff, then shampoo their hair twice. The first shampoo should clean the scalp of dirt, dandruff, and sweat. It's important to scrub the scalp firmly but gently, avoiding any harshness that could hurt the customer's head", she said.

"What is the second shampoo for, Miss Bessie?" Violet asked.

Williana, appearing distracted and not paying attention to Bessie's words, shot Violet a stern look.

"Would anyone like to tell Violet why we shampoo our customers a second time?" Bessie asked.

"We shampoo a second time to ensure our clients have a thoroughly cleaned scalp, which enhances the shine and beauty of their hair," Peach said with a smile. "During the second shampoo, we scrub the scalp until a thick, rich lather forms, resembling whipped cream. When the lather is just right, we rinse with very warm water. Afterwards, we wrap the hair in a clean towel, section it, and apply Royal Crown or Dixie Peach to the scalp. I also like to brush their hair to loosen it before proceeding further-"

"We know, Peach!" Williana interrupted, her voice icy as she kept staring at Violet.

"I'm sorry, Miss Bessie. I tend to talk too much sometimes. I really love what I do here, and that excites me. Please forgive my chatter," Peach said sheepishly.

"You did wonderfully, Peach. That's exactly the answer I was hoping to hear before you were rudely cut off," said Bessie, looking directly at Williana, who ignored her.

"There is enough time to learn more later, but we have twenty minutes before our customers arrive. If you're done with your coffee, make sure to tighten the lid to prevent spills and dispose of your napkins to keep the place tidy. Violet, come along and bring the towels with you," Bessie said.

"Yes, ma'am," Violet replied as she took another bite of her biscuit and finished her coffee. She brushed away any spilled crumbs, discarded them, and then followed Bessie.

'Thank you, Peach," said Violet. Peach smiled at Violet as she busily prepared for her customer. Clarissa took out two pressing combs and placed each one on the hot plates to heat.

As Violet moved with Bessie towards the back of the salon, Williana watched and then snickered at Violet's belly.

"Humph! No wedding ring means no husband. Looks like you enjoyed doing those nasty things to get a baby inside you, huh?" she muttered, loud enough for Violet to overhear.

Overhearing the offensive comment Williana made, Bessie stopped walking and hurried over to Williana's station, getting right up in her face.

"Is there something you need to say?" Bessie challenged.

"Uh, no, Miss Bessie, I was clearing my throat," Williana said,

Before any customer sets foot inside this salon, you make sure you use the remaining fifteen, now thirteen, minutes to tidy and clean your station, she said sharply, tapping her watch. "You continue to leave behind a messy and greasy station! Last week, you left a pressing comb on the hot plate next to open hair pomade tins. My God, you could have started a fire! And who would be responsible for that, huh?" she asked.

"Mine, yes ma'am," Williana murmured, her head tilting slightly downward.

"Get started on your tasks to clean up this mess," said Bessie. "Violet, come with me, dear."

Violet followed Bessie, who was muttering and shaking her head in confusion. Violet glanced over her shoulder and saw Clarissa still straightening her station. Peach was gathering her tools for a press and curl. Williana stood confidently at her station mirror, holding a comb, sectioning her hair, and scratching out large dandruff flakes from her scalp, oblivious to what Bessie told her to do.

There's something wrong with that woman, Violet nervously thought to herself.

"I apologize sincerely for what you just saw and heard," Bessie said as they stopped in a room filled with unopened boxes and shelves holding bushel baskets of salon supplies. "Williana was trouble from the moment I inherited this salon," she added with a heavy sigh. "The salon was owned by my cousin, who passed away ten years ago, and she left it to me in her will. I used to work here as a young hairdresser, about your age. As the salon gained more customers who were moving out from the South, she needed more help. That's when she hired Clarissa, and a week later, Williana. Even before her first week, she started causing trouble, first with the staff and then with the customers. She never kept her area tidy, and it was always messy. After I took over, she improved for a while, but it didn't last. Customers waiting over an hour for her often left because she would arrive smelling of sex and liquor. Things worsened because many of those women were maids with Thursdays and every other Sunday off to attend church. All I can say is thank God for Clarissa, who tracked down these women to do their hair. She's the one all the maids and older women go to. Peach enjoys styling the hair of younger maids and many church women. I do hair for anyone who comes in, especially if any of the hairdressers are running late," Bessie explained.

"So, who gets their hair done by Williana?" Violet asked.

Bessie glanced over both shoulders as if checking for nearby listeners. Then she waved her hand, signaling Violet to come closer. Since Violet was much taller than Bessie, she tilted her head forward to listen to what she was about to say.

"Williana does the hair for all the prostitutes," Bessie lowered her voice. "They come in only on Friday mornings, as they need to be out working from noon until well past midnight. The place gets crowded on Friday mornings to prepare for Friday night into Saturday, and some come early Saturday if they have work in New

Jersey. They pay well, and Williana knows them all. Some with light skin and peculiar-colored eyes can pass."

"Pass?" asked Violet.

"Pass for white," said Bessie. "Their mothers were light, to begin with, and they either married very light-complexioned Black men who were also passing or ended up laying with white men then having their babies. This has been going on since slavery."

Violet's eyes widened in surprise, her mind momentarily drifting to Maria St. Laurent as she absorbed this information.

Humph! That explains some things about her eye color and skin tone, Violet thought. But she quickly pushed thoughts of Maria out of her mind.

"I would've never realized she was like that; no wonder she's unfriendly and bad-mannered. I heard what she said to me when I walked past her," Violet said.

"Oh, believe me, I heard what she said, too! That's why I shamed her into cleaning up that filthy space of hers, humph! Even some of the biggest four-legged rats in Harlem wouldn't visit her station! They'd run straight back into their rat-holes!" Bessie said, chuckling. "But let us not discuss Williana and her prostitute customers because we've got a lot more things to do today. You're standing in the supply closet. The reason I still call it a closet is that when my cousin ran the salon, it was a junk closet. When I took over, I cleared it out and threw away the clutter. Once I was done, I realized how spacious it was and thought it would be the perfect place to store salon supplies. I started saving twenty-one-bushel baskets whenever I bought vegetables. I cleaned them and used them to organize shampoos, hair pomade, bobby pins, towels, and hair clips. Every Monday, please count the items in each basket. I have a slip with the date, the count, and space for any supplies the hairdressers might need. They will record how many they take, subtract it from the previous count, and write their name and the date on the slip. I also keep the contact details for our hair product supplier, including their phone number. Please call them when our stock is low, but always check with me first—I'm monitoring every dollar spent in this salon. Also, please collect the payments from customers after their appointments. Each hairdresser will provide you with a yellow slip that includes their name, the customer's name, and the charge. We charge $2 for a shampoo and dry with a hot comb and curl, and $2.20 for the same service but with Hump Hairpins and metal clamps for finger waves. For longer hair, a simple bob style with a hot comb and click tongs for tighter curls costs two dollars and a quarter. Every Friday, you'll exchange soiled towels for clean ones from Clyde, his wife Gloria, or Simeon, to bring back to the salon for Saturday".

"Oh yes, I met them, Simeon, Clyde, and his wife, Gloria. They're very nice and I had a lovely time talking to them. They seem busy, which is good for them. Everything you told me to do, I scribbled in my notepad", said Violet.

"The older woman who used to live there was a wonderful worker. You heard what happened to her?" Bessie asked.

"She only died, and it was horrible how she was found," Violet said as she jotted down the final detail Bessie had provided.

"It was dreadful," Bessie said, dabbing her eyes. "Her name was Paula, but we all called her Miss Paula. We attended the same church, met for tea once a month at either her flat or mine, and she had her hair done here. I was the one who styled her hair after she died. I couldn't get over what happened to her nose and face. Thank God her casket was closed. I don't know who was worse to do, Miss Paula's hair or that other woman's hair I styled-her name was Lena, that's it, Lena Collins."

Violet felt a surge of panic in her stomach and looked away, blinking rapidly.

Violet hesitated whether to tell her that the woman who was her stepfather's first wife — the one who left him had actually been replaced by her mother, Audine, as his second wife. This is becoming quite overwhelming!

"Are you okay, dear? What's the matter because you look like you were just spooked", said Bessie.

"I'm fine, Miss Bessie. I just realized I need to make sure to do the things you just told me every day, especially on Fridays. I want to show you how I will be a good worker," Violet said, smiling.

Bessie said, "I have no doubt you'll be a great worker. I only ask two things: be honest and tell me the truth at all times. If you can do that, you'll have a job here as long as you want." She continued, "Also, I need you to sit at the front of the salon to greet customers, show them where to sit, and wait until their hairdresser calls them. Some maids will arrive early and come in. When you receive payment after the service has been completed, please place the money in the wooden box I'll provide. I go to the bank on Mondays. Just make sure there are ten dollars in one-dollar bills each morning to make change if needed," Bessie explained.

"Yes, ma'am, I'll remember to do that", said Violet as she took notes.

"It's almost eight-thirty," Bessie said, tapping her watch. "Time to get back to work. Are you set?"

Violet cheerfully exclaimed, "I'm ready!"

Bessie had Violet go out first to switch off the light. As they returned to the salon, Violet saw two women outside the door, huddled together to keep warm from the cold.

"I'll let them in, Miss Bessie," Violet said as he hurried toward the door.

"Good morning, ladies! Please come in; it's freezing outside!" Violet said as she opened the door for the women, who were visibly cold and shivering upon entering.

"Oowwee! It's freezing outside! Thanks for letting us in. We were at the salon across from Harlem and waited so long that we decided to come here. I'm Althea Sayles, and this is my good friend Lizzi Dottin," she said, extending her hand to Violet.

"I'm pleased to meet you and Miss Lizzi. Allow me to take your coats. Miss Clarissa and Miss Bessie don't have appointments for another hour, so they can see you now. Are you both planning to get hot comb presses and simple curls today?" Violet asked.

"Yes, we definitely are," Lizzi said with a smile. "We have a lot to do since Thursdays are our only day off, so if they're ready, we're ready too!"

"Follow me, and I'll carry your coats to the back room to hang them near the radiator, so they'll be warm when you're finished."

Violet took their coats and led them to the stations. They first stopped at Bessie's station, where Bessie introduced herself as the owner. After closely inspecting her hair and scalp, Bessie decided to take Althea, especially after observing how Althea was scratching her short, thinning, unruly hair. Once seated and draped, they engaged in lively conversation as Bessie scratched out dandruff and then took her to the sink for a hair wash. Violet then escorted Lizzi to Clarissa's station. Clarissa and Lizzi quickly bonded when they discovered they were attending the same church. Lizzi explained she was "tender-headed" and asked Clarissa not to scratch her scalp too hard. Clarissa agreed, and within forty-five minutes, both customers had their scalps examined, washed, rinsed, their hair sectioned, oiled with Glossine pomade, and placed under hairdryers, all while engaging in more animated conversations.

Within minutes, Peach, Bessie, and Clarissa each had their regular clients arriving. Violet greeted, met, and accompanied them to their respective hairdressers. The salon quickly started filling up. Meanwhile, Williana was noticeably missing. Violet observed that whenever she took the customers' coats and purses to the closet across from the bathroom to hang up, Williana would slip away just seconds after Violet left, hurriedly heading to the front as more customers arrived.

Violet decided to watch her closely because something seemed off. She noticed that Williana was the only one not busy, as she took ten dollars from Bessie and Clarissa, the two early customers who appeared satisfied and looked lovely despite covering their freshly styled hair with hats.

"Thank you for coming, Miss Althea and Miss Lizzi. We look forward to seeing you again next Thursday," Violet said warmly as they left the room. Neither replied, which was unusual given their cheerful demeanor upon arrival. Violet observed Althea and Lizzi anxiously searching their purses. Althea glared at Violet with disgust before storming off.

The salon was busy with more than twenty-eight customers still present late in the afternoon. While they waited in the front seating area, Violet overheard snippets of their conversations, and all of them were maids.

"That woman expects me to stay late at work on Friday. She said she's having a late lunch with a "friend," but I know it's a lie. She's actually meeting the man she's been seeing for over a year at his hotel. I overheard her making the plans, so I know the truth!"

"The woman I work for just had a baby on Thanksgiving Day. That new baby doesn't look anything like her husband," chimed in another maid. "The baby was born with red hair, and both the mother and the father have blonde hair."

Another conversation in the corner got even livelier.

"Welp, on New Year's Eve, my friend Addie called in sick, so the other maid, Gladys, stayed on because she said she could use the extra money. Everyone at the dinner party was so drunk that they all ended up staying overnight. After staying awake until three a.m., Gladys finally went to bed and was sleeping soundly in the maid's quarters. Suddenly, she felt a hand squeezing her breast. When she turned around, she saw it was the host's husband. He covered her mouth and climbed on top of her. She described feeling him push his long, thick part inside her all night until she couldn't scream anymore. Recently, Gladys told Addie that her period is two weeks late."

The conversations, some quite disturbing, had Violet at times massaging her belly and dabbing tears from the corner of her eye. What snapped her out of her deep thoughts were customers leaving their seats to be served, and the ones leaving. Each time Violet said goodbye and thanked them for coming, she was met with silence. When she watched them from the window outside, the same scene repeated: they'd rummage through their purses, look up and point at her, then storm off. This pattern continued all day. Bessie also had to excuse herself from her customers several times to answer phone calls from angry callers insisting on speaking to her.

"Violet, could you come to the back, please?" Bessie asked anxiously after ending her eighth call. "Williana isn't busy today, so she will handle the front of the salon and take care of the payments while we talk."

"Yes, ma'am, of course," Violet said. She followed Bessie, who was walking quickly toward the supply room.

"Close the door behind you", she said briskly.

"Yes, ma'am, "said Violet as she closed the door.

"Violet, I've been told that several customers have reported money missing from their purses or coat pockets. One maid, who recently got her paycheck, had saved two weeks' worth of earnings to pay her rent and buy food. Now, her purse is empty! She has no money to buy food for her family and can't afford to take the bus back to her workplace! Oh, my goodness, Violet, you were the one collecting coats and storing them in the back room, where we keep our customers' belongings. Why would you take money? Is it because you need money for yourself or your baby?" Bessie asked with a tense, angry tone.

Violet remained motionless.

Did I hear her right? She's accusing me of stealing? Violet thought, horror-stricken. Baffled, Violet spoke for the first time.

"Miss Bessie, I would never steal anything that isn't mine, especially someone else's money! Since I started work today, all I've done is greet everyone, take their coats and purses, and have them sit down until it was their turn to get their hair done!" exclaimed Violet, who was close to tears.

"But why would they tell me that you took their money, Violet? How do you explain that before they arrived, they had money, and after you took their belongings, every single dollar, except what was needed for their hairdressing service, was missing?" said Bessie.

"Miss Bessie, I didn't steal anything from anyone! That is the truth," Violet said, her voice thick with tears.

"Violet, I'm sorry, but for my customers' sake, I have to let you go. Please gather your belongings and leave," said Bessie.

Violet shook her head in shock.

"Miss Bessie, I swear I didn't take anything from anyone!" Her voice trembled with desperation.

"Get out!" Bessie hissed, turning her back to Violet with her head bowed low and shaking it from side to side.

Violet grabbed her belongings, quickly slipped into her boots, and hurried out of the room. Trying to hold back tears, she tossed her head and walked straight ahead. The salon fell silent as she left.

"Humph! It looks like you got caught in more ways than one", Williana said, snickering.

Violet stopped abruptly and turned around to Williana, who sat at the salon reception chair and desk, smiling with a hint of arrogance in her eyes.

"What the hell do you mean by saying that to me?" Violet said, furious.

The women in the waiting area ceased their noisy chatter to listen in on every word exchanged between Violet and Williana, who found Violet's dismissal amusing.

"Look at you! It's plain as day that you ain't got no husband, you expectin a baby, you're desperate, and you're walking around town with High Roller-Gunn, the biggest gambler on this side of Harlem, hah! Is Gunn the father of the baby, or have you been sleeping with every man you meet here in Harlem?" said Williana, sneering.

The salon patrons gasped at what they had just heard.

Violet felt herself becoming dizzy and grew increasingly angry at the accusations from Williana, who was sitting back and laughing loudly.

"I want you to know I spent the entire day working hard to ensure customers were greeted warmly, but it seems you didn't serve a single customer all day," she replied, her voice growing angrier. "What I find strange is that for every two or three customers I helped, taking their coats and purses to the back, you would go to the back of the salon pretending to use the bathroom for ten minutes, never hearing you flush the toilet, or the water run from the sink to wash your hands. Now I wonder, who might be the thief? And one more thing: the baby growing inside me is from a man I loved, who died after being bitten by a snake. My child will grow up never knowing his father. Working here could have helped change things, but now everything's different. We'll manage, thanks to my stepfather in New Orleans. It's horrible and dishonorable to say such cruel things to me, and you should be ashamed! Listen to my words: the real thief is inside this salon, much like the red rattlesnake whose venom killed the man I loved,"

Violet exited abruptly, slamming the door and leaving the salon in stunned silence. Williana's eyes flashed with surprise as several customers hurried to the back of the salon into the room where their coats and purses were stored to retrieve money from their pockets.

They then returned to their seats, clutching their purses

tightly.

CHAPTER THIRTY-NINE

"So, Miss Bessie accused you of stealing?" Cee-Cee asked as she ladled leftover chicken and sausage gumbo over a mound of rice for Hubert, who had just finished work after spending the last two days at his employer's house. The lawyer he worked for gave him the next three days off and said he wouldn't need his driving services until Monday. He is representing a client accused of murdering her husband, who had battered her daily for twenty years.

"Yes," Violet said as she looked down at her steaming bowl of gumbo. "Miss Bessie mentioned that several customers have complained about their money disappearing from their coat pockets or purses when they went to pay after their salon appointments. They said I was the only one who took their coats right after they arrived, which is true. After each customer came in, I greeted them and then took their belongings to the back room, where coats and purses are hung up. I told Miss Bessie I would never steal and that I am not a thief! Why would I steal? Wayne sends me money every month, and you and Uncle Hubert advised me to save every dollar I get. Why would I steal from those women?"

"Sumptin just doesn't sound right to me," Hubert said briskly. "You just got here from New Orleans, Wayne's been sending you money, and by the grace of God, you have a roof over your head. So why would you want to steal from Bessie's customers? It just doesn't make any sense to me at all."

"I noticed someone in the salon," Violet said, raising her head. "There was a hairdresser named Williana. From the first time we met, she didn't like me. She looked at me with hatred and made nasty comments about me."

"What kinds of things did she say to you?" Cee-Cee asked as she started eating her bowl of gumbo.

"She was looking at my belly and my left ring finger. And said no ring means no husband," said Violet, dabbing at her nose with her napkin.

Hubert cleared his throat loudly and continued eating. Cee-Cee reached over and grasped Violet's hand.

"Violet, stop fretting because Williana is a no-good soul." Something in Cee-Cee's voice made her look directly up at her.

"From what I've heard about Williana, none of the maids who have Thursdays off will get their hair done by her. Besides being bad-mannered, she's nasty, doesn't wash her uniform, and she smells," Cee-Cee said. "Her customers are the prostitutes who'll wait until their hair is so unkempt that when they come to her, they'll come to her in droves, sometimes as many as twenty will show up. Bessie told me that she hates it when they come in like that, crowding her salon, talking loudly, and smelling of cheap perfume, but they will pay. Tell me what you noticed about what Williana was doing," said Cee-Cee.

Violet said, "Whenever I took coats from two or three customers, Williana would go into the back room shortly after, pretending to use the bathroom and staying there for a while. When she returned, she would sit in her chair doing nothing to assist in the salon. She'd either just stare at me or go back to the coatroom and remain there even longer."

Cee-Cee and Hubert stopped eating and looked at each other, their eyes flashing with shock.

"Williana is the thief," Hubert said with disgust.

"Yes, I was thinking the very same thing," said Cee-Cee.

"But how can I tell Miss Bessie what I saw? She doesn't want me back in the salon and is so busy she didn't notice what happened!" Violet exclaimed, exasperated.

"She's right, Hubert," Cee-Cee said. "How can we explain to Bessie that it wasn't Violet who stole the money from her customers, but Williana all along?"

"We both know Violet wouldn't dare do something so shameful. Bessie needs to witness it herself. The real question is, when will Bessie realize she has a thief working for her?" said Huber, shaking his head. His expression was serious and angry.

"That's going to be very hard to do," said Cee-Cee as she shoved a forkful of rice into her mouth.

"To do what?" Hubert asked.

"Opening her eyes," Violet said, "Miss Bessie needs to see what a mean-spirited woman Williana really is. She hasn't noticed it before because Williana is skilled at hiding her true nature to avoid getting caught."

After everyone finished their coffee, Cee-Cee and Violet cleared the table, stored the leftovers, and washed the dishes. Once they all said goodnight, they went to bed. Violet, however, lay awake staring at the ceiling and didn't doze off until she heard Cee-Cee and Hubert preparing for another workday. It was five o'clock in the morning.

While sleeping, she dreamt of Clarence outside her bedroom door, gently knocking and pleading to be let in. She heard the doorknob turning, but her legs felt paralyzed, preventing her from getting up. She tried to call out to him, but her throat was dry, and no sound came. The knocking grew louder, and she heard Clarence screaming to be let in because a snake had bitten him. Suddenly, she woke up to the sound of pounding on the front door, and someone called her name. Groggily, Violet got out of bed, put on her robe, and slipped into her slippers.

"I'm coming!" she called out as she hurried to the door. She adjusted her tignon and threw the door open. Standing there was High Roller-Gunn, dressed in what seemed to be a new coat, a matching derby, and smoking a cigar.

"Good morning, Violet," said Gunn as he tipped his derby to her. "Are you doing, okay? I was knocking on your door for a while, calling out to you. I didn't see or hear anything. Is the baby okay?" he asked, concerned.

"My baby is doing just fine, but I'm not," Violet said groggily. "Yesterday, I got fired. Miss Bessie accused me of stealing money from the coat pockets and purses of all the customers who came for hair appointments. I tried to explain that I would never commit such a terrible act!

I told my aunt and uncle that one of the hairdressers, her name is- "

"Williana Harperson", Gunn said, cutting her off.

"Yes, do you know her?" Violet asked.

"Everyone in Harlem knows who she is, especially the prostitutes. They all go to her for hair appointments, and she's also a troublemaker," Gunn growled. "She spread some nasty lies about one of the prostitutes, causing her to lose many customers and a lot of money. One day, Williana kept spreading more lies, but this time to the wrong woman. She didn't realize the woman was the prostitute's aunt. That night, ten of the prostitute's friends knocked on Williana's door, and ten of the prostitute's friends knocked her down when she answered the door. Those women beat the living shit outta Williana. You'd think she'd have learned her lesson from that ass-kicking. Don't worry, get ready for work tomorrow. I'll talk to

Bessie now and handle that greasy bitch once and for all," Gunn said. He rushed down the stairs, slamming the front door behind him. Violet quickly locked the door and ran to the window, just in time to see Gunn squeeze into his car and drive off without checking the traffic. She stood at the window, speechless at what she saw and even more shocked by what Gunn told her about Williana.

What kind of woman is Williana, that she doesn't care who she tells lies to? Violet thought to herself as she backed away from the window.

Violet returned to her bedroom to tidy up. After a quick bath, she got dressed and made a pot of coffee before preparing a light breakfast of leftover sausage and potatoes. She looked down and massaged her protruding belly. Clarence appeared to her in a dream. She hadn't thought about him in a while because of work, but it was also time to find a midwife to discuss care during her pregnancy. Cee-Cee, now working at the hospital, would know who to contact. There was no point in mourning Clarence anymore; he's dead and gone forever.

She sat on the edge of her bed, took out her writing tablet, and began jotting down the details of what was needed for her child's future and her own.

The salon lights were on, but it was empty inside. Gunn looked at his gold pocket watch. It was 6:45 a.m. The salon wouldn't open until 8:30 a.m., since today was Friday. A parked car, driven by a Black chauffeur, was directly in front of the salon. The chauffeur seemed unusually nervous sitting in his employer's car.

After about ten minutes, two women carrying large bushel baskets appeared, seemingly struggling with their overflowing loads. The fellow sitting in the car quickly jumped out of the driver's side to assist. He opened the rear door, allowing the women to load the baskets into the back seat, stacking them on top of each other. Before covering the baskets with a blanket, he paused to inspect everything. Satisfied with his approval, he reached into his coat pocket, pulled out a large wad of cash, and handed it to the woman, who looked unkempt and oily.

She smiled maliciously after counting the wad of cash. Unbuttoning her coat, she hid the money in her bra. She then said something that made the other woman and the man burst into loud laughter. The fellow and his companion quickly got into the car and settled in, while the unkempt woman ran back into the salon, turned off the lights, and locked the door. She then ran to the back of the driver's side, climbed in, and slammed the door shut. The man drove away swiftly.

"I knew it," Gunn growled. "That oily fucker Williana has to go."

Gunn started his car and made a U-turn, heading in the direction of The Southern Pot to get the morning usual for himself and Bessie, who would get an earful about what he had just seen.

CHAPTER FORTY

The ride back to Bessie's after stopping at the Southern Pot was quick, but today he felt unusually silent without Violet by his side. As he slowed the car at the red light, Gunn looked longingly at the empty passenger seat, Violet. Since her arrival from New Orleans, she had brought changes into his life. Though he continued to gamble and won hundreds of dollars daily, Violet made him think about the future, raising a family in a real house, not the rundown place he currently called home. He envisioned a proper house where they could build a life together.

Gunn thought to himself with a broad smile: My family. I know her time is near, but she needs a husband for her baby's sake — a role I will happily embrace. As long as I am here, they will have everything they need.

The honking horn behind his car broke his train of thought. Gunn nodded and smiled at the driver. As he drove the remaining five blocks to Bessie's salon, he reflected with pleasure on the idea of Violet as his wife and being a father to her child.

The salon's lights were on at Marcel's. Peach was attending to a customer, Clarissa was already hot combing someone sitting in her chair, and Bessie had a customer under the dryer. Three customers were in the reception area, but there was no sign of Williana.

Good, I'll be able to talk to Bessie alone while that oily bitch is-who the fuck knows where or cares, Gunn thought angrily.

Gunn stepped out of his car carrying two sacks of the morning food from the Southern Pot. Crossing the street, he opened the salon door and went inside. The salon was already filled with the scents of Dixie Peach, Royal Crown, and Glossine hair pomade.

"Mornin', ladies," Gunn boomed.

"Mornin'!" Everyone in the salon responded.

"The Southern Pot had a bunch of hot, buttery, golden-top biscuits, so I bought them all for you, hard-working women who haven't eaten anything. I'll place them here on the table, so please help yourselves. Enjoy!" he said.

"Thank you, Mr. Gunn, how thoughtful of you!" Several waiting customers took a wrapped hot biscuit and immediately started eating.

"Thank you, Mr. Gunn," Peach said happily. "I dashed out of my place without even a sip of coffee." She excused herself from her customer to grab two biscuits—one for herself and one for her customer, who appreciated the kind gesture. Clarissa nodded to Gunn, acknowledging her thanks in return.

Gunn tipped his hat to everyone and walked over to Bessie's station, where she was arranging her hair-styling tools to create finger waves on her sleeping customer under the hairdryer.

"Mornin' Bessie," Gunn said. "Got your usual, but I asked Moe, the cook, to add some bacon to yours." Gunn took out the wrapped biscuit, which was still hot, and handed it to Bessie.

"Thanks, but I'm not hungry right now," Bessie replied, seeming distant.

"What's wrong?" Gunn asked as he took a bite of his biscuit loaded with three pieces of bacon, dripping with butter and bacon grease.

"Let's go to the back and talk because I don't want any of my customers to hear this, and I definitely don't want Peach and Clarissa listening in," she whispered.

"Lead the way, Bessie," said Gunn as he gathered the food and coffee.

Bessie hurried past Gunn, who followed her into the supply room, which was usually well-stocked with bushel baskets and wooden crates lining the walls. However, several crates and spaces were noticeably missing, particularly some brands of hair pomades and shampoo.

"Bessie, what's wrong?" Gunn asked.

"The salon was robbed," she said angrily. "You see those empty spaces against the wall?" she asked, gesturing to several spots that were empty of crates of pomade.

When I arrived this morning, I noticed a lot of footprints on the walkway leading to the salon. I thought it was unusual because the salon opens early on Fridays. I immediately unlocked the door and turned on the lights. There were puddles of melting snow that created a real mess, she snapped. "When I tell you I was terrified, believe me, I was trembling all over." The tracks led into the supply room, where I noticed about four crates were missing, along with six crates of Glossine pomade. Each crate contains forty jars, and I bought enough to last until early summer. Oh, my Gawd, what am I gonna do!" she bellowed.

Gunn, who was intensely listening to Bessie's laments, rubbed his chin, and a sudden deep frown creased his forehead.

Gunn said calmly, "I know who took your pomades and also who took the money from the purses and coat pockets of the maids who came in on Thursday."

"What? Who was it?" Bessie asked, confused.

"Williana," said Gunn. "I came here early this morning, hoping you'd be inside the salon so we could talk about why you fired Violet. Bessie, she didn't steal that money, Williana did."

"Williana took the money from those maids who were here the other day? How?" Bessie gasped.

Gunn gestured for her to sit on some crates, then dragged a chair over from the corner.

"Let's start from the beginning about the second day Violet worked. Was Williana here that day?" Gunn asked.

"Yes, and I immediately heard her say some very mean and nasty things to Violet. I also had to warn

Williana again to keep her station clean. Well, what I'm about to say is very embarrassing, but Williana doesn't pay attention to her cleanliness. She smells like sour fish, her hair is messy, and she never comes to work wearing a clean uniform like Peach and Clarissa. Another thing I noticed was that Williana would stare hatefully at Violet because she was such a lovely-looking young woman. But what does all this have to do with Williana?" Bessie asked.

"When I talked to Violet, she mentioned that when she took your customers' coats to the coatroom, she noticed Williana leaving her station to go to the back to use the bathroom. The bathroom is right across from the area where all the coats and purses are kept, right?" Gunn asked.

"Why yes, it is", said Bessie.

"Violet mentioned that for every three or four customers, she would take their coats and purses to the coatroom. When she sat at the table near the door to greet everyone, she was also watching Williana. Like clockwork, Williana would quietly slip into the back as if going to the bathroom. How many times can a person piss or shit? Oh, and there's more I need to tell you," Gunn said, rubbing his forehead. "When I arrived early to see you, I noticed the salon's lights were on, and a black coupe was parked and running right in front of the salon. The fellow driving that car was a chauffeur. I know it because he was wearing a chauffeur cap and a dark suit. I waited to see what would happen. It turns out that it was worth the wait, because I saw two women come out of the salon, each carrying two-bushel baskets full of pomade. The chauffeur got outta the coupe to help load the baskets into the back seat. After they were packed, he reached inside his coat pocket and handed a wad of money to the woman, who turned off the salon lights and locked the door. When I got a closer look, I almost shit my pants; it was Williana," Gunn explained.

"Oh, my Gawd!" Bessie exclaimed in horror. "Now I understand why Williana was getting up and going to the bathroom three or four times yesterday. I thought she was just sick or something. So, what am I supposed to do now?"

"Come with me," Gunn said as he stood up from the chair. As soon as Bessie rose from the crate she was sitting on, Gunn was already inside the bathroom. He pressed his index finger to his lips to signal her to be quiet, then pulled her into the bathroom and locked the door.

"Shh," Gunn whispered. "See this picture you've nailed onto the door?"

"Yes," said Bessie, nodding in agreement with him.

"Where do you keep your tools in case something needs fixing around here?" Gunn asked, scanning the floor with his eyes.

"In there in the box underneath the sink," she said, pointing to a small wooden box underneath the sink.

Gunn crouched down and retrieved the box from under the sink. He opened it, saw several tools inside, and sifted through the hardware until he found what he was looking for.

Found it, a hand-crank hole maker! This plan of mine will catch that oily bitch and get her out of here once and for all, he thought to himself, grinning.

Gunn removed the small photo, which was hanging on a nail with twine. Taking out a pencil, he marked the spot with a small "x". Gunn carefully pressed the sharp drill bit into the wood and turned the handle. After fifteen minutes, a small, discreet hole was drilled into the door. The workmanship proved successful because Gunn was able to get a clear view of the coatroom.

"Bessie, come here and look through the hole I just made in the door," Gunn said, motioning for her to peer through the hole he had just created.

Bessie peered through a small hole that allowed her to watch as two customers entered the coatroom, took their coats, and left without noticing she was watching. Bessie turned to Gunn; her mouth open in surprise that the two women hadn't even seen her watching. The invention was incredible.

"All you need to do is go into the bathroom, lock the door, and keep the lights out. Make sure that when you do this, Williana isn't watching you go into the back. You'll have to be very careful. But be sure to keep the picture over the hole so nobody will know about it. After that, when Williana comes into the coatroom, watch her through the hole I made", said Gunn.

Bessie nodded and hugged Gunn, tearfully thanking him. Then, she peered through the hole again to ensure no one was coming in, slipped out the door just in time, and woke her sleeping customer under the dryer to start hot-combing her hair.

After cleaning the debris from the floor, Gunn hung the photo back in its place, snapped off the light, and exited the bathroom.

Striding back into the salon, it was filled with patrons getting their hair done. Williana was at her station with one of the prostitutes who was in the chair getting her hair styled.

"I see you finally made it in," Gunn said gruffly. Williana stopped what she was doing and glared at him.

"Humph!" she grunted back to him, rolling her eyes.

He leaned in close to Williana and said, "We'll see how much you'll be rolling those eyes of yours, sweetheart, because rats eventually get caught and devoured by cats."

The prostitute gazed at him with wide eyes, then looked up at Williana, who ignored him and hurried to Bessie's station. She was in the middle of pressing her customer's hair.

"Bessie, may I see you for just a moment outside, please?" Gunn asked.

"Yes, of course, Mr. Gunn. Judy, could you please excuse us? I assure you we will only be a moment," she said to her customer, who nodded and smiled at her and Gunn. Gunn tipped his derby hat to the woman. Bessie set the pressing comb back on the hot plate and wiped her hands with a towel. She and Gunn quickly moved to the salon's front door, passing the women eagerly waiting for their turn to get their hair styled for the weekend.

When Gunn opened the door, a powerful gust of wind caught them off guard. Bessie hugged her shoulders and shivered from the cold air.

"Okay, listen to me," said Gunn. "I hatched a plan for you. When you're done with that customer you're serving, please get her coat, give it to her, and escort her out. Then, when you get your next customer, have her hand her coat and purse to *you* and put them inside the coatroom. But before you return to your station, tell her you need to use the bathroom, then retrieve some pomade from the supply room for your station. What you're gonna do is stay in the bathroom, lock the door, and keep the lights off. Move that picture to the side and look through the hole. I guarantee that you'll catch

Williana and that woman sitting in her chair, going in there to rob your customers."

"Oh, my Gawd! You think it was Williana who stole from me?" Bessie asked.

"I'll put my life on it", Gunn said. "And one more thing, I'll be sending in my friend Berneice and four of her friends in here right after I leave. After they arrive, lock the door cause Williana and that oily bitch friend of hers will try to escape after you catch them".

"If it is Williana who stole from me, I owe Violet an apology and will want her back here immediately," said Bessie.

"I know, I already told her," Gunn said with a grin. "Oh, and take this," he pressed a ten-dollar bill into Bessie's shivering hand.

"What's this?" she asked, glancing at the bill.

"For your customer who had to wait while you were talking to me, and use the rest to buy some sandwiches tomorrow for your workers and Violet," Gunn said, rushing to his car. "I'll see you later."

"Thank you", said Bessie as she waved at him.

Bessie hurried back into the salon, greeting the women who were loudly chatting and laughing. After pressing and curling her client, she told her that she didn't need to pay because Mr. Gunn had covered it. Following Gunn's advice, Bessie collected her client's coat and purse. She saw her out the door, but as she said goodbye, she noticed five women in the waiting area whom she had never seen before. She gasped at the sight of the tallest woman sitting in the middle, whom she immediately recognized as Berneice. Bessie thought to herself, then made eye contact with Berneice, who smirked and nodded in response. Berneice then turned her attention back to her four friends, who were engrossed in conversation.

Bessie quietly locked the door and called her next client, Mrs. Jettman, who hadn't had her hair done in several months. They embraced warmly. Bessie gathered her belongings and asked her to sit at her station.

"It's so good to see you, Mrs. Jettman!" said Bessie as she swiftly snapped open a towel to drape over Jettman's shoulders.

It's been a long time since I last saw you in October. The woman I work for now has twin girls, so my hours have increased a lot. Honestly, Bessie, my husband wants us to start a family of our own because he's tired of me caring for other people's children," she said.

"I agree with your husband that you should settle in and start your own family," said Bessie. She glanced at Williana, who was finishing up her customer's hair.

"Uh, Mrs. Jettman, would you excuse me for just a moment, please? I need to hang up your coat and purse and make a quick stop to the bathroom. Oh, and I'm also going to get that special pomade that I know you'll be delighted with," said Bessie.

"Of course, and I'd love to see some of that new pomade," said Jettman as she pulled out her newspaper and started to read.

Bessie hurriedly took Jettman's belongings, trying not to attract Williana's attention as she moved to the backroom. She quickly hung her coat and placed her purse out in the open, even slightly unbuttoning it to reveal the few dollars inside. Bessie then slipped into the bathroom, locked the door, and kept the lights off, following Gunn's instructions. Slowly, she moved the picture hanging on the door to the right, uncovering the hole Gunn had made. Through it, she could see the coats and purses.

Suddenly, the footsteps and high-pitched laughter of two women grew closer: Williana and her prostitute client, Hazel.

"You sure we ain't gonna get caught?" the prostitute asked nervously, fidgeting with her tattered gloves.

"Hazel, please," Williana said in her menacing tone of voice. "That ole lady is too damn stupid to notice anything missing. I also took four crates of the pomade she uses this morning and sold every jar. Plus, I earned an extra twenty dollars by rummaging through the purses and coat pockets of women who came earlier. Come on Thursdays, because that's when the maids have their days off and get paid, so you'll have more money for me and you if you come to get your hair done," she said.

"Good!" exclaimed Hazel, cackling. "I need a much easier way to make money instead of just lying on my back. C'mon, Williana, hurry up before someone else comes back in here!"

Bessie watched with growing distress as the two women rummaged through the coats and purses of the hardworking customers, who earned barely twenty-five dollars a week to support their families in Harlem. Many of these customers were alone, with their husbands away working in New Jersey and only returning on weekends. For them, visiting the salon was a rare escape and a small reward for their hard work, only to have their money stolen by these two wretched women. Gunn was right; Williana was the one who stole all that money earlier in the week, not Violet! Bessie thought angrily. She observed closely as Williana pulled an envelope from the pocket of a blue coat and opened it.

"Girl, look what I found!" Williana whispered, her eyes wide as she gazed at the envelope.

"Whatcha got there?" asked Hazel, inching closer to get a look.

Williana pulled out eight crisp ten-dollar bills and four one-dollar bills and waved them in front of Hazel.

"Ooowee, I just hit pay-dirt!" Williana said, clapping her hands gleefully.

"Oh shit! You gonna share some of that with me, right?" said Hazel, smirking.

"The hell I am," said Williana as she put the money back in the envelope and stuffed it into her bra.

Suddenly, she heard the bathroom door burst open, causing her to jump and drop the wads of money she was clutching tightly.

"You lowdown, filthy thief, Williana! How dare you steal from this salon!" Bessie yelled, her voice trembling with fury.

Williana stood where she was with money before her feet fell to the floor. She was stunned.

"I saw both of you rummaging through the coat pockets and purses of all the customers here! Pick up that money from the floor, give back what you stole, and get outta here!"

"You didn't see anything, you crooked old lady!" shouted Hazel.

"Yeah, maybe you're the thief, Bessie!" Williana retorted, moving closer to Bessie, who held her ground against the tall, wild-looking woman looming over her.

"Get out of here right now! I saw you both steal money, and you have an envelope with fifty-four dollars hidden in your bra, you dirty home wrecker! I also have proof that you stole crates of pomade from the supply room earlier today. Mr. Gunn saw you and your friends taking the bushel baskets and gave you money. He even saw you get into the car with them and drive away! No wonder you were late this morning! Additionally, I now realize it wasn't Violet who stole the money from those customers earlier this week, but you, Williana, you!"

A large crowd of customers gathered, with Berenice and her friends in front. Hazel tried to escape and ran, but was quickly caught by two of Berniece's friends. They pinned her down, hitting and slapping her until she yielded. They retrieved the stolen money and handed it to Berniece, who then gave it to Bessie. The women then grabbed Hazel by her coat collar, dragged her to the door, unlocked it, and one of them forcefully threw her onto the snowy ground. Hazel landed face-first, slipped multiple times on the ice, and struggled to get up. During the fight, her coat was torn, and she was badly scraped and bruised on her knees, bleeding from her mouth. She spat blood and her broken tooth, moaned, and limped down the icy path, falling several times.

"So, what the fuck you going to do to me, old lady?" Williana asked, her voice trembling with panic, almost rising to a scream.

"You're going to give her every got-damn dollar you and that shit-faced dirty whore stole", snapped the deep voice belonging to Berenice, who stepped forward.

"Mind your fucking business, you giant bitch!" Williana yelled. She attempted to push past Berniece, who, with one hand, grabbed the front of Williana's soiled smock. One of Berniece's companions reached into Williana's bra and pulled out the envelope containing eighty-four dollars.

"That's mine!" shouted Peach's customer. "Oh my God, that's my rent, groceries, and money for my hair today!" Bessie handed the envelope to the visibly shaken customer.

"Let me go!" shouted Williana, who was now in a tight grip held by Berniece.

"She's not doing anything until every dollar is returned!" Bessie shot back.

Berniece signaled the other two women to search Williana's pockets, while one of them picked up the money scattered on the floor and handed the recovered bills to Bessie. Berniece also found a key inside Williana's smock pocket and passed it to Bessie's trembling hand.

"I want you out of this salon, and don't you even think of coming back here again! For years, you've been a liar, troublemaker, and thief. Your days are surely numbered and cursed," Bessie yelled. "You won't receive pay for the week you worked here, as that money will go to the women you stole from. Now, get out!"

Berniece and the four women with her forcefully dragged a screaming, kicking, and cursing Williana out of the salon. As they moved past Williana's station, Berniece grabbed the hot iron pressing comb still on the hot plate. They then took Williana to the alley around the corner, pinning her against the brick wall.

"What are you gonna do to me, you dumb-looking fuck?" Williana asked combatively.

"You need to make sure everyone you meet in this city knows you're a liar and thief," Berniece said.

"Miss Bessie is well-loved here and is a decent woman who avoids trouble. So, to show people what kind of person *you* are, you're going to wear the mark of a thief," Berniece added.

Then, without warning, Berniece took the searing hot pressing comb and pressed it to the side of Williana's face. Williana screamed as the searing comb burned her face, causing the smell of flesh to waft in the cold air. The sizzling and popping sound made her arms flail and convulse until the comb was cold. Berniece let it fall to the ground. Then she and her group took their time as they walked out of the alley and into the waiting car of High Roller-Gunn. After everyone was inside Gunn's car, with Berniece seated in front, she closed the car door, and Gunn sped off.

Williana collapsed on the filthy ground, writhing in pain as she clutched her burnt face, which would leave her permanently disfigured and branded as a thief and

liar.

Her cries of pain went unheard.

CHAPTER FORTY-ONE

February 1934

"You're learning quickly! Since I've shown you how to make finger waves using clips and by hand, we've seen an increase in customers, especially singers and dancers from local clubs and dance halls. I'm delighted you're back with us. I want to express how sorry I am for accusing you of stealing that money from our customers last month," Bessie said, lowering her eyes.

"Miss Bessie, I already forgave you because I knew it was only a matter of time before Williana would be caught, as she was careless, just like her station," Violet said frankly.

Bessie and Violet had just settled in a small corner of the supply room to enjoy their lunch. Their meal included sliced chicken, a thick piece of feather cake, which was the weekly special at The Southern Pot, along with piping hot coffee with brown sugar and cream. They sat on two sturdy wood blocks and a round wooden table.

"Miss Bessie, what happened to Williana after she was fired?" Violet asked as she unwrapped her sandwich.

Bessie took a bite and slowly and deliberately chewed the edge of her chicken sandwich, as if she were elsewhere in her mind. She took a quick slurp of her piping hot coffee.

"Well, from what I heard, Williana's outcome was not good at all," said Bessie. "It's still the topic of conversation."

Violet's eyes held a puzzled look.

"Berniece, a close friend of Mr. Gunn, arrived with four friends to confront Williana and her prostitute customer named Hazel. They entered the coatroom and began stealing money from customers' coat pockets and purses while they were getting their hair done. What those two didn't know is that I was watching them from the bathroom," said Bessie.

"Huh? How did you see them steal money from the bathroom?' Violet asked as she took a bite from her sandwich.

"With the help of Mr. Gunn. See, he drove over here early the morning after I fired you. He wanted to talk to me about hiring you back because it wasn't you, but Williana, who stole the money. Did you notice the painted picture of flowers hanging on the bathroom door from inside?" Bessie asked.

"Yes," said Violet.

"Welp, Mr. Gunn used the hand-crank tool on the door to make a large enough hole so I could see directly into the coatroom. I stayed inside the bathroom long enough to witness Williana and her whore friend Hazel steal money. What really got Williana in trouble was when Gunn saw her stealing bushel baskets of salon pomade. Earlier in the morning, she had arrived with a chauffeur and a woman. Gunn saw the man pay Williana for the pomade! When I saw everything with my own eyes, I got out of that bathroom so quickly it startled Williana! Yes, Gawd, she and Hazel tried to fight me, but Berniece came in just in time. Her friends prevented Hazel from escaping by locking the salon's front door. When Hazel was cornered, they took her purse from her hand and rummaged through it. They found the money she had stolen from the customers getting their hair done, all the cash in Hazel's purse, which they then gave to me," said Bessie.

Oh, my goodness, then what happened?" Violet asked.

"Berniece's friends grabbed Hazel, took her to the door, and beat the living daylights out of her. I heard they threw her onto the walkway so hard that she ended up losing a tooth. Humph, guess that puts an end to her being a prostitute and stealing," Bessie said, taking a bite of her sandwich.

Violet's eyes showed a hint of shock as she opened and unwrapped the cake slice. Her hunger was intense, now that she was in her fifth month of pregnancy. Her belly was visibly protruding, and she wore a white smock to fit her expanding figure.

"So, what happened next?" she asked, taking a bite of the cake slice.

"Then it was Williana's turn, and let me tell you, she was fit to be tied. Berniece dug her big hand into the top of Williana's uniform and pulled out eighty-four dollars belonging to Peach's customer, money meant for her rent and her family's food! I was furious and told her to leave my salon permanently. I also withheld her pay for the week since her theft was her punishment. After Berniece and her gang removed Williana, Mr. Gunn told me they took her to an alley nearby. I saw Berniece take the straightening comb that had been on the hot plate all morning, and Gunn said that Berniece pressed it onto Williana's face, making sure it cooled before removing it."

"Oh, my goodness, Miss Bessie, so half of Williana's face was burned?" asked Violet as she took a sip of piping hot coffee.

"Yes, it was", said Bessie, "When it was all over, Williana walked back to the rooming place where she stays. As soon as she went inside, she discovered that her room had been broken into. It seems that all the baskets and crates of pomade she stole from here were gone, and a huge wad of cash that she kept under her bed disappeared, too. She stayed holed up in her room for weeks without coming out, no food, no water, and no money. Then an infection where she was burned, followed by fever, came upon her. Weeks later, she was found dead by the woman who collects the rent money from the tenants. She said that the burn on Williana's face had blistered and had broken open. Pus and blood was everywhere on her pillow, and her bed was also soaked in urine and shit. But you want to know the sad thing about this whole story, Violet?" Bessie asked.

Violet, transfixed by the story, could only nod as she went in for another bite of her sandwich.

"During Williana's funeral, no one came to say goodbye, not even her regular clients like the prostitutes she styled hair for. I was called urgently to fix her hair for the service. When the undertaker finally opened her casket, I was shocked; the burn on her face was open, crusted with dried blood and pus. Her hair was matted, and she still wore that dirty, greasy, oil-stained uniform from her work that day. I told Mr. Dalewood, the undertaker, that there was nothing more I could do and suggested keeping the casket closed. He agreed, but before closing it, I whispered a goodbye and forgave her. After he shut the lid, I left. The next morning, I found Mr. Gunn waiting at the door with ten of his men, holding crates and baskets of stolen pomade. I was overwhelmed with joy and burst into tears. Mr. Gunn then instructed his men to stack all the crates right here," she explained, gesturing toward the neatly arranged crates and baskets of pomade.

"Oh, just before Mr. Gunn and his men left, he gave me a large wad of cash. I asked what it was for, and he explained it belonged to the customers Williana had been stealing from for years. This explains why many customers left the salon and never came back when my cousin was running it while Williana was doing hair. Now we understand the reason. I asked where Mr. Gunn found everything, especially the cash. He told me he and his men went to Williana's flat while Berneice and her gang were in the alley with Williana, and they took the crates and bushel baskets. Before leaving, Mr. Gunn returned to Williana's room and overturned her bed; the cash was in a roll tied with twine," said Bessie.

"How much money was found, Miss Bessie?" Violet asked.

"That wad of cash contained a thousand dollars, Violet," Bessie said quietly. "It represented ten years' worth of money up to the day she died that Williana had. She arrived at this salon with nothing but her uniform and left dead, wearing a dirty, greasy uniform."

Violet sat in stunned silence after learning about Williana's tragic death, but inside, she was troubled by the guilt of stealing Maria St. Laurent's husband, Clarence.

Am I any different from Williana? In many respects, I am also a thief. I stole Maria's husband, the father of her children, and like Williana, Clarence is no longer alive, Violet thought, feeling heartbroken.

"Sorry to interrupt your lunch, Miss Bessie and Violet," Peach said as she hurried into the supply room. "Your customers are ready for styling, and we need the hairdryers. Things just got busier with four more customers arriving!"

Violet tilted her head back to finish her coffee for the day, while Bessie watched her intently.

"What?" said Violet.

"You remind me of myself when I was starting as a new hairdresser," Bessie said, a hint of fondness lighting up her eyes.

"Really? How do I remind you of yourself?" Violet asked while cleaning the table after lunch with Bessie.

"Your determination to succeed is clear, but there's something inside you driving you to work so hard. If I didn't know better, I might think your heart and spirit have been shattered. Yet, that won't keep you down. You've risen again, even stronger. I believe that with the skills of the women in this salon and your intelligence as a young woman, this salon could become Harlem's top spot. However, we have a lot of work to do first. Are you ready to put in that effort, Violet?" Bessie asked.

"Yes, I'll work extremely hard, especially to make up for what Williana has done to you, the customers, and the salon over the years," said Violet.

"Then come on," Bessie said. "We have many customers waiting, especially for you." The two women shared a warm hug before entering a salon bustling with clients.

"Five-thirty sharp, ladies," Bessie announced as she locked the door. Peach, Clarissa, and Violet were slumped and exhausted, sitting on the chairs at their stations.

Friday went by very quickly, with twenty-four women coming in to get their hair styled, mainly for the upcoming weekend. That weekend, women planned to visit local club joints to listen to jazz, dance, and then return home to rest up for church on Sunday morning. Several women who had their money stolen returned to the salon after being informed that it was Williana, not Violet, who had taken their money. Bessie happily returned their money. Not only did they get their money back, but they also brought their friends to have their hair styled exclusively with finger waves by Violet, who was gaining a reputation as the best in Harlem.

"I'm so happy that tomorrow is Saturday," Peach announced.

"Oh, really?" Clarissa asked, curiosity evident. "What's going on with you?"

"Well, Lawrence Henson asked me to go out. He plays trumpet in the jazz band at the hall on 125th Street. I told him I'd go if he came to church with me on Sunday and then joined me for Sunday dinner to meet my family after service. And Violet, could you please finger wave my hair?" Peach asked.

"Of course, I'd be happy to do your hair. You promise to let us know how it all turns out?" said Violet.

A loud, heavy knock at the salon door drew their attention. Bessie looked up from her spectacles after counting the day's last dollar. Since Monday, the salon had earned a total of $200.

"I'll get it, Miss Bessie," Violet said as she stood up. Near the door, she noticed a man wearing a black derby looking in. It was High Roller-Gunn. Violet unlocked the door to let him in from the wind and cold.

"Evening, Miss Violet, evening, ladies," he said, tipping his derby to the women.

"Good evening, Mr. Gunn," they all greeted.

"You all are here quite late," Gunn asked, flipping out his pocket watch. "I drove by to check if you all are okay because I've never seen this place open this late. Is everything alright, Bessie?"

"Everything is fine, Mr. Gunn. Today, twenty-four women received hair services here. Our last client has just left before your arrival, and we're about to close, as tomorrow promises an even busier day. Several customers from three Harlem churches are expected tomorrow for the second Sunday baptism services," Bessie said as she shut the ledger.

"Tell you what, four of my men are outside, each with a car to drive you all home, so you won't be staying out late. Also, it's freezing. Bessie, since you're across the street, I'll have Earl and Berniece make sure you get safely into your building. If you're opening early tomorrow, let Earl and Berniece know so they can stay with you until everyone else arrives. I'll take Violet home," said Gunn.

"That's very kind of you, Mr. Gunn," Clarissa said quickly, as she hurriedly put on her coat and boots. "It's freezing outside, and I was worried about how long it might take to walk home."

Gunn nodded. Once everyone was ready to leave, Bessie turned off the lights and secured the door. Gunn guided Bessie and Violet by the elbows, one on each side, as they descended the icy stairs. Two of Gunn's men helped Peach and Clarissa. Gunn handed Bessie over to Berniece and Earl, who were shivering in the cold night air. After saying their goodbyes, everyone hurried into the waiting cars. Gunn signaled the drivers to start the engines. He opened the passenger door for Violet to get in. After closing the door, he quickly stepped out of the cold to sit inside, blowing on his gloved hands to warm them.

"Thank you, Mr. Gunn," said Violet.

"For what, Pretty Lady?" he asked.

"For making sure that we were all safe. We were all worried about how to get home since it's freezing," said Violet.

Gunn suddenly became smitten with Violet, with affection and concern flickering in his eyes. He closed his eyes, trying to think about what to say next.

"Violet, I need to talk to you about somethin'," said Gunn.

"Oh? Is everything okay with you?" she asked.

"Uh, I don't know. But listen to me, please. You're about to have a child soon, and you don't have a husband. People here talk, and I'm sure you don't want your son or daughter to be made fun of like I was when I was growing up. You need a husband and a father for your baby," said Gunn, swallowing hard.

Violet immediately felt her face warm with shame. How could she tell Gunn, who was becoming somewhat of a friend but still lacked full knowledge about her, and what had happened to Clarence? Even worse, she thought Clarence's wife, Maria, would be giving birth to her baby in May, just a month before her own due date in June. The whole situation was a complicated mess that she believed should never be revealed to anyone. She wanted to keep the web of deception and shame confined to New Orleans.

"Mr. Gunn, what are you trying to say?" Violet asked.

Gunn said, looking away, "I want to be the father of your child, and if you'll have me, I want you as my wife."

Violet's eyes showed a flicker of disbelief. Suddenly, Clarence's memories flooded her; his supposed arrival in Harlem, plans for a new life, and the understanding that all of it had been sacrificed for an empty promise. Gunn broke her thoughts.

"Violet, are you paying attention to what I'm saying to you?" he said.

"Yes, I hear you. I'm just a bit surprised by all this. My plan, or rather the plan for my baby and me, was to be with the man I had fallen in love with. Honestly, he was married, but I didn't care. When we first slept together, I fell in love with him so deeply that I knew I wanted more of him. The more he came to me, the more I desired him. After our third time together, I made a secret wish to have a child with him, and that's when he put our baby inside me," she said, looking down and massaging her belly. "His wife found out about us, but that didn't stop Clarence, the man I love. No, he went to his wife and told her he was leaving her for me and the baby we had. He also told his children, and that piece of hot news made them hate him. He gave up his marriage, family, farm, and business to start a new life with me," Violet explained.

"So, what happened? Did he change his mind?" Gunn asked.

"No," said Violet, turning to look at him. Her eyes darkened with pain as she continued.

"On the night Clarence was supposed to tell my mother and stepfather, my brother told them everything".

"He told them everything? How'd he know?" Gunn asked.

"He heard us; our noises woke him up. My brother thought someone had entered the house and was harming me. Instead, he saw Clarence and me. My mother was the one who threw me out of the house. My stepfather contacted my aunt and uncle, informing them of everything that had happened to me. After I moved to Harlem and settled into their flat, we were all sitting at the dinner table. During the blessing, he prayed to bless those in New Orleans who needed comfort during their loss. That's when my uncle and aunt informed me that Clarence was being buried," Violet explained.

"So, what happened to him?" Gunn asked.

"A snake bit him while he was collecting firewood for the woodstove. The poison quickly spread through his body, and he had no chance. Clarence died in less than ten minutes," Violet whispered.

"Jesus, I'm sorry to hear that," Gunn said in a consoling voice.

Gunn wondered why he was falling for her. She had been through so much, and he was determined to set everything right for her, gazing at Violet with intensity.

"Listen to me, Violet. I didn't have it easy either. I've killed some people. My first was my mother's lover. I came home one afternoon and found them together. Something inside me broke, and I ended up stabbing the motherfucker until he stopped moving. I ran outta there and well, my mother took the blame, confessing she was the one who killed him. She didn't survive long in jail; she got sick and died. I didn't know she had died for six months. The prison dumped her body in a grave with other dead bodies, so I have no idea where she's buried," Gunn said.

Violet sat still, her eyes widening in horror. Gunn remained oblivious to her expression and kept going.

"I also killed a woman I brought here from New Orleans. I didn't intend to, but I was not in my right mind at the time. She was a beautiful woman seeking to leave New Orleans and begin a new life away from her husband".

Violet thought nervously, "What did he just say? He killed two people, and one was from New Orleans." She fidgeted with her gloves, feeling a sense of familiarity.

"Mr. Gunn, since I'm from New Orleans, what was the name of the woman you were just talking about?" Violet asked, her eyes fixed on him with intensity.

"Lena, Lena Collins," Gunn replied. "She was a beautiful woman, but she didn't know how to obey me. She ran away, leaving my place in a big mess! She broke my window and stole money from me. Eventually, I found her and had to kill her. I also killed the woman who helped her escape. She was the laundress for the tenants in our building, and the three people living there now are in the same flat where she used to live. So, you see, we both have problems, which is why we need each other."

Violet stared wide-eyed into his acorn-colored eyes. Her face flashed with terror upon hearing that he had murdered three people, and the most disturbing detail was that the murderer of Wayne's wife, Lena, was sitting right next to her: **_Gunn!_** Despite this, Gunn wants to be my husband and the father of my child! Violet thought in horror.

"Mr. Gunn, I've had a long day, and after everything I've been through over the past few days, could we discuss this later? I want some time to think about what you've said," Violet said, her voice calm enough to avoid upsetting or changing his disposition.

"Oh, of course. So that means you're going to give my marriage proposal some thought?" Gunn asked.

"Yes, Mr. Gunn, I'd like to think about everything you just said to me because you're right, I do need a husband and a father for my baby", said Violet.

"You've just made me the happiest man in Harlem! Just wait, Violet, I will give you anything you desire and all the things the baby requires. I also have plans for myself once you become my wife," Gunn said happily, clapping his hands.

"Oh, and what's that?" Violet asked.

"To stop killing people", said Gunn sincerely. Then he closed his eyes, pressed a gentle kiss to her gloved hand, and, without delay, started the car to drive a terrified Violet home.

When they finally arrived at the tenement building, Violet let out a relieved sigh. Gunn's confessions about killing Lena were so shocking that her entire body stiffened with fear. After multiple efforts to straighten his car on the icy road, Gunn appeared content and helped Violet exit. As she stepped out, she slipped and fell into Gunn's arms, which caught her before she hit the ground.

"Are you alright?" Gunn asked, still holding Violet close to him.

"Yes, I'm fine, thank you for catching me, Mr. Gunn. I-"

Before she could finish her sentence, Gunn suddenly pressed his open mouth against hers. He thrust his thick tongue, which tasted like a foul cigar, into her mouth. Every nerve in her body screamed for her to say no! She quickly pulled away, confused and stunned by what had just occurred.

"I-I'm sorry that just happened", Gunn said, stammering,

"I need to get inside, Mr. Gunn", said Violet, pulling away abruptly. "It's getting late as it is colder out here. Can we go inside now, please?" said Violet.

"Of course, let me help you inside", said Gunn.

Shit, Got-damn it! What the fuck did I just do to her? I can't lose her because of my stupidness! She's nothing like Lena or the others! This one is going to be my wife and I ain't about to fuck things up with her or my future with her! Gunn thought agitatedly.

Violet immediately felt the embarrassment of what had just happened and felt the need to diffuse the situation before an outburst.

"Mr. Gunn, I appreciate everything you've done for me. If it hadn't been for you, I wouldn't be back working for Miss Bessie. I understand how you're feeling about me and my baby. Tell you what, I'll give everything we talked about a lot of thought, and then we can talk about it again when I get home from church on Sunday," said Violet.

Gunn's face lit up with a broad smile, feeling relief and a renewed sense of purpose for his future.

"Thank you, Violet. Because of you, I now have a chance to live the right way, and I promise that if you say yes, I will do everything for you and the baby. Who knows, we might even have a few more of our own," he said. "But all I ask is that you forgive my past transgressions", said Gunn.

Violet kept thinking about what he told her earlier, especially about murdering Wayne's wife, Lena. All she wanted was to go upstairs.

But I've done my share of transgressions, laying with Clarence, who was married. I hurt his wife and tore his family apart. He's dead, and I'm carrying his child, so I'm just as guilty, so we're both sinners, Violet thought with remorse.

"We'll talk about that later, but not now, because I'm freezing," Violet said.

"Oh yes, we shall talk about it soon", Gunn said, agreeing.

Taking her by the crook of her elbow, Gunn slowly led Violet up the stairs until they reached the inside of the building. The only sound was the heavy footsteps of their approach.

"Well, this has been a very busy day for me, Mr. Gunn, and I appreciate the ride home. I'll be working again tomorrow morning, so I'll say goodnight and thank you."

"You're welcome, Violet. I'm here to help you in any way I can. When you're ready to decide about me being your husband, just let me know. Goodnight, my beautiful lady," Gunn said, tipping his derby hat to her. He then left, walking up the long, narrow stairs to his flat and closing the door.

Violet opened the door and was surprised to find all the lights on, the smell of fried fish, and Cee-Cee setting the table. In the shadow of Cee-Cee's bedroom, she saw Hubert changing from his chauffeur's uniform into his regular clothes.

Violet greeted, saying, "Good evening, Aunt Cee-Cee, you're home early; hello, Uncle Hubert."

"Hi Violet, I hope you had a good day at work. Was it busy at the salon today?" Cee-Cee asked over the noisy sound of frying fish.

"Yes, it was very busy today, and we stayed later than usual. Tomorrow promises to be even busier," Violet said, hanging her coat above the radiator to dry. She removed her boots and socks, then went into her room to change out of her uniform. Wearing her favorite floral dress and slippers, she entered the kitchen and wrapped her arms around Cee-Cee's neck. Cee-Cee could feel Violet trembling. When Violet pulled back, Cee-Cee looked into her face, which was full of terror.

"Violet, what's wrong? Is everything okay with the baby?" Cee-Cee whispered nervously. She pressed her hand on Violet's belly.

"Aunt Cee-Cee, could you call Uncle Hubert now? I have something to tell you both," Violet asked.

The tone of her voice had Cee-Cee worried, so she hurried to her bedroom to tell Hubert.

"Violet, are you okay? What's wrong? Did something happen?" Hubert asked as he sat at the kitchen table.

Violet slumped into the chair and grabbed the edge of the table.

"I know who murdered Miss Paula, the woman who used to live downstairs in flat 101," said Violet.

"You, you what?" Cee-Cee stammered, dropping the plate of fish onto the table. She then sat down heavily in the chair beside Hubert.

"I know who killed Miss Paula," Violet repeated.

"Who was it?" Hubert asked, frowning.

"It was Mr. Gunn, the man who lives upstairs," said Violet.

"Oh, my Gawd!" Cee-Cee exclaimed, covering her mouth. "Who told you?"

"Mr. Gunn admitted what he did," Violet said softly, lowering her gaze. "Aunt Cee-Cee, you and Uncle Hubert, leave here before six in the morning so you don't see me leaving with Mr. Gunn. He takes me to Marcel's every day."

"Wait a minute, he's been to our home?" Hubert interrupted.

"Yes, sir, he's been here, but not inside. He appears to know exactly when I need to leave for work because he knocks at the door, ready to take me to work and pick me up from Miss Bessie's," Violet said.

"He picks you up at Bessie's, too?" Cee-Cee whispered, rising from her seat. "Violet, when you first came here, I told you about that man and advised you to stay away from him because he's no good! Now he knows our address! Why did you disobey?"

"Aunt Cee-Cee, I wasn't being disobedient to you at all! Do you remember? My first day of work was really tough outside with the snow and ice," Violet asked.

"Yes, of course, I remember that day because I was as worried about your safety as well as the baby", Hubert said. "But what does that have to do with you?"

"Mr. Gunn took me to work that day and showed me the alley I was supposed to walk through. The ground was covered in ice, and I could have slipped and hurt myself and the baby. That's how I've been getting back and forth to work. I'm very sorry about all of this, but I have even more to tell you," Violet said.

Cee-Cee, who was now standing, walked over to where Hubert was sitting and grasped his hand.

"There's more?" Hubert asked.

"Yes. Mr. Gunn also murdered Lena Collins, Wayne's first wife", said Violet.

Hubert shot out of his seat so quickly that the chair he was sitting in tipped over and hit the floor. Cee-Cee let out a shriek and backed herself against the wall, crossing her arms tightly over her chest.

"Sweet Jesus, my sweet Jesus," Hubert said, rubbing his head as he paced the floor.

Violet sat quietly, watching as her aunt and uncle responded to what she had shared. She knew their feelings but could only handle their reactions.

"I need to call Wayne about this right now," Hubert said firmly. "This can't be true — that you've been with a murderer who killed two people living here! My God, Violet, that son-of-a-bitch might have killed you!"

Hubert turned into his bedroom to get Wayne's phone number, but Violet stopped him.

"Wait, Uncle Hubert," she called out. "There's one more thing I need to tell you. Mr. Gunn not only murdered Miss Lena and Miss Paula but also the man his mother was seeing. He said he was only nineteen when he caught them together," Violet explained.

Hubert halted mid-step and stared at Violet, his eyes blazed with horror.

"Oh my God, Jesus save us!" Cee-Cee cried, bending over and trembling. "Hubert, what are we supposed to do? We need to call the police!"

"Absolutely not! Cee-Cee, sit down. I'm calling Wayne now to tell him what Violet gave me. Then I'll contact Clyde and Simeon to set up a card game for tomorrow night with that murderer. I'll handle this, but in the meantime, Violet, you'll be working tomorrow. However, please let Miss Bessie know that you need to leave early because you're feeling unwell. I'll have my friend Evans, a driver like me, pick you up and take you to Mrs. Pearlman's, the midwife Cee-Cee found for you. She hosts Saturday night fish fry and is an usher at church on Sundays. You and Cee-Cee will stay there until Sunday night. I'll meet you at Mrs. Pearlman's after work so we can all stay there until Sunday evening. She said she expects us for Sunday dinner, and I told her that's fine and we'd love to join her and her family.

"What's going to happen while we're all away from here, Hubert? I'm scared to death!" Cee-Cee said, brushing her trembling hand through her hair.

"Don't worry. Mr. Gunn will play his final card game tomorrow night. Go ahead and eat, and don't wait for me. I need to call Wayne and organize the card game with Mr. Gunn hosting," said Hubert.

He kissed Cee-Cee on the forehead, hugged Violet, and left to speak with Clyde and Simeon in flat 101.

CHAPTER FORTY-TWO

Hubert had a one-hour talk with Wayne. When Wayne found out that High Roller-Gunn was Lena's murderer, he was stunned.

"What was his name again?" Wayne asked.

"High Roller-Gunn", Hubert repeated.

"Hold on, Hubert, I need to grab something," Wayne said. After a moment, he returned to the phone.

"Hubert, I just realized something. When I traveled to New York to bury Lena, her minister handed me a sympathy card with a thousand dollars. The signature on it read "H-R-G": it's him, High Roller-Gunn, who murdered Lena! Oh my God, Violet was with him in his car, heading to her job?" shouted Wayne.

Hubert explained a plan to Wayne to prevent Gunn from visiting Violet and from lurking outside his flat in the morning to pick her up for work. After their talk, he went downstairs to speak with Simeon and Clyde. Hubert didn't come back until after eleven that night. By then, Cee-Cee and Violet were asleep in their rooms. Violet had a long evening helping Cee-Cee clean up after dinner and pack some belongings for the weekend, as they'd all return late Sunday. To avoid Gunn getting suspicious, Cee-Cee left their suitcases for Hubert to carry to work.

When Violet woke up the next morning, she found a note written by Cee-Cee on the kitchen table.

Violet,

When Mr. Gunn comes to take you to work, act normally. Do not act scared, or that'll spook him into acting crazy. Go to work as usual, but later, inform Bessie that you're unwell and plan to visit the midwife I found for you. Bessie knows her well, and the midwife prefers not to have men around her place, so Mr. Gunn will understand not to come by for a check-up. Tell Bessie you'll see her on Tuesday.

When you're ready to leave, turn right two blocks from the salon. A driver by the name of Evans will be there waiting for you. He'll drive you to Brooklyn, where the midwife lives. I'll meet you when I get off work. Be brave!

Love,

Aunt Cee-Cee

As soon as Violet finished reading the note, there was a soft knock at the door.

"Who's there?" said Violet.

"It's me, Gunn. Are you ready to go?"

"Uh-yes, I've just finished using the bathroom. I'll be right there", she said.

As she stood still, a tremor coursed through her body, marking the first time she felt her baby move in her belly. She gently placed her hand on her stomach, closed her eyes, then took a deep breath in and slowly exhaled. Once she regained her composure, she pushed Cee-Cee's note deep into her purse. Putting on her hat and coat, she moved to the door, which she then opened. Gunn was standing outside, looking at her with concern.

"Is everything all right?" Gunn asked.

"Of course. As I grow bigger, the baby needs more to eat, so I end up using the bathroom more often," she said with a nervous laugh, meeting his eyes.

Gunn furrowed his eyebrows in a frown. He wasn't entirely sure what was happening.

"Mr. Gunn, I assure you that the baby and I are doing well. It's just one of the many things that women go through. It's called women's stuff," Violet said as she lowered her hat to prepare and shield her face from the wind. "I'm ready to leave now," she added, heading out the door.

"Oh, okay. I want to make sure that neither you nor the baby is in any danger," he said.

Danger? What is he thinking? Violet thought to herself. Her stomach muscles tightened at his look, which suddenly grew dark.

"Mr. Gunn, with you by my side, how could I ever be in danger? Everyone in Harlem respects you, and since you've been taking me to work and bringing me home, I've never felt safer. Do you remember my first day at work, when that alley was just a sheet of ice? How could I be unsafe with you with me?" said Violet, brushing against his arm.

Gunn seemed pleasantly awestruck by Violet's sudden act of affection when she brushed against his arm. He smiled as if he took pleasure in imagining Violet as his loving wife and the mother of their future children, as well as a father for the one on the way, even though the child wasn't his.

It's settled, Violet will be my wife. This Sunday, I plan to visit the church she, her aunt, and uncle attend. I'll introduce myself and publicly propose marriage in front of everyone! Gunn thought happily.

"Are you ready to leave? The Southern Pot will be less crowded today because it's Saturday. Our breakfast should still be ready for me to pick up," Gunn said as he reached out to hold her hand, and together, they descended the narrow stairs.

A cold shiver ran down her spine as Gunn held her hand, as thoughts of that same hand had murdered three people.

After a quick stop at the Southern Pot for breakfast pickup, they headed to Marcel's Salon. Ten minutes later, they arrived at their destination. Gunn was able to park right in front of the already brightly lit salon. There were already two customers inside, one in Clarissa's chair, and Peach was rinsing her customer's hair.

"Hurry in, it's freezing outside!" Bessie said as she opened the door for Violet and Gunn, with Gunn handing her the breakfast sack.

"Good morning, ladies," Gunn boomed.

"Mornin', Mr. Gunn," they all answered.

"Bessie, can I talk to you privately?" asked Gunn.

"Of course, I was just finishing counting the new crates of pomade that arrived on Thursday. I had completely forgotten about them because things have been so busy since Violet started doing hair. "I tell you, she's a Godsend," said Bessie, looking at Violet with admiration.

"Yes, she is. After you, Bessie," Gunn said, letting her go ahead. They then entered the supply room together and sat down at the table.

"So, what's on your mind, Gunn? You seem happy today," Bessie asked as she took out and unwrapped her piping hot biscuit, dripping in butter.

Gunn reached for his mason jar, filled with steaming coffee mixed with milk and a teaspoon of brown sugar. He blew on it gently before taking several audible slurps.

"I've got something to tell you, but you have to keep it to yourself," Gunn said, taking another loud sip of his coffee.

Bessie, who was absorbed in her breakfast, looked up at Gunn, who was smiling so much that he appeared giddy. She put her biscuit down and dabbed at the corner of her mouth.

Gunn said, "I've fallen in love with Violet and plan to ask her to marry me after church tomorrow."

Bessie heard the smile in his voice, even though he looked serious. She set down her jar of coffee. Her eyes flashed with disbelief at what she just heard.

"Did you say you've fallen in love with Violet and plan to ask her to be your wife after church? Hah! When was the last time you attended a church service?" said Bessie.

"Why does that matter? I'm going to her church, and after the service, I plan to ask her in front of her aunt and uncle. Then, we will see the minister to set a wedding date; she'll probably want to marry before the baby is born, that's for sure. I can't wait for her to become my wife, for me to be a father to our child, and in a year or two, to start our family. I also intend to change how I've been living. This gambling is becoming too dangerous. I've seen too many lose their lives over money, and sometimes I wonder if I'll be next to get shot in the head," Gunn said. He took several quick bites of his biscuit and wiped his mouth with the back of his hand to brush away the buttery crumbs.

Oh, my Gawd, does he really believe that Cee-Cee and Hubert will let Violet, a lovely and smart young woman, approve of marrying this detestable man? Bessie wondered as she took a small bite of her biscuit.

"Bessie?" Gunn whispered.

"Huh?" said Bessie.

"So, what are your honest thoughts on me and Violet getting married? I trust you, so please be truthful. You're like a mother to me," said Gunn.

Bessie hesitated, thinking to herself that this would not sit well with Cee-Cee or Hubert at all.

"I'm going to be completely honest with you, Gunn," said Bessie, shifting in her seat.

"Okay, go ahead then," said Gunn, slurping his coffee.

"Leave Violet alone. She's not ready for a relationship because she's dealing with many problems. The man who impregnated her has died, and she didn't learn this until she arrived in Harlem. Her aunt Cee-Cee said Violet went into shock when she and Hubert shared the news with her. Additionally, her mother threw her out after discovering that he was already married. Cee-Cee mentioned that the wife of Violet's lover is dangerous; rumors say she hexed her husband, Violet, and Violet's mother. It's said that anyone trying to get close to Violet will die, as the wife has supposedly cursed her never to love again. If I were you, I'd leave Violet alone," Bessie said honestly.

Gunn experienced a sudden surge of panic in his stomach after Bessie told him that the woman he loves might be cursed. He dismissed her concern as nonsense and waved her words away dismissively.

"First, Violet needs a protector for her entire life, including the baby, and I am that person", he said, pointing to his chest.

"Second, she needs a husband, since what you just said about her mother taking the wraps off her suggests I must protect her from shame and gossip. Look at what happened to Williana; if anyone speaks badly of Violet after she becomes my wife, the same fate will come to pass for those who gossip. Lastly, I don't believe in those New Orleans curses or hexes; they're bull-shit, in my opinion. However, I respect you, Bessie, and I understand what you're saying. Still, it's too late to turn back," Gunn said.

"What do you mean?" Bessie asked with curiosity.

Gunn reached into his coat pocket, retrieved a small black box, and carefully pushed it toward Bessie.

"Open it," Gunn said, smiling widely.

Bessie gazed at Gunn until he gestured for her to open the box. She reached out and opened it, covering her mouth in surprise at the sparkling diamond ring inside. The ring was adorned with smaller diamonds that made the central diamond appear even larger.

"I don't think she'll refuse when she sees this. Would you say no?" he asked, with a slight smile on his face.

Bessie couldn't believe her eyes. The ring, dating from 1920, was stunning. But she wondered where Gunn had acquired it. Few Black women wore such engagement rings, even among those whose husbands owned businesses.

"This is beautiful," said Bessie, clutching her chest. She could feel her heart pounding, not just from seeing that beautiful ring but also from concern for Violet.

He grinned and declared, "I'm going to marry her regardless of her aunt and uncle's approval. I'll attend church tomorrow morning, and after she chooses the date, Harlem will witness a wedding like no other!"

After snapping the box shut and slipping it into his coat pocket, he rose, towering over Bessie.

"Welp, I gotta go settle some business before heading to a card game I was invited to. Humph, it seems the two brothers who took over Miss Paula's laundry business want to play poker. They mentioned that the stakes would be very high, totaling $300 between them. But I'm not worried because I plan to win every penny, hah! Whatever I win will go toward our wedding. Can you promise me one thing, Bessie?" Gunn asked.

"What's that?" said Bessie, as she took another sip of coffee.

Gunn said, "Promise me that from the moment I say, 'I do' on my wedding day until the day of my funeral, you'll be sitting in the front row, no matter what."

"Alright, I promise", said Bessie, nodding her head.

"Good, because I'll be looking for you," said Gunn. He slipped into his coat, put on his derby, approached Bessie, and embraced her. Then he departed.

Bessie sat quietly, observing the steam drift from her coffee. Then, she bowed her head, shut her eyes tightly, clasped her hands, and started praying earnestly for Violet.

Gunn stepped out of the supply room into the busy salon, now crowded with women. The number of women had doubled since he and Bessie talked. As he looked around, his eyes caught Violet, who was finishing up with her client, a striking woman with fair skin and hazel eyes, someone who would likely attract many young men if she went out for the night. Violet saw Gunn and acknowledged him with a glance. He smiled widely at her, mouthing "See you later," and waved. As he headed out, he tipped his derby hat to three women entering the salon.

Gunn hurried to his car to escape the cold and wind. Once inside, he picked up the small box holding the diamond ring, opened it, and admired the sparkling ring in the sunlight.

It was unfortunate that Brian McCracken, the white bank vice president, hadn't repaid the money he owed.

Gunn suspected McCracken believed he could get away with it, thinking he was a naïve Black man who would overlook the thousands owed from the last ten card games, as well as money from women he introduced for sex—some of whom wanted to join in—so McCracken could watch as he touched himself. Because McCracken ignored him, McCracken's wife had to pay the price: she lost a finger, and he shot her in the head. Gunn also took her fur coat, which Violet would receive after they married. He thought that soon everyone would know she was his wife, as he placed the ring back in the box and started his car.

"People ought to know by now not to fuck with me or else," Gunn said aloud as he drove off.

It was already one o'clock in the afternoon, and the salon was getting overcrowded, so Bessie had to turn away several women. It reached a point where Violet,

Clarissa, Peach, and even Bessie could take a quick run to the bathroom and sneak in a sip of tepid coffee and a bite from a slice of cake.

"When your customer sits in her chair, begin by immediately scratching out any dandruff, then shampoo twice with a very warm, quick rinse. I've never seen so many customers in all my years here!" exclaimed Bessie.

Violet started to panic when she saw two more customers quietly slip in after Bessie walked away, forgetting to lock the door and leaving a note stating that the salon was too crowded and would not accept any more clients for the day. The two women who sneaked in specifically asked Violet to finger-wave their hair.

Violet needed to leave the salon by three o'clock. After finishing a finger-waving service for one client, she noticed two newcomers entering, removing their hats, revealing very short hair, which made styling easier. She had one client under the dryer while she shampooed and towel-dried the other, preparing her for the hairdryer. As she worked on the second woman and placed her under the dryer, she also began sectioning and oiling the first client's hair with Glossine pomade, then started finger-waving her hair. Once finished, she repeated the process on the first woman. By then, about twenty minutes later, she was nearly done.

"Violet, may I have a quick word with you? It's a matter of urgency," said Bessie.

"Yes, ma'am, of course," Violet replied, a line of concern forming between her eyebrows. "Dora, could you please excuse us for a moment? I'm nearly finished with your hair anyway. It won't take long," she added.

Dora nodded and resumed reading her newspaper.

Violet entered the supply room after Bessie.

"Is everything alright, Miss Bessie?" said Violet, wiping her hands on the towel draped on her shoulder.

"Everything is fine. You've been working all day since before 8 a.m. After finishing with Dora, go home and rest. I've noticed your ankles are swollen. Go home, and I'll see you in church on Sunday and at work Monday morning," Bessie smiled and patted Violet's belly. "I'll also finger wave Peach's hair for her night out with the trumpeter," said Bessie.

"Miss Bessie, thank you, because I wasn't feeling too well, and it just so happens that I'll be seeing the midwife who'll be tending to me when the baby comes," said Violet.

"Good, once Dora is done, head to your appointment. I hope you feel better, dear," Bessie said empathetically.

A smile appeared on Violet's face as she and Bessie exited the supply room and returned to their stations, where their customers were already waiting for hair appointments.

At exactly 2:45, Dora's hair was styled with finger waves to perfection. As she headed to the door to leave, she received many compliments. Despite the freezing weather outside, Dora declined to wear a scarf over her head to shield herself from the icy cold and strong wind.

Violet snapped off and unplugged the hot plate used for the straightening combs.

Violet reflected that, from her experience with Williana, the lesson was to avoid being careless and dirty like she was. She then went to the back of the salon to use the bathroom and collect her belongings.

Inside her lunch sack, there was a surprise: two large slices of cinnamon cake. Violet couldn't help but smile and feel grateful for Gunn's kindness, but she was also aware that Gunn was a murderer. For reasons unknown, Hubert wanted her and Cee-Cee out of sight until Sunday evening.

"I'll see you on Sunday, Miss Bessie, and thank you for letting me leave early," Violet said as she waved to her, Clarissa, and Peach. She then stepped outside.

It's two fifty-five, Violet thought worriedly.

She hurried to meet the chauffeur, Evans, at the two long blocks ahead, but the walkways were icy, and many people were shuffling cautiously. Two individuals ahead of them had already slipped and fallen heavily.

"God, please protect me and my baby. Don't let me fall on the ice," Violet whispered in prayer. Tears welled

up in her eyes and spilled onto her face from the blustery wind.

A deep male voice from behind her said, "Hello, Violet. I was waiting for you."

Violet suddenly stopped in her tracks, startled by an unfamiliar voice. Her mind raced with the possibility that Gunn had sent someone to find her, filling her with fear. Carefully, she turned her head and saw a tall man with dark skin, his hat pulled low over his eyes.

"Are you Violet?" the stranger asked.

"Yes, yes, I'm Violet, but who are you?" she asked nervously.

"Come with me, the car is just over there," he said, pointing to a grand-looking vehicle that still gleamed as if it were brand new. "My name is Evans, and your Aunt Cee-Cee is waiting for you inside. She saw you leaving the salon, and because these walkways are hazardous,

I thought it would be safer to wait here for you. Humph, after seeing those two people fall, Cee-Cee was close to tears, worried about you. C'mon, take my arm and hold on tight. The car is right there," he said, gesturing to the vehicle.

"Oh, my goodness, Evans, thank you!" Violet said as they entwined their arms together.

"I was so afraid I would have missed you," said Violet, feeling relieved.

"Even if you were going to be a few minutes late, I wouldn't leave you. It's dangerous outside with all this ice and cold, and since you're about to have a baby, it's my duty to ensure your safety," he said.

The car was just a few steps away, but walking there felt like an eternity. They finally arrived, and Cee-Cee was already seated in the back. She leaned over to open the door and gently helped Violet inside. Evans closed the door as Violet and Cee-Cee hugged.

"Are you alright?" Cee-Cee asked.

"Yes, Aunt Cee-Cee, I'm feeling much better now. I was really scared of falling and missing the car to meet you. I'm so cold and tired," Violet said.

"You're going to be just fine now," said Cee-Cee as she drew Violet nearer, both clasping hands. Violet trembled, so Cee-Cee took out a wool blanket and wrapped it around both of them to protect against the cold.

"That better?" Cee-Cee asked.

"Oh yes, much better, my legs aren't aching as much," said Violet.

"Ladies, are you ready to go?" Evans said as he started the car.

"Yes, we're ready, Evans. Let's leave immediately. Violet is probably tired and hungry," said Cee-Cee.

"Yes, Ma'am," said Evans, tipping his chauffeur's hat to her. He looked both ways, then drove to Brooklyn.

Five minutes into the trip, Cee-Cee reached into her purse, took out an envelope addressed to Violet, and handed it to her.

"This is from Wayne," said Cee-Cee. He didn't have time to write you a letter, but that night, he spoke to Hubert, and he called again. You were asleep, so he asked me not to wake you. We ended up talking on the phone for nearly two hours.

A frown creased Violet's forehead as she took the envelope from Cee-Cee and tucked it into her purse.

Violet asked, "What did Wayne say, Aunt Cee-Cee? Is everything okay back home?"

Cee-Cee looked at Violet with sad eyes. She immediately looked out the window when the car slowed and stopped at the corner to allow pedestrians to cross.

"According to Wayne, no," she replied, turning her gaze back to Violet.

"Oh God, what happened?" Violet asked, trying to brace herself for more bad news.

Cee-Cee reached out and firmly grasped her hand.

"It's your mother; Wayne threw her out of the house," said Cee-Cee.

Violet asked, "I remember him mentioning this in his last letter. I still can't believe they just got married! Please, tell me again what happened after your phone call with him. Are there any additional details?"

"Yes, there definitely is. Your mother was stealing from Wayne for quite some time, even before they got married. He noticed small amounts missing now and then, but after they married, he caught her taking money from his pants pockets. She laughed it off at first, but she became more cautious. The money your father left was meant for your education at that teacher's school, but circumstances changed so that you couldn't use it. When you told Wayne about your mother taking what was rightfully yours, he got angry. He wanted to wait and see if she'd change, but her actions only worsened. She borrowed money from coworkers and never paid them back, falsely claiming she and Wayne were broke and that you called for money constantly, which isn't true! Hearing this, Wayne had had enough. The Sunday before church, they sat in his car, and Wayne told her that he had seen her stealing from his drawer and from coworkers. He told Audine that after church, her bags were packed, and she needed to leave his house because their marriage was over.

Violet's face was streaked with tears as she listened once more to the terrible news about her mother. It confirmed her worst fear: Audine really was a common thief.

Violet asked quietly, "So, what happened next?" since Wayne's letter mentioned some details about Mason.

"Wayne refused to let Mason leave because, a month before Wayne married your mother, he filed papers to adopt Mason. He suspected that if anything happened to her or if she planned to leave him, he would keep Mason at all costs. Also, since Louisiana doesn't seem to care about Black children, the clerk filed the adoption papers, and a week later, the judge signed and sealed them, officially declaring Mason as Wayne's son," explained Cee-Cee.

"Oh my God, Aunt Cee-Cee, so it is true," Violet whispered, her voice thick with emotion. "I know Wayne made the right choice by keeping my brother safe at home, where he has a place to sleep, eat, and be protected. Wayne loves Mason as if he were his own son."

Cee-Cee mentioned that it appeared she wanted to quickly start having many children to grow her family and imitate her neighbor, Maria St. Laurent.

"Wayne told me that Mason was really happy to stay with Wayne and is excelling in school. According to Wayne, Mason is even considering a future as a Minister".

"A Minister?" said Violet.

"Yes, it seems like he observed everything," Cee-Cee paused before continuing. "When you and Clarence were together, witnessing that terrible fight you had with your mother the night you left, and hearing about her being a thief, made him turn more towards the church. Mason has discussed this with Wayne, and he's eager to help guide him toward becoming a Minister," Cee-Cee said.

"Did he ever ask about me, how I'm doing since I left New Orleans?' Violet asked.

"No, honey, Mason doesn't talk about you. Give him some time, though. Wayne has been wonderful being a father to him. Eventually, Mason will come around," said Cee-Cee.

"And what about my mother? Where'd she go?" Violet asked flatly.

"Nobody has seen or heard from her. Wayne didn't even give her a ride to the train station. He made her walk five miles to catch the next train, and it was at night. I was terrified for my sister and prayed for her every night, asking God to watch over her despite her shortcomings in this life. Wayne also went to the courthouse to file for an annulment, telling me that, given the circumstances, it would be final right away, considering everything that happened," said Cee-Cee.

Violet thought to herself, surprised that their marriage was ending, and her baby would likely be born in the same month as their annulment, as she moved closer to Cee-Cee.

"There's one more thing I need to tell you," Cee-Cee said. "It's about Maria, Clarence's wife."

Violet experienced a shiver when she heard Maria St. Laurent's name. A look of terror crossed her face, prompting her to swiftly turn toward the window.

"I'm so sorry," Cee-Cee whispered, clutching Violet's hand. She glimpsed Violet's face reflected in the window, noticing a tear sliding down her nose. Cee-Cee then reached into her purse and retrieved a handkerchief.

"Here, take this," she said, placing the crumpled handkerchief into Violet's trembling hand.

Violet gently sniffed and blew her nose. Taking a deep breath, she slowly turned to face Cee-Cee and the news she was about to share about Maria.

"So, what's going on with her?" Violet asked.

'A lot is happening with her and the farm where her children live. It appears Clarence wasn't a wealthy farmer. He spent nearly a year in debt trying to pay off the farm after adding the smokehouse. Wayne told me and Hubert that Maria received a letter from the bank stating they would foreclose on the farm if she didn't pay ten thousand dollars in full within six months of the letter's date,' Cee-Cee said.

Violet sat with her mouth wide open, stunned by what she had just heard.

"Aunt Cee-Cee, Clarence never told me that! He said he inherited the farm after his brothers died. Since he was the youngest, it automatically went to him. That's also why he wouldn't have any trouble divorcing Maria because he was—"

"Gonna marry you? Humph!" Cee-Cee said, raising an eyebrow. "Violet, Clarence didn't plan to divorce Maria to marry you. Do you know why? Because he was broke! He might've left briefly to be with you, but his intentions were definitely not pure. Getting a divorce, leaving his family, and handling that land would've cost him thousands of dollars he didn't have. During his visits to check on the farm and his family, he probably would've stayed permanently. With five children and another on the way, do you really think he'd marry you, Violet? Especially without telling his wife that he was behind on payments. Wake up, girl. The moment he's tired of you, he'll go back to New Orleans, fix his marriage, and admit his transgressions", said Cee-Cee.

Tears welled up in Violet's throat, but she managed to hold them back.

So, Clarence wasn't planning to marry me after all. It appeared he wanted to avoid his responsibilities, work, and debt, instead choosing to spend time with me and reflect, she thought bitterly. "He was a damn liar! I gave up on my dream of becoming a schoolteacher!" Violet muttered angrily.

"Yes, you did," Cee-Cee said candidly. "There's nothing you can do except for you and your baby to move on. And there's one more piece of advice I want to give you."

"Yes, Aunt Cee-Cee, anything you say, I'll listen to you", said Violet.

Now I understand that you wanted to become a teacher, and working as a hairdresser in Harlem was the last thing on your mind. But look at where you are now in that salon. Every woman who visits Marcels talks about you, praising you as the best at finger waves! Keep doing that, but also ask Bessie to show you the business side of her salon. Find out how you can help her grow her money as she gets older, and one day, the Lord will call her home. Then what? Who will manage the place? You're a very smart young woman, and Bessie needs someone intelligent like you to help her. That salon could one day be your future. Your life in New Orleans as you knew it is behind you, honey. Harlem is now your home. It's time to look forward," said Cee-Cee.

She's right. I can never go back to New Orleans. My mother is gone, Mason has hate in his heart for me, Wayne is free to start a new life all over again, and Clarence is dead, Violet thought to herself, dabbing the corners of her eyes.

"Ladies, we're here," Evans announced as he slowly parked his employer's car. He then quickly moved to the back to open the door, helping Violet out first, followed by Cee-Cee.

"Be careful going up those stairs," Evans said well-meaningly.

"Hubert has already taken your bags and his. He mentioned he'll arrive around eight tonight. He also said he has the weekend off because the lawyer he works for is staying home to work on a major murder case. I look forward to seeing you all at church tomorrow morning. It was a pleasure meeting you, Violet," he said, tipping his hat to her.

"Thank you for waiting for me, Evans, and for driving me and Aunt Cee-Cee here to meet my midwife. I know we'll see each other again," Violet said.

"It was my pleasure. A few months ago, I experienced a situation like this one. I was waiting for a woman named Lena from New Orleans, just like you. Sadly, she was unable to leave Harlem and return home to New Orleans. You're very lucky to have a family to protect you from what happened to Lena. Take care," Evans said. He then got into the car, started it, and drove away.

Violet continued watching Evans drive away until his car disappeared from view. She was stunned by what she had heard Evans say about Lena, and at that moment, she realized Gunn's murder of Lena was genuine, and she might also be in danger of facing a similar end. After speaking with Cee-Cee, she felt a sense of hope as a new world of opportunities seemed to be unfolding before her.

"Come on now," said Cee-Cee, grasping Violet's hand. "Your midwife, Mrs. Pealman, is waiting to meet you."

Violet gently squeezed Cee-Cee's hand as they slowly ascended the stairs of the two-story tenant building, gripping the iron rail. Nearing the door, Violet closed her eyes and took a deep breath, smiling at the familiar aroma of clove, nutmeg, vanilla, and cinnamon, reminiscent of New Orleans pralines and sweet potato pone, which always brought her joy. For the first time since moving to Harlem, she felt hopeful that everything

would turn out all right.

CHAPTER FORTY-THREE

The Last Card Game

"Why didn't Violet wait for me to come and get her? As her future husband and the father of her baby, I need to know her whereabouts, especially if she's not feeling well. You should have made her wait here for me!" Those were Gunn's final words after a heated argument with Bessie, who refused to tell him where Violet was. After leaving the salon, he drove as quickly as possible to the tenement building where he lived.

After parking his Cadillac, he forced himself out. He hurried up the icy stairs, slipping on the pavement and straining to lift his over 380-pound frame while searching for Violet. When he arrived at her flat, he knocked on the door several times. No one answered.

"Fuck!" he muttered angrily before leaving, stomping upstairs to his messy flat. I'll talk to her later; right now, I need to win a card game against those rural assholes who love doing laundry. They're such a strange group, he reflected on, amused. "And why the hell do they want to play poker with me? Don't they realize who I am?" he said out loud.

The flat was uninhabitable. Two large rats darted across the filthy kitchen floor into a wall cavity, while hundreds of cockroaches crawled among moldy dishes left untouched after Lena's last meal on her night of escape. The foul smell of spoiled food wafted from the stove when Lena baked a ham, which was infested with mice and cockroaches feasting on the rotting meat. Gunn glanced at the chaos as he passed by, dismissing it and telling himself Violet would clean up the mess Lena had left.

Pulling out a dirty, oil-stained sack, he gathered the items piled on his kitchen table to clear it for the evening poker game. The two assholes said they'd bring a new deck of cards, whiskey, and at least a hundred dollars in cash to start. After assessing everything, Gunn went to a chair stacked with his unwashed clothes, which had been there since his return from New Orleans last summer. Digging through the pile, he pulled out two items: a rolled wad of cash totaling four hundred dollars and a .38-caliber gun in case things got heated. He carefully tucked the pistol inside his jacket pocket, then moved to the table and placed the money in the center. Gunn heard a soft knock on his door.

"Just in time," he muttered to himself as he hurried to the door. "Who's there?" he asked, his voice steady.

The voice responded from outside the door: "Simeon and Clyde".

Gunn threw open the door to reveal two men in plain clothing, contrasting with his tailored suit.

"Ah, hello gentlemen, ready to lose some cash tonight?" Gunn said, laughing loudly.

"Oh, I see you're planning to stay up till tomorrow morning, sir. We're the ones who are going to win!" Clyde said, laughing just as hard.

They entered the flat. The pungent smell of rotten food made Clyde's eyes water. Simeon wrinkled his nose and rolled his eyes as another rat darted across the room into a hole in the wall.

"Sorry about the mess, boys. After I win all your money, I promise to hire a cleaning woman to take care of this shit-hole", said Gunn, signaling them to sit at the table. "Did you bring everything I asked for?" Gunn inquired.

"Yep, exactly what you requested: a new deck of cards, three hundred dollars in cash, and a new bottle of whiskey," Clyde said. He set each item, including the cash, in the center of the table.

"Very good!" exclaimed Gunn. "I'm pleased to see that you both paid attention to the details of what I requested. Shit, maybe you both can work for me instead of washing clothes that smell of shit and sweat. I can guarantee that I'll pay you big money, so what do you boys have to say about this: if you lose, you both will work for me, okay?"

Simeon and Clyde exchanged glances; Clyde raised an eyebrow in curiosity, while Simeon nodded in agreement to the deal.

"Okay, Gunn, if we lose, we'll gladly come work for you for as long as you want," said Clyde.

"Good! I intend to win every game we play. I don't think you two realize who I really am, because I always come out on top!" said Gunn, clapping his hands.

"Looks like this card game will take a while, so let's begin. As the host, you open the card box, deal, and take the first turn," said Clyde, sliding the card box toward Gunn.

Feeling delighted by the gesture, Gunn accepted the box, broke the seal, and poured the new deck into his hand. He brought the deck close to his nose, closed his eyes, inhaled deeply, and smiled.

"Boys, I smell the sweet scent of money, and it's all heading my way," Gunn said as he shuffled the cards.

"Hah! We'll see about that! I plan on using my win to celebrate by going out dancing next week", said Simeon.

Gunn burst into laughter and said, "What are those country-ass style rags you're wearing? You'd better buy some new clothes, or you'll be the only one left in the club! Once the women see your countryish look, they'll bolt!"

Clyde looked at Simeon, who joined Gunn in laughter. Gunn, now sipping his third whiskey and refilling his glass, chuckled. After dealing five cards, Clyde and Simeon each took fifty dollars from their pockets and placed them in the money bowl. Gunn smiled at the two crisp bills and started arranging his cards.

Smiling at his hand, he reached into his shirt pocket, pulled out two fifty-dollar bills, and placed them in the money bowl. The group stayed silent, but Gunn looked first at Simeon, who was visibly upset with his hand; he could see the frown on his forehead, and then at Clyde, who was equally agitated and snorted at his hand.

"So, tell me, where are you all from, and what brings you to Harlem?" Gunn asked, his eyes lowered to his cards.

"We came up here from Florida, where it's much warmer," said Clyde.

"Yeah, we miss the palm trees, the sun, and the fishing. We used to go to a lake nearby and catch enough fish to last a week. Everything changed a few months ago when we received a call that our mother had died", said Simeon.

Gunn looked up from his cards.

"Sorry to hear that, son. If you don't mind me asking, what happened to her?" he asked.

"She was murdered," Clyde said. He continued to look at his cards without raising his gaze.

"Damn, sorry to hear that. You boys hear anything more about it?" asked Gunn.

"Nope, you know how white police treat our people. Any of our own who gets killed is no problem, just one less Black man or woman. They don't give a fuck about us," said Clyde.

Gunn drained his whiskey glass and poured himself another. He took a long swig, finishing the drink. Then, he forcefully slammed the glass onto the table.

"Here's a deal: if I win this game tonight, you boys will work for me for a year. You'll run errands, follow my instructions, and manage the numbers game in Harlem. Plus, your wife will do my laundry for free and clean my place weekly," Gunn said with a smirk.

Clyde looked up at Gunn, who poured himself his fifth glass of whiskey.

"What if we don't agree?" Simeon asked.

Gunn, still focused on his cards, reached into his jacket, pulled out his gun, and placed it on the table.

Simeon's stomach clenched instantly upon seeing the gun. Gunn is clever, but his unpredictability could pose a problem for all of us, Simeon reflected as he looked at the weapon.

"So, are we in agreement, boys?" Gunn asked.

"Agreed", said Clyde, not looking up.

"Good!" said Gunn.

"How are we doing with the cards?" asked Simeon.

"Raise", Gunn said, grinning, as he pulled another fifty into the bowl.

"Raise", said Simeon, tossing in a wad of tens and twenties.

"I fold, my hand is fucked up", said Clyde.

"Got-damned, we just got started! You folding already?" said Gunn.

"Yeah, I'm feeling pretty fucked up after we told you about our mother," said Clyde, wiping his face. He poured more whiskey into his glass and took a short swig.

"Well, what happened to her? It looks like that whole thing about her murder got you both with your minds wandering away from the game. Shit, I was planning to win," said Gunn, clearly frustrated.

"Well, it's like this: mother lived in Harlem, and we stayed in Florida while she and our father moved here. In fact, Daddy helped build this place," Clyde said, looking around.

"This place?" Gunn asked, surprised.

"Yep, this is the very place where you eat, sleep, and park your fat ass," said Simeon.

"What the fuck did you just call me?" snapped Gunn.

Before Gunn could grab the gun he had left on the table, it was already too late. He was too slow and drunk. Simeon had already taken it from him and aimed it at Gunn, whose eyes widened with fear. Clyde approached Gunn and leaned close to his ear.

Clyde shared, "Our mother was a wonderful woman who worked hard after Daddy died. She tried her best to bring us together, but it was too costly for all of us. Instead, she sent money so we could have food and clothes, and our grandmother, who still cared for us, could even afford a car thanks to Daddy's hidden savings. So, when we learned of her murder, we rushed here as fast as we could".

"When we went to the morgue to identify her body, half of her nose was destroyed because it had been hacked off. Only a fucked-up madman could do something so damn cruel. The white police didn't bother investigating, so we buried her next to Daddy. Many people here loved her," said Simeon.

"Wait a fucking minute, the woman who used to live here and was murdered—was she your mother?" Gunn asked, horrified.

"Yes, and we've finally uncovered that it was you who killed her! That beautiful young woman, Violet, who you've been slobbering all over, told her aunt and uncle. It appears you can't keep your greasy mouth shut about what you've done, so after you admitted to killing our mother, Lena, and your sick-nasty, whore mother, Hubert rightly called Wayne Collins, Lena's husband. Concerned you might harm Violet and her baby, Wayne told Hubert to inform us immediately about the killer's identity. It was you!" yelled Clyde.

"You lying mutha-fucka!" Gunn screamed. Lurching forward, he tried to snatch the gun out of Simeon's hand, but Clyde wrestled him and grabbed Gunn by the collar, flinging him against the wall. Clyde roughly plopped a drunk Gunn back into the chair at the table. Gunn's nostrils flared as he sat, heaving. His fists were clenched as if he were ready to fight again. There was a loud knock at the door.

"You two fuckers are gonna get it now!" Gunn shouted. "Come on in, whoever you are, just come right in! Violet, if it's you, no worries, sweetheart, I love you so much! Come on in, baby!"

The door swung open, and in stepped Devil Man.

"What the fuck!" Gunn screamed. "You fuckers set me up! Get the fuck outta my place!"

"Shut up, you fat piece of shit," said Devil Man, grinning as he quietly closed the door behind him. "It's been a while since I last came here. Same old dirty, stinking fucked-up place. You can't keep this fucking shithole clean, even if your life depended on it."

"Get your slimy, narrow ass outta here! What the fuck do you want?" slurred Gunn as he struggled to stand up.

"What I want is satisfaction," Devil Man said, stepping directly to the right of Gunn's position. Simeon quietly handed the gun to Devil Man from behind.

When I was a kid, my father was never around. He was always out and often harsh. It seemed like every afternoon; he'd disappear for hours. One day, I decided to follow him. To my surprise, he went to this place every day. I managed to sneak inside once. I saw him go up the stairs, and when he reached this dump, a woman opened the door, and they kissed like they knew each other. I went further up the stairs and reached the door. As I was saying, I looked through the keyhole, and there he was, my father on his ashy knees while that whore of a mother of yours pulled her blouse up and asked my father if he wanted a taste of her milk. Ain't that what you ustah do unto you was a grown man?" said Devil Man, sneering.

"Fuck you!" Gunn shouted, furious that after years of hiding his secret, it was now exposed to two strangers. Disgust flashed on their faces as Simeon and Clyde exchanged glances.

"When I heard you running up the stairs, I hid behind the dark stairwell nearby. I watched as you slowly turned the doorknob before entering. That's when I heard your mother screaming and my father begging you to drop the knife. I heard the sound of stabbing and him screaming for you to stop. After that loud thud on the floor and your mother's screams, I knew you had killed him. Then you ran out, covered in my father's blood, while your mother was crying and moaning. I stepped out from behind the stairwell and stood at the door. My father was lying dead on the floor, soaked in blood. I ran outta there vowing that when I grew up, I would find you!"

Gunn remained frozen, unable to move or speak. Everything had vanished, and escape seemed impossible. On the other side of the table, he saw Clyde and Simeon, both with disgusting expressions. Suddenly, Gunn heard the familiar sound of a gun being cocked. He shut his eyes.

"Violet," he whispered to himself, tears streaming down his face. Suddenly, a strong, foul odor flooded the room as he lost control and soiled himself.

Devil Man pressed the gun to the side of Gunn's head and squeezed the trigger. The explosion to Gunn's head caused his right eye to spill out of the socket.

Devil Man pried Gunn's hand open and placed the gun in it.

Devil Man said, 'Looks like he had a royal flush," as he turned over the cards in front of Gunn and examined them.

"Humph, that fat fuck was known to cheat. But I guess tonight wasn't his lucky night after all,"

"Simeon, you got that note?" Clyde asked.

"Yeah, I didn't forget it," said Simeon.

Devil Man observed as Simeon pulled a note from his pocket and pressed it into Gunn's left hand. Afterwards, he took his own and Clyde's whiskey glasses, went to the sink infested with roaches, and threw them in.

"I gotta ask you all something: what does the note say?" asked Devil Man.

"It says that he confessed to killing our mother, your father, and Lena Collins, including the dates and times of each murder. It also mentions that he felt sorrowful over the murders and that he'd rather be dead than spend his life in prison. He also says that he would like his good friend, Mr. D. Mann, to receive his car after his burial. Mr. Martin Gunn signs the note with today's date," Clyde said.

Devil Man roared with laughter at the idea of being Gunn's good friend.

"Got-damned, you all had this thought out really good!" said Devil Man, nodding in approval.

"Yep, we did, but we need to get outta here before people get suspicious. Everything is done except the money," said Simeon as he scooped up the cash from the bowl. He took the remaining playing cards and put them back inside the box.

"What are you gonna do with those?" Devil Man asked.

"Burn them," Clyde quipped. "We don't want any memory of what happened here."

The three exited the door, and as they left, three large brown rats scampered across Gunn's feet.

EPILOGUE

Two weeks later, a foul, deathly odor was coming from Gunn's flat. After Bessie verified his identity, she delivered his body to the funeral home where she occasionally worked.

She honored her promise to Gunn to sit in the front row at his funeral, as no one else attended. Sitting before his closed casket, she didn't realize that when he said, "You'll never see me here again," he was manifesting those words.

On Thursday morning, May 8, 1934, in New Orleans, Maria St. Laurent gave birth to a son, whom she named

David Levequè St. Laurent. She resisted having Clarence's name on the birth certificate, but the registry recorded it as "Avid" instead of David.

On the night of Saturday, June 13, 1934, Violet gave birth to a son in her bedroom. She named him Richard Clarence Margaret. The birth was difficult and painful, complicated further by a late-arriving midwife and extraordinary circumstances. That evening, New York experienced a fierce rainstorm with intense thunder, lightning, and hail.

After giving birth, her son continued crying nonstop, and Violet's cough grew worse, intensifying each day. Despite seeing many leading Black doctors in Harlem, none could identify the cause of her persistent cough, which troubled her continuously for years.

After a year, Violet met a man who admired her, one of the doctors treating her cough, and they fell in love.

He discovered a remedy that could suppress the cough for several hours, though it was not a cure.

He was an older gentleman and widower with no children who proposed to her during Sunday dinner, bringing joy to family friends, Violet's one-year-old son, Cee-Cee, and Hubert.

A date was set, and two months before their wedding, they planned to announce that Violet was expecting another child, but her fiancée disappeared mysteriously.

Violet was overwhelmed by stress, which resulted in her losing the baby.

He was discovered dead two weeks later, shot in the head by a single gunshot, seemingly murdered by his jealous romantic partner, his gentleman lover.

❖ *Pieces, Revised and Revisited*

❖ *Audine's Story: A Sinful, Cursed, Malevolent, and Deceptive Woman*

❖ *Sistahs of the Tarot Readers of the Truth*